---
★
---

Curious, excited, but at the same time anxious, frightened even, she tramped on, in the wake of the broken underbrush. After a time the "path" veered off—south or east—she'd lost direction, but could still hear Hamlet's snortings back where she'd tethered him. She needed to know what had been dragged here.

And she saw. It was the body of a man. He'd been strangled with—oh God, God!—Ophelia's reins—the reins were still hanging from his neck. She knew they were her mare's because of the way the reins were scraped and worn on the edges—a certain way Ophelia had of turning quickly and having to be brought back in line. The man's neck was a dark red under the dangling reins, the skin bruised an ugly yellow above the T-shirt with its cruel message of *Death To Brits*.

---
★
---

"A solid farm-based series."

—*Library Journal*

"The characters and setting are exquisitely created."

—*Round Table Reviews*

Nancy Means Wright

# Mad Cow
# Nightmare

**WORLDWIDE**®

TORONTO • NEW YORK • LONDON
AMSTERDAM • PARIS • SYDNEY • HAMBURG
STOCKHOLM • ATHENS • TOKYO • MILAN
MADRID • WARSAW • BUDAPEST • AUCKLAND

For Llyn

**MAD COW NIGHTMARE**

A Worldwide Mystery/April 2006

First published by St. Martin's Press LLC.

ISBN 0-373-26560-3

**Printed in U.S.A.**

# Acknowledgments

Thanks and gratitude to the following for their help with this novel:

Linda and Larry Faillace of East Warren, Vermont, whose sheep were destroyed by the USDA, and who granted me an open, generous, and insightful interview; Joy Smith of Springfield, Vermont, breeder of Lippitt Morgans, who introduced me to her stableful of gorgeous horses; Nancy C. Plimpton for her history of the Lippitt Morgan family; Tim Fitzgerald, expert on Irish travellers; and traveller Richard J. Waters, author of the fabulous Internet site: www.travellersrest.org.

Thanks, too, to my dedicated and helpful readers Chris Roerden and Llyn Rice, and again to Llyn, master engineer, who responded to the plethora of "how-to," "how-come," and "how-about" questions. To my legendary editor, Ruth Cavin, my assistant editor, Toni Plummer; my copy editor, Brenda Woodward; and my agent Alison Picard—I'm deeply indebted to all of you. To members of the Champlain Valley Unitarian Universalist Society, a welcoming congregation and continuing source of inspiration. To my UU writing group, and to David Weinstock and members of his Thursday workshop, who encouraged my writing in so many ineffable ways. And finally, to my beloved extended family for being there for me during the research and writing of this novel.

I read innumerable articles on Mad Cow disease in *The New York Times, The Wall Street Journal,* and in the Vermont newspapers *The Addison Independent, The Rutland Herald, The Valley Voice,* and *The Burlington Free Press,* including Barbara Eastman's superb column, "A Farm Journal."

Three books were also helpful: *Nan, the Life of an Irish Travelling Woman* by Sharon Gmelch, *Gypsies, The Hidden Americans* by Anne Sutherland, and *Bury Me Standing* by Isabel Fonseca.

# ONE

RITCHIE WAS WEARING black jeans ripped in the knees and a T-shirt that read *Death To Brits* on its soiled front. He'd bought it the one time he was in Ireland. When he bent to drop a paper full of droopy flowers on Nola's tray table, she saw the black stallion on the back of his shirt. The beast was bucking, its hind legs kicking up, the man on its back gone sprawling, top hat and all—an Englishman, she supposed, toppled by an Irishman.

"Fifteen minutes," the nurse said in a starched voice and, frowning, rustled out.

Nola understood the frown. Here they were in a Canadian hospital, with a picture of the queen on every wall! The queen wore a silly little pillbox of a hat on top of her bluish hair; the man in tights beside her was kissing her plump hand like it was a warm macaroon. Ha! To Nola, royalty was no better than poor Irish travellers like herself—in spite of the fancy carriages and the horse guards dressed to the teeth in velvet and lace.

"And where did you pick the flowers?" she said. "They got vases here, you know. Just ask the nurse. They might die, though, in the cold of this place."

Nola was always cold, even though the nurse insisted the air-conditioning was turned down. It was because of the surgery, the nurse said: brain surgery was a delicate matter. Nola had been in critical, she'd barely come through, they said. She didn't understand it. She'd simply collapsed one day on the New York farm and Ritchie dragged her over the border in his uncle's truck and up to this Toronto hospital. Canadians took in every sick body was the excuse.

"Never you mind," Ritchie said. Meaning he stole the posies off a cart or out of some florist's window. And then, when she reached out for them, "Leave 'em be—and get that white sack offa you, we're outa here."

"No, Ritchie, I'm not ready."

They'd got the tumor (fancy that—she'd had a tumor, just in front of the left ear it was), but she still felt the weakness, the pain in the left temple. Besides, they fed her three meals a day here, they said she was anemic; she wanted to take full advantage before they tossed her out.

The next she knew he was in the locker, throwing jeans and shirt at her, her rosary beads, her black purse, then sucking up the lemonade on the tray table with a little smirk, damn him. She'd been drinking it slowly, to savor it, it had just the right sweetness. "Up," he said. "Before the big nurse comes back. We gotta find Darren."

"Darren doesn't want to go back," she said. Ritchie's half brother, Darren, was fed up with the uncle's harsh ways. He'd left the farm three weeks ago for Vermont where he had a cousin on his nontraveller mother's side, and the cousin had got him work on a nearby farm.

"Uncle wants him back. And move your butt, we gotta hit the road."

"Hit it how, the road?" she asked. Uncle would want his truck back, he wouldn't want it going to Vermont. And their own pickup had died of old age the week before. She couldn't believe Ritchie was doing this to her, with her only five days before collapsing outside the cow barn.

He didn't answer her question.

"What about Keeley?" she asked. "I don't want the boy left there alone."

"I called Penny," he said. "She'll keep an eye on him."

Penny was their neighbor and Nola's friend; Keeley liked her. She was a counselor in Keeley's school—when he went to school, that is. Keeley was as shy as a chipmunk caught dozing on your front porch. Now Nola's twelve-year-old son was out for the summer and the neighbor had a part-time job—she couldn't always look out for the boy.

Nola didn't have to go to Vermont. She could ring the nurse, stay right here. She reached for the bell but Ritchie's hand clamped down on her wrist. "You stay," he said, "and you're on your own when they dump you outa here. I wasted a week already waiting for you. Darren could be in Mexico, and no one to say where."

She got up slowly—slowly was the only way she could do it. Tormey Leary was cheap; he'd never let them take the truck as far as Vermont, even if he did send Ritchie after his brother. If Ritchie expected her to walk, it might take a year—if she had a year to live. She staggered some, deliberately, on the way to the toilet. He didn't try to catch her, he'd know she was putting it on. She heard the woman in the next cubicle groan—that one was just out of surgery—gallbladder or something. At least she was beyond hearing Ritchie's talk. Nola looked at the puffy face in the mirror and grimaced. At thirty she was already getting lines from the hot work in the cornfields. She'd balked, but Ritchie wouldn't let up on her. He and his half brother had capital in the uncle's place; he was in the will, he said, they had to make a go of it.

"Hurry up, will ya." He was standing in the doorway, scratching his armpits, shuffling his feet. "No time for primping. You can do that on the road."

"I gotta sign out at least," she said. "I can't just leave."

"You can," he said. "You definitely can."

She was too weak to fight back. There wasn't even the guts in her to grab that last hunk of cake from the plate on the tray table. And they'd left the posies behind. "My flowers," she said, but Ritchie said, "Keep going."

On their way out down the echoey corridor a woman shouted, "Don't go! Bad luck if you go!" A man stepped out in the hall and narrowed his eyes at the dark-bearded Ritchie, but Nola felt it was herself the woman was speaking to.

Ritchie hustled her past the nurse's station, where the nurse had her nose in a computer, down the elevator, and out into the lobby, where no one paid attention to them, no one at all. Outside she shut her eyes against the dazzle of the late June sun. The traffic coming and going sounded like the outer space she'd seen once in a Disney film where the stars and planets and asteroids all spun crazily about one another. Her knees gave way under the terrible weight of her headache.

She leaned on Ritchie and this time he had to let her; there was a cop standing on the corner. If Ritchie was scared of one thing in his life, it was cops. One day she'd dare to ask him why.

For now, she was his captive. They walked right past the cop and around the corner to the truck and no one said a word. She, for one, couldn't have said a word if she'd wanted to, his arm was cramped so tight around her chest.

# TWO

As usual, Colm had fallen asleep after they made love. It wasn't that he wanted to; she could hear him straining to stay awake—all those groans and mutterings: "Love ya to pieces, Ruthie, let's live together, let's…." The leg and arm muscles shifting and twitching, and then the soft, sonorous breathing into her neck. And he was off to dreamland, leaving her wide, wide awake—all that adrenaline left over from the lovemaking.

Ruth was glad, of course, that they were lovers; it had been a long drought since Pete left—fully four years while she'd struggled with the farm and the three children. And Colm had waited all that time. Impatiently, yes, but waited—the old Irish bullshit about "no other woman" in his life since they'd first met in high school. Though when she called it "bullshit" he'd rear up on his hind legs and shout, "It's not fair, Ruthie, to say that word when a guy bares his soul to you. Would you like me to say 'You don't mean it when you tell me you love me'?"

No, she wouldn't. There were times when she had to back off and apologize. No more using the word "bullshit" now except out in the barn when she had to clean up the droppings. She got up to use the bathroom, was suddenly overcome with the heat. The sole air conditioner was in the bedroom and that one installed only this summer over her protests. Colm needed cooling, he said, to counteract the sweat that oozed the length and breadth of his body while making love. A normal Vermont summer had only four or five days in the nineties, but this summer they were already up to a dozen hot dry days and it was only the fifth of July. A suffocating thought.

She shoved open the window and the sound of an accordion poured in, and then a woman's sweet soprano. Ruth had succumbed in a weak moment when Colm had brought along a distant cousin to fill in for her hired man, Tim, who was taking a year off to explore Alaska. But the cousin had arrived in a pickup more battered than her own beat-up Toyota and began to unload suitcases, tents, cooking equipment, musical instruments. Then out came a dog, a potbellied pig, and three human females: two adults and a ponytailed girl barely out of puberty. They looked like gypsies, but they weren't gypsies, according to Colm: they were Irish travellers, whose forebears had come over after the First World War. Some had settled, like the herdsman Darren, who stemmed from a village in North Carolina; most were clannish and peripatetic and kept to their own kind.

Colm was quick to point out that *he* had no traveller blood: the kinship evolved through a perfectly respectable Irish grandmother who'd happened after the war to wed a handsome young traveller named O'Neill.

It was the younger adult, a thirtyish woman named Maggie, who was singing now—something about love and loneliness. They weren't quite the right words for Ruth, who had found love these days but who still needed her space for quiet thoughts. This was the first summer in years, in fact, that she'd had the house all to herself. Teenager Vic was a counselor at a summer camp and Emily was spending a month at the Jersey shore with a college classmate. Daughter Sharon, as always, was at home in East Branbury, with a dozen chickens and three crowing roosters that were the butt of threatening phone calls each week but that Sharon and the grandbabies refused to part with.

The singing followed Ruth as she padded back into the bedroom, and grew louder still when she pushed up the window. Colm was asleep, sprawled now across the whole bed. He was a restless sleeper, had only recently had himself taped and wired head to toe to discover whether or not he had a sleeping disorder. It might be sleep apnea, he said when she laughed;

she might find him dead one morning in bed—did she have no compassion?

She had no compassion at least for these relatives, who seemed already to have multiplied, for another female voice was joining in and it wasn't the high-pitched tremolo of the younger sister, Liz, or the quavery soprano of Maggie's grandmother, whom she envisioned squatting on the trailer steps, stroking her pet pig. This new voice sounded more mature, a kind of deep-throated contralto. A third instrument came in on the chorus of "Danny Boy": *Oh Danny Boy, the shades of night are fa-all-ing*…and then a male voice, slightly off key, bellowing *Oh sweet Ellen-a-Roon*…

It was too much. Too loud. Too jarring. They were revving up the cows in the pasture—she could hear the bellowings. Colm must wake up, he must go down and deal with them—never mind the sleep disorder. She shook him and told him so. "Colm, love—we can't have this." She snapped on the table lamp.

"Huh?" Colm looked startled, as though he'd seen an apparition. She supposed she did look ghostlike: hair hanging in her face, bags under her eyes she called udders—a joke, of course—but when she looked in the mirror they seemed to deepen and darken. Ruth hadn't particularly worried about her appearance until she and Colm became sexual partners, and now she found herself taking surreptitious glances even in the shiny milk pans in the cow barn.

"Listen," she said, and flung the window wide. One of the female voices hit a high C and Colm groaned. The males bawled an octave below. One of them attempted a harmony that came out a cacophony. A drum joined the chorus; then high-pitched laughter and more bellows from the pastured cows.

"Tomorrow's Monday. Workday," he murmured, but it was no excuse.

"They're your relatives," she reminded him. "And I work every day. I need the peace." Colm yawned and started for the door. "You can't go out naked," she said. "They'll think you want to join in the orgy." She threw him his shorts. He sat back on the bed to pull them on, maddeningly slow, examining a mosquito bite on his leg, just when the outdoors sounded like a whole rock-and-roll band.

When the noise went on for another quarter of an hour she went to see for herself. In spite of the light from lanterns set up on plastic chairs, no one seemed to notice her standing there in bathrobe and barn boots. She was only one of a crowd of a dozen raggedy participants, all beating on makeshift instruments: pots, fry pans, metal waste baskets, glass bottles. A pale, thin woman was clapping spoons together to a sentimental melody that the traveller Maggie O'Neill was belting out an octave above everyone else.

And where was Colm? Why, leaning against the John Deere tractor, grinning ear to ear, his unshaved face pink in the fire the group had made in front of the travellers' trailer. He was waving his hands to the rhythm of pots and accordion as though he were back on the old sod himself. She threw him a dark look but his eyes were on the woman playing the spoons—admittedly a beautiful woman: long lustrous black hair, curving cheekbones, and skin the color of milk. No, not milk but chalk, Ruth decided, for there was a sickly pallor about the face. Her hands were busy with the spoons but her dark violet eyes were gazing up at the half-moon as though any minute she would swing herself up on it and sail off to some quieter clime.

As Ruth watched, mesmerized, the woman appeared to shrink into herself, like a genie melting back into its bottle. In moments she was crumpled on the ground, curled up like a fetus. Was she dead? Playacting? Or simply passed out, drunk perhaps? The others, carried along by their music making, appeared to ignore her. The music crescendoed to its high, maudlin resolve.

At the end of the song a tall, lean, bearded man picked up the prostrate woman and, complaining bitterly—"Christ, Nola, and I got a bad back, you want to crucify me, huh?"—carried her beyond the lantern light and into a tent that someone had pitched several yards beyond the trailer. Which made Ruth all the madder because who had given permission for a second family and a tent on her property? This was a working farm, a hardscrabble farm; there were balsam and scotch pine trees in this area, Ruth's attempt at diversity. Already she saw where a row of seedlings had been trampled by callous feet.

"Look here," she shouted, and no one looked. Colm's relative, Darren O'Neill, was pumping up a new tune on his accordion. Maggie was arguing with him.

"That's not the tune," she screeched, "that's not it a-tall, you got it wrong."

"Is," he yelled, "is an alternate, you never sung it right, you don't listen."

"I do, I do, you got it wrong! Now put down that thing and let me sing it right."

Ruth marched forward, hands on her cotton hips. She wished she'd had on her working jeans—who could show authority in a bathrobe? "It's midnight," she hollered. "Do you know what time the cows get milked? Do you?"

The crowd quieted to a few whisperings, stared at her. Who was this creature come to put the damper on their party? "Now what kind of foolish question is that?" Darren said, smiling at Ruth. "Where you think I'll be at four-thirty this morning but in that bloody barn over there, milking your big beautiful herd?" He pointed at the red barn that seemed at this hour little more than a dark heap of boards. The moon had slid under a cloud.

Ruth stood there, awed by his insensitivity.

"Aw," he said, coming over to her, "five hours of sleep is plenty, I never needed more, ma'am, not even when I was a kid." He grinned into her face.

"Colm," she said, addressing the infuriating figure in the white boxer shorts. "This is your relative. Please explain things to him. And who gave permission for that tent?" She pointed to the tent where the bearded newcomer was emerging now, stomping over to the group of spectators squatting on the grass.

Squatters. The word came to her. They squatted on your unoccupied land until they claimed it for their own, and who could get them off? She'd heard that about the Irish. Who were these people anyway? Gypsies, she thought. She didn't care what Colm called them. Travellers like Maggie were surely to be classified as gypsies. Not European Roma gypsies, but itinerant wandering Irish-Americans who thought nothing, folk said, of taking the corn you'd just brought to fruition in your garden, or the ripe tomatoes or pole beans. Human raccoons! Come in an ancient pickup and a trailer painted a canary yellow.

Colm was whispering to Darren; the tall lanky fellow was all apologies as though he'd no idea the music could have disturbed anyone's rest. "Right," Darren said, "we'll put it all away and let you go back and have your night's sleep. We'll be fresh as buttercups in the dawn and you'll get a day's work out of me'll make you fall on your knees and shout a-men."

"And that?" she said, ignoring the bullshit (that word again but fitting this time)—she pointed at the newcomers' tent.

Darren squinted as though surprised to see it there, a thin plastic structure with tiny holes as though it had been attacked by a swarm of killer bees. He laughed. "Oh, that's just my big brother, Ritchie, come to take me back to Uncle's farm. The hired guy quit when he couldn't take Uncle's temper, and now he's short of hands. But would I leave you in the lurch? Aw, hell, you know I wouldn't—I swear—got a Bible around here?" He crossed himself with a flourish, glanced at Maggie for support; she trilled a few high notes. "Not this summer, not when I promised to stay, and Maggie here's got a concert next month, up to Burlington, in one of them cafés there. Good pay, too, I tell you, am I right, Mag?"

"Right," she said, and rubbed her palms together. She gave the younger sister a slap on the bum and sent her into the trailer, presumably to sleep.

"They're not staying, any of them," Ruth mumbled, and glared at the yellow trailer, which was clearly profiled now where the moon had swung back into view. Beyond the trailer she saw a second pickup that someone had driven into her pasture, mowing down a hundred new trees no doubt. And then a horse grazing on her scotch pine. She was dumbstruck with the audacity of it. And there was her lover, Colm, smiling, calm as a summer's night, thumbs stuck into the band of his white boxer shorts. They were all alike, the Irish—on both sides of the ocean. Not like her own rational Scots, who'd feel the weight of an awful guilt to be exploiting another's hospitality.

"Darren. Please. I want them out by tomorrow night."

"But, ma'am, the woman's sick—she had surgery, Nola did, two weeks ago—up to Canada," Darren said, looking innocent. "You can't throw her out. It's just till she recoups, you know, and they'll be outa here. I give you my solemn promise." He held out his large calloused hands as though a Bible might suddenly drop into them.

"Day after tomorrow then," Ruth said, relenting. "Tell your brother to find a place for the two of them. These are new young trees on this pasture. I need the income. And see to it that horse is out of here at dawn. Can't you see it's digging up the grass?"

She blinked, and the place was suddenly empty. The spectators, horse and all, had gone, crawled away it seemed, into the dark. Were they bundled up among her trees? Sleeping with the cows? What would she find in the morning? Her trees trampled, her pasture littered with bottles, jars, paper cups, burger wrappers?

She had to have her sleep. She had to be up at four-fifteen. The cows wouldn't wait. She stumbled back to the house. Colm was there at her elbow, all sweet talk and hands stroking her butt. Not a single apology for this mayhem in her life, this loss of sleep. She loved him: he was good, loyal, engaging, compassionate. He had a great sense of humor. But there were times he went too far.

"They would've sneaked over the border, I expect," Colm said. "I suppose we should call that hospital, but I don't want them in trouble."

"What hospital? Why would we call them? What about?"

"Why, that woman who died of variant CJD—you didn't hear it on the radio? They did an autopsy after she had surgery in a Canadian hospital and that's what it was, CJD, Creuztfeld-Jakob disease—the human form of Mad Cow."

Yes, she'd read about it, but oh, he was maddening, using those foolish initials. As if you could reduce pain, death, and disease to mere initials.

He went on with an ingratiating smile as though she were some kind of idiot, wholly out of the mainstream. "Comes from eating the meat of animals tainted with Mad Cow. They're making a call for a hundred patients who might've been infected from the surgical instruments after some young woman died of CJD. Or from a patch of brain sheathing they closed the incision with. And worse, a couple of them donated blood, might've lied about where they'd been—like in farms where they'd had Mad Cow. The hospital's closed down for now. They need those folks back for testing. For quarantining, I'd expect."

Slowly she put it together—her brain wasn't working too well at this hour of the night, especially after the rude interruption out in the pasture. Some young woman up in Canada had that incurable disease, and this woman in her tent, here in the Willmarth pasture, who'd been in that hospital and might be infected herself...

"Oh! Do you think it's contagious?"

"Contagious? Well I don't know about that. Could be, I guess. But over a hundred deaths in Britain and Ireland in the nineties—you read the papers, right? It attacks the whole brain, makes it look like a sponge, full of holes. Brings on depression, paranoia. You start seeing things upside down. You see things in surreal colors, you hallucinate—see bugs crawling all over the place. It eats away speech, memory. You turn into a vegetable. The worst, they say, is if you're infected it can sleep inside you for up to forty years—tens of thousands could already have it. And when it wakes up—bango!" Colm clapped his hands together. He was clearly enjoying the effect his words had on her. "Dead in seven days."

Outside, the accordion made a last trill, and was silent. The night beyond the bedroom window was black, the moon eclipsed by racing clouds. She imagined waking to a pasture empty of cows, like the sheep farmers up in East Warren who only three years before had their herd quarantined and then slaughtered because two animals had allegedly tested positive for a form of Mad Cow that could take years to prove. A livelihood removed, dreams destroyed. She'd felt sick for them.

"It could happen to me," she said, struck with the magnitude of it, the horror. "Oh, my God, it could." She flung her arms around her lover's neck. "Colm, we've got to get the woman out of that tent, back to that Canadian hospital!"

"Even then it could be too late for us," he said. "People will hear about it. Panic. Jump to false conclusions—you know."

She knew. She knew only too well. She felt the panic herself. She held on to him, needing solace. But he was already asleep.

# THREE

DEEP IN THE NIGHT Nola heard voices. She reached for Ritchie but discovered only the plastic mat they'd lain on nights since they left Canada—walking, stumbling, hitching rides after Uncle's truck broke down. One night they'd stayed in a shelter: that was heaven, a real honest-to-god foam mattress. Mostly, though, nights were spent on the thin mat, no pillow, her head a torture. And Ritchie wanting sex every night, when her head was hurting so bloody bad she thought she'd die. She just lay there and cried inside. If she fought him it could go worse for her.

The voices grew louder, arguing. It was Ritchie and Darren—they'd never got on. For one thing, Maggie was Ritchie's girlfriend first. Then Darren came between, married Maggie, his own first cousin; and the rejected Ritchie went to her, Nola. Nola with the pretty face—and the ugly scar on her breast. Yet for some reason Ritchie, the older by ten years, felt responsible for Darren, wanted him back on the uncle's farm. Blood sticks with blood, he'd say.

"Quit bothering me now," she heard Darren shout. "I ain't coming and that's that. I don't give a good goddamn he's our uncle, he got poison in his veins. It flows through him and comes out his filthy mouth. Now buzz off, Ritchie, leave me alone. I got cows to milk in the morning, a barn to paint. Go back to the old sumbitch, tell him I'm not coming."

"You'll be sorry," Ritchie said, his voice sounding desperate, threatening, the way it did when Nola crossed him, didn't do what he wanted, go the direction he pointed out. "You don't come you won't get a penny from me and Uncle. Sweet Jesus, this your last chance, I swear to God. The last!"

Ritchie stomped back into the tent and flung himself face-down on the mattress. His elbow hit her aching head. She cried out, but he hardly knew she was there. He was crying. Holy Mother, Ritchie was crying like a baby because his brother wouldn't do what he told him to do.

"Ritchie?" she said, feeling sorry, wanting to soothe. She tried to stroke his bare shoulder—but "Shut up" was the answer. "I don't need a mother. I need a woman. And not one who's forever moaning about her goddamn sick head." He flopped over, taking up most of the mat, shutting her out.

It was herself crying now, she couldn't help it. She was the one needing a mother. She'd never really had one, had she? Her mother always pregnant, running off, fetched back only to get pregnant again. And dead after the eleventh child, a stillborn missing a kidney. They'd burned that last one up, like it was a chunk of firewood.

"Quit that sniveling, will you?" He flopped over on his back. "Jesus, I could do with a fag."

He got up and went out; the night was quiet. Darren would have gone back to Maggie. Nola imagined him lying beside Maggie, arm around her plump body, kissing her, stroking her. Envy cut through Nola like a sharp blade. She had no one. Even her Keeley sometimes kept his distance—afraid of Ritchie, she supposed. Enola, her mother had named her. Turn the letters around and you got "alone." Her mother would of known that when she named her. Her mother knew it was a Donahue's fate to spin out her life alone.

Toward dawn Nola was squatting among the trees in her nightgown to take a pee—Ritchie gone God knows where—when she heard a cough behind her. She sat motionless, feeling an interloper here on this Vermont farm she hadn't yet seen in daylight. There were mountains, she'd been told, but she could see only the dark shapes of cattle in the pale lemony lights from the trailer and, beyond, from the owner's farmhouse.

"Nola?" It was Maggie, praise be, in a cotton nightie, a

burning cigarette between her lips. Seeing what Nola was up to, she handed over a papery leaf to wipe with.

Nola squinted, examining it closely to be sure it wasn't poison ivy—she'd had a bad experience just below the Canadian border. "Oak," said Maggie, who knew about leaves, shrubs, plants, and poison berries, and Nola took the leaf. She had always been in awe of her cousin Maggie, even when they were small girls in North Carolina, their families sometimes travelling together through the South, her father doing little "home improvements" like putting on a roof that would come down in the next big wind.

Maggie was the cousin who'd got away-because of her voice, that was. She could hit high C and hold it a full minute. When she was sixteen she'd won a contest, got a job in a local lounge, and begun to save a little money. Nola had envied Maggie for escaping the clan, never thought she'd have the luck herself, in spite of her pretty face, until she met Ritchie O'Neill in the bar Maggie sang at. He'd swept her off her feet and into a shiny new pickup with milk chocolates and promises of escape to a farm in New York State. It was Ritchie and his half brother Darren, who'd own the farm one day, Ritchie said, for the uncle never married, had no heirs—and wouldn't Nola be the grand lady then?

At first Nola said no. She wanted no part of Tormey Leary who'd swept in and out of town at drunken intervals, then swept out for the last time to "settle," he said, in the North. But Nola's father, still in Carolina, was even meaner than Tormey Leary. So Maggie and Darren were family now for Nola, Keeley, and Liz. Maggie begged, and Nola went.

"You're looking peaked," Maggie said and thrust out a hand to help Nola up. Holy Mother, but she could hardly stand up, she might's well be as old as Maggie's granny, who'd followed along to Vermont with her pet pig.

Nola shrugged a shoulder. She was cheerful enough by nature; it was Ritchie dragging her out of hospital and down country that had kept her down. Ritchie wasn't a man to argue with. Not that he'd ever broke her bones the way some men beat their women. Nola's dad would give her mother a regular clout each morning before he left for his day's scam, and hadn't her mother asked for another the way she'd stayed with him, though Nola and her sisters begged her to leave? And not just for the mother but for Nola, whose curse it was to be born with a pretty face and a body that a dad, whose wife was always pregnant, couldn't resist. She was working hard to forget all that.

"I want you should stay with me when Ritchie goes back to the farm," Maggie said, putting an arm around her cousin. "He's not good for you, Nola. He's not like his brother. Darren would never of dragged *me* outa that hospital! And you with your poor brain still addled. Why, you mighta kilt yourself coming all that long way and no wheels."

"We'll have them soon, wheels," Nola said, "Ritchie promised. He'll beg some money from Tormey and buy a second-hand pickup."

"Tell me another," Maggie said. "Uncle's truck all broke down in some dinky garage where you left it and he's gonna give Ritchie money?"

She laughed and hugged Nola, and it felt good. Nola could do with a little hugging. Though what she really needed this minute was a warm bath. She hadn't had a good cleansing since hospital—how she'd loved those backrubs! That sweet-smelling lotion the nurse rubbed on after the alcohol. She'd felt clean, really clean for practically the first time in her life. And she had a bed all to herself. No one to share it with, not little sisters or Ritchie. For a time she'd blessed even the brain tumor that brought her to that hospital, and the kind Scottish doctor who'd wormed the truth out of her about the old injuries. Like the time her dad had run after her, and she'd jumped on a horse standing in a nearby field, and when it reared, she fell off, hit her head on a stump, and he'd whacked her some more till she lay unconscious. Or the ugly scar he inflicted one night when he came home drunk, and swung a butcher knife around h body, and it slipped....

He'd felt bad then, he cried when she came to, and he wa all sugar for a time—till the next time he came home drun and then it was the old story repeating itself and no place to g clean of him. Except to leave home and go to New York Sta with Maggie and Darren.

Darren was coming out of the trailer, looking a young go with his hairy chest all bare and his fresh ruddy face—he wa younger than Maggie by four years. Nola had seen him look ing at herself, too, though he'd never tried anything. He kne Maggie and Nola were not just cousins but close friend They'd got even closer at the farm the brothers brought the to—their way of staying out of the uncle's path. Darren wave at the two women and then disappeared around the side of th trailer. The sun was struggling to rise over the mountaintop, th whole sky was pink with its climb. Nola wished she could ru up that mountain and dive into the warm core of it.

"I could do with a hot bath," she told Maggie, and Ma laughed and stubbed out her cigarette and said, "In this heat" Then Mag said, "They got a downstairs one in the big hous there. Ruth Willmarth lets us use it, once a day, sure and she let you, too, Nola. You see, her boyfriend's some kind of cousi to our men and she has to let us into her house. We got baco and milk in her fridge, too—our old GE's broke down half th time. I mean, she seems a good woman—she just lost it a li tle last night, that's all, and maybe we were kinda loud."

Now Darren was calling for Maggie and didn't Mag rac into his hairy arms like he was some magnet she couldn't kee away from? Off by the big house Nola saw the farmwoma emerging from a doorway, slim and windblown in a green rol and sandals, like she was some Venus rising out of the sea. No had always loved those goddess tales, wanted to believe them, though she was raised Roman Catholic. That religio hadn't helped against her dad, had it? Yet she told her rosar beads over and over, to ward off the bad things there in the shadows. She couldn't be without her rosary.

The thought of Venus rising from the sea made her long more than ever for that warm bath. She ran back to the tent for a change of clothing, grabbed panties, jeans, and shirt. She started toward the house, though keeping a separate distance from The Willmarth. When the farmwoman was out of sight, she went on into the house and through the kitchen—grabbing a doughnut, for she was suddenly hungry. She tried two doors before she found the right one and then she turned on the tub faucet full blast, knocking a hairbrush off the edge, but no matter. Flung off the nightgown she'd slept in for six days and nights—she never could bear to sleep in her day clothes—and slipped gratefully in.

She'd got the water too hot but it was all right, the hotter the better to clean the filth off her, all the long travelling miles from North Carolina to Tonawanda, New York; Tonawanda to Toronto, Canada; Toronto to Branbury, Vermont. She pulled the shower curtain across the tub, laid her head back against the white enamel. It felt soothing, cleansing, healing. She stretched her arms, yawned luxuriously.

She was wholly relaxed and half asleep when she heard the footsteps tromping into the kitchen, the banging on the bathroom door.

"It's occupied," she hollered. "I'll be out in a minute." But the door cracked open and footsteps pounded the bathroom tile. She could hear the breathing, heavy, like the intruder had been running. Then brawny arms yanked her up out of the tub and a hand clapped over her mouth to keep her from crying out.

THERE WAS NO SIGN of a tent at six that morning when Ruth went down in her green cotton robe to inspect first the corn, which was only ankle high and already scorched from the hot sun, and then, with even more trepidation, the scene of last night's "orgy." There was nothing among the seedling trees but the yellow trailer and Darren's pickup with its trailer hitch like a dropped anchor on a struggling pine. Darren stood bare-chested and cheerful, his long legs planted sturdily on the grass as though rooted there.

"And good morning to you, ma'am. By golly, I had the best night's sleep in the world. I'm ready to face them cows. Though a cuppa coffee would help, it surely would, it's the caffeine that moves my muscles, so to speak. You wouldn't happen to have the pot on, would you, before we hit the barn?"

Ruth nodded absently, she was a bit off balance this morning. "Sleep deprived" was the phrase—the worse because Colm, who was the partial cause of her lack of sleep, was still sweetly snoring; his real estate office didn't open till nine. The whole world, it seemed, was slumbering, not a car on Cow Hill Road at this hour. The mountains that rimmed her green valley were a pale lavender in the rosy dawn light. She hadn't yet put on the coffee, she wanted to see to the sick woman, have the woman's partner—or husband, or whoever he was—take her to the local hospital, have her tested for that disease. Then pronounce the disease negative, of course. In short, give Ruth a new lease on life, a future to work toward.

"Where is she?" she asked. "The sick woman?"

Darren smiled blandly, as though there had been no intruders, no fainting woman, no brother—what was his name?—carrying the woman back to the pup tent, his horse tethered on her land, his truck—or was it someone else's truck and horse? For there had been a dozen people here, at least, last night, mowing down her seedlings. She squinted, and sure enough, there were several rows listing sideways as though already stricken with this Mad Cow.

"Oh, my poor trees!" she cried.

"Hell, we'll set them right. Plants are tough. I'll tend to them after milking. Sorry about last night, ma'am, they were just a few acquaintances, you know, friends Maggie picked up here and there." He waved at his wife, who was walking briskly among the older evergreens, a sheaf of what appeared to be music in her hands. "I told them not to drive up on the grass, but you know how careless folks can be." He shook his head woefully as though he himself would never dream of driving on anyone's property, much less defiling it.

"But you said you'd put on the pot, hey? A bit of caffeine and I'm Mohammad Ali." He flexed his muscles, bulging them out like a prizefighter, and she had to laugh. It was hard to stay cross with Darren.

She led the way back to her kitchen; she was faint with the lack of caffeine herself. She'd give him his fix and then send him on to bring in the cows. No more questions asked about that woman. Let bygones be bygones. Tens of thousands exposed, Colm had said, and how could you track them all down? Why, her cows were healthy! She seldom had to call the vet; their milk was organic, pure—no BST or other additives. Organic milk came from cows that grazed out of doors, that ate corn and forage raised without synthetic fertilizer, herbicides, or pesticides. This was Vermont, land of milk and honey, and if there was occasional malice, well, it usually happened on other folks' farms, not hers.

"Just stop the music after ten and we'll all live together in peace," she instructed, and filled his mug with strong, fragrant Green Mountain coffee. "And bring in the cows, I'll meet you in the barn." She ran upstairs to pull on jeans and a sleeveless shirt. It would be another hot dry day; the sun was rising blood-red, the mountains fading to palest mauve with the increasing humidity. Downstairs she heard Darren singing something lusty, something with a woman's name, Mag or Nola. Wasn't Nola the name of the ill woman? Yes, she recalled hearing the brother call her that, and then Darren's voice afterward, saying, "Nola had brain surgery." My God! Ruth thought, and there the poor woman was in a tent, spread out no doubt on the hard ground, or at best on a thin mat.

She rebuked herself for ignoring the sick woman, threw her

robe on the bed where Colm was still sleeping sweetly on his side, his nose squashed into the pillow; she pulled on jeans and a blue cotton shirt. She should have brought the woman into the house, put her up in Emily's old room. How could she have been so thoughtless! A woman on her own premises, in need of a little kindness. Where's the old law of hospitality now, Ruth? she asked herself. If the pair returned she would sit the woman down, talk to her, make her see for her own sake that she must report to the authorities. What were Ruth's cows in relation to a woman's well-being?

But the farm is everything now, she thought: my life, my income—though with milk prices so low these days it was more outgo than income. County farms were failing, one by one. Vic was growing daily out of his clothes; Emily needed help for college books—the scholarship didn't pay for those. She had to think first of her own family.

Sitting down to pull on her socks, she relaxed. What chance anyway that the woman carried the disease? Probably one in a thousand. Ten thousand! "Quit worrying, Ruth," she said aloud. "Quit it, I said! Smile."

"Just what I been telling you, Ruthie." Sitting up with a sonorous yawn, Colm reached for her, pulled her back down to him, stroked her back, shoulders, arms, hair. It was comforting. Maybe she *should* let him move in. There was only Vic now in the house most of the year; the boy liked Colm; he needed a surrogate father.

"Colm, love," she said.

"I'm here, Ruthie."

"Don't go to work. Not today. I think I might need you."

"That woman, you mean? You went out there? I thought I heard you get out of bed." He was still holding her, making her relax in his arms. They were comforting arms, warmly muscled and smooth as satin; salvaging arms, holding her close. To hell with independence, she thought. Give me co-dependence—was that the word? Co-something anyway, like in her yoga class where she couldn't stand on one foot for more than a few seconds but when six women in a circle barely touched one another on the shoulders she could stand one-footed with ease.

She told him about the tent's disappearance and he laughed. "See? Nothing to worry about. Just an ordinary day coming up. I got an appointment at nine-fifteen with some retired couple wanting land to build on. You'd think a couple in their sixties would want a condo, everything done for them. And here they plan to start building, like they're just beginning life."

She smiled. She liked that idea. She hoped she'd keep on building in her sixties. That wouldn't be long now, she was already fifty-two. She hugged him, then wriggled out of his arms. She had to brush her teeth after the coffee; already the singing had ceased downstairs. She heard the kitchen door slam; Darren would be heading for the pasture, herding in the first group of cows. She had to prep them, get the milking machine going, the day moving before it got so hot she was all sweat. There was something to be said for getting up early in the summer, working in the cool. It was a kind of low-key limbo before the sun was all the way up. And the summer already so bizarre—not just the early heat but the odd travelling folk out in the pasture, and now this sick woman who'd come—and seemingly already gone.

Colm let her go. He fell back on the pillow—he'd sleep another hour or two, lucky fellow. She went into the bathroom to brush her teeth, her hair. She'd cut it short this summer to simplify her life. Simplify, simplify—she wanted to be one with Thoreau and his nine bean rows. She didn't want any traveller woman carrying some kind of plague. Bubonic, Black Death, typhoid, smallpox, AIDS, anthrax, West Nile, now SARS and Avian—so many plagues through the ages and never once touching *her* life.

Until now. She gasped when she went back downstairs and opened the door to the bathroom where she'd left her hairbrush last night. Hot steam and water curled out onto the kitchen floor; inside a small flood, her hairbrush floating in it, the bottle of liquid soap, a hunk of soggy doughnut. The old footed tub was still trickling—someone hadn't turned the faucet completely off. Water everywhere—who had taken a bath and left it running? One of the travellers, she supposed, though she'd seen them all, hadn't she, when she went down to inspect the trees? Darren's women were sitting on the trailer steps when Darren came out.

All except for the sick woman.

There was a tumble of clean clothing on the toilet lid: panties, jeans, a blue checkered shirt with a bottle of Tylenol in the breast pocket. The woman who had taken the bath had doubtless intended to wear this clothing, perhaps take a Tylenol. Then, since there was no evidence of shoes, she'd returned to the tent. But had somehow been prevented. Did she run back through the kitchen? Or did she escape through the window, wide open because of the heat? And stark naked?

There was no sign of dirty clothes she would have taken off, or a nightgown or pajamas, perhaps? Or had she come in her clean clothes—and before dawn?

And what about the man she had come with: Darren's brother, Ritchie? What part had he played in this?

She stood motionless a moment longer and then hollered for Colm. Hearing no response, she raced upstairs, shook the sleeping fellow, poured out the scenario into his groggy ear.

She realized as she gushed on: The woman was indeed missing, the woman who might be carrying a life-threatening disease. A threat not only to herself but to others. At least that was the way folk would look at it. The woman had been on the Willmarth farm, folk would rationalize; therefore she was contaminated. So they'd boycott the beef from the slaughtered bull calves—and worse, the milk that came from Ruth's cows. It was a disease, they'd shout abroad, that could affect the whole town, the county, the state. The whole country. The world—look at the way SARS had travelled in just hours!

"We've got to find her, Colm. We've got to know. She was taking a bath in my tub. She ate one of my doughnuts, I saw part of one in the water on the floor. She can't have gotten far. We'll have to inform the police. We have to find her. For her sake—and ours. It could mean my farm, Colm. *Our* farm—as you like to call it."

"Jeez," he said, and this time he was fully awake. He followed Ruth downstairs and into the flooded bathroom.

"Blood," he said, squinting down at the windowsill, screwing up his face. "We'd better call headquarters."

# FOUR

THE WHOLE COUNTY, it seemed, had heard about the missing woman and what she stood for. And the man who'd brought her here, gone as well. "Plague," said Ruth's older daughter, marching into the barn next morning in the usual getup: long flowered rayon skirt cut on the bias, bare, unshaved legs, and something that looked like a nightgown draped over the whole. But leaving the two darling grandkids in the car as though they might catch something, Ruth thought, as though already Ruth herself was contagious.

"Damn it, Sharon, we don't know she has something, you'll just make things worse using that word." Though hadn't she used it herself, just yesterday?

"Plague," Sharon said again, and choked out a list from AIDS to zebra mussels.

"She was in that Canadian hospital," said Sharon, who listened to Vermont Public Radio each morning and habitually quoted the bad news to her mother on the barn phone. Though this morning she'd felt compelled to come herself to tell the tale, as though Ruth didn't know the woman had bathed in her own tub and then disappeared—in such a hurry she'd left her clean clothes and the Tylenol. "The hospital authorities want the woman back. Good Lord—she was Colm's relative, right?"

"Wrong. Darren was his relative—the brother Ritchie, too, of course. Nola was the girlfriend, a traveler—from the accent, a southerner, though they have some language of their own, Colm told me, something called Cant—a form of Gaelic. Travellers are like gypsies, you know, the lowest caste in Ireland—the one that gets spit on and blamed for anything that goes wrong. They're sort of like the homeless here, but they hang out in clans. And all related in each clan, it seems—at least Nola and Maggie are. Colm said they're double first cousins, can you imagine? That means there's a relationship between kids born to siblings within one family who marry siblings within another."

"Whoa. Far out." Sharon had met Maggie, had even heard her sing on the village green, an impromptu noon concert with Darren on the accordion and Maggie in a flowing Indian skirt and sparkly top that barely hid her pendulous (as Sharon described them) breasts. Stuck in the ground beside them was a placard announcing her upcoming stint in a Burlington café. "But who's going to listen to her now in that café?"

"Oh come on. We don't even know if Nola has it, the CID."

"CJD, Mother. CID is a police department in London. You'd better learn the right initials."

"Oh, I know that. Don't torment me, Sharon. But I'm thinking now it's not as suspicious as Colm and I first thought. The poor woman had brain surgery, that's all. She was exhausted, I figure. She was taking a bath and heard a noise. She thought she'd be hollered at for taking a bath, so she took off through the window. Pure and simple, no hanky-panky."

"And what about that blood the police found outside in the grass? I heard it on the radio. I mean, how do you account for that?"

"On the grass?" Ruth hadn't heard about that. The police had arrived with a crime lab technician, after Colm, who worked part-time for the Branbury police, summoned them at five-thirty in the morning. The technician had photographed the soapy, watery mess, donned rubber gloves, and gathered up hairs and fibers; the police stretched a yellow crime scene tape around the whole kitchen. When Ruth complained she couldn't make coffee or eat breakfast, they enclosed only the bathroom. After all, the woman wasn't dead, was she? She was only missing. Wasn't she?

The affair was sounding more ominous now. She slathered the barn floor with a mop as though it were the bathroom floor—no blood, but shit and slobber and bits of hay, making for easy sliding. More than once Ruth had gone head over teakettle on that floor and landed on her butt. Darren was okay with the herding, milking, and planting, but he was no hand when it came to cleaning; he let Ruth do that. And Maggie wouldn't put a foot in the barn. The most her soft white hands could seem to do was pull a few weeds. At least the grandmother and young sister volunteered to feed the calves—in particular, the two Friesian calves Ruth had purchased, at Colm's urging, from the uncle back on the Tonawanda farm. The uncle had given her a "good price," and Darren had brought them to Vermont in June.

Today, though, Maggie was keening as though the traveller woman really was dead. Keening was a business with the Irish, Ruth had heard: folk often hired professional keeners for their wakes and funerals. Calamity, it seemed, brought traveller clans together; they revelled in one another's mortality.

"Cripes," Sharon said, going to the barn door, "it sounds like a whole army of wailers out there." Mother and daughter listened as the noise rose to a crescendo, trembled in the air like the eerie background music of a sci-fi film, and then fell, a long, cascading waterfall of potential disaster.

So they might have keened in medieval times, Ruth thought: to mourn the dead—or near dead—of the Black Death.

"Where did the keeners come from—at least twenty women and children?"—Sharon asked, but Ruth couldn't answer. It was as if they had been waiting in the woods and hills for the kill, and now, a ragtag army in colorful cast-off clothing, they'd converged on Ruth's pasture to warn of dire things to come.

"Go out and see. You'd fit right in, in that outfit, Sharon," and Sharon laughed. Sharon danced to her own tune, she didn't care how she looked—although her husband, Jack, had lately taken to making comments that Sharon would repeat, giggling, to her children: "It's parents' day at the Quarry Hill Day Care, and Mother will show up in a *loverly* new lace curtain." Though that wasn't really so funny: Sharon *had* worn a curtain to Town Meeting day when she was pregnant with three-year-old Willa, and even got compliments from her peers.

"I'll go down there then. I want to see for myself what's going on. I'm worried about you, Mother. They said on VPR—"

"What? They mentioned me? On public radio?"

"This is your farm, right? They said—" The barn phone rang and Sharon pointed a finger at Ruth. "Pick it up, Mom, and hear what they have to say. You've got to face it. Take your stand, prepare your defense."

"What are answering machines for?" said Ruth, and went on swabbing the floor. A sick heifer mewled in the rear of the building. It had foot rot. This was all the illness she was prepared to deal with right now.

"Even domestic cats get CJD," Sharon announced when the phone had completed its fifth ring. "Up in Canada, elk and deer. In Britain, cows, pigs, and sheep—you saw that newscast a couple of years ago, you were at my house. It was after I served that garlic cream soup we all got sick from. A British cow shedding weight, drooling, acting crazy—off balance, waving its head, threatening the vet. Then boom, dead as a doornail! All in a matter of hours."

"I wish you wouldn't say that: dead as a doornail. What is a doornail anyway?"

"Then that young woman in Wales—I saw the documentary. She took to sitting alone on her bed, staring out the window for hours at a time. The doctors called it a nervous breakdown, but two years later, there she was, paranoid and incontinent. A month before she died she went blind and couldn't talk or eat."

"Enough!" cried Ruth, forking hay into the sick heifer's stall. "That was ten years ago. They've got a handle on it now. Nothing in the news about all that for a dog's age."

"That's just it," Sharon went on, "the dogs—" The phone

rang again and Sharon stopped in midsentence to pick it up, listen, and smile triumphantly as though the caller had just corroborated her story. "One moment, please," she said, and held it out, a hand over the mouthpiece. "It's those women down the road, the ones with the Morgan horses. What do you call them?"

"Lippitt. Lippitt Morgans. The original Vermont Morgan. More rugged, ridable, and lovable than your government Morgan," Ruth said, quoting her neighbors. She wiped her hands on her jeans and took the phone. She liked those two women, had been witness to their civil union. They'd come from Poughkeepsie, New York, to have a ceremony when the new law passed, decided to settle on the Larocque farm and raise their horses after old Lucien went to live with his daughter.

This time, though, it wasn't about coming over for a cup of coffee, exchanging pleasantries, or the latest on how to keep raccoons out of the corn. Franny and Henrietta had been listening to public radio. They were worried about their horses. They had four full-blooded Lippitts; someone had just called to cancel a scheduled breeding with their mare.

"But why?" cried Ruth, all innocence—though she knew it was because of the missing woman. "There hasn't been a single instance of Mad Cow in America. Or in any horse anywhere, for heaven sake. Tell them that!"

"Those sheep," Franny said, reminding her of the destroyed Vermont sheep.

"And never proven. Never!" cried Ruth, her back to the wall. "And sheep don't get the actual Mad Cow. Look, Franny, let's be rational about this. Nothing's been proven about this traveller woman, either. Even if she has that disease, it doesn't mean she's contagious. You have to eat bad beef—the nervous system of infected cows. Let's not panic till we find her."

"Even then it could take days, weeks—months," Franny said in her low, croaky voice. Franny had been a summer stock actress before she aged and expanded and could no longer reap the bittersweet roles. Now she rode a horse as stout as herself and leaped up and down off her favorite mare as nimbly as a circus performer.

"Franny," Sharon said, grabbing the phone, "be reasonable. This woman was on the property exactly twenty-four hours. Mother never saw her before last night, never even heard of her, right, Mother?"

Ruth nodded and shrugged. She felt helpless—something like the embarrassed bare-assed sunbather she'd seen in a cartoon, greeting the UPS man. "The poor woman took a bath, which Mother has decontaminated—why, she used a whole box of Lysol on it after the police did their thing, right, Mother?"

No, that wasn't right. Ruth hadn't even touched it. The crime lab technician took all the samples. But Ruth let it go for now. She heard Franny's tragic voice crescendoing: her beloved horses, her bucolic life-in-the-country, her partner's health— for Henrietta had some mysterious ailment from a dirty needle in her experimental days, and could fall an easy victim to any modern scourge. Already the couple was anticipating the West Nile virus since an infected bird had been found just seventy miles north in Franklin County.

Ruth snatched back the phone. "What I'm trying to tell you, Franny, is there's nothing I can do. I have thirty-four cows. Don't you think they're in greater danger than your four horses? It's called Mad Cow for a reason, you know. Look, I could be the victim here. Do you think I've had a minute's sleep all night, worrying about my livelihood?"

"But that's why I called—to cheer you up!" Franny shouted from a half mile down the road. "I've been worrying about you, Ruth. I just wanted to tell you we're here for you. You can come over anytime and we'll have tea and commiserate. I have some antistress tea, I want you to try it."

"Thank you," said Ruth, and hung up, though she wasn't sure what kind of reception she'd get if she did appear on their doorstep. Would they spray the contents of a can of Lysol on her?

Ruth was waving good-bye to Sharon, who'd been summoned by a sibling fight in the car, when the phone rang again—eight times. It was Bertha Willmarth, her born-again ex sister-in-law, who called Ruth twice a week as a kind of atonement for her brother's abdication of wife and farm. Ruth held the receiver away from her ear and grimaced at the sick heifer who, as if in sympathy, was making a gagging sound.

Bertha and her peers had been researching in the local library and come up with some horrors that "You ought to know, Ruth. Listen: 'Mad cow is the cer-reepiest of all the, uh, pri-on diseases. It makes the Ebola virus look like chicken pox!' That's a direct quote from a piece in *Time*. Prepare, Ruth, prepare! If you'd come to my church we'd help. You know we'd be glad to have you." Her voice rose in pitch and volume; she began quoting the Bible: "'I am come not to call the righteous, but sinners to repentance.'"

"Thank you, Bertha. But I've never accepted the label of righteous *or* sinner, and don't expect me at your church." Ruth had to milk the cows on Sunday as well as every other day and knelt only to the bovine underbellies. She'd have to do a little praying now though, she thought, listening to the wailing out in the pasture.

"What *is* that noise?" asked Bertha. "It sounds like heavenly angels. Is it the radio?"

"It's the Tabernacle Choir, Bertha. I have it on to comfort me in this time of need." Ruth slapped the phone back into its wall cradle before Bertha could gush out a response.

A CHILD IN EACH HAND, Sharon marched into the pasture, through the crowd of travellers, who had brought their lunches, fiddles, and pennywhistles as if for a prolonged festival, and into the trailer where Maggie was warbling to the strum of a guitar. Sharon was intrigued by Maggie and her vagabond life; she often daydreamed in the tub about running off and setting up housekeeping on some remote mountaintop. Or perhaps by the ocean side, she hadn't decided which. She did long to travel but was held back by children and a forester husband who was too in love with the Vermont forests and clay plains to leave the state.

Inside the cluttered trailer, which was hung with red and yellow India print cotton sheets and racks of sparkly skirts and blouses, the grandmother squatted on a three-legged stool, peeling potatoes. She was dressed in an orange cotton skirt and low-cut black blouse that revealed the tops of her wrinkly boobs. A potbellied pig with a pendulous belly and stubby snout sat at her feet, munching on the dropped peels and making little satisfied *ouff*ing sounds. Seeing Sharon, it began a kind of *ha ha ha* pant that put Sharon quite off balance. But the old lady grinned. "She's just saying hello."

Sharon smiled back, decided she could do without a pet pig, and inquired after Maggie.

The grandmother waggled her thumb in the direction of a screened-off area in the rear of the trailer. "In there," she said. "She won't go out. She won't speak. She won't do nothing but worry about Nola and sing depressing songs."

And sure enough, the tragic words "Laugh at death, but weep for those who die before their time" came warbling out of the back side of the crowded trailer, which Maggie shared with her husband, Darren. The lyrics switched into Gaelic, or was it Cant?—sounding something like "Gory at thasp, keener…" and, well, Sharon gave up trying to decipher the words, and knocked on the wooden frame of the screen.

Maggie went on singing.

When Sharon entered anyway, after cautioning the children to "Stay outside and don't chase the heifers," Maggie jumped up from her mattress and grabbed Sharon hard about the neck. Anyone who would listen to her songs was apparently her friend, and Maggie had seen Sharon at her concerts. The younger woman waited while Maggie finished pouring the end of the song into her ear-in English now. The girl in the song had drowned and her lover sat alone on the bridge where the girl had leaped, beating his chest for the guilt of having betrayed her.

Typical man, Sharon thought. She thought of the missin
woman, Nola, and her lover. For she had a lover, didn't she
The man who'd come with her from Canada, who'd taken—n
abducted—her from the Toronto hospital? According to th
newscast, a witness had heard her protests. And if the fello
had abducted her from the hospital, wouldn't he abduct he
again, against her wishes, from the dairy farm? For it was Sha
on's theory that Ritchie had come in on her taking the bat
yanked her out of the tub, and hearing footsteps in the kitche
shoved her out the window, giving her a bleeding knee or shi
Then he sprang through behind her and hurried her off the farm

"So where is he? The boyfriend?" Sharon whispered whe
the last note quivered on the breeze that wafted in through th
cracks in the rear door, and then died away. "Where did he tal
your Nola?"

Maggie stuck her hands on her shiny yellow hips. "Wh
knows, the selfish bastard? Aw, and he's gone with her all righ
Don't want to see any cops. No, not him! Not with what he done

Sharon sat back on her heels. Here was something more i
triguing than any distraught lover running off with a sic
woman. Here was the hint of some hanky-panky, some fo
play. Had the woman drowned in the bathtub? Had he pushe
her under, then hauled her out? Had he disposed of her bod
somewhere and run off—not wanting the body dug up, give
an autopsy? And where had this lover gone? This monster?

"What did he do?" she whispered, gazing into Maggie
black mascaraed eyes. The mascara had run down her chee
from all the weeping and into the creases beside her full red lip

The eyes only gazed back soulfully at her. "'S not for me
say. Do you want me killed, do you? I never told Nola, and tha
a fact. Ritchie would of knowed where the telling come from

"But it might've saved her life to know!" Sharon cried, for sh
had decided that Nola was dead—if not a homicide, then a su
cide. Or maybe dead already from that chronic wasting diseas

The young sister burst into the tent and held up a small e

ameled box. A slim-hipped girl in her early teens, the sister was a match for Sharon's sister, Emily, in her tight jeans and stretchy pink tank top that showed the small pointy nipples of her pancake breasts.

"Can I have it, Mag? It's just the box for my earrings! Nola won't have no use for it now, will she?" The girl folded her hands together, pleading.

"It's locked, Liz," Maggie said.

"Well? There must be a key somewhere in her stuff Ritchie brought, and if not, there's always a way in, right?" Liz looked at Sharon for support. She was a smaller version of Maggie: carroty red hair, large, slightly oval eyes, and those deep pink Irish cheeks. "Pretty" was the word that came to mind; Liz and Maggie were both pretty. But the newscast had described the missing Nola as "a beauty"—a description sent out by the hospital, along with a photograph that was now in police files. Sleeping beauty, Sharon thought, envisioning the woman in the tub, her head floating below the surface of the sudsy water after the lover pushed her under and carried her inert body out the window…. Well, no, not sudsy, because the water was hard here on the farm, and Sharon's mother did not have a water softener. An unnecessary expense, her mother insisted, when Sharon came to take a bath because the well was always running low at her own house in East Branbury. As a teenager on the farm, Sharon would wash her hair and have to trudge down to the beaver pond to rinse out the dull iron. Already she'd noticed a lavender tint to her mother's graying hair. She must point this out to her.

Maggie grabbed the box, clutched it to her chest. "No," she said, pushing out her lips in a pout. "No no no no. It's Nola's box. She gave it to me for safekeeping. Though it might give a clue to Nola. Anyway, I don't want Ritchie to see it. Oh, he'll turn up somewhere, you can bet on that—he's a bad penny all right. Nola jumped out the window, oh sure, after he came in on her taking the bath. I don't blame her! She wasn't gonna let him steal her away again."

Here was a new scenario Sharon hadn't thought of: Nola fleeing alone and Ritchie in hot pursuit. And when he found her, what would he do? Cripes, Sharon thought, what *would* he do?

"Then if I decide—and if we can find the key—or maybe get it open some way or other," Maggie told Liz, "you can maybe borrow the box till Nola gets back. But not till then."

"Her and Ritchie aren't coming back," Liz said. "I heard Ritchie this morning talking to Darren when he was folding up the tent. He said he was going to buy hisself a pickup and go back to Uncle's farm, and if Darren wouldn't come he'd have the farm to himself when the old man died. He'd see that Darren didn't inherit a bloody acre of it. That's what he called it, a bloody acre."

"Is that so? And why would Darren care a fig anyhow? Why did Darren run off if he wanted to own some old farm with a million rocks and stones and some old doddering cows? Darren hates cows." Maggie glanced apologetically at Sharon. "Well, not all cows. It's just that cows is all Darren knows how to do. Except play music. But right now the music don't buy the food, you know. Even with me singing."

"I know what you mean," Sharon cooed in sympathy. Like her mother with this farm, she and Jack were barely hanging on, even with three part-time jobs between them.

"So here we are, right? Here we are," Maggie repeated, planting her two feet firmly on the linoleum floor of the trailer, her blue-black eyes watering. "I hope he's gone for good," she said between her shiny teeth. "I hope he never comes back. I hope Nola's alive somewhere and keeps hiding and he never, ever finds her."

But the cloudy eyes looking off through the trailer window betrayed that hope. For a moment Sharon felt disoriented, as though Maggie and her cousin had fallen into a deep hole and there was no way Sharon could pull them back out.

# FIVE

At first, looking out the bedroom window, barely awake, James Perlman thought it was a sheet, torn loose from his wife's clothesline. But he didn't have a wife—she'd gone off with that man who ran the hardware store. So now James sent his laundry to Mountain Fresh in town. The apparition was dressed in white, like a ghost. Only the ghost was moving fast, feet running so fast they were spinning but not gaining ground. Suddenly the feet were on top and the sheet plummeting. Decompressing into a crumpled heap, like a parachute—only a dark-haired head now, and in his backyard.

His first instinct was to leave the heap alone. But it didn't move and he felt compelled to see what the trouble was. He threw on a robe, took a heavy flashlight from a closet shelf. In Batavia, New York, where James was from, good Samaritans were usually hit on the head for all their goodwill, left for dead. He'd read a number of cases like that in the Buffalo papers. This was the reason he and Maureen had moved to Vermont. One of the reasons, anyway. The other—well, the other he didn't like to think about. Because, of course, it would never happen again. No, never, never! He'd told Maureen that—pleaded with her to believe him. She just shrugged. They hadn't been in Vermont more than ten months when Maureen met that hardware fellow and moved out. Like she'd been waiting for such an excuse.

The head belonged to a woman. And it wasn't a sheet she was wrapped in but a white nightgown. It had settled seductively over belly and breasts, and again he was afraid and he stepped back. The poet Emily Dickinson flashed into his mind.

His wife, a middle school English teacher, had made him take a poetry class with her. Most of it bored him but he was intrigued by Emily, her white dress, her fascination with death. James was fascinated, too; it was why he was a hospice volunteer. Emily was dead. And maybe this one was, too.

Gripping the flashlight he tiptoed to the woman, heard a groan. "Hello," he said, but no response. That was when he saw the blood on her sleeve, like she'd cracked her arm on something and broken the skin. Blood on her forehead, too, like something had struck it, though maybe she'd rubbed her forehead with the sleeve and that was why. And a purple bruise, or scar, where the top of her breast showed above the nightgown. She had something in her hand—looked like a necklace. He wondered if she'd stolen it. He said, "Hello, you're hurt." But still no reply.

He stood there, gazing at her. She was young, beautiful— the blood on the white gown. He thought of Poe's Annabel Lee, who died in her prime. Maureen had a video of that poem.

There was that hot, needy sensation in his groin the poem always brought. He didn't—couldn't—move.

Though his brain kept working. Should he call 911?

No, he didn't want to be involved with that kind of thing. Didn't want to be involved with police or nosy social workers. Not that he'd been formally indicted—there was no real proof. It was just a local scandal, confined mostly to the hospital where he'd worked as a male nurse. The offense was kept quiet—till word got out, some officious reporter put it in the Buffalo paper, and he had to leave the neighborhood.

He didn't want his past polluting his present. He had his twenty acres, his two dozen sheep that would fuel his retirement. He had a decent job with the counseling service. He was a caring person, he worked hard at hospice—had already helped three cancer patients to their final rest. The relatives had thanked him. One even sent a basket of fruit, invited him to attend her church, and he did, though he was bored. James was an agnostic, if anything.

But he couldn't leave the woman here on the grass. She was moaning louder, a wailing sound that rose and fell with her breath. "Can you walk?" he asked. But again no answer. He put down the flashlight—he didn't want to frighten her. Anyway, the sun was coming up, the mountains turning pink. He was still in his bathrobe—he slept in the buff these hot nights. James was a good person, he was! People back in Batavia had the wrong idea, his wife never understood. Sometimes his body overrode his mind.

He couldn't leave her lying on the ground. He took a deep breath, picked her up in his arms—she hardly weighed anything, and that was good—he was a thin fellow, weighing in at 155. "Slight," they'd called him in that newspaper article. He'd rather they'd have called him "slim" or "lean."

A car pulled up in front of his house, startling him—he almost dropped the girl. It was the mailman; he had a package in his hand. He might bring it up to the porch, and then what would he see? James imagined him describing the scene to a coworker: "This fellow Perlman, with a woman in his arms—in a nightgown. Was there blood on the sleeve? Should they inform the police?"

It was too compromising. James laid her on the grass behind a tree. The day was warming up, the air wouldn't hurt her. Later he'd go out and see. Bring her something to eat and drink. Bring her into the house maybe. He'd get dressed first, he didn't want to scare her. He'd made all those resolves since the trouble he'd got himself into. He ran around to the front of the house.

"Hello? A package for me?" he called to the carrier. "Wait, I'll come and get it. You stay right there."

It was a pair of Land's End denim shorts he'd ordered. The shorts had been back-ordered, he'd almost forgotten about them. He dropped the package on the kitchen table, popped two English muffins in the toaster. The woman looked like she could use some nourishment. He'd take one out to her, gain her trust a little, then go feed the sheep. Sheep were pretty easy to care for, they didn't have to be milked, like cows. Just fed, kept healthy, lambed and sheared once a year, then sold. If he did well with the sheep he'd quit the counseling job. He didn't like the suicides he had to work with, the weirdos he encountered. You couldn't reason with them the way you could with the dying. The dying were grateful for any crumb you could throw their way. A bath, a pain pill—they looked at you like you were their savior. He liked that. They trusted him. He'd never touched a dying female, not once.

Of course they were mostly old, the ones he cared for, wrinkled and saggy—he wouldn't want to touch them anyway.

Not like that woman in white out there on the grass. He watched her from his window: she was in a deep sleep, a sleeping beauty, trusting him, accepting his hospitality. He buttered the muffin, poured a glass of orange juice, placed them on a tray with a pansy blossom, and went out. Down in the pasture behind the house the sheep were grazing. He thought of the song "Sheep may safely graze"—how did it go? He couldn't carry a tune but he loved good music. Romantic music.

The woman was still asleep. It was a beautiful sight. "I'm coming," he called out. He was warm with his generosity. "I'm bringing food."

The woman opened her eyes, sat up-he could see it was an effort to do so. She looked like she might flee but couldn't get her legs to move.

"It's all right," he said, "I won't hurt you." He put the tray on a flat rock, stood with his hands at his sides to reinforce his words. She reached for the muffin, crammed it into her mouth like she hadn't eaten for days. Swallowed it down with the orange juice. She seemed to realize then she was wearing only a nightgown—she hugged her chest with her thin arms.

"I'll bring you something to wear," he said. "You can't go around like that. Where did you come from, anyway?"

The woman looked at him with huge violet eyes that seemed to consume her face. She didn't answer, just put a hand to her head. He saw a purple swelling on the temple, like she'd hit it on something—a little dry blood. It occurred to him that she might be running from someone. There was a place he knew in Branbury, the Healing House. He should take the woman there.

But not in a nightgown. "Wait," he said, "I'll be right back."

Upstairs he pulled an old housedress of Maureen's out of a back closet, a pair of hipster panties their adult daughter had left in a drawer, and ran back with them. The woman was up on her feet when he arrived—head arched back like she was challenging him. Challenging him to do what? He squinted into the sun and studied her. She lowered her eyes, stood absolutely still. He held out the clothing. When she didn't come forward to take it, he laid it on the rock beside the empty tray.

The dress and panties lay between them, spread out on the rock. He had that sensation again in his genitals. She saw him looking at the clothing and took a step back.

"It's all right," he said. "I'll go away while you put them on." He turned and started back toward the house. "I've coffee if you want any," he called over his shoulder. "It's hot. Then I can drive you to a safe place." He had business at the Healing House, in fact, a client to bring over in a day or two. She'd come from a threatening husband. He hated that kind of man. Himself, he'd never strike a woman—some fool reporter put false information about "brutality" along with his photo, and he was sick, sick at heart, sick to his stomach reading it.

"They'll take you in, it's a kind of shelter," he shouted back, already halfway to the house. He would definitely take her there. She'd be off his hands.

She didn't answer and he kept on walking. Then turned when he reached the porch. He was cooling down. He felt triumphant, like he'd walked a tightrope to safety. He couldn't see the woman at all now, assumed she was behind a tree, changing her clothes. He'd give her time to come round. He went into the kitchen and fixed himself a cup of coffee, then turned on the radio for the eight o'clock news. The White House defending war again, Dow dropping 120 points. Something about a missing Irish traveller woman, believed to be wearing a white nightgown. Wanted by a hospital in Canada—she'd left before being dismissed. A hospital, James recalled now, where another patient had been diagnosed with Creutzfeldt-Jakob disease. "A fatal brain condition," the newscaster said, sounding excited, "a spongiform encephalitis, a form of Mad Cow disease." The announcer gave a number to call if anyone had information about the woman.

He slapped a hand to his chest, massaged it. He had a terrible case of heartburn, his chest on fire. He thought of his sheep. Had he touched that woman? Oh, God—he'd picked her up. But he couldn't have her coming into the house. And Christ, here she was! Coming up the path, in his ex-wife's housedress, carrying her nightgown.

"No, no," he called out, "you can't come in. I'm sorry but you can't. I have sheep, I have a daughter—" Well, he didn't know where the daughter was now. She and her boyfriend had split up. She was somewhere out west.

He locked the kitchen door and yanked the shade. Waited. The knocking came once more and then stopped. When he peered out again through the window he saw her leaving. Oh, Christ, not into the sheep pasture!

But no, she was moving on down the road in that green print dress. She was sticking out her thumb. A beat-up car skidded to a stop, a man beckoned her in. He was sorry now for closing the door on her. She'd be better off with him, James Perlman. "Stop! Wait! Come back!" he shouted and ran toward the car.

But it started up again, churning up the roadside gravel, tires chirping. He saw the woman's head snap back.

He picked up the phone to call the police—then hesitated. The police would ask *him* questions, and he didn't want that. He didn't want them drumming up his past. Though why should they? He was getting paranoid. He was just a good Samaritan, trying to help the woman. He hadn't laid a hand on her. But

Christ, she'd left the nightgown on his porch—what was he to do with that? Burn it? He stood there, confused.

No, he should leave it for the police. Someone would want to examine it, take samples or whatever they did.

He suddenly despised the woman. Bad luck that she'd picked his place, of all places, to land on. Where had she come from anyway?

Then he remembered. The newscaster had mentioned the Willmarth farm. The woman had been camping on the Willmarth farm. He was trying to remember where it was. Not far—on Cow Hill Road, yes. A mile away as the crow flies. The woman had walked that mile, probably through the woods, to get to his road. Why had she done that? Why wouldn't she just give herself up, let them take her back to that hospital? Unless she already had some kind of dementia. The disease did that to people, he knew, made them unreasonable, confused. Crazy, running in circles.

He'd call the Willmarth woman, that's what he'd do. He'd heard about her taking on problems, resolving them. He had sheep, he'd tell her, he'd found his Eden. Life was suddenly precious to him, even without his wife. More so maybe without his wife, damn her. The Willmarth woman had to find the sick traveller, he'd make that clear. James had work to do in the barn, a sick lamb to look after—it was his first responsibility. He'd finish his morning's work and then he'd make the call.

FRANNY GATES WAS feeling more upbeat after the call to Ruth Willmarth. This was usually the case after she'd vented all her concerns and got the other person harried and sweating. It was like the Aristotelian theory she'd studied in theater school. You poured all your pity onto the tragic person and then you felt better, you felt purged, it was a catharsis. You looked at the post-theater world with fresh eyes, and even in November the trees were green. Franny had spent a summer understudying at the Stratford, Ontario, Shakespeare festival; she'd lived through

*Macbeth* night after night, and by the end of summer, even though she never got to perform the role, she felt she had been Lady Macbeth. She knew every line, every nuance, every twist of the heart and body. And always the grass was emerald green when she left the theater. Even afterward in the dark she could see the green in her mind's eye.

So Franny wasn't at all surprised when the phone rang and it was the woman who had broken the agreement to breed her government Morgan stud with Franny's prize Lippitt mare. And lo! the woman had changed her mind. "I want her," she gurgled, "she's a gorgeous creature, looks healthy as a newborn. The foal will be mine and I'm thrilled."

"I should imagine so," Franny said.

"But I want to wait a little, don't you know. I mean till they find that missing woman, give her a clean bill of health. Because the woman was on that farm up the road from yours, right?"

"Oh, really," Franny said, waving her arms, though no one could see her. "But we never step over each other's boundaries. I seldom even ride over there."

"All the same," the woman said, and asked if she could come over that afternoon—"and just take a peek at your mare?"

Ophelia was a gorgeous creature, it was true. Franny had fallen in love with her as a foal. Sired by True Diamond, a champion horse, Ophelia was of middling size, a light bay color, with bushy mane and tail; she was altogether smart and classy. If Franny hadn't been drawn to her partner, Henrietta, whom she'd met in Falstaff's Bar after the fifth performance of *Othello* that season, she'd have been happy enough to spend her life with Ophelia. There were nights she actually fantasized that Ophelia turned into a human being after midnight and the two of them rolled happily about in the hay.

"We-ell, after lunch then," Franny said. "Shall we say two o'clock? You can ride her if you like—perhaps a half hour? And we'll sign the contract? Set a date to bring your stallion over.

Ophelia should be in heat in two weeks or so. I don't know about that missing woman. Who knows when they'll come to terms with her? But I do have another breeder interested—a prize stallion with impeccable credentials. I'm not sure we can wait."

It was a lie, there was no other stallion panting at the gates, though there were possibilities. At any moment the phone might ring. Though with that woman missing from Willmarth's... She silently cursed the dairy farm. What stupidity anyway to allow gypsies to squat on one's land, a virtual encampment. She'd ridden past one night and heard all the singing, stopped to listen. What had Ruth been thinking about? She seemed a practical woman, but really! Gypsies! And now the whole neighborhood in peril. They'd come in with armed troops, she'd read, to take the sheep from those people over in East Warren. Imagine! Yet there was still no proof of any disease, and it had been five years since the removal. There was only the fear, the suspicion.

Franny and Henrietta had come to Vermont to avoid that kind of suspicion. For the most part folk left them alone here in Vermont. The fight had died down over the civil union legislation. Would it crop up again? There were still people trying to overturn it.

Oh woe. Alack a day! She felt a scourge coming on the land. "A plague of sighing and grief!" she quoted from one of the Henrys—she'd forgotten which. "It blows a man up like a bladder." And she and her partner in the middle of it.

She hung up the phone, then realized she hadn't said good-bye. But the woman had already committed to the two o'clock visit.

"Franny?" It was Henrietta, calling from the bedroom where she was still in bed at ten o'clock—she'd been up till two writing her fifth lesbian romance. The first four lay unpublished in a drawer.

"Orange juice in the fridge and freshly squeezed," said Franny, who was the breakfast cook, while Henrietta was pastry chef. "I made pancakes. You'll have to heat them up."

"You know I don't eat pancakes," Henrietta said, her voice groggy with sleep. Henrietta was on a new diet. She weighed 170 pounds and no diet had ever removed an ounce, not the Atkin's protein diet or Weight Watchers or a macrobiotic diet or Dolly Parton's portion control diet where you ate ten tiny meals a day, or the one where you could eat all the cake and ice cream you wanted just so you ate them all within a single hour. That diet had actually added 5 pounds to Henrietta's buttocks. Though Franny didn't mind a fat partner at all; the weight made her partner sexier than any skinny femme. It was seeing Henrietta's fat butt leaning over the bar at Falstaff's that had attracted Franny in the first place.

"You love my pancakes, you know you do," Franny yelled, and added, "Louella Clark is coming over at two to have a peek at Ophelia. She still wants to breed. But we have to hurry. Get up, will you? Make a batch of those chocolate orange cookies, we'll woo her with those. I'm off to the barn. Might take a quick ride with my—" She hesitated. She had almost said "my darling." But Henrietta was jealous of Ophelia. My, yes, Franny had to be careful. Franny needed both Henrietta and the horse. She wanted no ménage à trois, no jealous outbursts here.

"Shit, Fi," Henrietta screeched from the top of the stairs, where she stood in a pink polka-dot nightie that would envelop two Frannys, "I don't have the ingredients. I don't have any chocolate bits. I don't feel like going to the store. I had a bad writing night. The plot just won't jell. I think I need a new heroine. I'm sick of this tall, robust Caucasian."

"Try a gypsy," Franny called back. "A lean, hungry, violet-eyed gypsy beauty with a mass of curly black hair and skin like Snow White."

Then she realized she'd been quoting the radio description of the missing woman and she shivered. "No, no gypsy. Absolutely no gypsy. They're the worst kind. Troublemakers, the lot of them. Oh God, God." She ran out of the house, waving her arms, down the path to the horse barn. She was the pot calling the kettle black

"Ophelia," she called out, "Phelia, darling, Mommy's coming, we'll go for a nice ride in the woods. Phelia, baby!"

She ran into the barn, past Hamlet's stall. The stallion blinked down at her, stamping his hooves, as though upset about something. On the barn floor a pile of hay and manure, a broken slat, a saddle thrown down on its back—bridle and reins gone. Ophelia's stall empty. Empty! What? She opened her mouth to shout but nothing came out. There was no way the mare could have broken loose, she'd never have done that; the stall gate was latched.

Now it swung open with the wind, a grating sound like tears. Someone had opened it. Someone had stolen Ophelia. Franny collapsed back against Hamlet's stall and the stallion licked her neck with his long coarse tongue. "Where's Ophelia? Where's my darling?" she croaked, blowing into Hamlet's mouth for solace. But the stallion's huge moist eyes only gazed down at her sorrowfully.

# SIX

JAMES PERLMAN WAS IN HIS BARN, bandaging a lamb's shank where she'd been bitten by a neighbor's hound, when a shadow loomed in the doorway. There was the stink of an unwashed body, a menacing silence like Maureen's used to be—Maureen could keep silences for days at a time—she was a dragon breathing fire. Panic ran like freezing water down his spine. Strangers were not allowed in the sheep barn unless specially invited—and then James had a boot disinfectant to apply. There was the fear of foot-and-mouth disease, scrapie. That traveller woman brought the fear home. "Stop right there," he called out. "Did you read the signs?"

James wasn't going to be interrupted by an uninvited guest. He wasn't going to stop what he was doing. The lamb was a pretty little thing, perfectly shaped, she took the bottle like a baby. His poor hurt baby. He was always drawn to hurt animals and children—their helplessness, their fragility. He thought again of that woman in the white nightgown. He imagined her laid out on his sofa, grateful, like so many of the hospice patients, for his solicitude. He wouldn't try to touch her. He would just look at her, wait on her. That was all he'd had in mind back at that Buffalo hospital....

Now the man was all the way in the barn and James had to rise. He held out a warning arm but the man ignored it. The fellow began talking, using his hands, like he was desperate for answers. Angry that none were forthcoming.

James knew then who he was. He knew from the clothes he wore: the T-shirt that read *Death To Brits*. The bearded face with

he Irish hooked nose that wasn't ugly now but would domi-
ate the face in later years. The radio described him as the part-
er of the escaped woman—he'd been seen leading her down
he hospital corridor. And here he was, looking for his woman.
ames glanced about for his disinfectant but couldn't remem-
er where he'd stashed it. Besides, the man's face said he
vouldn't allow it.

"I seen her come this way," the man said, his big blotched
ands on his hips. "She been sick and we had an argument. I
vant her back. She's my woman."

*My* woman, he said, like she had no mind of her own—no
pinions, no rights. James didn't like that. He'd voted for the
oliticians who backed *Roe v. Wade*. A woman had a right to
er own body. He'd told himself that, even as his own body
ame down on that female in the recovery room. She was at
east fifty, she wouldn't bear any more children. What hurt did
e do her? He'd told himself that, too. She'd come on to him
arlier, hadn't she? But deep down he knew he was wrong. He
ated himself for doing it.

"I saw her, sure," he told the man—to get him out of the barn.
The man could be carrying that disease himself. He'd given
lood, the hospital said, he'd lied when they asked if he'd ever
een in the UK. "She went that way."

James pointed in a direction opposite to the one the car had
aken. It had actually been heading east, toward East Bran-
ury. Where the Healing House was, though he didn't men-
ion that to the man. After all, the car could have turned in
ny direction. "She was in a car. There's no telling where she
ot dropped off. Could've been a local fellow. Could've been
n his way to Burlington, who knows? Or Montreal. That's
ll I can tell you." He took a step toward the man, to nudge
im out of the barn. The lamb bleated in its pen, a pathetic
ound.

"You saw her," the man said. "I found this on your porch." He
eached into his pocket and pulled out the crumpled nightgown.

Held it up. James could see the spot of blood on the shoulder of the gown. He felt guilty then for not bringing it into the house. The man glared at James, like James had molested the woman, when he hadn't, wouldn't have touched her. Oh no, he was over all that.

"I gave her my wife's dress to wear," James said, feeling the bile rising in his throat. "I left it outside and she took it. She didn't come in my house. I was planning to call the—" He paused; he didn't want to use the word "police" in front of this man. He didn't know why. It was just the way the man was looking at him, scrutinizing his face like he'd seen James somewhere before. This man was from Tonawanda, according to the news report. Tonawanda wasn't that far from Buffalo. The fellow could have seen something in the paper, remembered something. You never knew. It was all so ugly. He had to get this man out of his barn, out of his life.

"I've told you all I can tell you, mister. She went off in a car. That way," and James pointed again. But Christ, now he'd pointed the right way! He reversed the direction of his thumb and the man narrowed his eyes. "Look, I've work here to do, I'll have to ask you to leave."

The man didn't offer to move. There was that aggravating silence. The lamb was bleating, needing help for its leg. James was frustrated, he felt desperate, bold. "I know who you are," he said. "You're that woman's boyfriend. They're looking for you, too. You gave blood in that hospital. It might've been contaminated and they want you for testing. You owe it to the public. Do you want to start a plague?"

The man's eyes were cold. What did he want anyway? James had said all he could say. He edged over toward the barn phone. He wished he had a cell phone; he'd go buy one today. He didn't dare take his eyes off the man. He'd heard about those traveller men. They could be violent; they were petty criminals, most of them. Irish. His wife, Maureen, was Irish—fiercely, patriotically so. James was English on his mother's side, Russian Je on his father's. He disliked the Irish in any form, traveller or no. They drank, they were rowdy, they told lies, they stole.

James was furious now, outraged. "Get out!" he screamed. "Out of my barn or I'll call the police!" Uh-oh, now he'd said the word.

The man growled in his throat and then spit on the barn floor—a disgusting wad of mucus. He turned on his heel, the nightgown wadded up in his arms. For a moment he held it out, stared at it, like he'd tear it apart. Then he stuffed it in his pocket, ran out of the barn. Up the path to the drive. James saw him standing on the edge of the road, looking in the direction the car with the traveller woman had gone. Then he crossed the road and ran off into the woods.

James went to the barn cabinet, pulled down a bottle of Virkon S. The label read "Recommended for the FMD virus." He sprayed it on the barn door, the door sides, the floor where the man had stood in his filthy raggedy shoes. He sprayed it on his own boots and pants, and on the sides of the lamb pens. He didn't stop spraying until the bottle was empty.

COLM WAS BACK by nine o'clock that morning and he brought disturbing news with him. He'd run into a pair of *Free Press* reporters in the local diner where he'd stopped for waffles and juice and they were talking up strategies for a piece on the Willmarth farm. "They were mouthing off a mile a minute," he told Ruth, "like they were on the verge of an orgasm. A big breaking story. Like a local anthrax case. They kept on about that traveller woman, wanted to know her story: How could they find out? Who could they interview? I kept my mouth shut, just listened. They call you, huh, Ruthie?"

"Not yet," she said, and pushed the pan of freshly made doughnuts in his direction. "And when they do, I'm not talking. I have nothing to say about anything. I mean, I don't know anything, do I? What do I know, Colm?"

Colm looked thoughtful where he sat in her kitchen munching on a doughnut. There were two platefuls. When Ruth was feeling stressed, she cooked an overload. The sugar had formed a mustache on his upper lip. If she hadn't been so alarmed at the thought of reporters she'd have giggled.

"We'll have to be the ones to work up a strategy," he said. "We can call up the fifth, you know."

"We?" she said, teasing him. "It's still my farm. My cows. You haven't moved in permanently yet."

"Yet," he said. "That word holds hope. But hey, I was here that night, wasn't I? I was upstairs asleep when the woman was down here flooding the goddamn tub. Jeez, I could of done something, I could of saved her." He looked forlorn, his sugary lip was quivering; a lock of graying hair was falling over his nose, into the sugar. Colm could use a haircut.

She reached over and patted his hand. He gazed back at her like a spaniel that had just been hissed at by a feral cat. Smiling, she squeezed his fingers.

The phone rang.

"Don't answer," he said. "You're out in the pasture. You can't be reached. That's the way we'll play it now."

The phone rang four more times and quit. A minute later Darren came running up the porch steps and into the house. "Can't you answer the bloody phone? It's for you, Ms. Ruth. I took it in the barn. I was baling hay—you got a bloody slim crop in this drought. Now I got to feed the calves. The calves oughta be Maggie's job but she's out of it, Nola gone and all. Christ on a cross, what a rough thing, Nola running off like that. Stupid, I call it. Who in hell's dumb enough to run away when she's sick?" He shook his head, ran a hand through his yellow windblown hair.

Ruth sighed, and waved him off. "Get Boadie. She'll feed the calves. She's always out there petting them."

It was Franny again. "Can't you answer the phone when a body needs you? I been ringing and ringing and then I get that gypsy fellow who doesn't know shit from shinola. It's terrible, oh God, terrible, the worst kind of tragedy." She broke into sobs. Ruth held the receiver at arm's length.

"They found the woman," Colm conjectured, "tests were positive. She has the CJD. Now what?"

"What's terrible, Franny?" Ruth said, waving away Colm's words. "Calm down now and tell me." Ruth had been through Franny's crises before. The last time it had been Henrietta with the chicken pox and Franny unable to cope.

There was a panting silence, unusual for Franny. Then a gagging sound, as though Franny were trying to catch her breath, trying to speak, but couldn't get out the words. "It's, it's—"

Ruth waited. Colm was grimacing, he was into the plate of doughnuts again. And after those morning waffles.

"Gone," Franny choked out. "Phelia's gone. Like drowned, only not even that. Just gone. Her stall empty. Nothing but a pile of turds and urine on the floor, she must've emptied her bladder when they took her, scared to death, my beloved. Ooh God." The sobs went on like a pot boiling over.

"Hang on, I'll be right there," Ruth said. It was all she could think of to say. She envisioned the mare gliding down Otter Creek with flowers in her mane, on the way to Lake Champlain where she'd slowly sink, like Hamlet's lady friend, into the roiling waters. Ruth hung up, mopped her perspiring brow with a hot hand.

"What is it now? Henrietta got the hives? Can't eat for a change?"

"Ophelia's gone, Franny's prize mare," she told him. "It's like losing a lover, Colm—Franny adores that mare. And somebody's gone and stolen her."

"Hey. Somebody left the barn door open, that's all. She got out. You're getting paranoid, Ruthie, you've got to keep your head."

"Maybe so. But the way things have been going around here lately, I'll believe anything. I'm going over to have a look-see."

"And if the reporters come? The health guys to get more tub samples?"

"You can deal with them, love, you know you can." She kissed him and felt the sugar crusted under her own nose. He kissed her back, taking dozens of small sips from her lips as if she were an ice cream soda. It was sweet and mesmerizing and for a moment she gave in to it. Until the phone rang again and she pulled away, leaving the answering machine in charge, and she took off for Franny's barn.

"I CAN DEAL with them, I *can,*" Colm told himself when the white Subaru careened into the driveway and the couple he'd seen at the Branbury diner leaped out and trotted purposefully up the steps and into the kitchen. He wiped his upper lip with a paper napkin; rose to his full five-foot-ten-and-a-quarter to greet them.

Colm longed for clarity. He just wanted to go back to his real estate office where he understood what was going on. The Connecticut couple wanted a farmhouse with a trout pond and a view of the mountains. It was perfectly aboveboard and simple as hell. After a short search he could undoubtedly find it for them—there was always a view in Vermont, if not a trout pond. But a missing woman? Even the FBI had been alerted, in case she'd left the state. Could they find her? A needle in a haystack, as the saying went.

"Ms. Willmarth is out," he told them, "and I'm just a friend." He put a finger to his lips to show he had nothing to say.

But already they were snapping pictures of the kitchen: the stove, the refrigerator, the bathroom door where the yellow crime scene tape was barring passage. One of the reporters, a middle-aged man in a short-sleeved, open-necked tattersall shirt and a pool of perspiration on his snub nose and forehead—for already the temperature had hit eighty-six—was leaning into the bathroom to get a shot of tub and window.

"Wait a minute here—you can't go in there. You can't photograph without a signed release," Colm cried, and flashed his police badge. He was only a part-time cop, but damn it, he was going to pull rank when he had to.

"Sure, sorry," the fellow said, the damage already done. Colm wanted to yank the camera off his neck but resisted the urge. It wouldn't do to irritate the press. Besides, the publicity helped—now and then.

The female reporter frowned at the cameraman, spreading vertical wrinkles under her nose. She was obviously older, fifties maybe. She knew the ropes; the thrust-out chin was steely. She lifted a "What can you do with these young jerks?" eyebrow at Colm. Then she cupped a hand around the corner of her mouth as if to utter a secret and said, "If anyone from the USDA calls, you haven't seen us."

"USDA?"

"Department of Agriculture," she said, dropping her hand. "They've warned us not to play this up—this CJD thing. Not to come here and poke around."

"Why's that? The woman's disappearance is already on the radio. There's no secret about it."

"Possibility of BSE—you know, Mad Cow—somewhere. Maybe here," the reporter whispered. "They don't want that spread around. There's never been a case of Mad Cow in the U.S. The government doesn't want that."

"And if there should be?" he asked, something sticking in his throat. He swallowed his coffee but it wouldn't go down.

"Denial," she said. "It never happened."

Colm didn't get it. And he didn't want to ask. "Doughnut?" he said, swallowing hard. He needed to spread goodwill, wanted good press at least for Ruth. After all, he wanted to move in here with her. He was sick of living in a mortuary— his father would have to cope without him nights. Colm was a domestic animal. He needed a woman to come home to nights, a hot meal, someone to sound off to, a little lovemaking—hell, more than a little. All those years of living alone...

Besides, he loved Ruth. Damn it, he just plain loved her. Always had. Always would. Never mind she called it Irish bullshit. Though he knew she didn't really mean that. Did she?

Uninvited, the cameraman stuck a doughnut in his pocket. The woman was pointing down toward the pasture, where Maggie was singing at the top of her lungs. Jeez, Colm just wanted to get out of here now, let the reporters have the traveller, bend her ear, make her talk if they could. He wanted to get back to the real world: the world of buying and selling houses and land. He was comfortable in that world.

Colm was a rational man. He'd never liked fairy tales when his mother read them to him. As a child he was scared of the supernatural: werewolves, ghouls, witches, vampires. And already this CJD thing bordered on the supernatural. Where had these plagues come from anyway? How could a virus like AIDS or CJD lie dormant inside a person or animal for up to forty years and then decide—whoosh!—to come out and devour the body? It was beyond his ken. He could help his dad fill a body with formaldehyde and cremate or bury it—but what did you do with a live woman who might be harboring a deadly plague inside her body?

It was like those fairy tales where the beautiful woman smiled at you, got you lusting after her, then offered a poison apple.

"Go ahead," he told the couple. "Down the path to the east pasture. Follow the voice. But there are seedling trees there, don't step on them."

The phone rang again, five times until the answering machine kicked in—a man's excited voice, wanting to speak to Ruth. He was a farmer, too, he had sheep, he said, on Bailey Road. Another kook, Colm assumed, worried about his animals, as if Ruth's farm could contaminate his, at least a mile away. Colm knew Bailey Road, it was full of large homes, newly built by down-country retirees. This guy must be the Perlman fellow his associate had sold land to, to graze sheep on. Got moved in and bango, the wife took off. Well, Colm had heard every story known to man in his real estate dealings: deaths, divorces, adulteries, even a murder or two. Those fairy tales mirrored reality after all.

He grabbed his briefcase and left the house. "See no evil, hear no evil," he told himself and hopped into his old blue Horizon. It started up after the second try and Colm was off to the real world.

Now SHARON WAS on her high horse. She filled the doorway of the trailer, holding the door barely open so the reporters couldn't see in. They stood there like minor deities: the man with the camera like a huge roach around his neck, the woman with clipboard and pen, practically panting with excitement. She was already describing the yellow trailer, Sharon supposed, the laundry spread out on the grass, a horse and pig grazing nearby, munching on her mother's trees, a small dog of indeterminate breed relieving itself against a half-grown scotch pine.

"Don't let them in!" Maggie hissed behind Sharon, and "Don't go out," to Liz and the grandmother. "It's none of their damn business. They're like lice in the hair. They want to burrow in and dirty you." She shook her own frizzy mane of red hair loose, then wrapped her arms defensively across her chest.

"If you have any questions, I can answer them," Sharon told the reporters. "I'm the farmer's daughter." Sharon liked that title, she had used it before with salesmen, land seekers, charities, religious kooks who came to harass her mother. Sharon liked to be interviewed. She'd been interviewed at length after she'd discovered that woman killed with an icicle up at Molly's Crotch, and surprised herself at how well she'd handled it. If only she could write or sing or act or become someone famous she would quite enjoy the notoriety.

But Sharon had no particular talent, except for the sheer act of living: she simply poured herself into life, that's all. She had a gift for people, her husband, Jack, would say.

"We heard the missing woman's cousin lives in this trailer. We'd like to talk to her—please," said the female reporter, and Sharon smiled.

"I'm afraid she's indisposed. Upset about her cousin, you know. There's nothing she can really tell you."

"How long has she known the missing woman? Were they really cousins? Where did they grow up?" the reporter asked, her pen poised above her pad. "Was the woman suicidal? Was she trying to drown herself in that bathtub? Where's the man she came here with? Night before last, was it?"

"Whoa," said Sharon, "slow down." There was a flash where the man was taking pictures. Flash, flash, flash, in all directions. Sharon pushed a wisp of honey hair back from her forehead, tilted her face for a better profile. Then laughed. How could she answer all those questions? "I've no idea," she said. "You'll have to make an appointment with Ms. O'Neill. I told you, she's unwell. Her cousin is missing, that's all we know. The man she came with is missing. Maybe they're together. Maybe they're not. No one knows. The pair arrived only night before last."

"How did she look?" the reporter asked in a hushed voice. "What were the symptoms? Jerking walk, poor balance? Dementia?" She was listing the symptoms of that CJD thing.

Now Sharon's back was really up. "None of those symptoms. Not a single one! She was tired, that's all. Plain old fatigue. Have *you* ever had surgery?"

When the reporter, taken aback, said, "Well, yes, but—"

"There's no reason to think she has that disease. None! There were hundreds of patients in that place. The hospital wants those people back as a precaution, that's all. I mean, you think just because she had surgery there she caught that disease? Aren't you jumping to conclusions?" She found herself moving down the trailer steps toward the reporters, making them step back.

The woman wouldn't give up. "I heard the cousin singing. I know she's in there. She gave a concert last month up in Burlington. The reviews were—well—" She wriggled her fingers up and down. "So—so," she said.

"What?" the voice screamed behind Sharon. "I got a beautiful one in that *Seven Days* paper. They called me lilting, lyrical, true-pitched, pure!"

"And dissonant," said the reporter, smiling. "Overly sentimental, too flashy."

"Nonsense!" Maggie stepped out, shoving Sharon aside. She had a news clipping in her hand. "Read this. Read it! They was talking about my dress when they said flashy, not my singing. You assholes quote everything out of context! Everybody liked my dress. I'm a traveller. Flashy colors is the way we dress. You want us to change just 'cause dull people like you wear black and gray and look like ghouls? Do you, hey? Hey?"

She began clicking imaginary castanets, doing an intricate dance step around the woman, hands waving in the air. The camera flashed and flashed, luring her on. Maggie snapped her fingers in the cameraman's face and he grinned ear to ear. The reporter was furious. "Make her stop that," she told Sharon. But what could Sharon do? The interview was out of control.

"Go home," Sharon told the woman. "Then she'll stop. She doesn't know anything. There's nothing to know! There's no contamination here. It's just fear you're spreading. You should be ashamed of yourself. Now go home and tell your paper to cool it."

The grandmother, Boadie, appeared in the doorway in a long purple and orange skirt and the camera flashed again. She glared fiercely at the female reporter, pulled a kitchen knife from her belt, and swung it in a wide arc about the woman's head. The reporter shrieked and dropped her notebook.

"Okay, let's get out of here," she told the man. "They're crazy, these damn gypsies. We'll come back later, talk to the owner." Then, "Quit that!" she shouted at the old woman as the knife flashed about her ankles. "You want to kill somebody with that knife? They'll put you in the funny farm."

"She's already in the funny farm," said the cameraman. "If this isn't the funny farm I'm a pig."

"Pig! *You're* the pig!" cried the grandmother and spit on his turning back.

Sharon picked up the notebook and tore off the page the reporter had been scribbling on; then handed over the notebook. The woman snatched it back angrily and stalked on up the hill.

Sharon's adrenaline was up; she felt good about the interview. She couldn't wait to describe it to her mother and Colm, describe how she'd saved the day. She couldn't wait to read the account in the paper. "Thank you," she hollered after the reporter. "Thank you for coming."

BOADIE STUCK the knife back in her belt and spit again in the wake of the reporters. She grinned when the man wiped the spit off his camera and turned to glare at her. Boadie had a long spit, she could reach up to two yards—she'd had years of practice. It was her grandmother taught her after the cops chased her parents, and horse and caravan ran off the cliff, killing them both. Spit at the fuzz, spit at fate, spit at the world, her granny had taught her. "They're all out to get you, you can't trust nobody. So spit, girl, spit." And Boadie did.

She'd spit at that no-good husband of hers, too; she wasn't one to let him beat her up the way some men beat their women. She wasn't named after that warrior female for nothing. Boadicea, the warrior's name was: belonged to some tribe and led a revolt against the Romans. Her mother said she was descended from that tribe. But then her grandmother'd always made up stuff so you never really knew.

One thing she did know from Granny Ward: They was descended from Irish bards—uh—huh, one of the oldest travelling families in Ireland. The name came from Mac an Bhaird—in Gaelic it meant "son of the bard." Bards, like travellers, her Irish granny said, travelled the countryside trading stories and poems for food and a bed. When the English tried to stop them, they had to go underground. Boadie's ancestors turned tinkers but they never stopped telling stories.

Like her granny, Boadie didn't like reporters coming to peer into her life. They'd only write up bad things, like travellers steal, travellers lie, travellers don't take baths, travellers cheat.

When Boadie never stole anything anyone really needed. What was an ear of corn when the farmer had a whole field full? What was a loaf of bread when end of day it was already going stale on the store shelves? Boadie knew how to dip the bread in warm goat's milk to give it moisture again. Boadie knew how to make do.

And she did take baths—once a week anyway. A bath a week was enough—saved on soap. Boadie couldn't fathom why there was all this talk about Nola taking that bath when the poor girl'd been on the road a week or more. It was just her bad luck, that's all, that Ritchie walked in on her. For Boadie seen him running on up there, oh yeah, it was after he took down that tent, rolling up her things with it, without her say-so, sure. Ritchie wasn't one to ask permission to do things. And now Nola was running from Ritchie.

"Go girl, go! Run for your life!" Boadie shouted in her head.

Boadie didn't like Ritchie, though sometimes she was sorry for him the way Uncle picked on him. She seen Ritchie cry once, he was so upset, and she wanted to go back and spit at Uncle. And she did—more than once she got him in the back.

But Uncle seemed to worship Darren. Boadie seen the way Uncle looked at Darren—like he was peppermint candy and Uncle couldn't wait to hold him and lick him down. But Darren wouldn't give his uncle the time of day. And Ritchie liked his younger brother, though there was jealousy there, Boadie saw that. Ritchie was head over heels about Maggie, but she'd run when she seen him coming. Still, Ritchie mooned after her.

Men.

Boadie'd had her share of men—some good, some bad—and now she was done with them. They mostly just wanted sex, drink, trucks, meat—in that order, and Boadie was sick of it all. When her husband suffocated after vomiting in his drink, Boadie got her first pig. A pig was pink and cute and smart; it was worth ten husbands. A pig didn't talk back, it didn't want sex with her—it just wanted food. It didn't drive a pickup, it just loved.

A pig was made out of stars just like herself. Somebody'd told her that once, about how we're all made out of the same stuff as stars. Boadie liked that. To think she'd been a star once. Boadie was Roman Catholic, yeah, but she didn't believe in all that heaven business. You got burned up when you died and your ashes went back in the earth and into the air and turned into stars. That's what Boadie believed.

Boadie went outside and picked up her potbellied pig where it was rummaging in the grass. It made a sweet squealing sound, let her cuddle it. When she held it to her chest, heavy though it was, it felt like she could defend herself against anything—reporters, cops, weird uncles—even death. Boadie wasn't afraid of death, no, not her. Boadie was going to turn into stars.


RUTH FOUND FRANNY and Henrietta outside the horse barn, slumped together in a pile of hay, their arms around one another. The three remaining Lippitt Morgans stood languidly in their stalls, tails flicking, bulging eyes gazing sadly at Ruth as though they knew one of their kind was missing—and one of them might be next.

"We've searched and searched," Franny said: "pasture, woods, trails—we called the neighbors. But really, there's no way she could of got loose. She's gone, that's all, Ophelia's gone." She dropped her head on Henrietta's fleshy shoulder.

"Stolen," said Henrietta, and hugged her partner. "The rope was cut through. Someone must've come in while we were asleep and taken her."

"But the saddle's still here," said Franny.

"But not the mare," Henrietta said, and Franny sobbed into the soft, saggy flesh of Henrietta's cheek.

Ruth had a moment of hope. "It could have been an accident then, the mare simply broke away. And someone will call in—you just wait and see."

Franny waved a freckled arm. "Rode her without a saddle.

Someone used to bareback. Like a gypsy," she said, pursing her lips, staring Ruth in the eye.

"Like a gypsy," said Henrietta, baring her teeth on the last syllable. "That man they talked about on the radio. I heard it again this morning. He was with that missing woman."

"The one who took a bath in your tub," said Franny, pointing a finger at Ruth.

Now Ruth was on the defensive. She was here to help a neighbor and *she* was under attack.

"We'll call the police then," Ruth said, "tell them about Ophelia. It'll make it easier for them to find the man if he has a horse."

"But that's just it," cried Franny, jumping up, knocking Henrietta back, squealing, into the pile of hay. "He won't have her for long. He'll sell her to somebody, take the money, and buy some other old nag. Buy a truck. Gypsies love their trucks, they paint them yellow and red—I saw that trailer on your land, Ruth. He could be in Orlando, Florida, by now!"

"It's only ten o'clock," said Henrietta, "how could he be?" When Franny frowned at her, she cleared her throat and told Ruth: "Oh my poor dear Franny. She had a breeder for Ophelia. Phelia was a prize-winning mare."

"Don't say 'was,'" Franny cried. "She's still alive. That man's not stupid enough to kill her! He just wants the money he'll get for her."

"Or he wants *her*," said Henrietta, and Franny said, "What do you mean by that, damn it?"

"Nothing. What could I mean?"

"You think he's going to mount her, do you? Rape her?"

"Of course not, Fran. We're not talking kinky here. I just meant he wants to keep her 'cause she's so beautiful. That's why *you* keep her, isn't it, Fran?"

"You're jealous," said Franny. "You've always been jealous of my horse. For God's sake, Hen, she's a horse, not a woman. Who could be jealous of a horse?" She clasped her hands together, lifted her chin, sighed. "But such a beautiful horse, oh dear God, those eyes, you can just float in them. And they're gone now, gone." She flung herself at the sturdy Henrietta; her partner caught her in a noisy embrace.

"I'll call the police then," said Ruth, needing closure to this frustrating session. They weren't getting anywhere with all these histrionics.

"Oh no," cried Franny, running after her. "They'll just botch it up. Why, they have guns. If there's a showdown with that man, they could shoot Ophelia!" Her face was a disaster, all quivers and gullies and tears.

"Colm," Ruth said. "I'll call him. He'll tell them not to shoot. Now look, Franny, we'll find her. Just leave it to Colm. He'll want a full description of the mare, of course, you can e-mail it to him at his office, okay? Moonlightcolm at shoreham.net." The women looked at her. "Moonlight," she explained, "because he has three jobs: Realtor, mortician, and cop. The only way to make a living in Branbury, Vermont. Now go in and contact him and then have a cup of strong coffee. Relax. We'll call with any news."

"We don't drink coffee," Henrietta said. "Only green mint tea. We grow the mint ourselves."

"Whatever," said Ruth, feeling powerless, the way she felt increasingly these days, and she jogged slowly back to her battered green pickup.

# SEVEN

NOLA HUNCHED CLOSER to the car window; the man was too quiet. He just sat there nursing a bottle of Woodchuck cider—5% alcohol, the label read. It was hard to talk anyway, with the radio blaring some rock tune that killed her head it was so loud. He'd locked the doors after she got in. She was sorry now she'd hitched the ride, but she had to get away. Already the sheep man who locked the door on her would be calling the police. They'd be after her, that was what Ritchie had shouted after he surprised her in the tub. He'd heard something on the kitchen radio-she hardly knew what he was talking about. "You didn't tell me you had that filth inside," he yelled. "Now I'll get it, too."

"What filth?" she'd said, covering the scar on her breast with her hand—Ritchie found it unsightly, and it was. "What you talking about, Ritchie?"

He'd stood over her in the tub, ranting about some disease. They were both doomed and it was her fault. "They're looking for you," he said. "That hospital wants to make a test mouse out of you. Now the police'll be on the case and they'll want to talk to me. You want me behind bars, do you? That guy I knifed died, they'll think I started it when I didn't. It was him. I was justified."

"What man died, who?" she'd cried, but he didn't answer. He put a hand on her head like he'd push her under and she panicked.

"Hand me a towel, will you, Ritch? I'll go give myself up." The thought of that hospital again was comforting, actually, she needed a long rest, good food, those backrubs. But she'd said the wrong thing. He was hollering about police again. He was dead anyway, he said, thanks to her. They were to get out of there, fast. He threw her a towel but it landed in the water, soaked through.

"All right," she'd said, stalling for time. "All right, but get me some coffee, will you? It's on the stove. I can smell it. I'll get ready."

He'd gone in the kitchen then and she'd jumped out of the tub, slipped on the floor, pulled herself up by the sink edge. Pulled on her nightgown—it was faster than jeans and shirt—grabbed her rosary beads from the pocket, she'd need them. Out in the kitchen she heard him grunt and swear. It was her chance. She heard him open the fridge—he'd steal what he could. The bathroom window was open, she shoved it all the way up. It was a short drop to the ground. She climbed out, scraping an elbow on a nail. It bled, but she hardly felt it. She made the jump and ran through the kitchen garden, trampling some plants—she couldn't help it, she had to get away. She was afraid of Ritchie, he'd almost drowned her. He would of drowned her—she'd seen the look on his face, a queer coldness in those black eyes. And she ran.

"Where you headed?" the driver shouted. He finished off the bottle of hard cider, grabbed another out of a cardboard carton on the floor. Offered her one but she shook her head. He was older than she'd thought at first: receding hairline, a hardness in the face brought about by time and bad luck, she knew the look. Her father had that look, her mother, too, after the father, full of drink, knocked her about for the millionth time. The look said, "I hate the world. I hate you." In America, that was the way most people looked at travellers. That was why they had to lie low, keep out of the news.

And here she was, making the news.

"Stop and lemme outa here," she shouted back. She didn't know where they were but what did it matter? She'd get to the cops, there was no point in running. She could die, running.

They'd lock their doors on her, like that sheep man. All she'd wanted was to use his telephone, call the farmer woman, tell her to tell Maggie she was okay, not to worry. She and Maggie had grown up close, their trailers side by side. How many times Maggie'd come to help put down the fights between her parents, save her from her father.

When the man didn't stop she shouted, "Take me to the police station. I need to talk to somebody there." She had her hand on the door handle. If he didn't stop she'd jump out.

He just laughed. "It's locked, baby. We're not stopping at no police station. Not on your life. We'll cruise a little, then we'll stop." He guzzled the Woodchuck, then let out a long belch.

"I can't hear you. Can you turn that thing down? I got a headache." She pointed at the radio dial. Her head was pounding, she felt ready to die.

He gave a harsh laugh and turned it down. "Got a headache, huh? Pretty thing like you? Got a funny way of talking. Where you from anyway?"

"North Carolina," she said. She didn't want to say New York; he'd probably heard a news broadcast. They might have mentioned she was an Irish traveller. "Scottish by birth. I might've got some of my mother's talk."

"Yeah?" he said. "Scottish." He tried to imitate the accent, but the word came out "Scoottish." "Got a lotta sheep there, huh? Mountains and stuff, like Vermont? I might like to go there, see what it's like."

"Sure, and you'd like it." Though she'd never been there herself, nor to Ireland, either. She'd like to go one day and take Keeley. Keeley especially wanted to go; he talked of Ireland like it was some paradise. She supposed she should ask this man a question but she didn't really want to get to know him. Not with that hard face of his. He could be another Ritchie and she couldn't bear that. Not that Ritchie was so bad when he was younger. It was just that a lot of bad things had happened to Ritchie, and, like layers of dirt, the bad things clung to him and weighed him down and now he couldn't seem to hold his head up. He just fought back at the world. It was maybe one of the reasons she'd stayed with him. She was sorry for him.

Anyway, where else would she have gone? She had no money of her own. No education beyond parochial school. And who would want a woman with an ugly scar on her breast?

"Got an idea," the driver said, throwing the second old soldier into the backseat. "We go to Scotland together, you and me. I got no girlfriend. One I had, left, she were a bitch anyways. You and me we'd make a team. Whatya say, huh? You running away yourself? Huh? Got no place to go tonight? You running away from some Joe?"

He reached out a hand and it slapped down hard on her knee. She let it stay. She was afraid of him, she wanted out of the car. But it wouldn't do to antagonize him. "Sure," she said, "we'll run away to Scotland. You pay for the tickets?"

He thought that was hysterically funny, he laughed and laughed. "Sure, baby, I'll pay. I'm rich. Saved up big bucks from the last job I had."

She didn't want to know what the job was. It could have been a robbery. Ritchie always had his radio on, like he was hoping not to hear his own name mentioned. He listened to news about thefts and bank holdups and killings, and once he broke down and cried when he heard about some criminal getting the gas chamber.

Nola just wanted out now, she was getting claustrophobic.

"I gotta take a pee," she said. "Can we stop?" They were moving beyond town; the houses were fewer and farther between. That was a worry and a comfort. But if she got out and ran he could probably outrun her. He had a flabby belly, short legs, she was a fast runner. But she was exhausted—it made them even.

He was looking hard at her, he suspected something. "Not here," he said, and put his foot on the accelerator. It was an old car, the odometer read over 120,000 miles. When the car got up over seventy it wobbled. She wasn't ready to die, not yet. She wanted to live a little, maybe find a good man who wouldn't mind about the scar—she wasn't married to Ritchie. She wanted a daughter, do for her and Keeley what her ma wasn't able to do for her, with her father spending what Ma begged or worked for on drink. Her mother had hated begging, she hated telling fortunes—all those lies.

They drove a few more miles into the countryside. The driver was quiet again, he probably had to pee himself. He put on the brakes a quarter mile beyond a farmhouse. "Okay," he said, "you can go take a leak, but don't go anywhere. You won't like it you start running off. You won't get far anyways."

God but it smelled good, the woods. He unzipped in front of her, started to pee. There was evidently more than that, thank God—he was moving into the bushes—it was her chance. "I'll be behind that tree over there," she called to him. A trail ran alongside the tree. She started running. Her head was beginning to clear, she hardly felt the pain. She only knew she needed to get away, over to that house. If they locked her out she'd break a window, climb in, she was that desperate. Or she'd crawl under the porch. When he came after her he'd think they took her in and he'd leave.

She heard him behind her, yelling. "Bitch, bitch—stop, bitch," and she kept running. She could see the slate roof through the trees, a TV aerial. Her whole body seemed airborne, her breath one huge pain in her side. The running was consuming her, she couldn't feel anything—feet, legs, head, torso. She was all air, hovering like some cyclone, headed down for the house.

She flung herself up on the porch; a chair was still rocking there, as though someone had been sitting in it and just got up. She banged on the door and no one came. She twisted the handle and it opened. Something was zooming toward her. She flung herself at the glittery object—something on wheels.

"Well, look what the wind blew in," a rough voice said. And then there were a dozen voices clucking over her.

THREE federal agents were in Ruth's kitchen when she got home from the horse farm. They'd walked in past Sharon's protests, her daughter hissed when she met her mother at the door. Then she had to leave—"Sorry, Mom, Robbie's dentist appointment." One of the men had a rim of sugar on his upper lip—she bristled at that! A uniformed woman was on her knees, inspecting tub, sink, and floor, although the police had already ordered it done, and appropriated the traveller woman's clothing. The trio took no notice of Ruth—she might have been a gust of wind that had blown through the door.

She cleared her throat. "I'm Ruth Willmarth, owner of this dairy farm." She stuck a hand on her hip for emphasis. "This is my kitchen, not a Dunkin' Donuts, thank you."

The man with the sugar on his lip looked over and apologized. "They were mighty good," he said, with a slight southern accent. "We're here, ma'am, from the—"

"Department of Agriculture," Ruth said. "The logo is on your shirt. We've nothing to hide here, a woman took a bath, that's all. The police were here before you. There's no proof she carries any disease."

"Oh no, ma'am," said Southern Accent. "We're just being cautious. Sometimes the police, well, they overlook things. Everything turns out negative for CJD—then hey, you're off the hook, you know, I mean unless they find that woman and she's—"

"Then we have to step in," said the second man, a short wiry fellow with a slightly hunched back and feet too big for his body. He was wearing a black Carhart jacket over a pair of white coveralls. His words came out like a shrill alarm.

"What does that mean, 'step in'?" said Ruth. Something had caught in her chest, she couldn't seem to breathe right—couldn't even get a cough out.

"Quarantine, ma'am," said Southern Accent, smiling, trying too hard to put her at ease. "Dis-ease" was the word that came into Ruth's head. *Not* at ease, no.

"My cows?" Ruth said. "Quarantine them so I can't sell the milk? So we milk twice a day and then throw away the milk?" She heard her voice getting huskier, full of phlegm. "Cows won't simply hang out in the pasture and wait till your department decides to lift a quarantine. Cows—"

"Ma'am, please, ma'am. Nothing's happened yet. You asked the question, we're just giving an answer." Southern Accent waved his hands. He bit into a second doughnut. It was like he'd taken a bite out of her. She felt the pain in her throat. One more bite and she'd bite him back!

"Just giving an answer," echoed Big Foot. He reached for a doughnut, too.

Ruth was ready to defend herself. She picked up the coffeepot. The woman came out of the bathroom with her samples, looked at the two men, and then at Ruth. "All set," she said defensively, and thrust out a hand at Ruth. "Look, ma'am, we're sorry for the intrusion. But we have to do it, you know. It's a terrible disease. If it spreads—well, it's like AIDS. It could kill thousands. We're just doing our job, believe me."

The pot was suddenly too heavy to hold. Ruth put it on the table and sank down beside it.

"Just doing our job," Big Foot repeated.

"But we understand," the woman said, "that you've had reporters here. We prefer that you do not—do *not* tell them we were here. Do *not* discuss our conversation with them." She fixed Ruth's eyes for a long moment, and then turned on her heel. The screen door slammed behind the trio.

The phone rang but Ruth's legs were too weak to get up and answer it. She might be getting arthritis in her shoulders where she'd forked hay for a decade. Arthritis was inbred in the Scots, that bitter highland climate. And then there was Vermont—though already the thermometer in the kitchen window read eighty-eight, and not yet noon. It was still early July and three days now of blazing heat. Ruth dabbed at her forehead with a paper napkin and it oozed sugar.

The world was out of whack.

The voice came loud and squeaky through the machine. "Ruth, are you praying? It's the only answer, Ruth. Ruth, keep praying. Pray the scourge doesn't reach you. Pray, Ruth, pray!"

"Oh, shut up, Bertha," though her sister-in-law couldn't hear her. "Just shut the hell up." She slumped over the table, her head in her hot sticky hands.

# EIGHT

MAGGIE WRIGGLED her butt to make herself comfortable on the futon. She'd never liked a bed, just a mattress on the floor. Liz and Boadie were feeding the young calves, and Maggie was finally alone on a hot Wednesday afternoon, with Nola's secret box in her hands. Nola had given it to her to caretake when she found Ritchie trying to get into it one day, and Maggie had brought it to Vermont. She'd been dying to open it and knew she shouldn't, but it might give a clue to Nola's whereabouts. Or so she reasoned.

Nola was not only Maggie's cousin, but her dearest friend. They were always together as kids. Nola's mother had been stuck on the importance of education, and with the help of Father Linehan, got the two girls into a parish school. They hated the head nun—if they whispered together she'd make them sit with their heads out the window, rain or shine, the window down sharp on their necks. Or she'd make them write *Jesus loves me,* or *I'm a sinner,* depending on the offense, a hundred times on the blackboard till their arms were ready to fall off. Maggie learned to read, but not stubborn Nola—not till Maggie taught her on her own, and then Nola went way past Maggie—Nola had smarts.

Maggie twisted a piece of wire and pried open the box. The lock was weak. Maggie knew about locks from her dad, who had a talent for busting them open. No one wanted to discourage his talent, because life was happier when Dad was caught and put away.

The lid snapped open. It was a tin box, hand painted, Maggie knew, by Nola's grandmother. The poor woman had faced up one last time to Nola's abusive father, been knocked clear across the room and into a shelf full of steel tools, and was never right in the head after that. She died one windy day hanging laundry—was found wrapped up tight in a sheet. Everyone knew it was bad luck to unwind a sheet, so all they had to do was bury her like that. It was all quite convenient, Nola's ma said.

There were trinkets in the box, a necklace with a silver spiderweb hanging from a red ribbon, a present from Maggie herself. Maggie and Nola were always exchanging presents, sometimes mingling their blood—it was very spiritual, very emotional. Maggie held the necklace up to the light. Nola loved spiders, she felt their webs were magical. Untangle them and you knew your future, Nola said. Nola never wanted to know her own future, though—she was afraid of the future because of her name, Enola, and what it meant spelled backwards.

So what was happening now to Nola? Maggie squinted into the silver web but it gave out no secrets. She could only hope Nola was all right, that she'd found a family to take her in and care for her till she was able to fend for herself. She'd never fend for herself, Maggie knew, while Ritchie was alive. It was like he wanted to own Nola, was jealous of everyone who ever spoke to her. And yet Ritchie never really loved Nola—he only wanted to own her. It was Maggie he still carried a torch for, since the day he first heard her sing, he said—didn't he tell her that over and over again? Maggie would tell him to cool it, she had her Darren—but it didn't stop Ritchie from sidling up to her, touching her, breathing in her ear. God, she hated that!

It was funny how two brothers from the same mother could be so different. But then, the brothers had different fathers, so maybe that accounted for it. She didn't know either of the fathers, so who could tell?

She laid the necklace carefully on the India print coverlet and pulled out two more bits of jewelry: a narrow gold ring with the initials PP—her mother's initials; a copper earring she'd worn as a pair in that nun's school and never since, because Sister Eileen had pulled one of them off after Nola sneezed six times in the middle of Sister's lunch prayer and Sister was pissed off and kept the one earring. Oh, but they'd had a good giggle!

There were yellowy clippings and letters—one from an old auntie—midwife who'd helped with Keeley's birth and knew who the father was—someone Maggie already suspected, yet it was still a shock for her to read the name. Another letter from Penny, a Tonawanda neighbor and school counselor, a kind soul who took Maggie, Nola, and Keeley under her wing and fed them home-baked strudel when they came to visit. The letter was dated June 22—after Maggie and Darren left, and a few days before Nola went to the hospital. Nola would have read it over and over, the way it was folded and refolded a dozen or more times.

Maggie started to put it away but then saw her own name mentioned and couldn't resist reading it through. She wasn't a good reader—she'd sung her way through those two years in the nun's school—but when she had to, she could sound out the words. She held the lined paper up to the light and, pushing her finger along the lines, read aloud through to the word "Maggie." Nothing important: just a recipe for Penny's strudel Maggie and Nola had asked for, and a plea for Keeley to attend school more often. He shouldn't be on that farm all the time, she'd said.

But then Penny wrote there was something she suspected, something Nola should know, and that was why this letter. It was easier to write, she said, than tell it face-to-face. Holding the page close to her eyes, for something had spilled on the paper—soda or something—Maggie read on. Her mouth dropped open with the double shock of the two letters. Her heart so heavy now she could hardly hold the paper, she needed two hands to support that terrible weight.

And the pain of knowing that now Nola knew.

COLM WAS BACK with lobster for lunch. Ruth couldn't even look at the poor creatures struggling in the steaming pot, and Colm making jokes like "Quit frolicking in there, you guys, and settle down."

If Ruth ate lobster at all these days it was in a stew, not on the claw like this, presented with ceremony, melted butter, small pincers her lover set down by her plate to crack the shells with. And then, while they cracked and sipped the wine he'd brought (not a word yet about moving in, but it would come as it always did, the schemer), she could think only of what was going on in her life: the travellers in her pasture, the missing woman, the possible quarantine of her cows.

And here she was eating lobster of all things, as if the world wasn't about to come crashing down on her!

The absurdity of it all broke on her and she had to giggle. "Silly man," she said. "Dear silly sweet man," and she gave him a hug. Which he returned, of course, turning her shirt into a hot buttery rumple.

Ten minutes and Colm was done with his lobster—once a slow eater he had lately turned into a gulper; he was always done way before her. He was holding up a newspaper, reading aloud the AP news: "'We don't know what the likelihood is that the cows have eaten contaminated feed—'"

"What?"

"From someone in Minneapolis," he acknowledged, and went on reading: "'Federal officials are monitoring cows in Vermont, Minnesota, and Texas for signs of Mad Cow disease, according to a USDA expert on the illness.'"

Ruth put down her fork, settled back into gloom. "Don't read it all, just paraphrase," she said. "Tell me the worst and get it over with before they come knocking on the door again."

"Two cows in Minnesota have shown symptoms," he summarized, waving his pincers for emphasis. "A USDA official named Leafmiller is monitoring them because she doesn't know if they were given contaminated feed before they were imported five years ago from the Netherlands. But she doubts there's any BSE." Colm began quoting again: "'BSE has never before appeared in the United States and the Department of Agriculture is determined to keep it that way.'"

"Even at the risk of hiding it if it happens?" Ruth said, recalling the federal agent who had all but said, "If anyone asks, we weren't here." She hadn't been able to fathom that remark.

"I wonder," said Colm, chewing on his lower lip.

"So she says she doesn't know if they ate contaminated feed?" A spot of anger pricked her cheek.

"She doesn't know, right, but hey, she doesn't want to take any chance of Mad Cow moving into our food supply. We'll have to trust her, Ruthie. To catch the disease, your cows would've had to eat feed made from infected animals—or, it says here, eaten infected animals' brains, spinal cords, or nerves. Or a single infected cow could contaminate the others. They don't really know. Not that they test every slaughtered cow like they do in Europe and Japan—they've been pretty lax."

Ruth pushed away her plate. She couldn't eat another bite. The pink claws reminded her of broken bones.

"You won't catch Mad Cow from lobster."

"That's not the point." She hoped he wouldn't ask her what was the point, because she didn't know. She only knew that something poisonous, like a dark red cloud, was hovering over her farm and wouldn't go away.

"Twenty-two cows were imported to Texas, three to New York, and four sheep to Vermont—they're all being watched. Scary, huh?"

"Those sheep are the ones they've already taken. And not just the four. They took the whole flock. It wasn't fair!"

"Nope, wasn't," he said, slurping a bit of leftover butter, rather enjoying her panic, she felt—having created it, for God's sake! "Those sheep were killed. At a government lab in Iowa.

Three hundred sixty killed from Vermont—their brain tissues tested. Four, they claimed, came out positive."

Ruth had read about it in the *Free Press*. "But the first time the tissues turned out negative! And the owners weren't allowed a second opinion, an independent tester."

There were too many inconsistencies. It was all too much. She shoved back her chair and sprang up. The claws went flying; one of them struck her wineglass and gave a sharp ring. She took it for a sign, a severe warning. For her, and her cows.

"Hey, where you going? I brought dessert from the Otter Bakery. Chocolate éclairs, Ruthie. You love 'em."

She was already at the door. She had to go down to the pasture. A letter had come in the mail for Maggie; she had to deliver it. She had to count cows.

"Nobody's taken your cows yet, Ruthie. You're getting paranoid. Come back and eat your éclair."

"You eat it, Colm. I don't want it. Nobody's going to take my animals. Over my dead body they will!" She was in the cupboard now, rummaging about.

"What are you looking for?"

"Pete's gun. He left it here for me. In case of predators. When I was single, you know, before you started to ooze in, you sneaky fellow—take over my bed."

He was up behind her, his arms around her waist, his face pressed into her neck. It felt good for a moment. But she had to find the gun, and she pulled away.

"You're not single anymore, Ruthie, love, we're in this together. You know you hate guns. You don't need one, for pete's sake."

"Don't say that," she said, opening drawers, flinging out pans, napkins, paper plates.

"Don't say what?"

"Don't say 'for pete's sake.' Pete's gone now. He married that actress. It's all legal. I'm a single woman."

"Not for long, though," he said, picking up what she'd

thrown down. "Tell me not for long. It's a cold, scary world out there, Ruth. Crime moving out of the cities, into the country. You need a man in the house. Full-time, you know?"

She held up the gun. It was an old hunting rifle, a Winchester 30-30—empty now, but she knew where the bullets were. On the very top shelf, aha, she'd kept them up high in case Vic, who was only ten when Pete walked out on her one day, picked up the gun and played army with it. True, she hated guns. She didn't know why she'd kept it. Though she was glad of it now. She might need it. And she knew how to use it—Pete had taught her. It wasn't crime she worried about, so much as the unknown, the insidious, the unseeable. Plague!

He was holding her tight again, making her put down the gun, turning her around, pulling her into his arms. It felt good, it felt secure. But did it keep out the plague?

He was sipping at her lips again, then pressing down hard, and she pressed back. "I love you," he murmured, and she felt herself nodding, murmuring back, holding on as though if he let go, the claws would get her, and she'd be lost.

THIS TIME FOR NOLA there was no getting away. It was the sheep man. He'd walked right into the spare white-walled dining room where the eight women were just finishing lunch—a good lunch, too: cheese, tomato and bacon sandwiches, fruit salad. Nola felt rested, nourished. For three nights now, since she'd stumbled up on the porch, she'd had a bed of her own. Well, in a room with two other women, but what the hell. To be alone in bed was the joy.

But this man. Why was he here—was he looking for her? Had he brought the police? There was something about the way he'd looked at her the morning she fled the farm, the way his eyes roamed her body. She lowered her chin and ate quickly. She had different clothes on today, a blue striped skirt and white blouse—he might not notice her.

But when she'd finished the plateful of salad and looked up, their eyes met. He stared, talking all the while to the director in her wheelchair, something about a woman who needed a place to stay, to hide from her husband. He was here on business then? All the same she didn't trust him. He'd locked her out when she needed his help; she couldn't understand that after he'd given her food and a dress.

The director, a big-breasted woman with blazing eyes and thin legs that dropped, useless, onto the metal footrests, wheeled into an adjoining room and the man followed. Nola saw her chance, excused herself from the table—no one knew her story, a woman had the right to privacy here, to keep her life to herself if she chose. Upstairs, Nola tucked her rosary beads into a pocket of the white blouse, piled the green print dress, toothbrush, underclothes, and pajamas they'd given her into a cloth sack, and tiptoed down the back stairs. She'd leave before he asked about her, gave her story to the director, frightened the woman. She was probably infected, they'd said; she'd heard the newscast, the women talking about it. One of them had glanced at her when they heard the missing woman was from the South. She'd told a lie, of course: "I've been living north of here. My man got to me, he gave me a concussion. came here to get away from him." She'd given a false name— Peg; embroidered a little, half believed the lie when she told it.

But the prying woman didn't believe her, that was obvious from the smirk—a comment about Nola's southern accent. And the director—Mother, they called her—had lifted her chin up out of the wheelchair, exchanged a sharp-eyed glance with the smirking female. Nola didn't know her well enough to figure whose side she'd be on.

And this man, who'd seen her only in a nightgown, would speak to the director, tell her the truth. Because he knew, all right. He knew.

"You're leaving, Peg?" The voice startled. It was Ellen in the doorway, a chunky, sweet-faced woman in her forties who slept in the next bed. Ellen had nightmares; Nola had heard her moan n her sleep. Now and then she'd give a shout, a warning to omeone she called Sweetie. A daughter maybe, warning gainst an abusive father? Ellen didn't say. Nola was sorry to eave Ellen; she needed a friend.

"Don't tell," Nola said. "I have to go. I have a daughter who eeds me." She didn't have a daughter at all, though she wished he had. Sometimes she fantasized about a daughter, a sister or shy Keeley. Keeley needed someone else to love—who oved him. God, but she worried about that boy! And more than ver, since that frightening letter from Penny.

"You have a daughter? I didn't know. How old? She sick?" Ellen looked sympathetic. Nola wished she could bring Ellen vith her. But she had to travel alone; with a companion, she'd e easy to catch. It would be comforting, though, to have Maggie with her. She touched the gold cross that she never took off er neck—this would be her companion. She'd already sent a ote to Maggie to tell her where she was—got a stamp and envelope from the director. She'd mailed it to the Willmarth farm— oped Ritchie hadn't seen it. She thought of going back to the Villmarths' to talk to her cousin. But then she might run into Ritchie. She didn't know if he was still on the farm or if he'd gone n to Tonawanda. Or if he was still looking for her… She hadn't ven looked back when she ran off, to tell the truth. Just kept running, heading across the main road, barely avoiding a milk truck. Then across a cornfield and through a hole in the fence into the ack of the sheep farm on the next road, twisting her ankle.

That had been the wrong move!

"Sick, yeah," she told Ellen, who was taking up the whole oorway with her wide girth. "She had pneumonia and I got to et back to her." She pushed past Ellen, kept moving. She heard male voice downstairs in the hallway, she had to get out.

"You'll be back? You can't stay with them, you know," Ellen houted, meaning an abuser. "They tell you they love you, then ey hit you the next time you look at them the wrong way or ed 'em something they don't like the taste of."

"Yeah, I'll be back," Nola called over her shoulder, thoug
she knew she wouldn't, and she slipped down the back step
and out the rear door. There was a vegetable garden behind th
house, two large maples, and a stand of papery white birche
Beyond, it was all woods, and then swamp, someone had said—
they weren't far from Otter Creek.

She couldn't see a path through the wood except the wa
she'd come by. She couldn't go down the main road, either, th
sheep man would see her, call the police. He'd probably alread
called, they'd be looking for her. She didn't want any clues tha
might lead back to the farm where Keeley was still living. Sh
didn't want the boy tangled up in this. Keeley had a problen
he lived in his own world half the time. Not autistic, no, no
that bad, her neighbor Penny said. But he needed help. H
needed it bad. He needed her!

She'd take Keeley away, she would! They'd make a life fo
themselves someplace where nobody knew them.

She threw the sack over her shoulder, slowly made her wa
into the woods, through the underbrush and furze. It was a li
tle past one, she figured. The sun shredded through the brus
here and there but was mostly obscured by the taller pines, the
thick trunks travelling up, and up, spreading canopies of prickl
leaves that kept out the heat. It was a strange feeling, like sh
was travelling through another time, another life, where an
minute she might run into an oxcart, an Indian, another trave
ler like herself—for hadn't her forebears been on the road fo
centuries? If not here, then in Ireland. She'd only twice seen
real Indian: when a woman came to the uncle's farm selling ba
kets and didn't say a word, just thrust the baskets under Un
cle's nose, and when Uncle sent her away, the woman stuck u
her chin like she didn't care and went off with her man. They
reminded Nola of her own life. Her father letting her mothe
sell the trinkets while he spent the money in the local bar. Nol
had wanted to run and hug that Indian woman, but she didn'
She was always slow to act on her impulses. Till now.

After a half hour's trudge she came on a trail that looped both ways. She hesitated a minute, deciding which way. Then, hearing voices to the left, she turned right. The angle of the sun told her she was heading north. She had to find a main road, take a chance, get a ride west toward Lake Champlain, cross the bridge she and Ritchie had come over four days ago, then head west again. Walking and hitching, she'd make her way back to the Tonawanda farm and Keeley. It might take days, maybe weeks, but she'd get there. Her ankle was better anyway, she hardly limped. She reached for her rosary beads—she needed help from above. "Hail, Mary, Mother of God," she began....

She heard a horse whinny and she halted. The vegetation was thinning out to a snaggle of vines and berry bushes; she was approaching a clearing. She moved cautiously ahead. A clearing meant she was near a road, but a human might be there and want to know what she was doing—if she was trespassing. In the South a traveller might be shot if a farmer found her on his land. Folk called travellers wild animals, crafty beggars. All that hate took away a traveller's freedom. Maybe that was another reason she and Keeley went north with Darren and Maggie. North, they said, meant freedom.

Freedom, yeah, till she settled on the uncle's farm and was no better than a servant. But things would change. She'd make them change—for herself and Keeley. There was no room for Ritchie in any future she wanted. She'd have to make him realize that if he caught up with her again. This time she'd tell him good-bye. Just—good-bye.

JAMES WANTED to get away from the director but she kept him talking. He wondered if she'd seen that woman leaving the table. The director was a tough old bird—never mind those lame legs. He'd seen her kind before. The old maid who could throw you over her shoulder if she got a mad on. He'd never liked that sort, always trying to manipulate men. A lesbian maybe. No sign of a man in this house! Their eyes threw daggers when *he* walked in. They turned their faces away. Of course, that's why he'd brought his client here from the counseling service. Some guy stalking her, getting on her back.

He'd seen the traveller woman through the office window, trotting on her small feet through a vegetable garden, into the woods, a coarse white sack over her shoulder. While the damned director kept on talking, never let him get a word in. Finally made him look at papers she'd drawn up for his client. When he finished signing papers and looked out again, the yard was empty.

"You like our view? Our stand of birches? Our women planted them," the director said, wheeling up after him. He could hear the irritating *click-click* of the chair.

"Yes, very nice," he said, deciding not to tell her about the runaway. If she didn't already know, let her find out for herself. "Nice woods. Creek down there, they say. The way it winds, you never know where you're going to come out on it."

"But you don't want to go back too far, you'll run into the Branbury swamp. Nasty place, that swamp. One of our people died in there once, running away from her husband."

"Oh?"

"Yes." The woman was beside him now, her eyes bulging up into his face as if she'd fix him here, dare him to take off after the damn gypsy. "He barged in. We'd told her it was a safe house, we'd call nine-one-one if he persisted. But she bolted back into the woods. And—" The woman's voice faltered.

"And?" he said softly, still looking out the window at the red maples, the stand of birches.

"He got her. Strangled her, left her body in the swamp. Of course, we called the police but too late. They found her."

"Oh dear," he said—what else could he say? He turned away from the window, saw her looking hard at him. Did she know something? His stomach made a noise, he had gas. He was uncomfortable, he didn't want to talk anymore, or hear her talk. He turned back to the window, wondering how he'd get away without making her more suspicious. Though it was foolish, he told himself; what could this disabled woman know of his past? He supposed she could have a client here from upstate New York…. Your past follows you, he thought. It's like a dark shadow.

He squinted. He saw what looked like a figure snaking into the woods from the east—a tall broad figure. He caught a flash of red and black on the back of the man's shirt. Then the bushes closed in on the figure and the landscape was empty again.

"Excuse me," he said to the wheelchair, "I have to go. I have an appointment at"—he glanced at his watch—"eleven o'clock? I'd almost forgot. I have to run."

He picked up the briefcase he'd left on the floor, and pasting on a smile, nodding at the shiny blur of wheelchair, he walked out. She called something after him and he replied, but had no idea what either had said.

NOLA CAME OUT into the clearing and there was the horse. It was the most beautiful creature she'd ever seen: a sleek glossy brown, like velvet, with a white star on its sleek head. It stared at her out of a rich brown intelligent eye, made a move toward her as if it knew her, knew she had oats for it, an apple. And she did, she had an apple in her sack, she'd taken it from the lunch table to eat later. She wanted to share the apple with this beautiful horse.

It took the apple from the palm of her hand, gazed at her through starry eyes as it munched. She leaned into the warm furry body, felt the breath heaving out of its lungs. She blew her own breath into its nostrils, and it nickered softly. She wanted to ride off on it, ride to the freedom she longed for. She was proud to be a traveller, her mother had been proud. No one was going to tell her what to do, where to go, where to live. "No one," she told the horse. "I'm free. I'm a free woman."

The horse snorted and its whole body quivered. She pushed herself upright, away from the warm belly. Someone was coming out of the brush. She ran back toward the wood but was yanked back, like she'd run into a wide elastic band. An arm grabbed hers, pinched hard and deep, till she cried out. He smelled of sweat and tobacco and drink. He swung her around to look at him.

"I didn't like it," he said raising a fist, "you running off like that."

# NINE

COLM HAD TURNED INTO a CNN news addict, and though she'd rather not hear the news at two in the afternoon, Ruth gave in and they sat on the sofa with the lunch Sharon had dropped off. The MUTE button was on, shutting out a commercial for bladder control—it always made Ruth want to pee, and how could she with a lap full of Chinese? Colm had his arm around her, he was eating with his right hand only, an art he'd perfected through numerous meals together in the four years since Pete had left. Every third or fourth bite he'd lean over to give her a Moo Shu Pancake kiss on the cheek—or lips, if he happened to aim right. She'd laugh, then swallow the wrong way, then cough until the news came back on.

The news *was* back on. Colm turned up the sound. The stock market was still down. That only depressed her, so she interrupted to ask about the latest news from the police department. Colm had a habit of checking in twice each day, in between his real estate and his mortuary dealings. It had been four days since the feds had come with their warnings of quarantine, but no results from the samples they and the police had taken. And, praise be, no quarantine. With each passing day she drew a breath of fresh hope.

"The missing traveller? The horse? Nothing at all?" she asked when he shook his head.

"Not a syllable. No woman, no horse."

"What have they done to try to find them? I mean, they can't just sit on their heels and hope woman or horse will show up at The Inferno for brunch and someone will call in a sighting."

Colm was half listening, CNN had his attention. He squeezed her shoulder to acknowledge her presence and took a bite of the Moo Shu. The blond newsperson was gushing on with her ill tidings. Everything had gone to pieces in the world: record low milk prices, a shaky stock market, the ongoing conflict in the Middle East, floods in Europe, an earthquake in China. "What can they do?" Colm said, getting around to Ruth's question. "Cops in five states and Canada are on the lookout for Nola Donahue. They've checked the Morgan Horse Farm—no Ophelia. They've called horse owners everywhere, put up posters—nothing. No horses galloping down the interstate."

She had to smile at the thought of a horse galloping down the interstate. "Franny's been calling here twice a day to see if I've heard any news. She says the police are just sitting on their butts."

"Jeez. She's been down at the station, too. The chief hides in the men's room when they come, but yesterday that fool Franny marched right in after him. He had his pants down, damned embarrassing."

"That'll teach him to hide."

There was another commercial about arthritis, a dog doing yoga—she liked that one. She'd quit yoga after the instructor got her twisted up one day like a pretzel. She hated to give up, but really! Who wanted to squat like a dog, on all fours? The only posture she could do to perfection was one called "the corpse."

Colm's plate was on the floor. He was moving in on her, both arms around her neck, taking those little sips from her lips again, *pup pup pup,* then a long one that ended with a small explosion of saliva. She had to laugh.

When he'd finished his dessert—*her,* he allowed—he hit the button again and the screen showed a farm in upstate New York. They'd found two sick calves on it—Friesian calves from the Netherlands. The beasts had begun shedding weight, acting skittish as kittens, according to the farmer, who'd shot them. At first he tried to hide the fact, but a neighbor informed the authorities. "It might be Mad Cow," the blond newsperson warned, her eyebrows locked tragically together, "a transmissible spongiform encephalopathy—TSE. TSEs are fatal and untreatable. They ravage the brain, causing symptoms that range from dementia to psychosis and paralysis. And are not caused by germs," she went on gravely, as though she were reporting the sinking of the *Titanic*, "but 'prions,' normal protein molecules that become infectious when folded into abnormal shapes. You can freeze them, boil them, soak them in formaldehyde— and they'll emerge no less deadly than before."

Suddenly a cow leaped onto the screen, as big as life: she was lurching crazily across a field, skin hanging loose on the bones; drooling, arching her back, waving her head, then charging headlong, mad-eyed, at the camera as though she would charge right into the viewer's home. Ruth cried out, drew back in horror—her tea spilled into her lap.

"It's an old film," Colm said, flinging an arm about her neck. "Some farm back in '98, in South Downs, England. Not New York. Far from here, Ruthie."

But it had been right in her living room! She let Colm rub and rub her neck and shoulders, but the image stayed behind her eyes.

The screen switched to a commercial on irritable bowel syndrome; Ruth felt her own bowels contract. She'd feel symptoms of every ailment they prescribed for—headaches, incontinence, heartburn, arthritis. Now fear. Colm was gripping her hand but she was too numb to feel it.

"Where in New York?" she whispered. "They didn't say."

"Government's probably trying to cool it," he said. "The media's jumping in ahead of them."

She nodded. "Maybe we should thank the media. Or should we? I don't know."

"Don't worry. Your calves are healthy, right? I saw the old lady bottle-feeding them." Her skin was turning blue where he was squeezing her hand.

"The White House has ordered…" the reporter went on, quickly changing the subject as if to say, "So what? We've got more important news. We're planning to invade East Mongolia, we think it has nuclear power."

"Upstate New York," Ruth said, realizing. "She did say upstate New York. That limits it. That's where that farm is—in upstate New York. Your relative's farm, Colm. Where I bought my two calves." At the time it had seemed a good deal. She grabbed the remote and hit the MUTE button. "So let's talk."

"Haven't we been?"

"About this latest. You know what it might mean, don't you?"

"Look, upstate New York's a big area. We don't know where this happened—the feds are keeping it on ice till they prove it's Mad Cow. Could be anywhere within a radius of three hundred miles. Let's not panic—yet."

"Yet," she repeated. Anywhere in New York was too close to home for comfort. When she'd first read about the disease it was clear across the ocean, in the UK and Europe, a safe distance. She'd never have thought of buying a calf from the UK or Europe. Upstate New York had seemed safe. A chill travelled her spine, like a spill of ice cubes. It seemed to be moving from farm to farm, that invisible plague, like a giant mowing machine, eliminating everything in its path.

She couldn't think what to do. She didn't want to think. She and Colm looked at one another in silence. "Oh God," she said, and buried her face in her hands. "If I'd never listened to you, bought those calves. You and your crazy relatives! How'd they ever find you anyway?"

It was fate, she thought, fate. His fate and now her fate.

"I told you," he said stubbornly, "but you'd only half listen. Darren's mother—she's a nontraveller—had some kind of genealogy done and Darren found it. Dad's name was on it—on the nontraveller side, I mean."

"Please, Colm—don't keep saying 'on the nontraveller side.' You sound so biased."

"Well, they do have a reputation. You heard about that woman who slapped her kid in the parking lot and they put her on the news and found she was an Irish traveller? Lies, thievery, beatings. NBC hit all the low notes."

"The old stereotypes," said Ruth, who had grown quite fond of Maggie and, in particular, the tough old grandmother with her potbellied pig. Boadie had fallen in love with the New York calves, was practically nursing them with her own saggy dugs.

They were quiet a moment while the TV flashed on in silence and the words "upstate New York" took on new meaning for Ruth. "Why," she cried, "if that's the Leary farm, it's where that Nola woman could have contracted it, that CJD. Good Lord, can you really catch it from a cow?"

"Mostly from eating infected beef, I guess. We'll have to find the woman to see if she did." He went on about women in Papua, New Guinea, who ate their female dead in a ritual of respect—and for the protein. "They were dying from something the tribe called 'kuru,' which means shaking or shivering—then stupor and death. They thought it a curse. Anyway, someone did autopsies. The brains looked like the brains of people with CJD. That kuru started spreading like the plague. I mean, it was the plague. And your cows are 'cannibals.' The meal they eat—from rendered pigs, chickens, cows."

"Stop!" she said. "Mine's an organic farm. My cows only eat grass and grains."

"But was the farm Darren bought those two calves from—organic?"

"Oh!" she said. She jumped up, she couldn't sit another minute. "But we don't know. We don't know it's our travellers' farm. We don't know! You're right, there must be hundreds of farms in that area. Thousands. Right, Colm, right?"

"Absolutely," he said. "Thousands of farms. We'll just have to hope, won't we?—that it won't affect—our farm."

"Our farm?"

"Yours, mine. Our children's."

"Yes." She gave in to his appropriation, patted his hand. Colm had no children of his own; she'd have to share with him.

She sat back down, leaned into him, and he put an arm around her shoulder; pulled her so close she thought for a minute he'd halt breath. But she didn't want him to stop holding her. They were partners now; he and she would be the wall that would keep out the curse—that *kuru* thing. Maybe she *should* have him move in for good, the way he wanted.

But what could a wall of flesh do against a bacteria—a "prion"—that you couldn't see, that could float in a dark cloud over the pasture fence, then ooze in through the barn door?

MAGGIE WAS TAKING an afternoon walk with her dog through the lower pasture, swinging her arms vigorously, singing to the birds, the cows—whoever would listen. A chickadee came down to perch on her hand when she held out a handful of sunflower seed. She warbled and it warbled back. Maggie was at heart an optimist, life wasn't going to get her down. For one thing, Nola was safe, at a place called the Healing House—she'd had a note. They were all women in there, safe from their abusive men. Safe from Ritchie—though Ritchie never hurt Nola bad, or so Nola claimed. But Maggie had seen the occasional bruise on her friend's cheeks and arms. She wouldn't put anything past treacherous old Ritchie. And wasn't there such a thing as verbal abuse? Wasn't it abuse to drag her forcibly from that hospital?

The black-capped chickadee flew away, its beige breast gleaming in the sun. The dog trotted off, investigating some interest of its own, and Maggie continued on her walk, deep down into the pasture. She squeezed through the wires on the fence and moved on down to the beaver pond. She could see the log and straw house where the beavers lived—it was thrilling. One night she'd left a carrot and the beaver took it, scrambled right up to her and took it! Maggie loved wild animals, all animals, though not cows so much. It was hard to love cows when you had to be mopping up their feces all the time. She picked her way through the wild raspberry bushes, a rhododendron that had grown leggy—years ago someone had lived here, there was still a stone foundation. She imagined a woman, youngish like herself, strolling through the brush where the leaves sang in the wind like silver dollars falling onto a table and clinking together.

Almost to the beaver pond she halted, stopped by voices. She knew those voices, they were as familiar as her own. The voices came toward her and she crouched down, ducked her head into her arms, her heart drumming. Neither voice would like being overheard. Even Darren had a temper sometimes—never abusive, but it could flare up, and she'd have to disappear, let it simmer down.

She heard the word "Uncle," and then Darren breaking in with the old tune: "I'm not coming back, Ritch, I tole you that a million times, now quit harping on it. Uncle's in trouble anyway, you know that. Can't pay his bills. Now this disease. I tole him his calves were acting funny. Soon there won't be any farm."

Ritchie said, "Come on, what disease? They was just off their feed, that's all."

"The Willmarth tole me," Darren said. "It was on the news. Some farm in upstate New York. You know Uncle got those Friesian calves—made me bring two of 'em here."

"Then he needs you," Ritchie said. "Needs the both of us."

"For god's sake, Ritch, what's with all this loyalty crap? I never seen much love lost between you two."

"He's blood, yours and mine. We gotta stick together. You're my younger brother."

"Yeah, and you love me, right? You love my woman, too, huh? What you did to her sister, thinking it was Maggie—"

"What? What did I do to her?"

The voices were rising now. "You know. You gotta live with it. So do I. You're a bastard, Ritch, a born bastard. I don't care you're my brother. And what you did to Nola—where's she at anyway?"

"I got her. She's not going anywhere."

"Hang on now! She's in that safe house, Maggie says. No men allowed. You stay away from her, hear?"

"No, I don't hear, g'dammit."

They were fighting. She heard the grunts and slaps, the cries of anger. Then one of them broke and ran back along the edge of the pond. She could hear the brush breaking, dead logs rolling into the water from the running feet. She heard Darren shouting. She heard the words "Nola" again, and "Uncle," and her own name, and then her dog came leaping through the underbrush, barking. She crouched lower but the dog found her. She held her breath, tried to shoo him away with her hands. The footsteps came closer. The dog jumped away from her and she heard Darren's voice: "Hey, pooch, what're you doing way down here? Come on, boy, too wet for you. We gotta get the prickers outa your tail." And luckily the dog followed.

She couldn't move for a time; she was trying to think through what she'd heard. Darren knew about Ritchie and her sister, and here she'd thought that long-ago pregnancy a secret from both men. But Ritchie still didn't know the outcome, she was pretty sure of that. And worse, Ritchie had Nola again, he'd got her out of that healing place. How had he known where she was? Now he was back here, nosing about. How many times had he been here? Did he see Nola's letter? He was obviously waiting for Darren to give in, go back with him to Uncle's. Uncle had Ritchie in some kind of bind. Blackmail? Money needs? Something about Ritchie's past? She didn't know. Uncle had no use for Ritchie, he just wanted Darren back. Maybe Ritchie's inheritance depended on his working there, that was probably it.

Oh, what did she know? Not a damn thing for certain.

When she pulled herself away from the prickers that held her skirt and sleeves she could hardly stand. It was like she'd grown old in half an hour. Like she was an old woman, older even than Mammy Boadie. Bent forward, trudging back up the hillside, back to a changed world.

And there was Ritchie, coming out of the trailer with a paper bag in his hand. How dared he! But he was the last person in the world she wanted to confront. She ducked behind the trailer, and just in time, for he glanced about like the sneak he was, and went running across the upper pasture toward the woods.

# TEN

WHEN JAMES PERLMAN heard about the sick cows in upstate New York—the Leary farm in Tonawanda, according to the Friday morning news—he reasoned that the gypsy couple might well have come from that farm. He'd tried to phone the Willmarth woman, but she was always "away from her phone," damn her. He'd have to go in person, there was no way out of it. He wanted to avoid reporters as well as police; reporters were always digging up one's ancestors, pointing a finger at someone a hundred years ago who'd robbed a bank or embezzled funds. Outrageous! Something should be done about the snooping media. They had the power to ruin lives, it wasn't right.

And there were his sheep. The one pair from Scotland, but perfectly healthy. No one knew about them. And he didn't want anyone to know. No, he had to team up with the Willmarth woman, they'd have to work up a defense between them against the world of so-called health and science. Not that he wanted to be chummy with that female—oh no, he just wanted his bases covered.

He found her in the back of the barn, examining a small bull calf, patting and probing it, peering into its mouth, like she was a dentist. He'd worn the wrong shoes. They were covered with pig shit after someone told him the farmwoman was down in the pasture and he'd gone there first. Then the pig woman said she was in the barn—Christ! Couldn't the farmwoman get rid of that crowd? He hoped she kept her doors locked. Those gypsy types were light-fingered.

She didn't lock up, though, according to the newscast. The traveller woman had walked right in to take a bath—disgusting

He came up behind the farmer, said, "Hello," and the muscles in her shoulders rippled. He saw an attractive woman, on the tall side, full-hipped, gray-brown hair pulled loosely up off her damp neck, fine freckles on the perspiring brow. Nice breasts, too, he thought, as she pulled her arms back and jumped to a standing position. Divorced, he'd heard, and there was that tweaking again in the groin.

"Didn't mean to scare you. The old lady sent me up here."

She was taking a stance, arms akimbo, like he was an interloper, come to steal her cows. She didn't say anything, just looked him in the eye, like he was meat she wanted to examine. Waited for him to explain. It smelled in here, worse than his sheep barn. More than that—it stank.

He felt more at ease now. She must think he was a government man, here about the Mad Cow scare, wanting to monitor her herd. He nodded. "James Perlman. I have a small flock of sheep a mile from here. I've been trying to call you but you're always, uh, unavailable."

She didn't seem a bit sorry that she was always unavailable. She seemed a tad more relaxed, though, her full lips gave in to what might be called a smile. He smiled back to show he understood, he was on her side. He thrust out his hand and she took it, though not with enthusiasm. "I know you're worried and I'm worried, too," he said. "My sheep are everything to me now. I'm trying to make a go of it up here. Still learning, of course, about sheep."

"And now you're afraid we have Mad Cow here. It will spread to your place. Someone will put your sheep under quarantine, take them away, barely compensate you." She patted the calf again, gazed at it as if to say, "Look. My calves are A-l healthy."

"Oh no, not quite like that." He didn't want her to think he was coming to accuse her because she allowed that encampment of gypsies—though under the circumstances she damn well shouldn't allow it! He'd never tolerate such a madcap gang. Even now he could hear singing down in the fields—female voices. It was intolerable. Who knew what diseases they'd acquired on the road? He'd been a nurse; he knew all the germs a person carried.

He spread his hands in truce. It was time to get to the point. "I have information about the missing woman." She looked up; she was interested. "Monday morning, it was, she wandered into my yard. She was in a nightgown, there was blood on it. I thought she'd escaped from the local hospital."

Now she was angry, her freckles thickened. She took a step toward him. For a moment he thought she'd strike him and he stepped back. "Why didn't you call the police? She'd have just come from my house. It would have relieved all of us here to have her back at that hospital."

"I didn't know where she'd come from," he said, determined to keep his cool. "Not then. I didn't think the police would want her—thought her one of the homeless. Then when I heard the radio report I tried to call you. But no one answered. I left a message for you to call back." He hardened his gaze. He wasn't tall, only five-foot-nine-and-a-half, but she was an inch or two shorter than he. His wife had been exactly his height; he'd never liked that. Maureen always wore two-inch heels, like she wanted to lord it over him.

The woman was contrite, she obviously remembered. "We've been under siege here," she said. "I can't tell you how many crank calls we've had, how many sightings. I can't respond to them all." She leaned back against the wall. He could see her breasts swell with the heavy breathing. A fly landed on her cheek and she brushed it off. She was quite—seductive. He stuffed his hands in his pockets, turned slightly away so she wouldn't see his growing erection.

"Then what? Where did she go? What direction? Did she speak to you? Did she seem distraught? Was she alone? No man with her—in the background maybe?"

"Alone," he said, and told her the story. How he'd brough

food to her, how he'd offered his ex-wife's clothing—he emphasized the ex-wife, to show his availability. He told how she'd flagged down a car and gone off. "Run off," he said, not wanting to tell how she'd banged on his door. "I tried to stop her, but she wouldn't. It's happened twice now."

"What? You saw her twice? Look, you'd better come back to the house with me. I'll call my friend Colm Hanna, he's a cop—part-time anyway. You can tell him the story. You'll need a good excuse for not getting to us right away."

She was taking an attitude and he didn't care for it. "I told you, I tried," he said. He picked his way slowly behind her where she was heading for a back door. The stink was bad, the manure slippery underfoot. The July heat, the drought, made the smell overbearing. She was in heavy boots, she was used to the cow shit. Cows were bigger than sheep; they were messier. He was in his good shoes, his visiting shoes. Already he felt them heavy with dung.

"So where was the second time she ran off?" she asked when they got to her kitchen. She gave him coffee—that was some compensation for her attitude. But she was a no-nonsense kind of female, he saw that. She was beginning to remind him of that head nurse in the Buffalo hospital. She'd suspect him of having his own reasons for not wanting to contact the police. He was uncomfortable; his bowels were beginning to loosen.

He told her about the Healing House, his job, the abused woman he was taking there. How he'd seen the traveller woman again—and no, he didn't recall what she was wearing—maybe the green print dress of his wife's. For some reason he decided not to tell her he'd seen the man Ritchie twice as well, the second time charging into the woods behind the Healing House, like he'd been hanging about, looking for the woman there.

He thought of that other woman the director had told about, killed in the swamp, her body rotting no doubt when they found her. He clasped his hands together to keep them still.

"She disappeared again after she saw me in the dining room. Like she didn't want to see me. Like I'd call the police, have her taken away. She seemed paranoid, that's why I knew I had to talk to someone." He put his elbows on the table, leaned his chin in his hands—a sincere kind of gesture, he felt. "I figure you and I are in the same boat. Both of us exposed to this woman. Our animals at stake, our livelihoods. I thought you'd know the next step to take. It isn't always the police, is it?"

He held her gaze a moment, saw she was coming round to his point of view, saw the attractive face soften. Police weren't always the answer for her, either. He'd heard the scuttlebutt.

"We'll get Colm here," she said. "You might be right after all. About the police, the bureaucracy. They might scare her off. Colm's an insider, so to speak, but we can trust him. This happened when?"

He felt she'd decided to trust him, and he relaxed, unclasped his hands, slurped the coffee. "Yesterday afternoon, she was on foot—out toward the Branbury swamp, I believe. She's somewhere in the neighborhood still, I'm sure. We can get a search party together. We've got to find her, get her back to that hospital, have her tested. Get us all off the hook."

"Or on it," she said. "Hooked like a steer, right through the eye."

He clapped a hand to his face. The eye stung, like she'd thrown acid in it. His bowels were acting up again; he didn't want an accident in front of this woman who could talk about a hook through the eye. He was in her hands now, he'd let her take the lead. He was glad he'd come, glad he'd told her about the woman. So she'd back him up if the police did come, accuse him of something.

It was terrible to be accused, whether or not you did it. The humiliation, the sick feeling in the gut. The shame of it in the eyes of the public. That was the worst of it: people looking at you, judging, suspecting.

Already the Willmarth woman was dialing, calling that Colm fellow. The one who worked part-time for the police.

How far could one trust the guy? The thought of police made him sick to his stomach. He'd been wrong to come, wrong to offer his story. No one would have known, suspected him of any implication if he'd stayed home, minded his own business. He couldn't talk to any policeman now, part-time or not. He was feeling sick, in a minute his bowels would let go. He wished now those gypsies were out of the county, out of the country, back in Canada at that hospital. He wished he'd taken things into his own hands, given them money, made them return. He wanted to find them—the man in particular. The man was the worst of the pair. He didn't trust that fellow.

"I've left a message for Colm—he's out with a client," Ruth Willmarth said. "I'll have him call you. Perlman, you said?"

"James, yes. And I've got to get back to work. I'm already late." He pushed up out of his chair, and bolted. He had to get to a bathroom, hadn't wanted to ask the farmwoman. Wouldn't want to use that bathroom anyway. He revved up the Honda, headed back to his place. Almost hit a dog that ran out in the road—swerved just in time. Stupid dog! Just standing there in the road, an old hound dog, like it had ten lives.

THE POLICE SAID the thief had probably taken Franny's mare off in a horse van, left town with her. They said Franny must prepare herself for not getting Ophelia back. But Franny consulted a psychic, who told her Ophelia was still in town. So Franny was going to ride her stallion, Hamlet, through all the town trails, however obscure. Ophelia knew Hamlet's smell, his whinny—she'd whinny back. Franny had a map of the town. If Sybil Moon was right, she'd find Ophelia. At the very least she'd find evidence of her, a clue that would lead to the recapture of her adorable mare.

Sybil Moon couldn't tell Franny exactly where, but knew she was somewhere in the area. And it made sense. That man wouldn't leave without his woman, would he? Though God knows where she was! Escaped from him at any rate, at least that was the rumor. But the police were wrong. There had been no evidence of a van coming up to the barn—only Ophelia's tracks leading out of the barn and up the back trail into the woods. This was clearly the work of a horse thief, and Irish travellers were famous for stealing horses. Oh yes, she'd heard that all over the place. The fellow was still hiding her mare somewhere in the woods—that's what the psychic said. Or maybe the swamp, Sybil said, though Franny hated that thought—her darling horse mucking through the Branbury swamp.

The landscape was a spider's web when she set out at dawn, a shining layer of mist enveloping the underbrush. Only the tops of trees visible, like they'd been cut in half but still grew, disembodied, on top. She felt like one of Arthur's knights, riding forth in search of the sacred chalice. While her companion lay in bed, snoring softly with the radio on. She'd kissed her lady Henrietta good-bye on the lips—it was indeed a sacred moment.

Yesterday she'd ridden through the north end of town. Today she'd follow the psychic's advice and ride to East Branbury, and into the adjoining swamp. She was wearing her rain jacket, riding boots, bluejeans, cell phone clipped to her belt—prepared for come what may. The psychic had not only mentioned the swamp, she spoke of something that might lie in it. A surprise of sorts. Her mare, Franny thought, an immense love swelling her breast.

Henrietta's radio had sputtered something about a sick animal—but far away in upstate New York, where people were trapped in snow and ice all winter long—worse than Vermont. It was nothing that could affect her Ophelia. For Ophelia was alive—exhausted perhaps, traumatized, but alive—the psychic had felt that. Franny had two red apples in her backpack, a carrot, and salves for the mare's hide in the event she'd been ridden hard. When she got the mare back she'd weave a garland of flowers. Like Shakespeare's Ophelia—only unlike the drowning woman, her mare would be alive and galloping home.

She took the main road for two miles, then veered east onto

Swamp Road, a dirt road that led to a covered bridge over Otter Creek and to the place where in 1776 the widow Ann Story had dug a tunnel for her five children and held out against the Indians and Tories. For weeks Ann had holed up there, listening to the enemy glide past hunting for the gunpowder Ann had stored inside her cave. Franny was working up a one-woman show, using Ann's persona. Franny had married, had one child before she realized her true sexuality—that child, sadly, had died in adolescence of leukemia. But Franny knew what it was to defend one's offspring against the enemy. In her case the enemy was the child's father, who had spread lies like manure on the veggie garden. Now Ophelia was Franny's child.

A narrow trail led into the swamp, where hunters ventured during deer season. The place was full of deer, otters, muskrat; it teemed with life. She examined the ground for hoofprints but saw none. Or if there had been prints, they'd been erased by fog and other animals. A snake skittered across their path, yellow eyes popped up, and then vanished. But brave Hamlet kept to the path. He was a sturdy fellow, she felt he would bring her to the mare. The way was thicker now, murkier; Hamlet had to slow his pace. After a quarter of an hour the path divided and she hesitated; then took the one to the right that led deeper into the swamp. There was no sign of human life here, few came to this wet place in summer. But there was the rich gold of swamp marigolds, of white saxifrage, and thick pink and white honeysuckle.

It was almost impossible now for Hamlet to walk: he'd lift a hoof and then it would sink into the murk and tangle of briars. Yet the stallion ploughed onward, as though he knew more than she did, was leading her to some fateful conclusion. Finally she tethered him to an alder and slogged on herself, not expecting to find the mare. Not even the smaller Ophelia could navigate this ooze—what monster would force her?

Yet someone had been through here. She came upon trampled and broken underbrush, like something had been recently dragged. She could see the outline in the path—or what could be called a path. A wavy, zigzaggy outline that the surf might make when it broke on shore. And beside it, omigod! a footprint. No, half a print, just the muddy heel of a shoe. And then the heel itself, broken off a shoe, but so muddy you couldn't tell the color. Whether man's or woman's it was impossible to say. One couldn't judge from a heel. Platform shoes were so chunky these days; she preferred the tiny satin heels of another century. She left the heel there—just in case it turned out to be important.

Curious, excited, but at the same time anxious, frightened even, she tramped on, in the wake of the broken underbrush. After a time the "path" veered off—south or east—she'd lost direction but could still hear Hamlet's snortings back where she'd tethered him. She would find her way back. She needed to know what had been dragged here.

And she saw. It was the body of a man. He'd been strangled with—oh God, God!—Ophelia's reins—the reins were still hanging from his neck. She knew they were her mare's because of the way the reins were scraped and worn on the edges—a certain way Ophelia had of turning quickly and having to be brought back in line. The man's neck was a dark red under the dangling reins, the skin bruised an ugly yellow above the T-shirt with its cruel message of *Death To Brits*. Feeling woozy, she grabbed a sapling for ballast; stood there, breathing hard to get her strength back.

She'd been right then, it was that Ritchie, the one she'd heard about on the radio, the one who'd abducted the missing traveller woman. Someone had strangled him and taken the mare, because she was no longer in sight. Franny lifted her chin and listened, but heard only a bird trilling overhead, a creature swishing through the tall grasses, a gurgle where something had splashed into the murk. There was no mare, no Ophelia. Franny had found the surprise the psychic had warned of—but it wasn't her darling horse. She had found her thief, but not his murderer. A new thief had come along to steal the mare and take her—where? Was he riding her without reins? What would he do with her?

And was the murderer still in the swamp—perhaps, this very moment, watching her by the traveller man's body?

Panicked, wanting the reins back but not wanting to touch the dead man—knowing anyway she should leave him to the police—she staggered out of the clearing. Stumbled back to Hamlet and flung her leg up over his broad back where she felt, somewhat anyhow, safe. Then she unclipped her cell phone and called Henrietta.

"Omigod, I found him, Hen—that traveller fellow. He took her all right, but the reins got him— Wha? Yes, strangled him! Never mind, Hen, I'll explain when I see you. Just need to call the police—what's the number? It's stuck to the phone, you've seen it there, damn it! Go down and look it up, will you? Dead, yes, I told you, he's dead! And she's gone, Hen, she's gone. Ophelia's gone. Without her reins. And God knows where… No, don't come out here, you can't come here, Hen, you'll get your feet wet and catch cold. You know what happens—last year it was bronchitis. Hen, please, please hang up and let me call the police, will you? I'll be home when I can!"

# ELEVEN

SHARON HEARD ABOUT the murder on the radio. It was breaking news, with few details, but one telling fact—that Ritchie fellow's death. So she drove straight to Cow Hill Road, careening up the drive, shoving Willa and Robbie before her into the barn, where her mother was swabbing the decks. Zelda, her mother's most ornery cow, under the weather with milk fever, bellowed when Sharon passed her stall, but Sharon was too excited to bellow back.

Uh-huh, her mother madly sweeping—same old routine, like nothing at all had happened, like a man hadn't been killed. Like his companion—whom the police suspected now of murder—hadn't disappeared without a trace.

Out of the corner of her eye she saw the commotion down in the pasture. And not just cows mewling, but pickups gathering: women, children, dogs. That keening again, like a croaky warning of Armageddon. One traveller dead, another on the lam. Worried all over again, she clutched her children's hands: three-year-old Willa, five-year-old Robbie: sturdy, healthy, lively children. She ran back with them to her car. Better not to bring them into the barn. Superstitious, yes, but Sharon was a mother. She shut them in the car with coloring books, a doll, Robbie's *Thomas the Train* book. "Stay," she ordered, "stay. I'll be back soon. I have to talk to Rooster." Rooster was the children's pet name for their grandmother, Ruth.

"What are you doing here?" Rooster asked, after she ran out to give the children a hug. "Don't you work Fridays? What's all that sweat on your brow? You look like you've been running the mile in ten seconds."

Sharon told her, watched the horror ooze slowly across her mother's face. "Ritchie O'Neill?" her mother said. "Are they sure?"

"The T-shirt with the stallion on it. Franny found him, I told you. Early this morning. Mother, you don't listen. He was wearing that shirt he arrived here in—Maggie described it to me, she said it stank with sweat. Well, he's dead, gone, strangled to death. And get this. With Ophelia's reins."

"Good God." Ruth put down her mop, reached for Sharon. Sharon opened her arms. Never mind the cow shit, it was her mother. This was terrifying news. "Still breaking news," Sharon said when Ruth mumbled something in her ear about "Nola? They think she'd been there, she might have done it?"

"Well, they didn't *exactly* say, but they suspect her, yes. He's a big man, they said. But hell hath no fury," Sharon quoted from somewhere. Sharon had created the scenario in her mind: Ritchie riding up on Nola in the woods—maybe even the swamp, though the news said something about a dragged body—and Nola, in self-defense, wrapping the reins about his neck.

"But she was a sick woman," Ruth insisted. "She was still recovering in that Healing House."

"Healing House? She was there? How'd you know that?" Sharon didn't like her mother holding back information, she wanted to be kept informed. Her mother could be spacey. She needed Sharon's help now and then.

Ruth told her about James Perlman's visit and Sharon said, "Ha! Another suspect."

"Oh stop that. He's a little odd, but perfectly normal. He had work at the Healing House, that's all. He should have informed the police, yes, but I suspect he's a little prejudiced, a little scared, like the rest of us. The travellers aren't real people, according to people like James. They're not like us regular working folk."

Down in the pasture the keening was working up to a crescendo; mourners were gathering—some northern clan maybe, related by marriage. Whether they knew or liked Ritchie or not wouldn't matter—he was one of them. He had to be mourned.

The barn phone rang and Sharon ran to pick it up. It was Colm. "I've already told her," Sharon said, and handed it over. She picked up the mop and finished washing the yukky floor while her mother said, "Oh, oh. How terrible. Oh dear, that poor woman. Sharon never mentioned the horse." When her mother hung up Sharon said, "Well I can't think of everything! Now what? Anything new?"

"The horse is gone. Poor Franny. And they traced Nola back to the Healing House—the director called in to confirm she was there, protesting a mile a minute that she didn't know who Nola was. So Nola's gone again."

"On the horse, they think?"

"Could be, who knows? But they've no evidence that Nola even met up with Ritchie. The police are down there now, looking for whatever they look for. Footprints…"

"Footprints in the Branbury swamp?"

"There might be something—an imprint on a rock or dry spot, a hunk of fiber on a berry bush. I don't know—something to connect them to whoever did him in. Franny did find a heel from a shoe, I heard. But it could be anyone's, lovers go in there to neck, I understand. I refuse to believe it was Nola who killed him. The police are just looking for motive, that's all. And Nola would appear to have that."

The phone rang again. Ruth said, "Don't answer it." But Sharon's arm reached out automatically. "Oh, Franny. Oh, you poor thing, finding that dead body!"

After that it was Franny's voice pouring words into her ear, shouting details that Sharon loved to hear—straight from the horse's mouth, so to speak. "Strangled. With her own reins. Phelia's reins! And she's gone now, my beloved's gone. That woman took her." And then a non sequitur. "Did you hear that a horse up in Argennes was found dead, infected with West Nile virus? And two birds dead with it. Dead, Sharon! She could have West Nile as well as CJD! If it isn't one thing it's another. It's a dying world, Sharon, dying! Rome—falling in a day."

"Good Lord," said Sharon, and passed the receiver to Ruth.

"Strangled him with Phelia's reins!" Sharon heard Franny shriek again over the line.

"Mom-mmm, Robbie's being mean to me, tell him to quit." Willa was at the door of the barn. Sharon ran to her, scooped her up. "I told you to stay in the car. Now back we go, little worm. Oh, golly gee but you're hea-vy! You're getting so b-i-g."

She staggered back with the child. Sharon was a small woman, short and roundish where her sister, Emily, was tall and svelte—cockeyed genes, you never knew. She deposited Willa back in her car seat. But no Robbie. "Now where did that child go? Robbie? Where are you?"

"Oh dear," said Ruth, looking anguished. "Go find the child!"

"Mom?" The answer came from the farmhouse porch. A man and a woman were standing there beside the little boy. They waved at Sharon and strode down toward her. The woman was dressed in a severe black suit—she looked like a nun. In dark gray and black-striped tie the man resembled an undertaker. The Suits, she thought, and looked down at her ankle-length Indian skirt with the blue denim shirt hanging out over it, her scuffed sandals. Her outfits were Sharon's protest to the world. "Mom?" the boy called, "they're looking for Rooster."

What did these Suits want with her mother? Sharon didn't want to think. "Well, she's not here, my mother's gone to town. You'll have to telephone her. Try in a couple hours. Come on, Rob, get in the car." She shooed him off the porch.

The woman came down from the porch, practically skipped on down in her zeal. "Tell your mother she'll hear from us about the calves."

"What?" Sharon paused. These people were buying her calves? "What about the calves?" she asked.

The woman smiled, an oily smile. Sharon narrowed her eyes. "What about what calves?" she asked again.

"I'm sorry, but I can't say," the woman said. "I can only say it involves a devastating disease."

"What disease?" said Sharon, sticking her hands on her cotton hips. She hated pretentious talk. "Spell it out." Though she knew. Of course she knew.

"Bovine spongiform encephalopathy," said the woman, still smiling that oily smile like it was sheer delight to say the words. "Your mother purchased two suspect Friesian calves that originated in the Netherlands. Oh yes, we've proof of that. We'll have to take them as a precaution—someone will come for them. I'm sorry, but we can't take any chances. Don't worry though, she'll be compensated. Given fair market value."

"What value is that?" Sharon asked, but the woman just smiled. "Oh not to worry, oh no." Now Sharon was on her high horse. She reared back, pulled up her bones to meet the woman's height—almost. She saw the man towering in the background; he was a challenge. "Compensated!" she cried. "Who can compensate a livelihood? Who can compensate a life? Those little black and white calves are perfectly healthy. I just saw them. All Mother's cows are healthy. Well, one down with milk fever—nothing to it. Mother's in there now nursing her."

Oops—what had she said….

"We'll want to tell her firsthand," said the woman, grinning at Sharon's mistake. Then, seeing Sharon's mouth quiver, the woman turned sympathetic. "My name is Leafmiller. *Ms.* Leafmiller. I'm here to, um, clear matters up. I know, dear, you were just helping your mother. You meant well."

"No, I didn't mean well," Sharon shouted. "And neither do you!"

Already the man and woman were marching down the path toward the barn, like Tories and Indians two centuries before, preparing to set the barn on fire. All they needed were torches. Or guns to shoot the cows with. For that's what they wanted, Sharon sensed. They wanted to take the cows. They wanted to destroy the farm. They wanted to ruin her mother's life.

"Stay put and don't move!" she shouted at the children, who were now back hanging out the car windows. She raced on down to the barn, squeezed through the door ahead of the enemy.

"Mother," she cried. "Don't let them in. They want the new calves."

Ruth Willmarth loomed up in the alley between the stalls. She had her arm around Zelda. Ruth named her cows after famous or literary women: Zelda was the wife of Scott Fitzgerald, who stole his wife's stories. It was almost as if the bovine Zelda knew. Sharon threw an arm around her mother's waist, and together mother, daughter, and cow faced the enemy.

Zelda fixed the feds with a wild dark eye. Sharon smiled grimly to see them take a giant step back.

Two WEEKS from tonight was Maggie's concert up in Burlington and everything was going wrong. Ritchie dead in a swamp and sympathetic travellers swarming in to weep or celebrate. Well, mostly celebrate, she figured, the way they were lounging about, cooking up fancy foods, dancing and laughing, and only the older women keening. At least Ritchie had no parents to speak of—the father in prison somewhere and the mother he shared with Darren in a nursing home now, with Alzheimer's.

And Darren. Darren, who hadn't picked up an instrument in two days to practice with her, was back in the barn, working up a sweat like he owed The Willmarth a month's work to be done in a day. What was his problem anyway? "We're supposed to be rehearsing. Why isn't Darren here?" she hollered to anyone who'd listen.

"You know, don't you, Mag?" It was Mammy Boadie, rocking away, peeling potatoes, the piggy squealing where she had it hemmed in with her feet. Maggie had given her grandmother that potbellied pig for her seventy-fourth birthday, and now the creature was driving Maggie nuts. It ate too much for one thing. It was growing an enormous belly that waggled when it walked, like a pendulum in a grandfather clock. Boadie slept with it in her cot—one day she'd find herself on the floor, and serve her right.

Maggie waited. Boadie usually answered her own questions.

"Guilt," Boadie said. "He hated that brother of his, and now he feels guilty. Oh sure," she went on when Maggie held up a finger. "You know bloody well, Mag. Ritchie got to you first, and Darren's never forgot it."

"They're brothers. They got blood ties."

"Half brothers. That don't make 'em bosom pals and you know it. Then Ritchie got in all that trouble back in '92."

"What trouble?" Maggie asked, though she knew. Though she didn't know how much her grandmother knew about the affair. She picked up Darren's guitar, strummed it. Glanced out the window to be sure Liz was outside the trailer and not listening. She wanted Liz brought up right; it wouldn't do for the young girl to know all these things. And Liz had bad genes to fight as well.

"Damn it all, Mag, you know what trouble. It was that high school teacher. The one got to Ritchie in the first place."

Now Maggie's blood was up. "Wasn't the teacher's fault. It was Ritchie started it. Seduced the teacher and the janitor caught them making out and she got fired. She was a good teacher, too, it wasn't fair." The teacher was only twenty-one—too young for pupils like Ritchie. And then she took an overdose. It was a scandal that rocked the town and gave a bad name to travelers—like travellers weren't already bad-mouthed enough. He'd come crawling back to Maggie after that, said he took on the teacher because Maggie had refused him; said he was in love with her and there'd never be anyone else. And the worst was, it was true. Some loves were just plain destructive.

"Guilt, okay," she said, to placate her grandmother. The potato peels were flying. The pig was shrieking, it was being bombarded. "So let's drop the subject, huh? I'm sorry I started it. Darren's glad Ritchie's dead, have it your way. I just don't happen to believe it, that's all. You know what family is to us travellers."

"They got an outsider mother. Outsiders get in, blood's polluted."

Maggie didn't hold with all that—sometimes outsiders brought in good blood. Besides, Darren's and Ritchie's fathers were second cousins with the same name, so that made the tie closer. Though Darren's dad was an honest fellow and Ritchie's father a petty criminal. The New York uncle was a brother to Ritchie's outsider mother. If there was an outsider who polluted, it was the uncle.

"Sometimes," she agreed, "sometimes there's pollution."

"Always," said Mammy Boadie, who nurtured her prejudices the way she fed her pet pig. She was getting up, knife in one hand, pig in the other. Her wiry frame was stooped—there was osteoporosis there, arthritis in the right hip, yet Boadie was strong. She could carry that potbellied pig for miles if she had to. And back in New York she'd split wood without breaking a sweat. She favored the left leg now as she limped to the sink, kicking aside a pile of magazines, and dropped the peelings into a wire basket. The pig leaked on her dress and Maggie grabbed it and opened the trailer door.

"No! Don't let it out! Someone'll steal it—no-oooo," Boadie screeched.

Maggie let it go, watched the urine ooze into the grass. The pink ribbon around its plump neck hung wet with pee. She sighed, propelled the pig back up the trailer steps. Damn thing weighed a ton and it was still a youngster. "Better take off that dress," she told her grandmother. "It's soaked."

"What else I got to wear?"

"I'll find you something."

The trailer door popped open and Liz appeared, her slight frame wriggling with what she had to say. She was wearing the teenage uniform, as Maggie called it: tight green tank top that outlined her small breasts, and bare midriff over tighter jeans. She looks like a praying mantis, Maggie thought. Maggie waited while the girl poured out her news.

"…Yeah and he's here, Uncle's here. Darren called him about Ritchie, I was here when he called—he got Uncle's cell phone. I know it's him, I know the truck. It's got a New York license. He's in the barn with The Willmarth. She don't like it, I seen how she looked when he was talking. I looked through the barn door—I been feeding the calves."

Maggie put her hands on the girl's shoulders, dug in. "What was he saying?" She wasn't surprised, though. Ritchie was dead; the uncle was here, she supposed, to see his nephew into the earth. Do his duty by blood and family. Maggie was glad they wouldn't have to deal with Ritchie's father—he had two years to go, she'd heard, for the latest rip-off.

"I couldn't hear. I didn't dare go in close, I didn't want him to see me. But he was asking for Darren. And Darren went out the back door. I seen him when I went to the barn. Darren didn't want to see Uncle."

"Oh Mary Mother of Jesus," said Maggie. "What now? We don't have a body. The police got it. Nola's gone." She felt her nose filling up. She missed her Nola. She blew into a Kleenex. Liz wiggled out from under her fingers and went to the small fridge to pull out a soda. It was warm, she complained, the fridge wasn't working right. On the way back she knocked a pan off the sink with her elbow. It clanged, and jarred Maggie's nerves—this crowded trailer! "And Uncle won't leave till he takes Darren back with him," Maggie complained. She clapped her hands to her aching temples. She was up in outer space somewhere with all that had happened. "You can count on that. The man's a leech. Let him near you just once and he don't let go."

Now Maggie needed to find Darren. Darren was a strong man, but he didn't always use the best judgment. Darren didn't like Uncle. But he couldn't bring himself to make a complete break. There was the question of inheritance, she supposed— though he denied he wanted any of it. "Where'd he head, what direction, Liz? Tell me, huh? I gotta find him."

Liz waved an arm toward the back pasture and glugged her soda. "Somewhere out there, I dunno."

Maggie knew. She knew where Darren went when he wanted to be alone, when he wanted to think. It wasn't the beaver pond—must've been Ritchie who arranged that meeting. "Liz, help Mammy Boadie with that potato pie, will you? I got to find Darren." When the girl didn't offer to move, stubborn, infuriating child she could be—those bad genes again—she raised her voice. "Help her, damn it, I said. Now go!"

Liz curled her fingers into fists, and went to help with the pie. "I hate potatoes," she said under her breath.

# TWELVE

THE UNCLE WASN'T a big man, as Ruth had thought from the way Darren described him. Instead he came on as a handsome but slight fellow: slicked-back graying hair with a little tuft in front like a Walt Disney bird; smooth ruddy skin and that self-confident, mocking, Irish-blue stare that tried to take your measure in a glance. His shoes squeaked as he walked. He introduced himself as "Tormey Leary from the Tonawanda farm. You heard of that, I suppose—whole world has by now."

Soft-tongued, with a tremulous smile to show he was suffering too, he snatched at her hand, full of apologies before she could utter a word. What could he do? He'd sold her the Friesian calves in good faith; they were born of Netherland's best, he'd no idea they might be contaminated with BSE. It was the USDA who allowed him to bring in a dozen cows back in '93—and then they'd closed the door.

"*If* they're infected," he said, his tone changing, becoming bitter. "They took my pair, you know, say they could have this dang Mad Cow thing, traced 'em back to that Dutch farm where they might've got bad feed. But got no proof. They got no goddamn proof. Just keep saying they can't tell us what the proof is. Sound like the White House, eh? They just think, they *think* it's that Mad Cow—Christ, I hate that word! And now my whole lot—two hunnert cows—in quarantine. Feds threatening to take 'em! Just to put down the public's fears—you betcha. There's no proof. But I'm holding out for real money, I am, they're not gonna take my cows without real honest-to-god compensation. If I'm gonna retire I'm gonna retire *big*."

Not a word about Ruth, of course: how she must feel, what would happen now to her livelihood. Just rattling on about himself, his cows, his farm, his money. Not a word about Ritchie. Did he care that his nephew was dead? He patted the rear end of the skinny adolescent boy who'd followed him in, and sent him outside. The boy was a big-boned fellow with arms and legs that had outgrown his clothing and huge eyes that seemed to plead for help when they looked back at her. She smiled at him but he averted his eyes.

"Darren told you then," she said, sitting down on an upturned pail, offering him the three-legged stool Zelda had sprayed when the feds came. The uncle was a farmer, he shouldn't mind a little cow shit here and there. She noted that he was wearing a good pair of black gabardine pants, nicely pressed and creased, more suitable for a funeral than Ruth's barn—those squeaky black shoes. "I mean, about Ritchie—the details?"

"Jesus, it's a turrible thing, turrible." Tormey Leary pulled out a white handkerchief, cleaned the stool with a deft twist of the wrist, lowered himself onto it. He was attractive, yes, she had to admit that. A little belly, but to be expected for his age-late fifties? Early sixties? Actually, the too-handsome kind she disliked, that didn't appeal to her at all. She'd had her day with handsome boys in school. Freshman year of college she dated one of them—discovered him one night in bed with a girl down the hall. She measured all handsome men by that experience—fair or not.

"You've no idea who dunnit, no?" He squinted those blue, blue eyes at her, cocked his head, straightened his tie. My God, a farmer with a tie? A bright red one at that.

"The police are working on it," she said, folding her arms across her chest. Her lawyer, too, though she didn't tell this uncle. At Colm's urging, she'd told her lawyer the story—she might need outside help. A simple farmer taking on the government? It was crazy! Here was Ruth, dressed in her oldest pair of jeans, ripped in the knees; it gave her a disadvantage and

Tormey Leary knew it. He was giving her his saddest, most ingratiating look.

"Somewhere things went wrong," he said. "I brung him up
to be a good boy after his daddy went to prison. My sister
couldn't care for him, she had lupus—it gets you in the nerves,
you know, toes and so forth—then something got her brain. But
somewhere Ritchie went wrong."

"Oh?" Ruth kept an eye on the barn door. Any minute those
men might come for her calves and she wanted to be ready.
Though she didn't know what attitude she would take with
them. Be stoic and let the calves go as Colm and the lawyer suggested? Or fight the agents? It would be a happening, she
guessed. But she'd glean what she could out of this man. Ruth
was, by nature, nosy.

"Question of a little scam here and there, you know. Ritch-
ie's father in and out of jail—that should explain something.
Ritchie in deeper'n that—now he's dead, I guess I can say it.
Fellow he killed, you see, a bar fight. Ritchie claimed the guy
attacked him. But I know. I was there. It's not a story for ladies."
He smiled to show gleaming white teeth—dentures, she bet.

She didn't press for details.

"I'm Irish but I'm no traveller," he insisted. "It was my sister married into that bunch. My grandmother come from Cork
couple generations ago. Upright farmers they was, left me a bit
to start the farm with. I worked hard, miss, I'm telling you. And
now they want to do me in, take my herd, my whole herd,
miss! But not without compensation, like I said, unh-uh, no sir."

Ruth hated to be called "miss," it made her squirm. "Yes,
Mr. Leary. But now my farm is in danger as well, you understand. I wasn't aware there was a question about the Friesian
calves." She didn't want him to forget that it was his idea to sell
her the calves—she wondered if he'd known they were suspect
before he sent them on with Darren. But no, she thought, no
one could be that irresponsible. "So someone who Ritchie
dunned might be guilty of his death—are you suggesting that?"

He shifted on his stool; his shoes squeaked. "Oh I don't know that, miss. But maybe, yeah—we should look into that. Though the dunned are mostly in my area—greater Buffalo, you know. That's where Ritchie mostly lived before he went south to stay with his father's family. He was twelve then. It was me brung him up as a small boy."

"So you said. Have you any other ideas? About people who might not like him? He wasn't a pleasant man, I gather. I only knew him briefly, but he wasn't kind to his, um, companion. She was trying to get away from him, you think? After he took her out of the hospital? That was cruel, wasn't it? The woman was exhausted. She might be lying dead in some woods for all we know."

He looked startled, went almost white. "Nola," he said, his voice cracking. "We gotta find her, you and me. That's one reason I come, spite of all the trouble I left behind on the farm. I brung the boy, you know, her son."

"Ritchie's child?"

"Ritchie allus said no—afraid of the responsibility, you see— but yeah, I'd guess so. Would've been back in '91—Ritchie was down in Carolina then. Anyhow, thought that might help bring her back if she knows the boy's here. If she gets the news from someplace. Missing his mother, sure. And worse'n that."

She watched him intently. Zelda mewled in her stanchion and she absently pulled on one of the cow's black ears. Zelda's tail threw up a flurry of hay.

"Plague," he said, dusting his hair where bits of hay had landed. "What they say she might have. I don't believe it. It can't be from my farm. She just had a headache, that's all—we gotta prove that. Always this headache—something her pa done to her, I hear." He rubbed his head as though the pain had rubbed off on him.

"She had a tumor, I understand, that's why she was in the hospital. She's lucky to be alive, Ritchie taking her out early like that."

He rose from his stool. He wasn't going to let a man take all the blame. "Should of gone straight back when they told her to. Let 'em test her. Find out she don't have no disease. Now she got us all in trouble; coming to look at my herd just because a her. If I find her, she'll know it all right!"

Ruth didn't like the threatening voice. But he'd struck a common note. They both wanted to find the woman, have her tested, find her negative. Get back to work on their respective farms. For a moment she felt warm toward him.

"Though it was Ritchie's fault," he said. "He wasn't good for Nola. I told her that. She wouldn't listen."

Couldn't listen maybe, Ruth thought, with Ritchie dominating her. But who knew what the relationship was? Relationships were complicated. Ruth had heard of women going back to the lovers who beat them. Was it just out of fear? Or something else... Did women think they deserved the beating?

She couldn't think. All Ruth wanted now was a normal day. Get up at four, milk the cows, put them out to pasture, then coffee and cereal and homemade doughnuts for breakfast. She had a new recipe from her beekeeper friend, Gwen, for honeydipped doughnuts—she wanted to try it out.

She could hardly imagine that normal day: how idyllic, how life-giving.

"She'll show up, poor woman," Ruth said. "One way or another."

"Sure, but when? After they've got my herd? They got 'em all in quarantine now, whole goddamn two hunnert of 'em." He said nothing about *her* herd, and she frowned. There was no kindness in the face, just the eyes, like a cold lake. She disliked him. Felt sorry for Nola, for Ritchie even—what kind of childhood had Ritchie had? The uncle hadn't asked about Ritchie's body: if he could take it back, bury it on the farm—he had expressed no remorse.

"I'm sure you'll want his remains," she said.

"Oh, I do, sure, yeah. Want to give um a good Catholic

mass, a burial. Got a burying plot on the farm, goes back to the Revolutionary War, you know. Got a soldier in there fought at Manassas."

"I believe that was the Civil War."

He smiled, spread his fingers. "War's war."

"True," she said. "But I'm afraid you'll have to wait for the body. The state medical examiner has it now, they're doing an autopsy."

"What? Who give 'em permission for 'at? Nobody asked me." He rose halfway from the stool, met Zelda's penetrating eye, and settled back down again.

"I'm afraid the police have jurisdiction in a homicide. They'll need to know what he ate that day, what was under his fingernails; if there were any hairs or fibers on his body. They'll take prints off the reins Ritchie was strangled with, check the DNA."

"Oh?" He looked confused, worried, as though he hadn't expected such meticulous research, the body cut up and examined, the fingerprints. There might have been concern for his nephew, though she rather doubted it—not from what Maggie had said about the man: how he preferred Darren to Ritchie, how Ritchie and the uncle never really got along. There was evidently something dark in that past between the uncle and Ritchie, maybe between Tormey and Nola. Maggie hadn't said and Ruth hadn't wanted to pry. Some things you didn't want to know.

"So you left Buffalo yesterday, did you? As soon as Darren contacted you with the news? Friday morning—or early afternoon? It's a long drive—maybe eight hours?"

"Tonawanda," he corrected.

But he didn't say when he had left. Darren had called a cell phone, he said, so Tormey could have been anywhere. Where *had* he been? "Of course, you were concerned when you heard Ritchie left here and didn't show up at your farm," she said, swatting a pesky fly. Though she kept one eye on him, to read his face.

The face was inscrutable. He was a man who knew how to control his expressions.

He was getting up on his squeaky shoes, and she rose to meet his eyes. But the eyes were gazing elsewhere: at the milking machine, the stalls, out the window at the calves in their white pens—two of them siblings or at least cousins of his animals, who authorities said might already have BSE. She'd isolated her calves, just in case.

"I need to see Darren," he said in a thick, guttural voice as if he'd been swallowing phlegm. "I was told he'd be here."

"Far down in the fields. Mending fence." She waved her arms in a vague direction. "I hope you have boots with you. Furze, briar bushes, nettles—you know what a pasture can be. And we've had almost no rain this spring so the ground is dry and rutty. I doubt we'll get a second cutting of corn."

He grunted something and got off his stool. He didn't look so handsome now; she could see the folds of dry skin, wattles at the jawline. She walked him to the door and saw him go over to examine the Friesian calves, critically, the way a farmer would, but without touching them. Then he stalked off, jerking a thumb to indicate the boy should follow. The boy did, but slowly, reluctantly, plodding along as though he had chains on his ankles. This was Nola's boy, he'd said—a sad-looking lad who hadn't yet uttered a syllable in her presence.

The Friesian calves were part black and white Holstein, hardly different from her own Holsteins, maybe a little smaller; flat-muscled, long-legged. Like her Holsteins, they had faces like maps: black islands on white seas. She'd loved them at first sight; they didn't look sick to her, not a bit. But because of this man and his suspect calves, they'd be taken away for testing, maybe slaughtering. Like those East Warren sheep, driven off at dawn to Ames, Iowa, and slaughtered—"euthanized" was the word. She didn't want that. She couldn't accept that without proof. She wouldn't allow it!

She squared her shoulders and went back to work, grabbing

the shovel, throwing manure back into the pails, cleaning stalls. She gave Zelda a hug. She could never bear to lose Zelda, her ornery beloved cow! She'd had enough worries without all this Mad Cow scare. It was like a triple whammy: a year of low milk prices, poor crops, and limited feed supplies because of drought. When she finished the barn chores she went out to feed the calves but found the grandmother already there on her knees, nursing one of the new calves with a baby bottle. She was crooning to it, some Gaelic lullaby. The song might have come down from her mother or grandmother perhaps—over the seas and into the mountains of North Carolina. The language sounded strange, Ruth couldn't possibly reproduce it. Yet it fascinated.

"Good morning," Ruth said, and as though nothing had happened—murder, the bereaved uncle's coming, a missing woman, disease-the traveller woman stopped singing and grinned, exhibiting two gold-filled teeth and an upper middle one missing.

"Nothing to smile about, I reckon, not with that bastard come to stir up trouble," Boadie said. "Wouldn't surprise me one bit if *hisself* didn't kill Ritchie O'Neill. Just to get him outa the way. He's mean enough to do it, you better believe it."

"Out of the way?" Ruth asked, something choking her throat, settling in her chest like a swallowed object.

The woman didn't answer, just went on feeding the black and white calf, clucking at it. "Little darling," she said, "oh you little sweetheart, you."

MAGGIE FOUND DARREN mending a fence in the far pasture. There were a dozen sheep there, along with a llama to keep out predators. Maggie loved that wooly-haired llama—it had soft upright ears and large soulful eyes. It never spit at her. The animals belonged to Carol somebody, a friend of The Willmarth. The Willmarth rented out the pasture, she'd told Maggie, to help pay off the money she owed the ex-husband who walked out on her one day like the bastard he obviously was. Maggie wouldn't have been surprised to see the sheep gone, whisked away because of the scare. But there they were, all fourteen, heads down in the summer grass, the llama keeping watch beside them. They'd nibbled the field bare, looked like. She waved at the blond-haired woman who was tending them—a woman in a pale blue shirt and designer jeans who looked more like she ought to be pouring tea at some charity than tending sheep. But who ever knew? Maggie had been around long enough to know you couldn't judge by appearance alone.

She stuck a tongue in her cheek, looked hard at Darren. She supposed he'd find the sheep woman attractive. She'd seen the way he looked at Nola sometimes. He was a good man, faithful to her as far as she knew, but men were horny, they were fickle—her mother had taught her that. Nola had a pretty face, one could say a beautiful face. There were a few times back at the farm before Nola took sick when she'd caught Darren talking to her, once with his hands on her shoulders. And Maggie had looked away. It was better that way, keep the peace. Her mother had taught her that, too.

But then Maggie wasn't about to kowtow, whimper around him, wrap herself in Saran Wrap like she'd seen in some magazine ad just to keep him home. She'd take her chances.

"You know who's here?" she said.

"You'll tell me." He was on his knees, straightening an old post that had fallen and left an open, saggy space in the fence.

"Don't tell me you didn't see him—dear Uncle Tormey. Come to find you, my lad."

"He's here 'cause of Ritchie. Even so, won't do him a bit of good to talk to me. I'm not going back."

"He's lost Ritchie, he'll be after you hammer and tongs, you wait."

"He won't get me, I told you."

"What'll you do, then? You can't stay here much longer—

the hired man's coming back in the fall. Where'll we go? Not back to Carolina, I'm telling you, we burned our bridges there."

"I got ideas."

"Yeah? What ideas?"

"Never mind. Just never you mind. But you're in the plans, love, don't worry 'bout that!" The post in place, he sprang up, grabbed her, spun her about, setting her off balance until they fell back together on the grass. A sheep bleated beyond them, a second came to nuzzle its rear end.

"Don't get ideas from that," she yelled, throwing a pebble at the sheep. "We gotta talk. He'll be out here looking for you. The Willmarth'll be sending him on down." She pushed his hands away where they were reaching under her skirt. She rolled a few feet in the grass, then jumped up, hands on her hips.

She looked down on him where he lay on his back, sucking on a stem of sweetgrass. She had to laugh, he looked so sweet himself. But she had questions to ask him. Questions the police might want to ask. She didn't want Darren implicated in this murder! Like where was he last Thursday night when the police, she'd heard, thought Ritchie was killed? Darren wasn't in bed, she reminded him, when she woke to go out and take a pee. And the pickup was gone. It was three o'clock, too early to get up and milk. How was he going to explain that?

She threw the question at him. "Not that I misbelieve you, Darr, but the police'll come around asking. Talk to your cousin Colm, he can tell you."

"They think it's Nola done it, why'd they want to talk to me?" But his eyes were a scared blue, she knew that look.

"Come on, they'll want to talk to everybody who knew Ritch—even me—but you was his brother. They find out you didn't get along, you and him—well, you know." She didn't want to tell him she'd deliberately eavesdropped the afternoon before Ritchie died, but she had to make him think about these things. She didn't want him accused of anything, she couldn't live with that! "They got a way of making you talk, it's like giving you ipecac, you know, so you throw up."

"I was in town at the 7-Eleven, that's all, getting cigarettes. I woke up, couldn't sleep, didn't want to bother you. I was worried about Ritchie, if you got to know. I mean, he *is* family. We gotta take care of family."

"We didn't take care enough, though, did we?"

"Reckon not." He looked distressed. His hands shook a little where they pulled at a daisy in the grass.

She gave it to him straight then. Stood over him, her legs over his legs, looked down at him, made him look up at her. "I overheard something Thursday afternoon. Didn't mean to, but I did. I might's well tell you."

"What? What you hear? Huh?"

He was smiling, trying to belittle her, the way he did sometimes, make her sound dumb, like a nagging wife. She didn't like that. She said, "Ritchie was here. I heard his voice. I was taking a walk—rehearsing, you know, so they wouldn't have to listen to me sing up there. Didn't hear all you said, didn't want to eavesdrop, you know."

"Yeah, sure, you didn't."

"I didn't! And didn't want to see Ritchie, have him see me. But he was here all right. I want to know what you was arguing about. Was it Nola? I need to know. What about you and Nola? If you done something you gotta tell me, and I'll try and understand—just so you quit doing it."

"Wasn't about me and Nola," he said, jumping up, grabbing her hands hard, till she cried out and he released them. "It was about—well, going back to Uncle, you know, same old thing, and I said I wouldn't go, you know, all that."

He was lying, there was more than that. She saw it in his face, the way his mouth twitched, eyes blinking, muscle throbbing in his cheek. But she wasn't going to tear up the pea patch. She wasn't going to stir up the old family secrets. Enough had happened lately, with Nola gone, Ritchie dead. Their lives all in pieces, in a matter of days. It was like she was living through a nightmare.

"Okay," she said, "okay. I didn't see Ritchie here, I didn't hear him. No problem at all, if the police ask. I was just taking a walk, singing to the birds. Right?"

"Right." He took her two hands, pulled her to him, nuzzled his prickly cheek in her hair. This time she smiled. She didn't care what Darren had or hadn't said or done. She loved him. Darren was hers. He was her man and come hell or high water she'd stick with him. She'd stick like goddamn glue.

Ms. LEAFMILLER from the USDA phoned while Ruth was making herself a peanut butter and fluff sandwich for lunch. The woman's voice was soft and sympathetic, but firm. "We're coming for the Friesian calves," she said. "Tomorrow morning. Please have them available. Furthermore, the State of Vermont, in consultation with our APHIS, will have to put the rest of your herd in quarantine where we can monitor them."

"What's APHIS?" Ruth cried. She was going mad with these initials. "And what proof have you? None, my lawyer says! I want to know exactly why you're taking these calves."

An hour before, Ruth had received a call from the Vermont state veterinarian—a sympathetic fellow who'd come to examine the calves, who seemed to be on her side. But who, like her lawyer, said she'd do best at this point to comply with the feds. "They'll put you out of business if you don't," the vet warned.

Leafmiller muttered something about Animal Plant Health—Ruth lost the rest of it. "I'm sorry," the woman said when Ruth made a noise in her throat that might have sounded like a growl. "But if this gets out of hand and into the food chain, it could be a disaster for the country. We understand that this is very difficult for you, but it's our duty, our mission, to protect American agriculture. We have an emergency here." Her voice rose to a high pitch. "An *extraordinary* emergency. BSE is on a list of pathogens that the terrorists might weaponize. Did you know that? Since 9/11."

"Wait a minute here," said Ruth. "You don't *know* these calves are sick. You can't tell me how you know." But Leafmiller went on.

"Perhaps you read about that woman in Glasgow? Who died this past April, a month after giving birth to a baby boy? Diagnosed with Creutzfeldt-Jakob disease—the human form of BSE? Died from eating contaminated beef—perhaps a decade earlier, who knows? Only married three years!" the woman cried, sounding horrified, aggrieved. "But the baby tested negative so we—so they—well, the disease was possibly not passed on. There's hope."

"Hope?" said Ruth, thinking of the dead mother, the bereaved husband.

"Hope that your calves will test negative."

Sure, Ruth thought, but the tests, she'd heard, were inconclusive. They took years. For the East Warren shepherds the tests were being done on mice, and only when the mice took sick from the tissues injected into them could it be diagnosed as Mad Cow. But since the disease could incubate for more than forty years—and if no mice took sick—why, she could be an old woman by then! Her farm gone, her way of life. What would be left to pass on to her children?

"They're not sick!" Ruth cried, balling her fists, feeling the blood up in her head. "I won't let you take them. You're not to quarantine my cows. What does that mean anyway, quarantine? I can't sell my milk? Can't sell my bull calves? Is that what it means?"

"I'm afraid so," Leafmiller said, sounding like she'd been bereaved herself, and went on with her litany: "Our mission, as I said—"

"I won't do it. I won't let you have them." Ruth was beside herself now, she was out of control. She slammed down the phone. Immediately it rang again and she let it. She was too distraught to go back to work. Her hands were shaking, her cheeks turned to jelly. She was falling apart.

"Ruth," the answer machine intoned: "She's carrying it, that Enola woman, *she's* the plague—you better believe it, Ruth. She killed that man. Now she's spreading plague across Vermont—across the country, Ruth. You better get her back before we all die, Ruth. All of us. Can you keep this on your conscience, Ruth? Can you sleep at night?"

"Bertha, shut up!" Furious, Ruth picked up the phone, pictured her former sister-in-law on the other end: the dyed orangy hair, the thin red lips, the shiny black pumps, the sanctimonious mouth. "I don't want to hear this, Bertha. I don't need to hear it. She is not spreading it. We don't know she has it. It's fear, Bertha. That's all it is. Fear. Hate. And you're spreading it, you're the one spreading the plague—you!"

"You'd better go find her, Ruth, it's the only way to stop this thing, this plague. Find that plague woman—"

Ruth dropped onto a stool, the phone still in her hand, the disembodied voice coming at her like bad apples falling off a tree. Mad, bad, and dangerous—that was Bertha. That was what they were calling the innocent cows. That was Ruth's world this summer. A mad-summer's plague. A plague of fear, like rotting fruit. Ruth dropped the phone. It banged on the floor and buzzed like some alien bird, flown into the sanctuary of her kitchen, chilling it.

When Colm barged into her kitchen a quarter of an hour later, filling it with life again, she ran to him, buried her head in his chest, held on to him as though he would keep her from falling over the edge of the world.

"Ruthie," he said, holding on so tight she could hardly breathe, "Ruthie honey. What is it, Ruthie? Something's happened, tell me. Those damned reporters again? The feds? My cousin's uncle?—I heard he was here."

"All of the above," she mumbled, not letting go of him. "All of it, and more."

"More? What's *more*. Tell me, huh? what's *more?*"

She told him about the phone calls. "We've got to find that woman, Colm. We've got to find Nola. And not because of what Bertha said. I mean, we have to get her to that hospital, we have to know she's free of that disease."

When he began to mutter about police, feds on her trail, she clapped a hand over his mouth.

"We, Colm. You and I. *We* have to find her."

She heard him sigh. Finally he removed her hand and said, "You're nuts, Ruthie, you're just plain nuts. But I love you. God, how I love you."

NOLA knew she couldn't keep the mare with her much longer or she'd be found. She didn't want that. She had one thought in mind and that was to get to Tonawanda, find Keeley, and take him away—maybe even to North Carolina. To the clan, who would hide them, nurture them, let them live in peace. Never mind her father—she'd stand up to him. She'd changed with all that had happened these past few years. She was stronger now—if not physically, then mentally.

But the mare was company, she ate apples out of Nola's hand—shared them, those early, barely red apples she'd taken from this orchard by the lake. It was so beautiful here on the shore of Lake Champlain, she wished she could settle here, start a new life. Yet she was a runaway, an outcast—terrorist, they called her. Was she? She was hiding from cops the way Ritchie used to hide—though he'd died without telling her all his past, she could only guess. And she didn't want to know—she tried to think of him more kindly now he was dead. He'd had a bad upbringing: that swindler father, the cruel uncle. The abused turned into abusers, she'd heard that. And Ritchie never really hurt her bad, had he? Not really. Not till he found her that night by the edge of the swamp. Not till they'd had that awful row. Not till—well, she didn't want to think of what happened after that.

The terrifying image of Ritchie, with those reins wrapped three times around his neck, lived just behind her eyes. She couldn't blink it away. She couldn't bear to touch the reins after that, just left them around his neck. She led the mare off by its bridle—no saddle on her anyway, but Nola rode bareback as a girl, she didn't need a saddle. Somebody, she'd figured, would find Ritchie. She wanted to be miles away by then.

She had to turn her mind away from what happened, she had to think of the present—how to keep out of sight. Beyond the orchard was the bridge that led to New York, on the narrow part of Lake Champlain. She could see the sign from here, it said Crown Point, NY, 9 miles. From there it was—she didn't want to think—oh miles and miles to Tonawanda, the western end of the state of New York. Could she ride across a bridge on a mare? Or even lead her? Someone would see, even at night. Nola, a bareback rider, with a rope taken from that orchard barn to serve as reins. They'd be looking for a woman with a mare—a woman last seen in a white shirt and blue striped skirt—she'd heard that on the barn radio after she tethered the mare and crept into the empty barn.

No, she'd have to leave the mare here, outside the barn. It was a quiet time in the orchard, no one picking yet. The apples weren't ripe, she had a bellyache from eating them. But it was all she had except berries, a loaf of bread, and a chocolate bar she'd got from that Healing House. She didn't know where the mare had come from, so she couldn't leave a note. But they'd have heard the radio news—the animal would go back to its rightful owner. Nola put her arms around the mare and the mare nickered back. They were friends now, they were practically soul mates. They'd been through hell together. To hell and—not back yet, no, not yet. She had to reach the New York farm, she had to find Keeley. She had to get him away from Uncle.

Uncle. The man she hated most in the world. Hated for what he'd done to Ritchie as a kid. What he'd done to Keeley—she worried about that. Even Ritchie—she'd found him in the bed-

room once, hands lifted like they'd come down hard on the boy
He'd looked up startled; she saw the tears crowding his eyes
his hands clutching like they'd strangle the bad desires. The
he'd followed her out and yelled at her for coming in on him
He was just saying good night to the kid, that's all, he said. Wh
did she have to follow him round like a suspicious cat? She'
pulled into herself then, kept her silence, ignored him till h
stomped out of the trailer. Then she went to Keeley, poor Kee
ley, who was wide awake, trembling. Keeley, who seldor
spoke his heart, even to her.

She held the mare close, so close she could hear the hea
beating. She was filled all at once with love and hate for th
world. One glancing off the other, like two sides of a coin, lik
they were one.

She whispered good-bye, gave the mare a last embrace, an
ran off into the woods beyond the orchard. She'd wait till nigh
fall and then she'd cross the bridge—on foot.

# THIRTEEN

BOADIE WAS FEEDING the Friesian calves, the pig loose and rooting in the nearby grass. She loved to watch it. She loved the way its little tail curled and then twitched as it frolicked in the grass. Since they took it early from its mother, it needed to find something to chew and suck on. Boadie had an old sock for it in the trailer—out here it was sucking on a thick blade of grass. The pig she had before this had its tail docked by the farmer— poor thing spent its life keeping its poor clipped tail out of the mouths of its penmates till she rescued it. It was happy in its prison, the farmer said. Happy, ha! Happy with no sun, wind, rain—straw to sleep on? Just a hundred other miserable pigs all squeezed together? That was happy?

If Boadie'd had her way she'd of taken all the pigs, every one, let them roam on Uncle's farm. Let them have their freedom. To go where they wanted. She'd made the mistake of coming to Uncle's farm so she could be near Maggie and settle in one place. But then was sorry. That trailer—she could hardly turn round twice in it. And one of her favorite pigs—she found it on Uncle's dinner table! Hated Uncle for that. Hated him! Hated Ritchie, too—it was Ritchie turned in the pig.

Now the first calf was done eating, and she put down the pail. It moved against her flank, licked her cheek with a fat, scratchy pink tongue. It was grateful, so grateful. She rubbed her cheek against its hide and it mewled softly. Herself, she'd had seven babies, breast-fed them, and they all grew up. The way this heifer calf would grow and birth and feed its own. No one was going to take away this calf. Or take away the other one calling for her now, wanting its turn, its pail of grain. No one was going to take away her pig, rooting happily in the grass. Boadie was as happy now as she'd been in her whole life. It was like everything was coming together at this one moment in time: bright sun, blue mountains over beyond the red barn. Grass so green it turned your eyes to emeralds.

Even the horse cantering up the dirt road now, with its rider shouting something Boadie couldn't comprehend, didn't disturb her peace. Till horse and rider swerved into the driveway, kicking up gravel, striking Boadie in the forehead, like a shatter of glass.

Who was this now? She squinted, but couldn't see for the dust. She reached out a hand to touch the shotgun she kept close by. Nobody was going to take her babies. Nobody was going to take away her good day.

THERE WAS A COMMOTION outside the barn where someone was riding a horse up the drive. Ruth saw it was Franny, bareback in jeans and purple shirt. She was waving her arms, shouting, "Ophelia, it's Phelia back, Ruth, and she's all right—though she has a hurt foot, we'll have to work on that. But the feds don't want me to keep her, they want her quarantined 'cause that woman had her, that Enola female who killed that man. I mean, Ruth, I just got her back and now *they* want to take her! But Ruth, I'm telling you, oh I'm telling you, they'll take her over my dead body!" Franny flung her arms dramatically in the air. It might have been a sign of victory—or loss. Or both, Ruth thought, poor woman.

Ruth ran up to caress the mare and pat Franny's leg that was flung over the animal's belly. Ruth was both delighted and sorry. They were birds of a feather now, two women under siege. "She looks beautiful," she told Franny, "she looks in the pink of health. Don't let them take her, don't."

"It's cruel," Franny agreed, "it's cold-blooded, it's inhumanly callous."

Ruth glanced at the white pens where Boadie was fussing over the Friesian calves, a shotgun at her feet. Since the traveller had heard about the feds, she'd not let the animals out of her sight except to go back to the trailer and sleep or eat. Before Franny arrived with her mixed news, Ruth had been resigned to letting the agents have the calves for testing. "You can't win over the USDA," Colm had insisted in his pragmatic way—she'd told him about the state veterinarian's warning. "At least they're not taking your herd for good just to monitor them. You have to realize, Ruthie, they do a lot of good around here." He'd outlined their mission. But Ruth could think only of her cows.

"I won't ever, ever let them have her!" Franny cried. Making a clattery turnabout, she cantered off down the dirt road, alternately throwing kisses and giving the finger to the absent feds. "Once more unto the breach!" she shouted back, and disappeared into a blur of road dust.

Ruth smiled grimly. At least something positive had happened—Franny had her horse back. And Nola was still alive—one of the orchard hands recalled seeing a woman leading a mare. The witness didn't know which way she'd gone after that; police were chasing in all directions.

Still, Ruth couldn't shake off the fear of bad times ahead. The cows were ruminating in the pasture, heads down in the grass that was already yellowing in places where they'd cropped it. With no rain now for two weeks and the corn coming up short, drought was a major concern. When she looked up she saw only bright sun, beating down on her head, scalding the tops of the calf pens. Dust was settling on the clover by the side of the road, on the old green pickup, on Ruth's barn boots, on her eyelashes—she rubbed her eyes with a fist. It was as though she were going blind, not knowing what to do, where to turn.

Except to work. Yes. She went back to the barn to work. There was always sweeping, mopping, scouring equipment after the morning's milking. She tossed clean hay in the stalls, scooped up a huge pile of manure into the old wheelbarrow. The work felt good; it was a way of coping, if not a cure. Her muscles ached but her back was strong; she had energy enough for two women. She would get through this crisis. She would go to that apple orchard on the lakeshore, speak to the person who had sighted Nola—it seemed the place to start. Though where it would lead, she had no idea. She had never felt so vulnerable, so superfluous.

"Superfluous," she hollered at Zelda, stomping in her stanchion, "I'm just plain superfluous!" At its root, she recalled, the word meant flowing all over the place but never settling, never knowing. It figured.

Outside the barn a truck pulled up, its brakes grinding. There was something ominous about the sound. The Agri-Mark truck had come and gone to pick up milk, but with the quarantine, there was none to pick up—she couldn't sell the milk, it had to be dumped. Dumped! She was crazy with the thought. She stood up tall, the broom in her hands, ready to swing if needed. Don Quixote, she thought: flailing at windmills. The truck doors slammed. Two doors, two people getting out. She waited, feeling a moment of paralysis, the broom stuck to her palms. She heard voices: a man's, then a woman's. They were outside by the calf pens. She heard the woman's voice low and sympathetic; heard Boadie's answering screech: "No, no! Can't! Won't!" A torrent of Cant, the travellers' language. And then a man's oaths, chilling the air.

The broom clattered to the floor, and Ruth ran out. The agents were there: hands outstretched, gesturing, appealing, while Boadie held them at bay with her shotgun. "Can't have them, not my babies!" she hollered. She lunged forward and shot into the air. The feds stepped back. She ran at them, howling, shooting to one side and then the other, knocking a clipboard out of a hand. "Not my babies," she yelled, "not them! Not them!" until the pair scurried back into the truck. She gave off one more volley that peppered the back of the truck, shattering the rearview window.

"The woman's crazy," the male agent cried out the window. "This is a felony! You can't keep us from taking those calves. We'll be back!" The truck roared off down the road, its big tires wheeling up a screen of dirt and gravel.

Boadie stood there, holding the shotgun in her shaking hands, then lowered it slowly. Ruth ran to her, gave her a bear hug. She couldn't speak, she found herself weeping. The calves were bawling in their pens but there were still eight of them, eight healthy calves, including the Friesians. They gazed up with big frightened eyes—the shooting would put them off their feed. The pig cowered, squealing, in front of the pens.

"Thank you," Ruth whispered to the old lady, then turned to face Darren and Maggie, who had heard the shots and come running. Franny was galloping back on her mare, throwing up dust and gravel in Ruth's face. "What happened? Is anyone hurt?"

"God love us," Maggie said, and grabbed the shotgun out of her grandmother's arms. "You want to kill yourself, do you, huh, Boadie?"

The uncle stomped up behind them, blustering on about what the feds had done to him—"Ain't nothing, nothing, compared to what they done to *me*." As if this was some kind of contest, Ruth thought—who deserves the most pity? "But you can't fool 'em with that," Tormey said, pointing at the shotgun. "They'll just bring in the big guns, you wait and see." He turned to Franny, gushed out his woes to her—Ruth heard the word "Ritchie," and Franny's eyes widened.

Carol came dashing up from the rented pasture to throw her arms around Ruth. "I heard the shots. I saw the truck when I was coming up from the field. I figured it was you keeping them out. You're crazy enough to do that! But I want to tell you, Ruth, I'm not moving my sheep. The llama stays, too. We'll face this together."

"Well, they're safe for now," Ruth said, hugging her slender five-foot-three friend, who had probably never handled a weapon, except to wrap a toy gun as a birthday gift for a son.

Herself, Ruth felt like a Civil War general, standing, unscathed, at the rear of the action, pronouncing victory.

But knowing it a false victory, knowing the enemy would be back. Knowing she had little or no chance at all against a foe a hundred times her size.

# FOURTEEN

RUTH AND COLM HAD HAD an argument, so Tuesday morning Ruth was on her way alone to the orchard. It was useful, Ruth thought, having Colm around, but it was divisive as well. The problem was that he had double loyalties: first to her as an individual, and then to the police. She came first in his loyalties, he always said that; but he was paid by the Branbury police—and could he betray them? "Not really," he argued. In this instance the police, aided by the FBI, were hotly pursuing Enola Donahue and wanted no interference by a female farmer who was herself harboring suspect animals and a group of equally suspect Irish travellers. Since Monday morning's shoot-out (so-called by police), she was even more out of sync, and she must—according to Colm, "play it cool, Ruthie. So stay home, please? Let them have the calves. They'll compensate you, for chrissake."

She'd howled at that. What was a few dollars for a pair of innocent calves she'd fallen in love with? And what of the old traveller woman who'd moved her pallet up beside the pens, along with pig, shotgun, pail, and nursing bottles? Already Ruth owed *something* to Boadie. One couldn't desert one's allies, few as they seemed to be—but growing, she had to admit. The phone calls were coming in faster now: Carol, of course, vowing to keep her sheep on the farm "come what may," and Franny and Henrietta ready to come and fight "at a moment's notice, Ruth, call us, damn it!"

And yesterday evening her local orchard friend, Moira Earthrowl, had called the Champlain Orchard to ensure a hospitable welcome and a lineup of apple workers for interviewing. "You helped us out of a hole, Ruth, we want to give back."

What more could a besieged woman ask for than help from old friends? "Go back to work, Colm," she'd told him in an early morning phone call. "Ignore me. I'll do what my heart tells me to do."

"I know you will, Ruthie," was the answer. "Holy God but don't I know you will. Your heart's too damn big." She'd imagined her lover making the sign of the cross. Though he wasn't a practicing Catholic, he liked that dramatic gesture.

The lake was coming into view as she rounded the last bend. A sign read Bridge to New York State, and her heart gave a lurch. She imagined Nola moving stealthily across at nightfall. For now, though, she needed clues to the woman's dress, her state of health, her direction—for she might have run anywhere, up country or down country, attempting to elude the authorities. Surely by now she knew they were on her trail.

But there was no telling what the rigid authorities would say or do when they apprehended her. Ruth wanted—needed—to find Nola first.

The orchard owners were there to greet her: a plump, plain-spoken, middle-aged woman in jeans and plaid shirt; a stoop-shouldered man in overalls, tall as an apple tree—both smiling creases into their apple cheeks. It's funny, Ruth thought, how one grows to resemble one's trade. There was something horsy about Franny, for example. Did Ruth herself resemble a cow? Oh my.

"They're here in the barn, ready for questions," the woman said. "Though I have to tell you the Vermont police have already been here. And it's only the one worker who had a glimpse of her, I'm afraid. But maybe someone else will remember something. I do hope so. I can only imagine what you're going through." She gave Ruth an impulsive hug and for a moment Ruth felt light-headed, a child struck dumb.

There were at least a dozen workers standing about in the apple barn, looking awkward, a couple of them giggling. One surly fellow looked as though he didn't see why *he* should be interrogated; another was jiggling a leg and making odd facial contortions. It was that girl's nervousness that made Ruth ask if she could interview each worker individually. "It will only take a few minutes," she promised the owners, "especially if most have nothing to add. I know you have work for them to do."

The woman owner spread her hands and smiled, as if to say "Anything for a fellow farmer," and gave the orders. The workers would wait outside the apple barn, and the surly fellow, who was evidently the overseer, would send them in one by one. The orders squeezed his face into a lemon.

For Ruth it was like her school days when she'd been asked to get up in front of the class and ask the questions but couldn't think what questions to ask. What could she ask, except Did you spot this woman? Can you tell me anything about her? But then the questions came in a flood. What was she wearing? Did she come into the barn? Might she have listened to the radio? (It was on, low, over by the cider press.) Did she appear ill? Frightened? And what about the mare? Did it seem to have been ridden hard? Was it sweating? Limping? And so on.

The responses were mostly negative. Until the anorexic-looking young woman with the trembly face and hands diving in and out of her jeans pockets inched her way in and allowed that uh-huh, she had seen a woman tethering a mare to a maple tree outside the barn.

"I tole the officers that, I don't have nothing to add. I was coming out of the barn when I seen her. She was looking all scared to see me and she run off. I didn't know what to say to her, why should I speak to her? I didn't know she'd of killed somebody."

"We have no reason to believe she killed anyone," Ruth said. "She was running from an abusive man—at least, that's our thinking. And there was no reason for you to speak to her. You did nothing wrong. We're just glad you spotted her, that's all."

The girl gave a tight-lipped smile, leaned back against the

barn wall, and went on with her justification. "I been cleaning the apple barn, that's what my job is. I been swabbing it down, though it's hard work, all that juice from the cider press, smelling something turrible. Stinking really. How was I to know some killer woman's out there with a stolen horse?"

"Of course you didn't," Ruth soothed. "Now can you tell me what she looked like, what she was wearing? That's where you can really help us."

"They already axed that, the cops. I tole them she was wearing something white on top. And blue on the bottom, that's all I 'member. It was blue. Kind of stripy blue."

"Pants? Dress?"

"Don't know, I was in a hurry, it was quitting time, I had to get home. I take care of my dad, he's got Parkinson's. Shakes up a storm. Drops everything. Breaks it, too."

"I'm sorry. But think hard. Striped blue—might've been a skirt?"

The girl cocked her head and thought. "Might've. Yeah, I guess. But she was in one hell of a hurry."

"She ran off?"

"Limped off, yeah, like she'd had a fall. Yeah, I 'member that. She were wearing a skirt, yeah, I 'member now, 'cause I wondered how in hell she'd rode that horse in a skirt without a saddle. Must've been all she had to wear."

"She was sick," Ruth explained, "she'd had brain surgery. Her male companion took her out of the hospital too soon. Did she look ill to you? Bruised maybe, scarred? I really appreciate your thinking about this, you've been such a help so far."

The girl gave a weak smile, stuck a tongue in her pale cheeks, appeared to be thinking. "Yeah, she had a bruise on her face. I mean, I 'member thinking she looked like an apple—a drop, you know, the way they bruise, kind of yellow. Come to think of it, bruises all over her face like somebody hit her. Lumpy, you know. Creeps, I remember thinking that. Funny how it just come to me. Lumpy."

"Fresh bruises."

"Well, bruised apples isn't fresh long. They rot fast."

"Yes. Well, I am grateful." Ruth smiled at the girl. "I've just one more question because I know you have to get back to work."

"Yeah, I don't get this barn cleaned by ten o'clock he'll clock me." She waved at the barn door, where Ruth could see the overseer standing, arms folded, looking, well, sullen.

"Where did she run? What direction? Do you think she might've gone over the bridge?"

"Not then," the girl said, bolder now, her cheeks calm, hands more at ease where they hung loose. "Not till later. Not till it got dark. Then I saw her again."

"Oh?" Ruth held her breath. This was new. Something, evidently, the girl had not told the police.

The girl stood taller, lifted her chin, her eyes were electric with what she had to say. "I was taking a walk with my boyfriend—it was late Saturday night, down near the bridge. I didn't want to tell the cops—my boyfriend got in a little trouble—I mean nothing serious, just a break-in-he won't do it again, he promises."

"Uh-huh."

"And I seen her. 'It's her,' I tole my boyfriend. 'The one what left the horse, the one they say killed somebody.' He got all excited then, wanted to go stop her, thought there might be a reward, you know? So I says, 'You want to talk to cops, do you?' and he says he guesses not."

"I can imagine. And then?"

"And then we just watched her look all round and when she thought no one saw, she went over the bridge."

"Limp over?"

"Limp, yeah. She had a little limp. Left leg. Don't know how she rode that mare. 'Less she'd walked it all that way."

"You couldn't see where she went when she got to the other side?"

"How could I? Least a mile long, that bridge. It were night.

Only reason I seen her at all was there was a light near the start of the bridge. She just limped over, that's all I can tell you."

"And you didn't think to tell anyone until Monday that you'd seen the woman?"

"I don't work Sundays, do I? Why'd I tell anyone before then? Look, I gotta get back to work or he'll kill me." She tilted her head toward the overseer, who was coming into the barn.

"Thank you, thank you so very much," Ruth said, and smiled at the fellow, who frowned back. "May I ask you a few questions?" she said and he said, "I don't see why. I got nothing to add to what anybody said. I do my job and that's that. I never saw the woman. Never wanted to."

"Well thank you. That says it all." And Ruth left the barn.

New York, she thought, as she drove back along Route 125 toward Branbury. And why would Nola want to go there? Had she any reason, any goal in mind? There was the farm she'd come from, of course, but from all accounts she didn't like the uncle. Did she know he'd come to Vermont? Not likely. Then again, there was the boy. She would want to find him. But the boy was with the uncle now, in Branbury. Ruth would have to see to it that the media announced that fact. So if the woman were to hear a radio or read a paper, she would return to Vermont.

How did Nola and the uncle get along? The uncle and the boy? She would have to talk to Maggie, she would have to talk to the uncle. She would have to find Nola before the traveller woman heard about the uncle. Perhaps she should visit that New York farm and talk to the farmhands there. And who was Nola anyway? Mentally as well as physically. Ruth needed to know more. Much more.

But how could she leave her farm? There were federal agents coming for her calves, maybe for the cows they had already quarantined. She had to be there.

And who had killed the man Ritchie? Was it really that sick woman, Enola? The bruises the apple worker described suggested a motive. Or was it someone else who hated the man,

for his or her own reasons? Before she went traipsing off to
New York she'd start with the ones closest to the uncle: She had
them all on the farm now. Maggie, Boadie, Darren, the uncle,
the boy Keeley—though he was hardly more than a child. When
Nola came back to find her boy, as perhaps she would, Ruth
wanted to have answers for the desperate woman.

BACK AT THE FARM she found all hell had broken loose. Two
armed men had hold of Boadie. One of them had her pig and another her shotgun. Boadie was screaming and so were Maggie
and Liz. Agents were loading the bellowing calves into a white
truck. Not just the Friesians, but all of the calves, she saw: all
eight, Jane Eyre's new calf and Charlotte's—and Esmeralda's!

Ruth leaped out of her pickup and ran at the men. "What do
you think you're doing? You can't do that! Those others aren't
Friesians, they're my own Holsteins, born this year on my land.
You have no right to take them, no right!"

"It's the farmers who have no right. No right to question the
USDA—you should know that," one of the agents said, smirking, and went on with his work.

An ancient Colt wobbled into the driveway behind the truck
and Sharon leaped out, hollering. "They can't get away without hitting my car. And I won't move! Mom, I got 'em blocked
in. They're not going anywhere." She opened the back door, un-
loaded two children and two dripping ice cream cones—then
shooed her crew into the house.

The men seemed oblivious to Sharon's car; a ruddy-cheeked
fellow was trying to hustle the pig out of Boadie's arms.
"Ma'am," he was saying, "ma'am, we're just taking it for tests,
if it's healthy you'll get it back." The fellow looked as though
he'd be glad to have lightning suddenly strike, just to get away
from the clutching, hitting, shrieking old woman.

"My piggy, my darling, my sweet piggy—you can't have my
piggy!"

Sharon ran to the defense, followed by Maggie and Darren.

Together they wrestled the pig from the agent's arms. The fellow looked pleadingly at his colleagues, who were loading in the last calf. Boadie shuffled off with her pig, back toward her trailer. One animal saved, anyway. But what of Ruth's calves? Their mothers were out in the pasture. They'd come back for milking—and no calves. And Elizabeth, eight months pregnant. Ruth thought of her son, Vic, kidnapped as a boy—how distraught, how grieved she'd been.

"Get the tractor," Ruth hollered at Darren. "Close in that truck. Sharon, drive my pickup in front so they can't get out that way." She threw keys at her daughter. "They can all leave in their one car. The truck stays here. They have no right, damn it! No one told me they'd take all my calves! Sharon—get my rifle out of the pantry."

The young agent laughed, and the other scowled at him. In minutes the truck was blocked in, Ruth was pointing her Winchester at the men. "Just following orders, ma'am," one of them told Ruth, backing away from her hunting rifle. "Just doing my job."

"Then get a new job," Sharon yelled.

"You're obstructing justice," the man shouted. "You'll be sorry, you don't move those vehicles. Put down that thing. You can't get away with this."

"So you said. You'll move in a tank, sure. Now leave," Ruth said, feeling the breath well up out of her toes, out of her heart. "If you want your truck back you can get it later, after we unload the calves. For now, just go. Go, I said!" She cocked the rifle. Couldn't think if she had bullets in it.

They went, the young agent, who wasn't laughing now, and the three scowlers. They promised to return after they reported this second mutiny to the proper authorities. They were just following orders, one of them shouted again. He didn't give a damn about the calves, "We were just doing our job!" His voice died away as the Buick backed out of the drive.

"Now start unloading," Ruth ordered. "And move those calf pens. Darren, find a place behind the barn that a truck can't get to. We have to circle the wagons. We're in the right here—it's on our side, you all know that."

"Brava, Mom," said Sharon, grabbing Charlotte's calf by the collar, hustling it down the back slide of the truck. "You won the day."

"The day," Ruth said. "Maybe just that. Just the day."

"You can live a lifetime in a day," said Sharon.

"Sweetie, sweetie, sweetie, swee wee wee," Boadie crooned to her squirming pig, "swee wee wee wee wee."

# FIFTEEN

THERE WAS NO placating Ruth, Colm knew that. Still, he tried. He stood over her where she had flung herself back, exhausted, on the horsehair sofa. Standing gave him better leverage. He loved the woman, but jeez, she was hard to control. Not that he wanted to control—Colm was a man of the twenty-first century (more or less)—but he at least wanted equal influence time.

"You have to give up fighting the feds, Ruthie. They're bigger than you are, they're an organization."

"I hate organizations. I hate the establishment. I hate—"

"Ruthie, please. The sixties are over. This is two thousand—"

She covered her ears, scrunched up her eyes. "I don't want to hear your argument." Her forehead was one wide wrinkle.

He sighed, sat down on the edge of the sofa, but she didn't move to give him room. She had to understand. This was bigger than both of them. This was a plague. "Two contaminated calves, Ruth, can lead to a total wipeout. The whole of Vermont sick. The world. You have to open your eyes."

She sat up, grabbed his arms, pinched. "But that's just it. We don't know they're sick. We don't know that Nola woman is sick—not with CJD, anyway. There's no grounding for this. You read this morning's *Free Press*. They've lowered the Mad Cow death forecast. Only one hundred thirty-two people have died of it-and most of them in Britain."

"I read it, yeah. And they admit they don't know. They just don't know. It could still be a hundred thousand, the way it takes years to incubate. And there's no blood test to find out how long it does take. Some Nobel prize neurologist saying we don't" know where and how prions move through the body before they show up in the brain."

"And they tried to take all my calves, Colm, all eight of them—with no prior notice!"

She wasn't listening to him, that was a fact. He sighed, and kept trying to quiet her. "So that was a mistake. The head honcho called this morning to apologize—you told me that yourself. The guys who came for them got it wrong. Human error, that's all. You got to allow for mistakes. They only want the two calves."

"But the rest are in quarantine! I can't sell the bull calves, I can't sell the milk from my cows. We still have to milk but then we spill it into the ground. And we're not supposed to tell anybody! As though Agri-Mark wouldn't know, for one, when they come for the milk and we turn them away." She had a point there, he thought. "They might as well lock me up, Colm, build a wall around the farm, put up a sign that says *Polluted*." She put her face in her hands, pushed her fingertips into her skin.

"Ruthie, don't cry. I can't stand to see you cry."

"I'm not crying. I'm angry. I'm furious! I'm a one-woman mad machine!"

She *was* crying, spilling snot and tears all over the black horsehair sofa. Okay, he wouldn't mention it again. He pulled her up into his arms, and she didn't resist. He let her weep all over his clean blue cotton shirt; tears soaked his khakis. He'd have to change his clothes before his next client appeared, but it was okay.

"Cry, love, get it all out. Cry for the woes of the world." He was astonished at the vibrato in his voice, rather admired it. But she didn't seem to notice.

"I'm not crying," she shouted, jumping up, rolling him off the sofa. "I won't cry. Crying gets you nowhere. I'll fight, that's what I'll do. Now go make me a cup of strong coffee, Colm, and let's plan our strategy. We have to find Nola. And soon."

The police had been looking for Nola for over a week now

with no luck, but he decided not to mention that. He poured two mugs of coffee, sat Ruth back down, and draped an arm across her shoulders. "Okay, Ruthie. You go first. What're your thoughts?"

"She's gone over the bridge," she told him.

"Huh?" It was the first he'd heard of it. "What makes you say that?"

"A worker I interviewed saw her go."

"What? And you never told me? You never informed the police? Our men interviewed those workers, too, and no one came up with that."

"There are two women in your department, Colm. Must you call them all 'men'? Anyway, it was only this morning I found out. When I went to interview the workers."

He sighed. She drove him completely nuts sometimes, bonkers.

"Well anyway, this worker did," she said and waved away the police—men and women. "So now I want you to go down to the radio station and see that word gets out about the uncle and Keeley being here in Branbury. You see, I figure she's planning to go back to that farm and get the boy. Just a hunch, you know, but it makes sense, don't you think? If you had a child, you'd want to go collect him, see he was all right, wouldn't you? Get him off that New York farm where they had two sick animals?"

"Now you're admitting they might have that disease."

"I am not, Colm! I'm just—oh, you know. Stop plaguing me."

They couldn't have a conversation without that word, but he let it go. "She's going after the boy she thinks is still there. Okay, good thinking. So let's get a map and plan out her route."

Ruth was sitting now with her chin in her elbows, gazing at the walls she'd painted a bright yellow one day last fall after they'd had an argument. He couldn't recall what it was about, but she'd slapped on the paint, needing "sun in her life," she'd said. Today she looked mostly nostalgic—that was the word.

Looking like it was her own son she was desperate to find. Ruth had been crazed with worry over Vic that time he was kidnapped. There'd been no talking to her, she would have raced around the world looking for the kid.

"So we'll alert the New York cops in case she hitches a ride or stops somewhere?"

"Wait." Ruth lifted her chin, she was coming back to life. "First the radio. We want her to know that Keeley's here, and turn around. I don't want police stopping her till she gets here. I want to talk to her myself, put her at ease. I want to see her with Tormey Leary—see how she reacts to him. Where was he when Ritchie was killed? You ever think of that, Colm? Your darling cops are so sure it was Nola wrapped those reins around his neck."

"They're not my darling cops, Ruthie. I just work there a few hours each week. If it hadn't been for my grandfather—"

"I know. The big hero. Killed in action, stopping the rumrunners down from Canada."

Colm was proud of that feat, actually. He didn't like Ruth's deprecating tone of voice. Sometimes he fantasized about that grandfather: imagined him chasing the predators, stumbling into an ambush, getting shot by a desperado.

Colm didn't know how he would have reacted to those smugglers. He didn't think he'd have had the courage to pursue them. He didn't feel he could live up to the family legend. He'd rather just trudge along in real estate, help his dad in the mortuary. But he needed the money. Moonlight in Vermont.

"So, Ruthie, you think the uncle might've done him in? How'd he know where to find him?"

"That's for us to figure out. He's on my list for this afternoon. You just put on your cop hat and get that message out to the media, and I'll interview the uncle. Talk to Keeley, as well. The boy seems a loner—hasn't said a word since he got here, but I suspect he could tell us something."

Colm was dubious. "I tried—but the kid just walked away."

"Colm." She had that stubborn, I-don't-want-to-hear-it look on her face that drove him bananas. "We can't just sit back and let this plague thing take us over. We have to fight. We have to take steps. Small steps maybe, but keep moving, keep pushing the bad stuff away. Now go. Some time or other she'll be in a car, or wheedling a meal out of some reluctant housewife. And hearing a radio."

"Sure, Ruthie. But you let the agents have the two calves, okay?"

She just sat there with that look on her face, so he didn't pursue it. "Go now," she said, pointing a finger at the door.

"Can I finish my coffee?"

"Take it with you, Colm."

He sighed, picked up the coffee, and went. There was no point arguing.

Outside he ran into his cousin (so-called), Darren, on his way into the kitchen, and Colm warned him not to go in. "She's in a mood. Upset about those agents taking her calves. You might meet with resistance."

"Uh-huh." Grinning, Darren winked at Colm and walked in anyway, letting the door bang behind him.

So much for influence on *anybody,* Colm thought.

THE FEDERAL AGENTS came back for the Friesian calves the next morning—not to slaughter but just to test, they promised, though Ruth believed little the feds said. She let them have the two calves. What else could she do? The old lady was in the trailer, according to Darren, napping in her chair, the pig at her feet. She'd be furious when she heard. Oh, well. Ruth's choices were lessening. It was like losing flesh, turning slowly into a skeleton. Tomorrow she'd look in the mirror and she'd be nothing but a bunch of bones strung together. How would she milk the cows?

Today then she must act, use her head, try to find out things. What things?

Ask questions, she answered herself, probe a little. Get under the skin of the interviewee.

And here was young Keeley, as though she'd summoned him, entering the barn on slow knobby legs, his head cast down, giving him a double chin although he was only a child—two years younger than her adolescent Vic. But a big-boned child, his body doubtless grown beyond his powers of judgment. When she spoke the boy looked up, all eyes, it seemed, dark violet eyes like his mother's, narrowing now to see her reaction to his coming. His lips moved, but no words came out. He gazed up at the barn rafters. A wisp of hay fluttered in the air and landed on his nose. He blew it off.

She waited. Finally, he said, "Help."

She looked hard at him. How was she to interpret the word? She said, "How nice, Keeley. I can use the help. But you know what? I can use a cup of iced coffee, too." When he looked dubious, she said, "I have cider—and honey-dipped doughnuts. You like doughnuts?"

The slight shrug said that he did, and he followed her back to the house, patted the yellow barn cat that was dozing on the front steps. He sat down beside it.

"You can bring it in the house if you like. I've some dried food for it."

He followed her in and she let him feed the cat, sit with it in his lap, stroke it with one hand, munch on a doughnut. He kept his eyes on the cat.

"Cats gravitate to a barn. We've always a small army of them. Does Uncle tolerate them in his barn?"

Still gazing at the cat, he said, "Kills the kittens. Puts 'em in a bag—drowns 'em." He looked as though he might cry.

"I'm sorry." It was all she could think to say. She poured the cider, coffee for herself. Sitting opposite the boy, she smiled. She wanted to gain his confidence. "So you like living on a farm?"

He shook his head. "I want—to go home. Find work."

"Home?" Home, she supposed, meant North Carolina. "What kind of work would that be?"

He looked at his hands, wiggled his fingers as though he was fitting something together. His lips worked to find the right words. He patted the cat furiously. It was wriggling to get away but he held it down. "Ritchie," he said at last, "he threw out the train I was painting."

"A model train?" He nodded.

"That wasn't nice. It was hard living with Ritchie?"

Keeley was doing funny things with his mouth, as though he had a toothache. He said, "He wasn't nice. Wasn't nice to my mother."

"What would he do to her? What would he do to—you?"

Keeley was looking evasive now, she'd have to go slow with the questions. She offered another doughnut and he took it. The cat jumped off his lap and he looked bereft, like the animal had rejected him. He crammed the remainder of the doughnut in his mouth and chewed slowly, eyes on the cat, which was now over by the empty dish.

"But Uncle was nice enough to you?"

He was choking on the doughnut. "Here, drink some cider." But too late, pieces of doughnut flew out onto the table. She handed him a paper napkin and he cleaned it up, carefully.

"You must miss your mom. Do you think she's gone back to that farm looking for you? I heard her speak warmly of you."

It wasn't true that she'd heard Nola speak of him, but sometimes a white lie helped. The boy looked at Ruth for the first time. "I want her—to take me home."

"You have family there still? In North Carolina?"

He nodded. "My dog."

"You couldn't bring the dog to New York with you?"

"Ritchie said no. I'm glad Ritchie's dead," he cried, jumping up, balling his fists. "I hate—hated him. I hate Uncle! I'm afraid—"

"Afraid of what? Who?" He was sobbing now. She put out

a hand but he pulled away. "I want Ma," he cried. "Ma's not sick—she got nothing bad like they say."

"I know," Ruth soothed. She kept silent a moment while he patted the cat, which was over by the refrigerator now. "You hate Uncle, do you? Do you think your mother hated Ritchie and Uncle, too?"

He stared at her, the eyes huge in his face, like moist grapes, a tongue stuck in his cheek. He didn't answer the question.

"Enough to hurt him maybe?" She was going out on a fragile limb, crawling out there where the limb might break. The violet eyes burned into her. The cat squealed and it sounded like a whiplash. He stared at her a moment longer, then wheeled about and dashed through the door, pushing it shut with his left hand—leaving her with the question.

Would Nola kill to keep Ritchie from hurting her again? From hurting Keeley perhaps—for the insinuation was there....

Outside the barn the calves stood on black and white stick legs, whining for their mothers. The two closest pens were empty—the emptiness seemed a presence. Ruth felt too drained to go back to work. She was still staring at the pens when Boadie came hustling up, all mouth, blazing eyes, the shotgun in her blue-knuckled hands. "Where they? Where they calves?"

It was like an army charging down, ready to fire. Ruth threw up her arms. "Don't," she cried, "stop! We're allies, aren't we? The calves are gone, Boadie. Being tested. There's nothing we can do about it. Either of us. They're just—gone."

The old woman looked as though she might crawl into one of the pens herself. She threw down the gun and thrust her arms high. Then she dropped to her knees and ho-owled out her protest.

The remaining calves howled with her, a mournful bellowing, like babies in a doctor's office, all crying because one cried. And for no reason they could understand.

IT WAS TOO EARLY in the summer for vegetables to ripen. Nola found only lettuce and a few early peas, hard as buckshot to eat, but she had to take nourishment. She'd been on the run for days now—weeks, it seemed. She could feel her flesh shrinking away, her belly bloating the way starving Africans looked in the newspaper photos.

"What're you doing in my mama's garden?"

A small girl stood before her, dressed in blue cotton shorts and pink shirt, her yellow hair in pigtails. Her stance was defiant; she was the kind of spoiled kid Nola despised, the kind who'd said and done mean things to Nola as a girl in that convent school. Once a girl like this had put a butterfly net over Nola's head and pinched her nose and made her cry. Afterward in the bathroom Nola stepped on the girl's foot, pushed her into a stall, where she slipped and banged her head against the toilet. When the girl told on Nola, the sister got out a switch, made Nola go without lunch and write, *I'm a sinner,* a thousand times on the blackboard. Her wrist ached for days after that.

But in her heart she never repented.

"I'm hungry," Nola said, staring the creature down.

"Then go buy yourself some lunch. This is my mama's garden."

"Jennifer? It's time for lunch. Didn't you hear me calling you?" A young woman stepped out through the grove of trees, then stopped, surprised to see Nola. The woman was a larger copy of the child, with tan denim shorts and blond hair in a ponytail tied with a pink ribbon.

Nola stood erect, the lettuce in her cupped hands. "I can work for you. I can clean your house."

The woman laughed. "Just for a head of lettuce? You're welcome to it. Take it. But first come in for a bowl of soup. Pea soup—I just made it."

"She stole the lettuce, Mama," the little girl said, her lips pursed.

"She's hungry." The woman motioned for Nola to follow.

Inside, the house was immaculately clean, one could practically eat off the waxy linoleum floor. There would be little to clean, except a few dishes in the sink. The woman set a hand-made bowl of pea soup in front of Nola. There were bits of ham and bacon floating in it. Nola approached it slowly, gazing at the silver tablespoon. Yesterday she'd eaten a raw potato out of a garden and a bit of meat left in a dog's dish. Then thrown up half the night, where she lay in a woodshed. Her back and head still hurt from the rough wood floor—the shavings weren't thick enough to cradle her sore bones.

The woman set a hunk of buttered bread beside the soup bowl, then sat across the table from Nola. Now, Nola felt, the questions would begin. Who are you? Where are you going? Why are you homeless?—for that was what Nola appeared to be, though she had no travelling bags with her. She had nothing, just empty pockets and a sack with a shirt, skirt, and dress that desperately needed to go through a wash.

But the woman asked no questions. She just talked about the hot weather they'd been having, and how dry it was—her garden so parched she had to buy her lettuce from the store. "It was all wilted, what you picked," she said. "You wouldn't have gone far on that."

Nola felt now that she owed the woman some explanation. "I'm on my way west," she said. She didn't want to say Buffalo, or Tonawanda—the place had been in the news. Though she hadn't heard any recent news. She hadn't dared hitchhike, and this was the first time she'd been in someone's kitchen. There was a radio here, but it was mute. She was glad of that, actually, she didn't want to arouse any suspicions. This woman was kind, the bread was homebaked and delicious. It had olives and walnuts baked into it. "It's really good," she said.

The woman seemed thrilled that Nola liked it. She said, "I'll write out the recipe for you," like Nola was a neighbor dropped in for a cup of tea. The woman scribbled the recipe on a pad and Nola had to smile. As if a homeless woman in a dirty skirt with a torn hem could go somewhere and bake bread! This blond woman, she felt, was living in a dream world. The pretty daughter, the pretty clothes, the immaculate house. The woman seemed to want to help her, offered food and a warm bath—even the Tylenol Nola was brave enough to ask for. Dear God but she needed a Tylenol!

She was swallowing a second pill when the husband walked in. He looked surprised to see Nola. She hid her hands in her dirty lap. He narrowed his eyes at his wife.

"She was hungry," the wife said.

"They always are. You're a magnet for the homeless." He gave a sharp laugh and then tousled the little girl's hair; sat down and drew her onto his lap. The child said, "She was stealing from our garden. It wasn't nice." Safe in her father's lap, she glared back at Nola.

The woman set a bowl of soup in front of her husband, a glass of red wine, and some buttered bread. He looked at it and made a face. "You got any plain bread? You know I don't like olives."

"But they're baked into the bread, it's a new recipe, I thought—"

"Grace?" Nola saw the woman wince. She's afraid of him, Nola thought. The husband made her think of Ritchie. Nola had all too often been afraid of Ritchie, especially when he was into the drink. Ritchie was like a burning fuse; one never knew if or when it would explode.

Though now Ritchie was dead, it wouldn't explode anymore. Was she glad of that or sorry? She pulled the rosary beads out of her pocket, fingered them under the table.

"Have you got a tongue?" the man asked her. "Where did you come from? Where do you live—or do you just go around raiding people's gardens?"

Nola dropped the rosary, and the little girl scrambled off her papa's lap to pick it up. "It's a necklace," the child said, holding it up, grinning. She draped it around her neck.

"It's my rosary," Nola said, feeling the anger up in her throat. She reached out for the beads and the child ran off with them into another room. The mother started to go after the child and the husband stopped her.

NANCY MEANS WRIGHT 165

"Sit down, Grace," he said. "We'll get it back." He didn't scold the child. He turned again to Nola. It was like she was a mouse he was playing with. "Now answer my question, please. You're eating my food, you can answer my question. I asked where you came from. You're southern, I can tell that. These are foreign parts to you."

Nola sat paralyzed. She couldn't think of the right words to say. "I—I don't live anywhere just now. I'm going to find my son, take him back, um, south."

"That's where she lives," the wife said, patting Nola's arm. "She lives in the South."

"Then you're in the wrong place," the man said. "This is Johnsburg, New York, you know? It's not the South." He looked curiously at Nola, his mouth hanging open a little. He was a big man, not tall but husky, with small white hands that had never seen a day's manual labor, or so it appeared. Ritchie, though, had worked hard all his life, she had to hand him that. Even when he'd put on cheap roofing, or tar on a driveway, it was hard work. His hands were rough, red, the skin raw in places, and scarred. It had been terrifying that night to see those hands that had always been busy, lying lifeless in the swampy grass. For a moment she'd wanted to pick them up, massage them, but couldn't bear to touch them again.

She was suddenly angry. He'd deserved what he got. He deserved it! He'd cheated too many people. He'd killed a man. He thought she didn't know, but she did. Maggie told her that, the night she arrived in Vermont. Maggie had heard about it from Darren.

"You wouldn't be one of those Irish travellers now, would you?" the man said. "They've been in the news lately—that woman who beat her little daughter? Girl not much older than my own?" He frowned at Nola, like *she* had beaten *his* daughter.

Nola stammered, "I'm not going south yet, I have to find my son, I told you. We got separated. We have a place to live." They didn't exactly, but she wasn't going to tell this man. It would be

only a step from Irish traveller who beat her daughter to Irish traveller he'd read about in the newspaper. The one who killed her
man and was spreading some kind of cancer. "I have to be on my
way," she lied. "My son is waiting for me in the next town."

"You haven't finished your soup," the woman said, standing up with Nola.

"I've had all I can eat. Thank you, but I got to go." Nola
started out the door. The man was still sitting there, watching
her, he looked like he was thinking hard. She went outside,
moving carefully to avoid suspicion. The woman trotted after
her with the loaf of bread. "Edward doesn't like it anyhow, take
it." Then, "Oh, your rosary beads! I'll get them from Jennifer."

Nola saw the man reappear in the doorway. "Never mind,"
she said, and went off toward the road. The man was still standing there, staring at her. He wasn't done with his questions. Before long he'd put it all together.

"Thief," the child yelled from a window. "Stealing our food.
You ought to be in jail!"

Nola walked rapidly now, around a bend in the road, then
veered off into a copse of trees. She'd seen a shiny black automo-
bile in the driveway—she didn't want the man coming after her.

In the underbrush she threw up the bread and soup. She
thought she'd spewed blood, but discovered it was bits of pi-
mento from the olives. But she had the rest of the loaf, it would
carry her through two or three days. She didn't want to take
from anyone's garden again. She didn't want to go into anyone's house. She would have to live on berries and mushrooms,
though she didn't know which ones were poisonous. She
wished she had Maggie with her, Maggie knew herbs and
plants. With Maggie she'd be able to survive.

But Maggie was back in Vermont, and Nola was headed
west. She'd have to take a chance and get rides now and then,
she could never walk that far. But she'd get there.

"I'm coming, Keeley," she said aloud, lifting her face to the
sky. The sun hammered her temples with its fiery knuckles.

# SIXTEEN

JAMES PERLMAN LIFTED the edge of the curtain to see who was banging on his door. He didn't like what he saw. It was a pair of agents from the Department of Agriculture. What did they want with him? He'd told his story to the local police—the Willmarth woman had argued him into it. Luckily the police were single-minded about the missing woman: they didn't ask about himself, other than his name and current occupation.

But Christ, his occupation was the problem, he discovered, when he let them inside the kitchen—a man and a woman, like a couple of walking badges, hardly human with those painted-on smiles. Could they inspect his sheep? Were the sheep U.S. born—or had he imported any from abroad? Did he know those sheep were suspect, might have ingested contaminated feed? Did he know about the farm in East Warren, the slaughtered sheep, the suspect ewes?

"But my sheep are healthy," he cried, standing up because they refused to sit down—their badges crying "Power, we have Power over you." "You can see for yourself. Come on and I'll show you."

The Smiles went along, seeming to agree with him, to sympathize—that was what Power was, that aura of benevolence. He knew it well. Power was the female supervisor in that Buffalo hospital: a large, pickle-faced woman with dots of rouge on either cheek and a buglelike voice that split his eardrums when she spoke. It was she who'd walked in on him when he was with that woman in the recovery room. It was the first time—the first time it had happened! Even as he mounted the patient he hated himself, told himself it would be the only time. He'd watched the woman when she came into the hospital for her colonoscopy. He knew her to be a sleep-around woman, married to an older man who couldn't do anything for her—James wasn't taking advantage, no. She would have given it to him free—she as good as offered when he asked if she was finished dressing. And she said she was finished. But then she stood grinning at him, a big lusty orange-haired female, her pale blue johnny open to the world. Then they heard a female nurse coming, and she tied the loose strings of the johnny and he bent to his job: attaching the IV to her arm.

The feds were talking about the weather, the heat, the drought. Wells were going dry in nearby towns. It was too bad, it made people cross and grumpy. "You can't think we like doing this, taking and testing animals," the female agent said, "but we have to think of the greater good. We can't have this disease taking over the country. Your small sacrifice could save a nation."

The woman was looking at him closely now. He wondered what she might know. That dead man, Ritchie, had known about the hospital incident, James was sure of it. But Ritchie was dead, he wouldn't talk. James wondered where this woman came from. He didn't dare ask. His offense was on record if someone wanted to do the research. The supervisor had caught him in the act. Then the patient had started to wake up from the sedative and she was smiling—James was sure she was smiling to see him. She wanted it, she'd asked for it.

"We've traced a pair of suspect ewes to you," the man accused, "brought from a farm up in Greensboro." He thrust his pimpled chin in James's face like it was James's fault, all that paperwork and tracing his sheep from Scotland to Greensboro to Branbury.

"I had bought a pair, yes," James said, "but I sent them back when I heard about the contamination. My sheep here are healthy—I can show you their papers." He'd bought the pair because East Friesian sheep were famous for their dairy production. Anyway, the ones he'd bought were not from the same Belgium farm as the East Warren or Greensboro ones. The feds were painting everyone with the same brush. You lived in Belgium, had sheep—therefore they were sick. He despised it, he despised that kind of irrationality, that prejudice. When the hospital supervisor blabbed about her discovery, the red dots in her cheeks like strobe lights, everyone had shunned him. He was a pariah, an object of hate and suspicion. He'd wanted to kill that officious head nurse. She was jealous, he'd told himself. Christ, no one would want *her!*

The feds were examining his sheep: probing, judging. For once, the smiles left their faces; they couldn't find anything wrong. Finally they shook his hand, out there by the pasture fence. "This is just a preliminary visit," they said. "You'll hear from us. We have to be overly cautious, you understand."

James watched them walk away, talking to one another, laughing. The woman had a big butt, she was wiggling it—she was no better than the patient in the Buffalo hospital. James liked his women small and compact. Like Maureen, his ex. Maureen had stuck with him through all the hooplah; then when they came to Vermont and began a new life—she left him. Angry tears crowded his eyes, thinking of it. Even his daughter out in California rarely called.

Christ but he felt alone now. Thirty acres and two dozen sheep and no one to talk to. No one in the whole neighborhood, in fact—though to tell the truth, there were few he'd really want to sit down and have a drink with. Not those kooky lesbians with the horses. Not that crazy beekeeper, Gwen, who grew the marijuana and nightshade and asked to keep bees on *his* farm—he'd told her where to go! Not the Willmarth woman with her silly bovines named Jane Eyre and Elizabeth and Oprah. (James never named his sheep, why would he?) Christ, but there were a lot of weirdos in this small town! He hated that Willmarth woman—hated her for letting that crew of thieves camp on her land.

Hated her for bringing all this suspicion on him and his sheep.
It was time to do something about that woman. But what?
Letter in the local rag? Phone calls? Anonymous calls? He
didn't know, he couldn't think—he was too upset from the
agents' visit. But the public should know what the dairy farmer
had done. He'd think of something. She wouldn't get away
with it.

There were still tears in his eyes. He prided himself on not
giving in, even when they threw the book at him in the hospital. But here he was, blubbering away like a baby. He blew his
nose hard into a Kleenex, then picked out the rest of the tissues,
one by one, and shredded them. Threw them into the air, where
the wind picked them up like bits of chipped ice.

HENRIETTA WAS reading aloud from the manuscript of her lesbian romance novel. She had the heroine, a sexy Rubenesque
female with flaming red hair, lying naked on her bed. Henrietta loved the color red—her bedroom was furnished with a red
carpet, red print wallpaper, red curtains with tiny red roses
climbing and embracing. Her heroine looked up, smiling,
plump arms draped over her head, when Jalousie walked in.
"'Jalousie, is that you?' Rubena asked."

"Who?" said Franny.

"Jalousie. I changed the name. It was Maria, but Maria's
such a common name. I need something more metaphoric, you
know, a name to suggest character. Jalousie's jealous because
Rubena went to that bar with Ivy, and Jalousie found them there
together, sipping out of the same martini glass."

"Oh," said Franny, who was trying to make an omelet out
of Egg Beaters. She'd lately discovered her cholesterol was
high, and with all the anguish she'd been going through she was
worried about heart attack. Her mother and grandmother had
both died at the age of sixty-eight and Franny was taking no
chances. She'd visited a naturopath who prescribed an over-the-
counter drug called Red Yeast Rice; she swallowed a caplet

every day now, hoping to ward off the inevitable. It turned her urine canary yellow, and that was interesting.

Henrietta settled herself in her red cotton nightie in the kitchen rocker and read from her manuscript. "'Ivy's a wimp,' Jalousie said, pointing a wicked finger at Rubena, who was standing there in the driveway, holding the bridle of her beloved bay mare. The mare had been stolen—"

"Wait a minute," Franny said. "Where did this bay mare come from? You said Rubena was a nursery school teacher. You keep changing names and occupations and you'll never make sense. Besides, you're stealing my story—"

"That's what writers do. Something happens in their lives and they add it to the manuscript. A stolen mare is dramatic stuff."

"I thought this was a romance, not a mystery."

"Well I'm thinking of changing it to romantic suspense. It'll sell better in today's market. And when they prove it was that Nola killed that man that stole your mare—"

"You think it was Nola, do you? Look, Hen, Ruth Willmarth said Nola's a small woman. And that Ritchie was pretty big—around five-ten, she said, and all muscle, you know—the yukky good ole boy kind." Franny flipped the eggs and they came down in the pan with a slap. The grease shot over into the next burner.

"Sure, it was a crime of passion. I figure he hit her for the last time—that's what Irish male travellers do. They drink and then they hit their women. That's what that NBC documentary showed."

"Media hype—they're out for sensation. I'm betting on the uncle. Did you see that uncle when he came to Ruth's?" When Henrietta shook her head, "Well, I did. And there's something slippery about him. My hackles went right up. You see, I caught him in a slipup. He introduced himself to me and I said—you know how I like getting right to the point—"

"Don't I know."

"Yes, well, I said, 'Who's tending the farm while you're gone—three days now, is it?' I mean, I didn't know it was three days, I just guessed. And he didn't argue. He said he had a good hired man to do the work-cows have to be milked anyway, even though they're in quarantine—"

"Franny, get to the point, please. How is that a slipup?"

"Hen, think for once. Think! It means he was here the Thursday night when that Ritchie fellow got murdered. The uncle could've done it. When I said the word 'Ritchie,' a certain expression came over his face. Oh yes, you doubting Thomas, it did! The uncle was afraid of Ritchie. Dead or alive, I'm telling you!"

"How's Ritchie going to hurt him if he's dead?"

"Oh God, Henrietta, you're so dense." The eggs were burning in the pan and it was all Henrietta's fault. Franny sighed and turned them out onto a plate anyway. She'd have to eat them charred. She shoved a piece of bread down into the toaster.

Henrietta said, "Answer me, please."

Franny turned to face her, hands on her denim hips. "Because, dummy, he killed him. That's my theory. If he killed him he'll go to prison. For life! Or else fry in the chair. And some smart reporter will dig out the story behind it. Maybe the uncle stole Ritchie as a baby from some rich family and Ritchie found out and the uncle didn't want him to talk. Remember the Lindbergh baby? One theory is the father or a close relative stole that kid."

Henrietta snorted. "Who'd want to steal that hairy old Ritchie? You see the picture in the papers? Yuk. Anyway, my bet's on that Nola woman. Never mind the uncle. It was Nola."

Franny was disgusted with her partner's obtuseness. She marched over, leaned two hands on Henrietta's rocker, halted its rocking. "I saw Ritchie, remember? I'm the one who found him. No small woman like Nola could've strangled him like that with the reins. Not a big-muscled fellow like that."

Henrietta pushed out her bottom lip and stared back at her partner. "What about your darling Lady Macbeth—'unsex me here!' ho ho ho? What about that ferocious Emilia in *Othello*? You get a woman mad enough she can do anything. I could kill if anything happened to you."

Franny sucked in a breath, taken by surprise. She stared back at her partner. "Oh Hen, you idiot, you darling. I do think you would. And so would I." She leaned down to pull Henrietta up out of the rocker and give her a hug. The manuscript went flying, and Henrietta complained, but Franny just laughed and kept hugging.

The women were putting the manuscript back together, page by page, when a knock came at the door. Franny said, "Shit. Who's that?" She yelled, "Knock, knock, knock! Who's there i' the name of Beelzebub?"

It was two men—big men, the good ole boy type that Franny abhorred. They were dressed in dirty gray workpants and cheap blue shirts. They wouldn't appreciate the greeting from *Macbeth*. Beyond in the driveway was something that looked like a horse van. Not her horse van. This one belonged, she saw from the emblem on the side door, to the U.S. Department of Agriculture. Her hackles were really up now. She knew why the feds were here; she'd been warned. They were going nuts, they were rounding up all the farms in the neighborhood.

She smelled the burning toast and something burned inside her brain. She ran to the cupboard and took out the old .22 revolver her father had given her when she came out of the closet and he realized she'd be living without a man in the house.

A woman could kill, oh yes, if it came to the loss of someone, some creature she loved. "Go away," she said. "You're not taking my mare. Go away." She lurched forward, waved the gun. If that old traveller woman could do it, so could she.

The men backed off, shrugging. One of them giggled, like he didn't think she could pull it off, this shooting, and she shot over his head but heard only a click. The revolver had no bullets—she'd meant to buy some, but kept putting it off. The men smiled and pretended to be frightened. They said, "Oohh," then got in the truck and drove it up the path to the barn. "We're just doing our job," one of them called back. "You gotta sick mare, she got to be tested."

Franny and Henrietta ran after them, shouting, pummeling the men on butt, back, and shoulders. The men laughed. They'd just been hired to drive a truck, they said, but they knew a mare from a stallion. One of them led a whimpering, snorting Ophelia out to the van and, too overwhelmed even to cry, Franny jumped in after. If they were taking the mare, they'd take her.

Henrietta climbed heavily up onto the tailgate. "I'm coming too," she cried. "Give me a hand, Franny."

"Get out, out!" Franny hollered. "Who's going to take care of the other horses? You stay home, Hen, and try to drum up bucks if they throw me in jail."

"Crazy," Franny heard one of the men say, as Henrietta got out and wailed beside the van. "Nutty's a fruitcake."

"What'd you expect—they *are* fruitcakes," the other said and they both guffawed.

"Brutes!" Henrietta picked up a fallen branch and swatted the fellow with it.

Franny balled her fists. If she'd only bought the bullets. If she got through all this intact, if she got Ophelia back, the pistol would never, ever misfire again. A woman had to protect herself. "Never ever," she told the mare, and she covered the mare's flank with kisses.

THE UNCLE WAS lodged in town in the Branbury Inn. He was staying there while they did the autopsy on Ritchie's body. He had his computer, he said, he could keep in touch with his foreman by e-mail. With his cows in quarantine, what could he do back in Tonawanda "but chafe at the bit?" He'd made reservations for Keeley as well, but Maggie insisted the boy stay with her and Darren. Ruth hadn't heard the boy object.

They met for a drink at the Branbury Inn. The uncle had suggested Ruth's house, but she wanted to keep the interview on neutral ground. The inn was a nineteenth-century building, decorated with oriental rugs, mahogany paneling, and Early American reproductions. Tormey was seated on a bar stool when she arrived, in loud conversation with the female bartender. They were talking weather: how hot it was, how dry, how cold here in winter. The uncle was thinking he might settle here; it was always snowing in Buffalo. The bartender was smiling. The uncle was personable, leaning forward with his drink, elbows on the polished bar. It was three o'clock, he was the only customer.

Ruth came up behind him. "Shall we take a table?" She didn't want the bartender part of their conversation, although the uncle spoke so loudly the bartender probably would be— along with anyone else who came into the room. Ruth was sorry now she hadn't met him in her kitchen.

"Why, hello there," he said, getting up, his face florid from the drink—something foamy and yellowish. He'd had more than one, that was obvious. He grabbed her hands as though they had been long acquainted and she felt suddenly woozy, almost sick to her stomach. Why was she here anyway—what did she hope to find out from this man?

He ordered a drink for her, didn't ask what she wanted. It would be a surprise, he said—his favorite drink. Women liked it, he added, winking at her, as though he'd offered it to a hundred women and they all got down on their knees to thank him for it.

"Iced coffee, please, if you have it," she told the bartender, "and I'll pay." She wanted no gifts from this man whom she instinctively disliked.

The first question that came to her mind was "Where were you on the night of...." But that was too blunt, too obvious. So she began with his background. She'd like to know more about him, she said—as a fellow dairy farmer, like herself, in trouble. That was the approach she'd take.

"Well, born and raised in Carolina when my mother left my

old man, but eventually moved north to the family farm. I was the only one of three willing to take it on, back in '94 when the old man passed on."

Ruth could relate to that. She didn't think any of her own three would take over the farm. Her Vic seemed completely allergic to cows these days. She'd received a postcard from him recently, picturing a sandy beach with girls in skimpy bikinis hanging out on it. "Love this sweet ocean," he'd scrawled, "like to spend all summer here." Ye gods. Was this her innocent young Vic?

She asked about Ritchie and Darren, and he told her the story: How he took in his sister's boys after her illness and after Ritchie's father was first jailed in Virginia for a series of burglaries. "Wasn't easy, I'm telling you. Darren—he was a good boy, stubborn sure, but a hard worker. But that Ritchie. Jesus H. Christ. A troublemaker. Always minding *my* business, he was. Never liked the farm. Kept running back to Carolina, taking Darren with him. One day—" He stopped, pressed his lips together, took a long swallow of his foamy cocktail. His fingers traced a scratch in the tabletop.

"Yes?" she said. "I understood he was in some trouble. Maggie mentioned something about roofing repairs, dunning people?"

"Oh that," the uncle said. "That's the least of it. That's the traveller influence. The father's side. The father's mother was a whore."

Ruth was taken aback. "Literally?"

He leaned a scarred elbow on the table. He liked to shock. "Well, she didn't live in a brothel if that's what you mean. But she liked her men. Anyway—what was I saying? Well, my sister and I was close till she started to get funny in the head, and then she gave up her part of the farm. And my brother and I had that, uh, misunderstanding."

"Misunderstanding over—?"

"Land. Just land. The farm. We inherited it together after my sister pulled out, see? Split down the middle—only Mike, he wasn't interested in farming. So I farmed it and Mike took some of the profits. But I wasn't about to give him half. I did the work, right?" His face grew coarse, impassioned as he spoke, his voice bitter. He tightened his hands around his glass. "And Mike stalked off. Went off to Alaska—something about a fishing boat. But the boat sunk and Mike with it. He didn't need the land then, right? It was just and right I got the farm."

"Your sister gave up her rights. But what about Darren and Ritchie? Were they next in line?"

"Yeah, oh sure. But it's mine long's I live. It's in the will," he added in a half shout.

"You'd like Darren back, I understand. You sent Ritchie to fetch him."

"You bet I did. Darren's a good worker. I need him. Farm's all his now when I kick off—only one interested, only heir I got."

"What about Nola? With Ritchie gone?"

He bit his lower lip, looked contemplative. Then he banged his glass down on the table. "They wasn't married, was they? Nothing legal there. Nope, when they clear up all this mess, land goes to Darren."

"And to Maggie? Maggie helped on the farm, didn't she?"

"No, no, not a hell of a lot. Well some, maybe. She did some cooking. A lot of singing." He smiled. It was the first smile she'd seen from the man.

"Nola worked there, too?"

He shrugged. "Nola was okay—though she had an attitude—know what I mean?"

Ruth didn't know. She waited.

"Well she helped where she could, cleaned the barns—some of that. Tried to make up for Ritchie. Ritchie didn't pull his oar."

Ruth was amused by the water metaphor. "Even though he was in the same boat with you."

The uncle didn't get the pun. "Right. Made more trouble'n he was worth, even as a kid. Like this accident he caused—tractor. Tore my arm half off! Can't lift it above my head. It was

Ritchie's fault. He wants to drive, see, and I says no, but he jumps in the seat and roars off and I jump up to stop him and he keeps going, fast, and Holy Christ! my arm's caught in the wheel!"

He raised his arm in its white short-sleeved shirt to show he could only lift it to the height of his shoulder. He looked grim. Angry. There was a fresh scar, as well, on the arm that ran from his elbow to his neck, as though someone or some machine had attacked him there.

She pointed it out. "Ritchie did that, too?"

He stared at her, unanswering. She kept her eyes on him. He said, "Not Ritchie. How in hell could Ritchie done it when Ritchie's dead? Scar's got nothing to do with Ritchie, or anyone else for that matter. I fell out of bed, 'at's all. I'm diabetic, I got poor balance. Slipped on the rug night before I came here. Bleeding like hell, but okay, okay, I can tolerate it." He sat up straighter in his chair, stared belligerently at her.

"And when was that?" she asked. "When did you leave for Vermont?"

He blinked, seemingly confused. "It was a Thursday," he said finally. Then drew in a quick breath: "No, I was in the Horizons Bar Thursday. Left home Friday, sure." He narrowed his eyes at her. "It was after Darren called me about Ritchie. That's when I come here. Why'd I want to come any sooner?"

She cupped her hands around the glass of iced coffee. Waited.

"Well, I'd sent Ritchie to fetch Darren. All them bloody feds on my farm. Hey, look, lady, I was fighting for my farm. I'm still fighting. They took my Friesian cows, got the rest quarantined, goddamn 'em, the sumbitches. Why'd I want to come here any sooner? Answer that." He glared at her, stuck out his lower lip. He hadn't shaved that morning, the chin hairs bristled. She heard his shoes squeak when he shuffled his feet.

It wasn't a question one could answer. Ruth smiled grimly, thinking of Ritchie, his violent death, according to the coroner, the way the mare's reins had been wrapped three times about his neck.

"You'll have to tell me," she said, and sipped her iced coffee. It tasted warm and bitter, as though the coffee beans hadn't been fully ground, the ice already melted; and she left it in the glass.

# SEVENTEEN

HOME, RUTH FOUND six women seated in a circle on her lawn. They were dressed in black pants or skirts, black blouses—one wore absurd patent leather pumps with purple trouser socks. Each had a red circle painted on her forehead. Ruth felt crippled, unable to get out of her truck. It was like a time warp, back to an earlier century—the bubonic plague, the red circles on the doors to mimic the rosy rings on the plague-ridden bodies. "Ring around a rosy," she thought: the nursery rhymes that children sang, unaware. "Ashes, ashes, we all fall down."

Now the women were singing the words, their high voices splitting the quiet of the hot summer air. They were acting out the words, standing on tiptoe, waving their black cloth arms in the air; then, at a signal from the leader, falling down on the grass and lying facedown, as though dead. One of them had a sign on her back: *GYPSIES MUST GO*.

Down in the pasture she heard a wailing sound, as though the travellers had already been stricken. Over by the barn, Boadie crouched in front of the calf pens, mouth open, body trembling with fear. She could oppose a man coming for her beloved calves; she didn't know how to confront a superstition.

Ruth's heart was pumping hard—not with fear but with rage. The leader was her sister-in-law, Bertha: old superstitious Bertha, with her church cronies. Ruth jumped out of her truck, slammed the door, and charged ahead. "You get off my lawn, you Neanderthals! At once! How dare you come here and frighten my guests. Go!"

Guests, yes, the travellers were guests on her property. They were taking sanctuary here, they had every right. She would not have them frightened off. She yanked Bertha up by the sleeve of her black polyester blouse, looked her in the eye. One of Bertha's black pumps twisted as she rose. Bertha said, "Ow, quit that, Ruth."

"Then leave. Right now. And take these foolish women with you."

"When you send those gypsies away," Bertha whined. "They're the ones causing the trouble." Her plump arm swung out in the direction of the trailer, came back full circle to point at Boadie. She clutched at Ruth's sleeve; her knees bent, and wobbled. "Send them away, Ruth. For your own good. Then close off the farm. Get rid of these sick cows. That's what they're telling you to do. Did you read today's paper?" The red painted lips spit out saliva.

Ruth stepped back, she had a pain in her stomach. "What in today's paper?"

"All those letters. To the editor! Oh, not my work, Ruth—other folk. Other farmers. They're all afraid. Of what could happen to their own animals. It's not fair, Ruth. You've got to think of others. You can't be so selfish. Think of your children, Ruth, my nieces and nephew. I called my brother about it—Pete still owns part of this farm, you know that. He wants you to let the cows go. It won't be so bad. The land will be in quarantine for a few years, then it can be used again. You can start over, Ruth."

For the East Warren shepherds it was a six-year quarantine. No animals allowed to ruminate on their land for six years!

It could happen to her.

The women were marching down into the pasture, singing, "Ring around a rosy, pocket full of posies...." One of them held up a cardboard sign with red lettering: *GYPSIES KILL. GYPSIES MUST GO.*

"I don't want to start over!" Ruth yelled. She was feeling irrational now, out of control. That nursery rhyme, the red paint on the wrinkly foreheads. But her feet stood glued to the ground.

She heard Boadie wail and the calves bellow; she found her legs and ran to quiet the old lady. "Stop that noise, Boadie, stop it! They're just a bunch of ignorant women come to stir up hate." She yanked Boadie up from her crouch, tried to hug her, but Boadie wrenched away.

"They're witches—witches!" Boadie wailed. "They're after Maggie and Liz. They'll take my piggie. They're putting a spell on us. I got to stop them!" She ran down after the women in black, her arms flailing. Ruth could barely keep up with her. It *was* like a spell, Ruth thought.

"Ashes, ashes," the women sang, "we all fall down." And they tumbled in a dark heap in front of the trailer.

Maggie appeared in the doorway, her carroty hair loose in the wind. She grabbed a pitchfork by the side of the trailer, rammed the nearest black butt with its sharp tines. The woman screeched and rolled into a fetal position. The pitchfork attacked a second butt, and a third; then everyone was screeching, the pack running back up the hill. A panting Boadie snatched up the sign and ripped it in three pieces. The women straggled slowly, hollering, up toward the driveway where Bertha had left the church van; Maggie kept after them with the pitchfork. A prick in the butt, a prod in the back of a plump black-stockinged leg. Bertha had lost both of her patent leather pumps; they rolled into a fresh cow pattie.

"Go home, witches!" Maggie shouted, waving the pitchfork, "back to your dens. Back to your cauldrons. Leave us alone!"

The women piled into the black van, Bertha at the wheel. "We'll be back, Ruth," Bertha screeched out the driver's window. "You'll hear from us again. You can't win. We've got God on our side!"

Mercifully the van drove away. Maggie stood panting, grinning, on the hillside, the pitchfork dangling in her left hand. Liz ran up behind her, crying. Boadie trotted up behind the pair, the potbellied pig in her arms. The pig had grown since they'd arrived, but the old lady wasn't going to let it free. "One of them tried to take her. She tried to take Blossom," she whimpered. "They would of killed her."

"They're too squeamish to even touch a pig," Ruth said, gathering her senses. "Now stop crying, all of you. And thank you, Maggie, you were wonderful!" Ruth took the pitchfork from Maggie's arms—it belonged in the barn, she noted—and hugged the young woman. She felt the return hug and knew Maggie was weeping, too. All those centuries of hate! Ruth hugged harder, felt the strong arms around her own back.

Lord, but it felt good to be hugged. So good. It felt like, well, firm ground under the feet, a cup of strong coffee, the children home, safe, in the house. When Colm's battered Horizon drove up into the driveway and he jumped out with a copy of the local *Independent* in hand, she pulled away from Maggie and ran to hug him.

"Jeez, Ruthie," he said, "you got a stranglehold on me here, easy now, girl." But he was hugging back. His body was warm and solid in her hands. She didn't want to read the newspaper he'd brought. "Not now," she said. "Let's go inside and sit together on the couch. That's what I need now."

He scooped her up, carried her over the threshold of the kitchen door. She heard herself laughing like a schoolgirl. She couldn't help it. Colm was laughing, too. They were both laughing.

Outside by the calf pens, Maggie was singing, "Red is the rose, blue is my heart…." Boadie's trembly soprano joined in, and then Liz's sweet contralto.

"They're singing a love song. Gets me in the mood—how about you?" Colm said, and pointed upstairs.

"Colm, what about the cows? They have to be milked." She glanced at her watch. Well, she did have almost an hour. It would be kind of nice to…

"Half an hour, Ruthie, that's all—a little time-out, huh?" He put her down, circled her waist with his sturdy arms, and moved on through the kitchen. Giving in, needing him, she let him lead her up the scuffed oak stairs.

FRANNY WAS IN JAIL. She was the only woman in residence, so she had a room to herself. She thought of Virginia Woolf, a woman's need for a room of her own, and smiled at the irony. They'd taken Ophelia from her: two men, both smirking. "Just for testing," they told her—"Calm down, go back in your house." But she didn't want to go back in her house. She wanted to be with her mare. She'd fought and they'd had to restrain her, summon the cops, who took her to the local jailhouse. What could a woman do against all those men? She bit the cop, heard him yelp, reached for him again, but he slapped on the handcuffs.

The worst of it was she couldn't seem to cry. It was like it had all happened in a dream. Her precious mare gone and Henrietta trying to summon up bail. But who could dig up five thousand bucks when you could hardly get enough together each month for the mortgage on house and barn? It was a nightmare, and she just wanted her day mare.

She couldn't smile at her own pun. "Ophelia! Phelia, baby!" she shouted, and the words bounced back from the bare prison walls and struck her in the temples.

She sat on a stool in a semidaze and vegetated. She was a dun-colored vegetable, shapeless, amorphous, like a rutabaga or a head of loose-leafed lettuce. Or an onion that you peeled and peeled—and what did you have? Nothing. No name. No mare.

"Franny? Franny, love! I've got you a lawyer. He's here with me now. Franny?" The cell door grated open and there was Henrietta, like a summer's day in a hot pink shirt—was it still summer? Or had a whole season passed since they locked her in here? Hen had a young man with her; his face was a fuzzy peach. Wide green eyes, open green collar to match—at least no tie; Franny loathed men in ties. He might be eighteen—could you be eighteen and hold a law degree?

"Franny, love, I'll have the money for you by Monday, I've borrowed on my Merrill Lynch. Only one percent interest, it's nothing at all, sweetie. We'll get you out of this hellhole. Oh my

God, is that supposed to be a toilet? Gross!" Henrietta pointed to the scarred potty in the corner. Franny had used it and it wouldn't flush. Hen marched over and slapped down the lid.

The lawyer's name was Calvin Bottum. The name reminded Franny of the unflushed toilet. He was a pleasant sort of fellow but too young, oh my, much too young. "What can *you* do to help?" she asked skeptically, when she'd told him her story and he'd taken copious notes.

"We'll give it our best shot, that's what we'll do," he said with a grin that showed rows of shiny white teeth. His face fairly glowed. He actually resembled an *unripe* peach. "We can sue?"

It was a question. She gazed back at him. "How much would that cost? What good could it do?"

He spread his hands. "You might win in the end," he opined. "If they find the mare healthy."

"Well, of course she is!"

"Yes, well then you can sue for damages. Heartache, headache, mental trauma, and so forth." He was warming to the subject; his cheeks grew more peachy still. "Now if you'll give me carte blanche I'll do some homework. I'll want to know more about this man Ritchie. All I know is he gave blood up in that Canadian hospital—illegally, oh, yes. I've done some homework. Without owning up."

"Owning up to what?" Henrietta asked, her face as plump and pink as a sunset. She patted Franny on the arm—pat pat pat. Franny moved away; she wasn't in a mood to be patted. She just wanted to get out of here and find her baby, her adorable mare. It was horrible, horrible! To think what that sweet mare was enduring. What indignities, when Phelia was a full-blooded mare, descendant of True Diamond, in turn descended from Moon Glow, over in Royalton, Vermont, where the Lippitt Morgans came from.

"I understand he'd been in western Canada, buying calves for his uncle. Oh yes, I've done a little homework all right." He appealed to them for approval—those dazzling teeth. "Didn't own up at customs. You know—when they ask if you've been on a farm? And then he gave blood. No telling who has that blood in his system now."

"Oh my God." Henrietta threw up her arms—she was so emotional, Henrietta. It drove Franny crazy sometimes. "Isn't that irresponsible?" Henrietta said, appealing to Franny.

Franny didn't respond. She was confused. They wanted Ophelia because the mare might be carrying something bad, something spread by that contaminated man who stole her. Now they'd taken the mare to test for that bad thing. Should Franny have let them have her earlier? Was her precious mare really contagious to someone else? She couldn't think. The words "responsibility," "accountability" entered her head, words the Republicans were always throwing about and annoying the hell out of liberal Franny, making her feel guilty when she didn't want to feel guilty.

"Isn't that irresponsible?" Henrietta said again, and Franny said, "We don't know that that man stole her."

"What? But Franny, you said—that is, you were so sure— I mean, how else would he have got the reins around his neck?"

"It's not proof. It might have been that Nola who took her, found the man, and wrapped the reins around his neck. You don't know, no one knows."

"But Nola's contaminated too, right? I mean she was with that man. We know she was with that man. Sleeping with him, right? The newspaper said they used those infected instruments again in the hospital after that other woman died who had whatever those dreadful initials are—"

"CJD," Calvin Bottum said. "Creutzfeldt-Jakob disease. The only way to prove one has it is to examine the brain tissue— but of course by then the person is already dead." He grimaced at the irony of it. His cheeks colored.

"You mean, they'd have to kill that traveller woman to test her?" Henrietta asked, and the lawyer shrugged.

He was showing off, Franny felt. He was definitely too

young to defend her. Those teeth looked as new and gleamy as a child's first teeth. She had no confidence in lawyers anyway. It was hopeless, the whole thing was hopeless. Moreover, she didn't like the inference that only in death could the disease be proven. "Oh, my poor innocent Ophelia," she whispered.

She held herself rigid, her eyes wide to keep the tears at bay. Whatever happened, she would be stoic, she would cope. "Get me out of here, Hen, I want to see Phelia. I want to know she's still all right." She turned to the lawyer. "I want to know where they took her. Find that out for me, will you?"

She had to trust this child lawyer—what else could she do? She smiled wanly at him, and he patted her shoulder as if *she,* forty-six-year-old Franny, was the child and he the mature adult.

COLM GOT UP TWICE in the night to pee and woke Ruth each time—he'd had too much wine. A bad day was his excuse for the surfeit of wine. A house he thought he'd sold had fallen through when the young couple decided to divorce, and then Tormey Leary had gone to visit Colm's dad at the mortuary, tried to borrow money, and his dad was peeved, and summoned Colm.

"I mean, why should Dad lend him money? They hardly knew each other, they were barely related," Colm said, coming back into the room after a third trip to the bathroom. "And now this guy wants to exploit him. You know Dad would never get the money back. Not from that fellow. I mean, the guy's practically bankrupt—can't sell his milk."

"Uh-huh," Ruth said. She didn't want to think about "bankrupt." She'd been in a sound sleep and now Colm was engaging her in an unsavory discussion.

"So the guy gets all heated up because Dad won't lend him the money and the guy goes Irish and starts crying, saying he wants to leave farming, go to Alaska, and start a new life. But he needs money for that. The only thing that saved the day for Dad was a new body arriving at the mortuary. Dad asked Tormey if he wanted to help embalm the fellow and suddenly Tormey had to leave. But he'd be back, he said, sounding desperate for the money. Dad just rooted his feet to the floor and buttoned up his lips. He wasn't about to change his mind."

"Your father was right not to lend him money. Now will you please get back in bed? I have to milk in"—she checked her watch—"oh Lord, in two hours."

She'd had a bad day herself, with those kooky women marching on the trailer, then the four letters to the editor she'd forced herself to read in the local paper—people she didn't even know, full of unsubstantiated fears, protesting she was keeping her cows on the farm when they might be spreading Mad Cow. Or SARS. When there hadn't been a single case of SARS in that Toronto hospital when Nola was a patient. Why, she wondered, did those letters all at once start appearing? It was as though someone was organizing the protest. Bertha maybe?

Colm lost his footing on a rag rug and crashed onto the bed. Crack! A slat sprang loose under the mattress and the bed tilted. "I'll fix it in the morning," he said.

"It's already morning, Colm, and I'm wide awake. So fix it now, please, sweetheart, or I'll be rolling over on top of you."

"Would I mind that?"

"Please, Colm?"

He got up obediently and shoved the slat up onto the bed rung. It was a fairly new queen bed but poorly put together, so the slats had a tendency to slip out—at least they did when Colm shared the bed. Humming, he shoved up the mattress on his side and secured the slat. The sound of his humming at three in the morning got her laughing. The cockeyed slats seemed a metaphor for the absurdity of her life now, everything falling apart: a dead man, a missing woman, pirated heifers, and madwomen with red circles on their foreheads singing nursery rhymes on her lawn. And now letters to the editor calling her irresponsible, a spreader of disease—just because she wanted to keep her farm, her livelihood.

She felt like Alice falling through the rabbit hole. "Queens never make bargains!" she shouted. Colm laughed with her as he crawled back into the bed. He kissed her on the lips, those little sipping kisses like he was lapping up a bowl of soup or slurping a piña colada.

He rolled back over on his left shoulder and a second slat banged loose.

"Leave it," she said. "Just hold me so I won't fall on the floor."

"If you fall," he said, "it'll be on top of me. I'll keep holding on, Ruthie. You can count on me."

"I know," she said, as the bed sloped downward—and she clung for dear life to her lover.

COLM BROUGHT IN the morning Free Press and there it was on the first page: WILLMARTH CALVES SUSPECTED TAINTED WITH BSE. The feds, he thought, would be pissed to see it.

Though how could they expect news like this to be swept under the rug? He scanned the article; it said little beyond a few known facts. The Friesian cows had originated on a farm in the Netherlands where Mad Cow had struck down two other cows. The article did not say how the USDA knew that these calves had the disease. It ended with a mention of the calves found on the Tonawanda, New York, farm owned by Tormey Leary, and the fact that all the calves, including those on the Willmarth farm, would be taken to the government laboratory in Ames, Iowa, presumably to be slaughtered.

What would upset Ruth as much as anything, Colm knew, was that her picture headed up the piece as if it were herself, and not the calves, who were ill. The photo showed Ruth pointing an irate finger at the camera—not a flattering photo, most likely taken by the reporters who had first invaded the farm when Nola Donahue defected. The caption under the photo read, *"Woman farmer protests USDA taking her calves."* Ruth, he knew, hated the term "woman farmer."

The newspaper stung his hand, like a hot pan you pick up off the stove. He dropped it on the kitchen table, wished he could burn it so Ruth wouldn't see. But if she didn't see it someone would tell her. And undoubtedly she'd receive some kind of missive from the USDA informing her of their findings—whatever their findings were—the article didn't specifically say.

Should he take the paper to her? Try to pave the way for the bad news? How could one pave the way anyway? He had no lilies or roses to spread in his path. Just ill news that would devastate her. She'd made it through a husband's defection, a son's kidnapping, a daughter's dangerous love affair, and kept her sanity. But this time he couldn't predict her reaction.

In the past at least the farm had remained stable; the cows were milked twice daily; milk prices went up and down, but she kept her equilibrium. Now the farm was in serious danger of going under. An extraordinary emergency, the feds had called it. Jeez.

He had a nine o'clock appointment at the Realtors' office, he had to leave. He could take the easy way out and roll up the paper, stuff it back in the blue plastic container hooked to the mailbox, pretend he'd never read it. Then let her call him and howl.

But they'd promised one another to be honest, straightforward, "in sickness and health"—all that sort of marriage thing, even though she was still putting off any wedding. Colm felt their relationship to be a marriage, for they'd been together almost continuously since the travellers moved in and she hadn't objected. She needed him, he knew that. God knows he needed her! They loved each other—in or out of wedlock, it didn't matter, he just wanted to be with her.

He called the office, cancelled the appointment. He'd wait here until milking was done, greet her with coffee and the bad news. He wouldn't let her face it alone.

# EIGHTEEN

THE DRIVER Nola had hitched a ride with went suddenly quiet. She'd been talkative at first, a thin gray wiry woman with small nervous hands and broken nails, driving fifty in a thirty-mile zone. She'd bombarded Nola with questions. Now there was only the drone of the engine, the car slowing down like she might dump Nola right here in the road.

"You can let me out at the light," Nola said. They were coming to a crossroads. They were in a large town called Minesville, about a third of the way to Buffalo, according to the map she'd bought with her last dollar bill. The thruway junction sign was up ahead; she might catch a ride with someone headed to Buffalo. She'd had no news of the outside world for days now—though most of all she worried about Keeley, about leaving him with Tormey. Her neighbor, Penny Thornton, had promised to keep an eye on him, but you couldn't always count on a busy neighbor—Penny had grown children who were always coming home with problems. Nola wondered, too, what the police were up to, what they thought they knew about Ritchie's death.

Ritchie's face came into her head as it so often did—and mostly with those reins wound about his neck, his skin gone shades of green and purple. It was hard to conjure up earlier, more pleasant images. They'd lived off and on together for years now. Not good years, but there were some lighter moments—especially in the beginning, she had to remember that. Like the time he'd brought her a fistful of wildflowers on her birthday and said, "Let's go to the diner and celebrate," and they did, and made love that night on the sofa, giggling, because they could hear her brother snoring in the back of the trailer. And the time on the farm when she'd sprained her right arm, was trying to wash up after a meal, and he took the rag from her and did all the pans, scrubbed them clean while she just sat in a chair and watched a show on TV. Then he'd sat down to read a car magazine while she read the paper. They were like a long-time married couple.

But mostly there were the bad times, like when he'd come home drunk—before they'd left Carolina for the New York farm—his face like a dead man's face, and she was in the rocking chair, peeling carrots for a stew. He dropped to her feet and, clutching her legs, said, "I'm sorry, I'm sorry," a dozen times over. And wouldn't say what he was sorry for, but she smelled the lilac scent on him. She knew that scent—on a sleep-around woman in their clan. She'd pushed him off and run out into the woods behind the trailer and sobbed out her hurt and anger. And what did he do but lose his temper and shout that it was no use apologizing because she never understood him. And then he knocked her to the ground and gave her a mean kick.

Was she glad he was dead? Maybe, yeah. Well, not glad so much as relieved, like a hundred pounds had fallen off her back and now she could stand up straight. Guilt and all.

The light was green—she'd been in outer space—and they'd driven past the corner. The car was speeding up. "I forgot to remind you," she told the woman. "Would you mind stopping at the next light?" There was a light two blocks ahead, it would probably turn red by the time they got there.

But the woman just clutched the wheel like she was some race driver and zoomed around a corner just before the light. Before Nola could catch her breath—for she was feeling spooked now—a red brick building came into view, a sign read MINESVILLE POLICE DEPARTMENT. "Not here!" Nola cried, but the woman pulled up in front and jammed on the brakes. "You're going in here," the woman said.

"What? Why?" Nola asked, her nerves shooting off like

fireworks. The woman didn't answer. She was keeping her distance like she had a killer female in the car and didn't want to be stabbed or shot. Nola reached for the door handle, ready to run, but the woman was quicker. She slipped out and locked the doors from the outside and Nola was trapped. The woman ran into the police station, her heels kicking up like brown hooves, her hair ashes in the wind. The metal door clanged behind her.

Nola looked about for a heavy object, her heart thumping. If she could break a window... If she could get her body through the rear right window, which was open a third of the way... She'd lost weight from the running and the lack of food, she couldn't weigh more than a hundred pounds—she might make it. She climbed into the backseat, yanked on the window, but it wouldn't open any farther. "Hail Mary, full of grace," she whispered, wishing she had her rosary beads, but even rosary beads wouldn't open the window for her. She recalled a rat that had come into her trailer once, how she'd gone after it with a boot. How it slithered through a hole so tiny you'd think it could never make it, but the sleek body shrank to a gray streak and it vanished.

Nola knelt on the seat and examined the window. When the head got through, she recalled from helping a neighbor midwife, the body followed. It was the height of the window that was the problem—heaving her body up to push through.

She heard voices: the woman's nasal tone, and then a man's deep bass—the cops, sure. She grabbed the edge of the window and stuck her head out, sucked in belly and breast—her breasts were pancakes anyway—gave a giant push with her legs, and thrust through. Her dress ripped. It was like diving into an empty pool, landing on her palms. The pain racked her bones; it was hard gravel, a mean landing. But she was out. The cop was shouting, the woman too: she jumped to her feet and ran. The police station was on a corner, she rounded it; there was a mall up the street, people milling about. She ran into the mall, heard the whistles, voices shouting, "Stop! We need to talk. Stop!"

She didn't need to talk to any cop. She had to get to Tonawanda. She didn't want to land in any police station. The thruway was close by, she'd get a ride—they couldn't stop her now.

She ducked into an elevator, going down. Huddled there in the corner. Ignored a child's stare at her ripped clothing, got off with two other people, entered the crowd again. Had she lost the cop? She didn't know. Something on the loudspeaker, calling her name. "Nola Donahue," it called, "Nola. We want to talk to you, Nola...."

RUTH'S COWS were grazing, heads down in the field, like an artist's still-life drawings: The maternal Jane Eyre with her half-grown heifer, the spirited Esmeralda, and Charlotte 2 with her calf, born in the spring. There was loudmouth Dolly; Oprah, always first in line for food and hollering for it; Elizabeth, who'd been speared in the side by Ruth's ex-husband's mistress but pulled through and was pregnant again. And feisty Zelda, out of her sick bed, off to herself like the balky independent she was. Ruth knew them all so well, their quirks and personalities. They were her surrogate children, she'd birthed and milked and fed and nurtured them in sickness and health; she loved those cows.

How hard it was, though, to look at them and imagine them dead. Colm had shown her the *Free Press* article at eight that morning, sat her down on the sofa, his arms circling her, as if he thought she might suddenly collapse, to read the bad news. At first she just stared, she couldn't believe what she'd read. Her calves sick? Her new calves that gazed up with eyes like rich brown butter; then, released, galloped off after their mothers like young mares? Healthy, she'd have bet her life on it. Healthy!

She'd got on the phone then and called those agents, was put on hold for twenty minutes while Colm mumbled soothing words into her ears—his arms made the scenario absurd and impossible. When a human being came on the line, she expected a retraction. It wasn't her calves sick, no, couldn't be. They'd made a mistake. It was the newspaper getting it wrong.

And then the harsh truth. The apologies, for not getting right back to her. They'd intended to call today; some "arrogant" reporter had gotten there first—like it was the media's fault that the calves were taken, would probably be slaughtered; that her whole herd was now in quarantine.

Quarantine! She'd shrieked to hear the voice say it; it was like a death sentence. Her whole herd in danger of being taken away. "Zelda won't accept that," she'd hollered into the phone, and when the agent on the other end was suddenly quiet, she realized how irrational she sounded. The agent talked on and on about shared responsibility, the spread of disease, her deep apologies—"but for the good of the whole...."

She thought of the ancient ritual of stoning. An innocent woman sacrificed "for the good of the whole." Something wrong somewhere.

Afterward, Colm had mixed her a strong drink. She had one in her hand now, watching the cows—already dead in her vision. Seeing the field empty, the grass wild and overgrown, her friend Carol's sheep—gone—for they, too, would be taken. Her whole universe, empty—because of two calves brought over by Colm's Irish traveller relatives and sold to her. It was like a blaze of lightning, unexpected, striking her barn.

She balled her fists. She was angry at Colm, angry at the intruders. For the travellers were intruders. The letters to the editor were right. If they'd stayed where they came from, left her alone, none of this would have happened. She'd be milking daily and selling her milk—for a pittance maybe, but selling it. Paying her bills: to the vet, to Agri-Mark, to Allstate Insurance; paying off her ex-husband so the farm would be wholly hers.

She heard Maggie behind her somewhere, singing. Singing! When the world was dying in front of her eyes... She wheeled about, stumbled up the slope to the trailer where the woman was waltzing through the young trees and warbling, as though she had a whole audience at her feet.

"Stop that singing," Ruth cried, "stop it! Get out of here. I don't want you here. You're bad luck. You've brought us only grief. You're killing my cows! Now go in and pack. I want you off my land by tomorrow morning, the whole lot of you. You hear me, do you?" She knew herself irrational—couldn't help it. She was possessed, she was one huge ball of rage.

Maggie stopped singing. She stared, openmouthed, dropped her arms at her sides. She ran, wailing, into the trailer. Ruth ran blindly past, up to the barn, where strong arms grabbed her, turned her about, held her close.

"Mother, I heard," Sharon said, "Colm called me. Mother, it's all right, we'll get by. I'll help, a friend of mine will help in the barn. You've been getting calls from neighbors. They'll help, too, they promise."

Ruth broke away from her daughter, ran into the house, staggered upstairs, off balance—flung herself on her bed, buried her face in the pillow. It was all she could do, she couldn't work in the barn. "You'll have to help, yes, Sharon," she shouted at her daughter, who'd followed her up into the room. "You'll have to milk till they come for the herd. I want my cows content till the last minute. I can't do it myself, Sharon, I can't. I'm like—like I've had a stroke or something."

She pushed her face into the pillow. She was dry-eyed, she couldn't even cry. "You're in shock," she heard Sharon say, "I'll call the doctor."

Ruth couldn't protest. Her arms and toes were tingling, her brain and body separated, her mind hovering somewhere up on the white ceiling. No, she had no mind. She was empty, she was a black and white silhouette out in the pasture. If you touched it, it would crumble to dust.

She lay there, even when she heard voices a million years later, creaking up the stairs; someone talking softly, squeezing her arm, puncturing it with a needle, and she bore it, she couldn't resist, there was nothing left in her to act.

SHARON FOUND MAGGIE in hysterics—it was all too much. First her mother going to pieces—her pragmatic mother who usually took everything in stride. Then there was this Irish traveller who'd become Sharon's cheerful friend—but weeping uncontrollably, flinging clothing, pots, pillows, potatoes into a sack while the young sister washed dishes with a mad look on her face and the grandmother scolded the pig who had wee-weed on the linoleum floor.

"Blossom never does it, never, she's clean, she does her business outdoors," Boadie said. "But Maggie's got us upset, says we have to leave again. When we just got here! A week ago just!"

"Two and a half weeks ago, Mammy," said Liz.

"Don't contradict!" shouted Boadie. She rubbed a paper towel over the mess on the floor, then marched outside with it.

"Well, you're wrong," said Liz. She kicked aside a pile of clothing on the floor and then clanged a fry pan into the full plastic dishrack.

"You don't have to leave. Of course not, who told you that?" Sharon asked, though she knew. Her mother going bonkers, losing her temper—that was nothing new, but this time she seemed to be diving headlong over the precipice.

Still wailing, Maggie stretched out her arm and pointed a finger in the direction of the farmhouse.

Sharon drew her down onto the plastic sofa. "She's upset; she's in shock. I had a home health nurse come and give her a sedative. You have to understand, Maggie, this is her whole life. Mom's a workaholic. The cows are more than her livelihood—they're her life since Dad went off with that Violet woman."

Maggie looked interested. She quieted. "He did? Why?"

"Well, I don't know why," Sharon said, settling onto a stool. "Seven-year itch maybe. Violet was an actress in a film they were putting on in town and Dad decided to be an extra. He never did like farming, anyway. It was his dad owned this farm. So he was bored, I guess. Greener pastures—or so he thought. Violet's an ass," she concluded, "I hate the bitch."

"Then do something about it," Maggie said. "Knock her about a little."

"They live in New York City," Sharon said, although the idea appealed to her. "Is that what you'd do? Has Darren ever given you reason to, um, want to hit him?"

Maggie blew out her cheeks, narrowed her eyes. "One time especially."

"Want to talk about it?"

Maggie looked like she would. She bit her lips together. Then the words burst through. "It was the worst thing. Nola's my cousin, you know, we got the same grandmother. We went to school together. I mean she's eighteen months younger than me, but I got a late start. We did things, we were close."

"So then?" Sharon felt the drumming in her chest, the anguish over what was about to happen. Nola coming on to Darren. Or vice versa—was it Darren's fault? "Nola came on to Darren? Or Darren came—"

"No no, not Nola—though I seen Darren looking at her. I mean, I got fat thighs. Nola's got everything right where it's supposed to be. Who wouldn't look at her? She's paranoid about that scar her dad gave her, but you don't see that when she's dressed. Sometimes I think Darren's got the hots for her, but I never caught them in anything. Besides," and her voice softened, "Nola'd never do anything to hurt me. You wanna see something?"

"Uh-huh."

Maggie pulled up her sleeve and stretched out a bare upper arm. Sharon saw a tattoo. It read: *N&M* in intertwined hearts.

"Oh, sweet," Sharon said. She'd had a close childhood friend once, but they'd only exchanged a little blood, and then the friend stole away Sharon's boyfriend and that ended that.

"But what was the worst thing?" Sharon asked. "Who?"

Maggie looked at Liz, who was quietly wiping dishes. "Dump that dishwater outside," she told the girl. "Go help Mammy Boadie with her pig. She's all upset about that pig wetting the floor."

Liz stomped outside and slammed the trailer door. Maggie sighed. "That girl. She's got the worst of Ritchie. She's got his temper."

Sharon drew in a breath. "Liz is Ritchie's daughter?"

"And my sister Nan's—she's a year younger'n me. That's what I was trying to tell you. Liz doesn't know, though Boadie does. He got Nan one night when she stayed in my bed, and he thought she was me. Darren was gone—this was back when he'd just come into my life. Boadie was asleep, or Ritchie thought so, though he didn't care, he was that full of drink. Nan screamed and clawed—you look behind his ear. He's got a scar won't heal up."

"I can't look—he's dead," said Sharon.

"Yeah. Well, I hated the bastard. I was his girlfriend first, you see, before Nola. Then when I chose Darren, Ritchie was furious. I don't know why. Like I said, Nola's prettier'n me."

"Nola doesn't sing. She's quieter, I understand. You have a lot of charisma."

"Yeah? You think?"

"Definitely." Sharon patted Maggie's arm, grinned. She sometimes wondered why her own husband, Jack, had picked her out in that Sadie Hawkins dance they met at. She wasn't any glamour girl—never dressed up or wore makeup—but lots of bounce, Jack said; she got the adrenaline rolling in his body, gave him energy. She drummed her feet on the floor and smiled.

Sharon stood up; she'd promised to help Darren with the cows. She had no great love for the smelly beasts, but she wanted to see her mother through this trauma. "You couldn't possibly leave now, Maggie, so unpack that sack. Besides, Mother needs Darren, he's all she's got here to help. Cows may be in quarantine but they still need to be milked. Mother needs you, and your family. Liz has got charisma, too, just hasn't had a chance to show it, I think. You love her?"

"Of course I do, I'm her aunt."

"Ever tell her? I was told she was your little sister."

Maggie didn't answer. She got up and emptied out the sack. Liz came back in the trailer and Maggie said, "We're staying, Liz. You go get Boadie and help in the barn. Barn might need some cleaning. Darren's out discing. Cows gotta eat, quarantine or no. You know that, you were on Uncle's farm."

Liz's face puckered and Maggie squeezed her shoulder. "We'll have rice pudding for supper tonight. You like the way I make it. I'll do the dishes and maybe we can take in a movie after. That new Harry Potter film in town."

Liz's face brightened then and Sharon took her leave. "See you two," she said. "Have fun with Harry."

"Oh," Liz called after Sharon, "I meant to tell you. There was a man out in the field, looking at the cows. Seemed like he was counting them."

"Uh-oh," said Sharon. "Feds."

But if there'd been a man in the pasture, Sharon thought, he wasn't there now. She wished Harry Potter could come and save the farm. But she doubted even a wizard could help at this point.

NOLA SNATCHED a newspaper off a bench, and holding it up in front of her face, moved with the crowd out into the hall. There was something familiar about the face that stared back at her from the newsprint, but she couldn't place it. She couldn't place anything at this point. She entered the first dress shop she saw, thinking to find a quiet spot, pretend to be shopping. It was a store geared to teenyboppers—bright-colored tank tops, glittery stretch pants, and loud rap music. Ordinarily she wouldn't be caught dead in a place like this—today she found it a haven. Still feeling the panic in her chest, she snatched up a black cotton top and pair of jeans and ducked into a dressing room. She

ood motionless, holding the clothing in her hand, her heart
ouncing about like a rubber ball. Outside in the store girlish
oices rose and fell and giggled and squealed.

She gasped to see herself in the dressing room mirror. It was
ie first mirror she'd looked in since The Willmarth's bathroom
nd it was a shock. A stranger stood there, her face pale and
ruised, the cheekbones curved and raw. A puffy red scratch
in the length of one cheek. The skin hung slack on her arms;
ou could barely read the initials on the *N&M* tattoo. The dress
ie wore was so filthy and ripped she might have been one of
ie homeless, just in off the streets.

She *was* homeless. She had to accept that.

She yanked off the dress, left it in a heap in the corner of the
ubicle. She couldn't look at the mirrored image another min-
te. She stepped into the jeans—they were too long and she
olled them up. She'd grabbed a size 6 shirt—too small but she
ot it over her head, yanked it down over her starved breasts.
.t least it was black—it wouldn't call attention to itself. She
ill had her sandals, she'd at least thought to stick her feet in
iem before she left The Willmarth's—but the soles were worn
iin from all the running and walking. She sat down on the stool
o massage her sore feet. Afterward it was painful to pull the
andals back on, but she had to, she couldn't go barefoot.

She ran her hands through her hair, trying to comb it. She
ouldn't have been surprised to see it gray, but the mirror had
old her it was still dark, in spite of the trauma, the surgery, the
nxiety. It was a dull, lifeless brown, though, in need of wash-
ig. When she got out of here—if she got out—she would find
 stream somewhere and wash it and her body. Even without
hampoo or soap, the clean water would remove some of the
rime. Her scalp was itchy—was something crawling on it? She
ombed again with her fingers, then shook her head vigor-
usly, horrified at the thought of lice or ticks. She'd had them
s a child and the nuns had scrubbed her scalp with Lysol. It
as mortifying. She'd reeked for days.

Someone knocked on the dressing room door and her heart gave a crazy lurch. "It's busy," she called over the noise of the heart. She held on to the latch.

"Do you need any help? I didn't see you go in," the voice said, so close Nola could hear the woman's hoarse breathing. A fat woman, Nola thought—she'd seen her when she came in, trotting laboriously after a customer.

"No, ma'am, I'm just trying on a shirt. Making up my mind. I'll be out in a minute." Nola wished she'd picked up two shirts and two pairs of jeans—the saleswoman might not have noticed. She could walk out in one outfit like she'd come in with it and pretend she was returning the other to the racks. She wasn't a thief, a klepto—she'd been horrified once when Maggie stuffed a nightie in her bag and got away with it. But this time Nola was desperate. She was a refugee. Worse, she was a fugitive.

"Do you need another size?" the voice persisted.

"No, no, I have the right size. Please. I'll be out in a minute." When the saleswoman walked away she picked up the crumpled dress, tucked it under her arm with the newspaper. The photo leaped out at her this time and she knew, with shock, who it was. The Willmarth looked stricken, like she was pointing at some monster coming at her. The headline said her calves were sick with that disease they said Nola had. Nola felt for her rosary but of course it wasn't there. She missed it terribly, she needed to atone. If she got out of here she'd find a church, a priest. She needed to confess. She had so much to confess! Terrible things. This scourge, for one. Had she brought it on people, like that Chinese child she'd heard about who got sick with SARS and then infected millions of others?

The thought made her nauseous. She had to get to a priest. She'd spotted a Catholic church as she ran from the police station—she'd go back there and seek sanctuary. She should have thought of that before. She'd go to a confessional, pour out her soul, her sins, cleanse herself before she moved on west.

Because she had to move on, she had to get to Tonawanda. She had to find Keeley. They'd been separated far too long—he needed her. He was still so young, a child of her own youth. She hadn't wanted him at the time, knowing he'd be without a father. But now he was everything to her.

She had to find him, she had to get him away from Uncle.

She opened the dressing room door a crack and peered out. The saleswoman was slapping blouses back on a rack. A group of teenagers were rolling in, swooping down on the racks and tables, laughing, chattering, grabbing up shirts and running to the mirrors. This was the time. Clutching her rolled-up dress and newspaper—she'd toss them into a trash can—Nola slipped out, made for the entrance.

"Miss. Miss!" It was the saleswoman, she'd seen Nola. "Stop, miss! What've you got there? You'll be stopped outside. You can't get away with—"

An alarm sounded, a high-pitched shriek that split her ears. To her left a pair of cops were running toward the store, and for a moment everything blurred: shops, shoppers, cops—if she didn't keep moving she'd turn into a pillar of salt. Already she felt the salt in her throat.

She ran out a door marked EXIT and found herself in an alley. A warehouse loomed to the left so she turned right and ran to a parking lot. She dodged in and out of cars and trucks, found an open door in a car, and, exhausted, crawled in and curled up on the backseat. She no longer cared; she couldn't go on. Footsteps and voices approached, increased in volume, and thumped on past. She closed her eyes and sank into a semi-slumber that slowly deepened into sleep.

SOMETHING WAS WRONG with Zelda. She was acting strange. She'd leap into the air, then crash down on her bony knees. Then up again, twisting into an impossible S—tail slashing the muzzle, hind hoof pummeling the jaw; mouth wide open and foaming—bellowing out her anguish. Lurching about the pasture—

udder heaving. Slamming against the bewildered cows, crashing again and again against the electric fence. Then through it—a howl more human than bovine—racing to the beaver dam. Leaping in, thrashing about in its brown waters. A shot! and a shriek, the cow sinking slowly into the reddening deep. Zelda!

"What is it, Mother? Mother, it's Sharon. You were crying out. Mother. Wake up. Answer me, Mother!"

Ruth was swimming. Thrashing and beating through the bloody murk, clutching the cow about the throat, hauling it out, up onto the bank. The trees dead here, bare hollow logs chewed by beavers. The cow a crumple of skin and bones; one accusing eye glaring into Ruth's. Gleaming in the sun like a shard of splintered glass.

Ruth sank down beside it and wept.

# NINETEEN

JAMES PERLMAN turned down the aisle in Shaw's Supermarket and found himself face-to-face with his ex-wife. She had a look of triumph on her broad rouged face, as if she'd caught herself a big fish. Maureen liked fishing, she liked squeezing worms onto the hook. It made James sick to watch—he felt himself to be that worm, at least in Maureen's eyes. She had always looked down on him—at least ever since her father had tried to discourage her from marrying him. "James won't amount to anything, you'll see," Maureen would quote her father as saying. And smile as she quoted.

"Well, James," she said, "I see you've been in the papers recently. Those letters to the editor? Was that a good idea? Putting yourself in front of the public like that?"

He wondered how she knew. He'd used a fictitious name. But he didn't respond to her innuendo. There was no point, she'd just shove him back on the hook. "I have to get to a meeting, Maureen. I can't stand here and talk."

A young woman was hustling down the aisle, pushing a cart with a baby in it. She was an attractive woman; she caught James's eye and smiled. He smiled back. He was embarrassed to be seen with Maureen. He turned away, but the ex followed him with her voice. He loathed that voice, it was always accusing. Like there was still scum on the dishes he'd washed; upstairs toilet not flushed; front door unlocked—they might've been killed in their beds, according to Maureen.

"I'm Irish, remember?" Maureen said. "On my mother's side?"

How could I forget, he thought, her mother was all she

talked about, her "darling" Irish mother, who brought her up "the right way"—Roman Catholic. And he, born to a Jewish father and a Methodist mother, both of them nonchurchgoers and proud of it.

"Those O'Neill brothers aren't real gypsies at all," she went on—"the papers said so. They're Irish, James. You can't paint everyone with the same brush just because you hate me. That's prejudice, James. P-R-E-J—"

"I can spell, it," he said. He kept moving. He'd forgotten what he'd come for. He had two items in the cart, he'd push it to the express checkout. He'd get in his car and go home. He didn't really have an appointment, he just needed to get back to his sheep.

"You're spreading rumors, James—you did that in the Buffalo hospital, remember? It was one of the things got you in trouble? Rumors about the head nurse? When you had no cause, you were just getting back because she'd caught you—"

He wheeled about, stared into her made-up face. "Who's spreading rumors now, goddammit! What'd you tell everybody on the street about me back then? Why'd we have to move, huh? Because of you. You! It's not rumors I'm writing about—it's facts. You read the papers lately? Those calves got the BSE thing. It could spread to my sheep."

"Sheep don't get BSE, they get scrapie. You should know that."

"Never mind. The feds are already after me, they paid me a visit. It wouldn't of happened if those Irish travellers hadn't appeared. And they're still there! That Willmarth woman lets them stay."

She was pushing her hot pink face toward his and if there hadn't been two carts between them he'd have slapped it. "And don't you spread any Christly rumors in this town, you hear? I don't want to have to move again. You keep your mouth shut, hear?"

The lipsticked mouth was leering at him, made him sick to his stomach. He ran with his cart and accidentally rammed the cart with the baby. He nodded his apology and the young mother frowned at him. They were all alike, women. He was glad, yes, glad to be living alone. There were three people lined up at the express checkout. He thought he heard Maureen breathing behind him. He hated the woman. He hated the poets' names she was always dropping, like she was some genius herself when she couldn't put two lines together—he'd seen the crappy verse she wrote each year for their daughter's birthday. Moon, croon, swoon and all that mush. He hated the Irish she gabbed about—their boozing, their poetry, their blue eyes (his were coffee-colored brown), their talk, their endless talk talk talk like they were some brilliant misunderstood race and superior to the mixed English Protestant and Russian Jew he stemmed from. "Never mind Shakespeare and Dante," she'd said to him one day. "Read Yeats and Shaw, they say it all." And that was the beginning of the end with him. Never mind he couldn't understand a word of Shakespeare—the Bard was his fellow man, and he didn't want him slighted.

Who was Dante, anyway? Well, never mind. He threw the Charmin triple roll of toilet tissue, the Gillette foamy shaving cream, and the latest copy of the *Independent* on the counter and tugged out his wallet. While the three women ahead of him were checking out, he eyeballed the paper and nearly choked. There was a photo of the Willmarth woman, her finger pointing right at the reader, right at him, James Perlman, like he was to blame, like she too looked down on him. Like he was her next victim.

And then the headline: WILLMARTH CALVES BELIEVED TAINTED WITH BSE. It was like a grenade exploded in his face. It was here then, they'd proved it. That off-balance, brain-rotting disease that could translate into even scarier initials,.TSE and CJD. Already *he* might have it; it was like a bomb ticking inside the heart, and one day—bango! It went off and you wasted away, fast, like a top spun out of control.

But before that—his sheep, his precious sheep he'd spent his savings on, the precious little money left over from the divorce… She'd socked it to him, wanting half of everything—their former house, their sailboat, his annuities, his hospital pension—even though she was the one who left him. Christ, it wasn't fair!

She sailed past him with her cart, chin high, like he was some scum she'd stepped in and then wiped off her shoes. He hated her, the Irish bitch. Hated her!

"Sir? Do you have a Shaw's card?" The girl behind the counter was frowning, waiting for him to pull out his card. She couldn't be more than sixteen, a plump teenybopper. He'd have to watch her or she'd overcharge. Her name was Eileen, according to the name tag she wore on her maroon blouse.

Irish, he thought, and slapped the orange Shaw's card down on the counter.

Let her pick it up.

FRANNY WAS OUT on bail, but there was no bail for her mare. The child lawyer was no help at all. He couldn't stand up against the feds, they had Ophelia—wouldn't say where. It might be the knackers for all Franny knew. She was sick at heart. She was just going through the motions now with the other horses, long cheerless rides in the countryside. Hamlet was quiet this Sunday afternoon as they entered the swamp woods, like he knew what was going on. He was off his feed; she worried he might go on a hunger strike. Horses knew, they couldn't speak but they knew, they intuited, they were smart. She dismounted, leaned her head against him to hear his heart beat, and he nickered softly, cocked his head. They stood like that for long minutes. The swamp was almost dry here from the intense heat: leaves and brush crackled underfoot. Ophelia was gone, Hamlet knew that. The feds didn't care, they saw things in black and white, there was no gray. It was like being lesbian, Franny thought: a label they slapped on you because you were different. Lesbians burned their bras, lesbians hated men, lesbians were aggressive, they were antisocial, they wore their hair short and their boots low-heeled with spikes to kick men with.

Franny wore her hair long and so did Henrietta. Franny liked men to talk to-at least she had until the feds came along—now she was wholly disillusioned. Henrietta had been married once, had a grown son living down in Jersey—a son who no longer spoke to her after she divorced her husband and had a civil union with Franny. Hen didn't mention him very often now, but Franny knew it was a sore that wouldn't heal. The bastard. The blind, biased bastard.

Well, that was one man Franny could do without.

She'd poured all this trouble into the ears of the congregation in the local Unitarian Universalist church, a place where lesbians, blacks, Jews, gypsies—you name it!—were welcome. Everyone groaned during the Joys and Concerns when Franny told about the feds taking her horse. People rushed up later to fling their arms about her, wanting to help. All kinds of compassionate people: straight, gay, black, yellow, white.

But what could they do? The feds had the mare. It seemed hopeless.

She tethered Hamlet and trudged through the brush to the area where she'd found the dead man, the one who'd stolen Ophelia. The place was still beaten down, a yellow crime scene tape strung loosely around it and partially ripped. This was the second time she'd been here since the terrible discovery; something kept drawing her back. Like there was more to know, more to find. She bent her back to it, poured all her concentration into the dumb work of searching the bushes. Stems and limbs snapped, leaves dropped off, withered from the heat. She pulled up broken nests, dead branches, an occasional empty bottle, although few, it seemed, had come here.

She found nothing; she hadn't really expected to. She made her way back to Hamlet, offered a carrot from her pocket, and this time he took it. He'd been pawing in the dry muck, made a hole with his hooves: dry leaves, prickly limbs, and dampish earth were heaped up on either side of the hole. And in the center of the debris, something shining. She leaned closer to examine it, and sucked in her breath. It was a small gold cross—attached to a narrow black leather ribbon. She held it up to the sun, squinted. It looked like it might have been bitten, the way the leather was all jagged as if from teeth—a mare's teeth? As if the mare had fought back, tried to bite the hand that kept it captive. She turned it over, but saw no initials. The word "evidence" came to mind. This was evidence, something the police had not found. The cross might have belonged to the person who stole Ophelia.

Would that Ritchie have worn a cross?

Yet it was a small cross, like one a woman would wear.

Nola, she thought. It was that Nola. The papers said Nola had killed Ritchie, and now she knew. The scene came clear in her mind. Nola had taken the mare, and Ritchie, the horse trader (according to the papers), had found her. There had been a struggle, and Nola, on the mare, strangled the man with the reins. Ophelia had fought back, pulled the cross from the woman's neck, bitten through the leather, and the cross dropped into the underbrush.

The traveller woman had had the mare, oh yes. She knew how to ride without a saddle. Gypsies were brought up riding bareback, were they not?

Call the police, an inner voice told her. She unclipped the cell phone from her belt, held it in her hand.

But police were prejudiced, too, police were just good ole boys who wore badges. Would they believe her? They'd looked at her suspiciously enough when she found that dead man. She'd seen cops on TV, shooting a dozen bullets into an African-American who was only a suspect—no proof at all! She'd taken part in the New York City peace rally where five thousand cops on foot and horseback piled up barriers to keep her and thousands of other peaceful demonstrators away from the main speakers. Fear in the air like a guided missile.

All that targeting of people who were "other," like herself and Henrietta.

The thought that she, too, might be prejudiced entered her mind, but she tucked the thought away. Her mare came first, before any person, traveller or nontraveller—well, after Henrietta, that is. She wanted her mare back. She wanted the person who took Ophelia punished. It was only right. The police, she told herself, would bungle the job.

She punched in the number of the Willmarth farm. Ruth had smarts. Ruth would know what to do with the gold cross. Ruth had those travellers there. The travellers, she bet, would know whose cross it was.

THIS TIME COLM let the phone go on ringing. There was nothing more he could say to people. She's fine, he'd lied to the few he talked to; she was simply blown away by the bad news. She'd rally and fight—didn't she always? But jeez, the messages were piling up on the answering machine. Sympathetic farmers, worried farmers; understanding neighbors, angry neighbors.

Something now on the machine about "evidence." That horsewoman, wanting to speak to Ruth. "Desperately, Ruth, please, something I found. Call me back, Ruth, at once! Oh, Ruth, they won't let me see my darling, won't tell me where she is, Ruth I can't—"

Mercifully, the machine ran out of space.

Colm poured a little booze into his third cup of coffee. He'd taken an afternoon off work, told his dad he couldn't help in the mortuary, just plain couldn't. Ruth was his responsibility now. She was upstairs sleeping, she'd slept sixteen hours straight since they'd given her the sedative. Sharon was out in the barn with Darren; she wanted Colm to help. But he had to be here in case Ruthie awoke, didn't he? Anywhere, frankly, other than in the barn with those huge salivating, defecating animals.

In some ways, he almost hoped the cows *would* go. She'd

move to town, they'd rent an apartment or house together, live like ordinary folk. He could train her in real estate. She'd be good at it; she liked people, people liked her.

The phone rang again and the throbby voice filled the room. Franny had been an actress—good thing she'd quit. "Ruth, I can't just sit here with this thing in my hand. You're probably down in the pasture. I'm coming over now. Now, Ruth! I'll find you."

"Jesus," Colm said aloud, and poured in more whiskey. Already his hands were shaking.

Someone knocked and then crashed through the kitchen door before he could answer.

"I came to take a shower," Maggie said. "I need it, Colm. Boadie was giving the pig a mud bath and the bloody thing shook all over me. It was me give her the damn pig and I'm sorry for it now." Her muddy self confronted him, like she needed his permission to take a bath.

"Be my guest," he said. They had all the blood samples— why not use the bathroom?

But Maggie wanted to talk. "How's she doing? She come out of her funk yet?" When he spread his hands, she said, "I had a cousin spent a whole year in her room after she lost her boyfriend, wouldn't come out. Her mama put food by her door and found the plate empty in the morning, so she must of come out to take the food. But she never went outside, nuh-uh. Mother of God, a whole year this went on!"

Colm didn't need to hear any more good news. There was a black Mercury rumbling down the road, passing the farm for the fourth time since he'd arrived. Vermont license, but too clean, too free of dust to be a Vermonter in the driver's seat. He didn't like it. But what could he do? He waved Maggie into the downstairs bathroom, listened to the shower run, watched the steam pour out from under the door. He went upstairs with his cup, stood over the bed where Ruth was asleep on her side, a fall of hair covering her face. He wanted to talk to Ruth about that rented car. Full of feds, he bet. "Ruthie?"

There was no reply, only the deep, erratic breathing, an occasional moan like she was dreaming of lost cows. She was still in her barn clothes. Sharon had tried to undress her but Ruth would have none of it—she'd fought even in her sleep. If she didn't come to by tomorrow morning, Colm decided, he'd take her to the hospital. Of course, Ruth had no health insurance, couldn't afford it—she'd be furious if he took her to the hospital.

Another thought occurred to him. She hadn't peed in hours—had she? He pulled back the covers, but the bed was dry. Jeez, she must have to do something…. "Ruthie?" He said it again louder, then shook her. This was getting to be ridiculous, she had to wake up and face life. Colm's great-great-grandfather had come over from Ireland during the famine. He'd buried his parents and left his farm: he knew what it was to lose everything. Ruth had to learn to face adversity.

"Ruth, wake up, goddammit. They need you in the barn."

She opened a rich brown eye, it glared at him through the tangle of hair. Then shut again. She pushed deeper into the covers. The voice came back at him as if from underwater. "Go 'way. Leave me 'lone. Go 'way."

Downstairs a familiar voice was hollering: "Ruth—Ruth? Ruth, it's Franny, I have something to show you I found in the swamp. Sharon said you're upstairs in bed. It's important, Ruth, it can't wait. Ruth? Can I come up?"

"Jesus," Colm said, and ran downstairs to ward off the woman. And was knocked over by the smell of horse. The heat intensified the smell; he clapped a hand to his nose. At the same time, the bathroom door opened and there was Maggie, a mere towel between her bare self and the world. Her red hair was wet and wild, her head haloed by steam. "I forgot to bring clean clothes," she said.

"She was taking a shower," he told Franny, aware of the stupid grin on his face. "My cousin's wife," he added, seeing Franny's open mouth. "My third cousin, to be exact. Well, maybe fourth, I don't know. They're the ones who live in the trailer.

You two've probably met. You just didn't, um, recognize her."
He pointed.

"I came to see Ruth," Franny said, her blinders on, and
started upstairs. She had something dangling from her fingers.
Colm couldn't make it out because of the steam hanging in the
air from Maggie's shower.

"You can't go up there. She won't see you. She won't see
anyone." He held her back by the arm.

"What's that in your hand?" Maggie cried, and lunged toward Franny. Her towel fell off and Colm had to look—what
else could he do? He gave up, sank into a chair. It was too much.
Too too damn much. Naked women, hysterical women, crazy
women! He was wishing he was back in his father's mortuary.
Dead people didn't shout and run around naked.

"That was Nola's. What were you doing with that, you!"
Maggie held up the object. Colm saw a small gold cross hanging from a leather cord. It looked like any gold cross to Colm,
but Maggie seemed to recognize it. She was turning it over in
her hand, pressing it to her chest. Colm tried not to look at Maggie—but what could a man do? He was here first.

"I knew it! It was Nola took Ophelia from my barn!"
Franny cried.

"What? She never!" yelled Maggie, waving a towel, like any
minute she'd wrap it around Franny's neck. "Nola's afraid of
horses. Why would she go and steal one?"

"She had one later, didn't she? They saw her and my baby at
that orchard." Franny smiled grimly, she had reason on her side.

"That doesn't mean she stole it in the first place." Maggie
wrapped the towel about her torso, grabbed up her bundle of
dirty clothes, stomped out of the kitchen.

"It's evidence. I found it in the swamp. You can't take evidence!" Franny cried, and ran out after her.

Colm let them go. He wasn't in cop mode today. He just
wanted Ruth back in his life.

Though it was an interesting thought. The traveller woman

stealing that horse. Possible, he supposed. Even if she was leery of horses, it was a means of getting away. Besides, who could believe what Maggie said? Colm had had a few bits of dialogue with Maggie that didn't add up.

Or had someone gone to the swamp later and planted the cross? He had to think of that.

The thought struck him that Nola might have ridden the horse into the swamp where she'd feel safe, and Ritchie found her there and she strangled him. A furious woman could strangle a bigger person than herself, he was certain of that—he knew his Ruthie. The fury could do it. If so, he thought, they'd have to find Nola. And soon.

Through the window he saw the two women running down into the pasture. Franny was gaining on the younger one. Goddammit, he didn't need to have to break up a fight between two screaming females. But jeez, he'd have to go into his cop mode, run them down.

He dashed outside. "Hey! Stop! Will you both stop? Let me have the damn thing—it's evidence."

"Evidence! What did I tell you?" Franny hollered back over her shoulder, and kept on running.

SOMETIME IN THE MIDDLE of the night Ruth staggered up out of bed, stood a moment, ghostlike in her tan coveralls, then headed for the closet. Afraid of what she might do there, Colm led her to the bathroom, where she peed in silence. He might have been a nurse, or no one at all—certainly no one of importance to her.

He handed her the toilet paper and she wiped herself, pulled up the coveralls, then turned and shuffled back zombielike into the bedroom.

He wasn't going to let her get away with it. He turned on the light, shone it in her face. "Ruthie. It's me, Colm, your lover. Talk to me, Ruthie."

She rolled over on her left side, her rump bumping up whalelike under the sheet.

"Ruthie, we have new evidence." He described the gold cross, told how he and Franny had wrestled the cross away from a shrieking Maggie. "It was a scene, I'll tell you. The potbellied pig got loose in the middle of it, the old lady running after, screaming like a banshee. Maggie pulling Franny's hair—then throwing potatoes at me, a whole bushel basket of 'em, jeez— I'm all black and blue. Look." He dangled an arm in front of her face. Tried to make her laugh.

Ruth didn't move. But she was awake, he knew she was awake. He knew the strong, raspy breathing of her sleep mode—and this time it was shallow.

"So this proves Nola did it, right? We'll get the prints off the cross, prove it. She strangled him with the reins and then took off with the mare. Franny thinks the mare got into the fight, too, bit the cord right off Nola's neck. Quite a scene, huh?"

Ruth burrowed deeper into the pillow and finally Colm gave up. He needed the sleep himself. He'd promised Sharon he'd get up at four-thirty and help prep the cows. It was a dirty, smelly business, prepping cows, but his conscience made him agree. His watch read one-fifty. Less than three hours till he'd have to get up. He'd have to sleep fast. He turned out the light.

He spooned into Ruth's back, shoved an arm under her pillow, and draped the other arm around her breast. She always liked that position: it was intimate, warm, loving; she'd give soft sighs that made his eyes water.

Tonight there was silence. He sighed, but kept his arms around her. He was afraid to let go.

# TWENTY

COLM WOKE UP to a series of screams from outside and, sitting up, cried, "Wha?" Ruth made a gurgling noise in her throat when he pulled his arm out from under her pillow but she didn't move. There were more screams, a loud banging on the kitchen door. A flickering light filled the open south window, but it wasn't yet dawn. His watch read three-ten.

"What's going on?" he hollered, and Darren's voice yelled back, "Trailer's on fire. Call somebody!"

The screams grew louder. Colm dialed the fire department. "Willmarth farm," he shouted into the receiver. "Fire down back in that trailer. People sleeping there. Hurry!"

Though he doubted anyone was still sleeping with all the noise. He stuck his bare feet into shoes and started out the door.

"Wait," Ruth said.

He turned and there she was, sitting up, the whites of her eyes reddish, like a feral cat. "I'm coming," she said. "No, don't wait. Just go. I'm behind you. It's those letter writers did it."

"Huh?"

"The ones who wrote the letters to the editor. They hate travellers. They hate me."

"Ruthie, no—it's probably Boadie left a candle going. Damn pig knocked it over."

But Ruth was awake and talking. She was running out behind him in bare feet. "Put on your shoes," he called back, but her feet kept slapping along. He was done arguing with her. He ran. He heard cows bellowing in the field, Maggie's mutt barking, the pig squealing—Old MacDonald's farm on fire. Then the fire engines, streaming into the drive, men unreeling hoses, feet stomping the ground—what would happen to Ruth's Christmas trees?

Ruth's voice rose above the other noises, directing them to the trailer—though who could miss it? Flames were leaping out, smoke coiling into the air—the trailer was frail enough to begin with. Figures were pulling stuff out the back: lamps, rugs, screens, boxes, and more boxes. "Watch it!" he cried. "Firemen coming. Don't go back in, you'll get burned."

No one listened. He made out Darren and Maggie—the latter dressed in a thin nightie—but at least dressed. Boadie, clutching the pig to her chest. Liz, leaping out of the back of the trailer, collapsing on the ground, and Maggie running to her, screaming. The firemen racing down with their axes and hoses. There was water everywhere, soaking the earth, the trees, people, animals. "Good for your trees, anyway," he hollered at Ruth, but she wasn't listening.

It was like facing an oncoming wave. Colm backed off and ran into a drenched Ruth. She shoved past him in her wet coveralls, her hair flat to her scalp, shouting orders, like she was the fire chief. She was pushing the old lady out of the spray, ordering Liz, "Stay put, dammit, you want to die from smoke inhalation?" Ordering Darren and Maggie, "Take your valuables up to my kitchen. They'll get watersoaked here, trampled on. And don't look back!"

Colm wasn't immune to her orders. "Colm, go back to the kitchen and see to these people, quiet them down. Get them something to drink—hot cocoa."

"Cold milk?" he suggested, a furnace himself. "Iced coffee?"

"Just do it," she said.

AFTER THE FIREMEN LEFT and the place was a charred desert (or so he imagined), when he and the angry, weeping travellers were sitting around the kitchen, dripping onto the scuffed linoleum—the door cracked open and Ruth reappeared.

"Well?" she said. "What happened? How'd it start?"

The weeping and wringing of hands ceased; they looked at one another. No one spoke.

"You were all sleeping, I suppose," Ruth said. "No one left a cigarette burning? Maggie?"

"Not me!" Maggie cried, "I'm extra careful, I never—"

"A burner going on the stove?"

"Turned it off. I always do." yelled Boadie. "'Less Darren left it on, he was the last one up."

"Not me," Darren said. "I always check to see if Maggie dropped a fag or Boadie left the burner on. Or Liz didn't snuff her secret candle after lights out."

"I never. Didn't! Don't!" the women cried, and then went quiet, their eyes pleading with Ruth for support.

"Sometimes," said Liz, pointing at her sister and then at Boadie, "you do." Then it was a brouhaha as the three females lashed out at one another. Colm put his hands over his ears. All he wanted was to go back upstairs and sleep. But now they had four guests in the house. And a pig. Jeez.

"Okay," said Ruth, "Colm and I will go back down with a flashlight and take a look. Don't touch anything down there— nothing! There's no rain in sight. Your things won't get wet out there on the ground."

"They're already ruined from those hoses," Boadie complained, and Maggie burst into loud sobs. Darren put his arms around her and rocked her.

Colm shut his eyes. He couldn't take all this, he couldn't. Was he still supposed to go out—he checked his watch—in one hour and prep the cows? The cows were probably spooked, too, by the yelling and the fire. God knew what mood they'd be in. He'd once been kicked and fouled with manure, helping Ruth tag the cows' ears. He wouldn't want to repeat the experience.

Ruth was busy pulling pillows, sheets, and towels out of a downstairs closet. She ordered Maggie and Darren into daughter Emily's room—"a double bed there, Keeley can have the couch, and Boadie and Liz, you can have Vic's room. Vic won't be back till late next week. By then—well, God knows what by then. We'll just have to get you another trailer, that's all. You have insurance?"

"Just minimum insurance—I didn't read the fine print." Darren shook his head woefully.

"We'll worry about that in the morning," Ruth said. "You coming, Colm?"

"So everyone gets to sleep but us?" Colm complained as they went out into the charred night. A blanket of heat enveloped him; he waved it off but it clung to his skin. This time at least Ruth had pulled on her boots. She seemed full of beans; after all, she'd had almost twenty hours of sleep. His joy at Ruth's revival was over; he just wanted to go to bed. He wanted the travellers to go back to New York. Maybe they would, with their trailer burned up—that was a hopeful thought. It was a fiery, smoking ruin when the firemen departed.

But Ruth had him by the wrist, dragging him with her, down into the scorched pasture where the astonished cows were standing in line behind Zelda, staring at the ashen remains; he could see their dark silhouettes in the half-moon that, oddly enough, was still shining down at three-forty-five in the morning. But then, everything was out of sync these days. He remembered that black Mercury, patrolling the road.

"Let's wait till daylight, go back to bed," he argued, his last shot. "We won't find anything in the dark."

She was pulling him onward, as though they were heading down into Hades. The downward slope increased their momentum, they were practically running—Ruth so crammed with energy he could hear the adrenaline pumping in her toes.

"It was arson," she said. "You bet your boots it was arson. Someone—some *ones*—who wanted these people out of here. Who wanted my farm destroyed."

She was yanking him forward so fast he was flying. "Jeez, Ruthie, have a heart." But her fingers were steel on his wrist.

They were at the trailer site now, the ground was still soaked from the hoses, the fire done but the air a reddish color, smoke curling up into it—an unbearable stench. Ruth was sweeping her flashlight around in wild circles. The light landed on something, passed by, then came back. She stooped for a closer look, then cried out loud, a whooping cry like a savage with his trophy scalp.

*GYPSIES MUST GO,* the watersoaked sign read. She waved it in Colm's face.

"It was that bitch Bertha set it," she said. "You bet. Her and her circle of witches. But she'll be sorry. Oh, but she'll be sorry! I'll kill her. I'll just kill her!"

"Calm down, Ruthie," Colm said, ducking, where the sign was swinging about his head. "We don't know it was Bertha." Though himself he wouldn't put it past the kooky woman. She'd stirred up enough trouble in the past. Still, he couldn't have Ruth confronting her. Not in this killing mood. But Ruth was rampaging on. She was heading back up the hill—that was a good sign. With luck they'd grab an hour's sleep before dawn.

Though it wasn't the house Ruth was headed for, dragging the sign with her. It was the barn.

"You coming?" she called back. "I could use your help."

Jeez. What could he do but follow?

CHILDREN'S VOICES woke Nola. It was barely dawn. She glanced up, a sign read SKY VIEW MOTEL. Car doors opened, a woman's voice said, "Hurry now, guys, we gotta hit the road. Angie, stow those bags careful—don't drop anything! Look where you're going, Seth."

A heavy bag dropped on top of Nola; she sat up, stared into an adolescent boy's eyes. "Hey," he said, and his mother said, "Just settle down and keep quiet. I can't drive when you're all yelling and fighting."

Nola put a finger to her lips and quietly slid out the far side of the car. She banged into a small girl just getting in and the girl dropped her package. The child shrieked and the boy gave a high-pitched giggle. "What's going on back there?" the mother yelled, and craned her neck about.

Nola fled.

She was disoriented now, she didn't know where the street was she'd first run down, the one with the Catholic church. For that was her goal: to find a priest, go to confession. She felt slightly more energy from the sleep in the car, but her body ached from the uncomfortable position she'd assumed between hair dryers and kids' toys. Her upper body was heavy on her hips and legs, it was like she was carrying a dozen bags full of groceries. She could hardly move her legs. If she ran into the cops she wouldn't be able to run. She thought of giving herself up to the police, taking a chance they'd understand her story.

Yet how could they, when she hardly understood it herself? It was like one of those nightmares of running and running and never getting anywhere. She'd had brain surgery, she'd been hustled off to Vermont and left some infected woman dead in the hospital behind her—they wanted her back. And then the world began to close in on her—it was like a tug-of-war. Ritchie was wanted, too, he'd given blood, and lied about the farm he'd come from in the States. Lied about the drugs he'd taken, too. Ritchie—turning violent, angry, wanting her to flee with him, and her wanting only to be her own self. Enola—Alone—wanting to escape Ritchie.

But then he'd caught her, and afterward the terrible thing, the unspeakable thing, happened.

And now she was running from the whole world, like she was carrying the sins of a million people on her paper-thin soul, and people were hunting her down to throw stones, make her their scapegoat, cleanse themselves.

It was a dark morning, starting to rain, and she felt safer. She moved out into the street. Seeing a woman coming in the opposite direction, she asked, "Ma'am, can you tell me where I can find a Catholic church?" When the woman looked at her, she felt she had to explain. "I'm due there for a—a breakfast meeting and I seem to be, uh, lost."

The woman shrugged. "I'm new in town, too. And I'm not Catholic. But there's three or four churches all in a row on Main Street. You can go look there." She pointed a stubby finger to a street on the left.

Nola thanked her and moved in the direction of the finger. She found herself back on the main street; the mall she'd run into was at the far end. She'd moved, it seemed, in a wide circle; her chest burned to realize that. To get to the church she'd have to pass the mall. She could either go back down a side street and then take a street she'd been on earlier to avoid the mall, or she could walk straight down Main on the opposite side—the fastest way—past the mall, till she reached the church. She decided to chance it. The police wouldn't expect to find her on Main Street, would they? No, she decided, they would not.

But the church door was locked. Only an outside light lit up the outer steps. The weight in her chest was terrible now, she could hardly walk. But she had to get into that church. Why had they locked it? At home in Carolina there was always a door open into the sanctuary for a soul in need. There must be needy Catholics here in Minesville. She ran around behind the church and tried all the doors.

None were open. She wept in her defeat and sank down on the back steps. She'd have to wait. Though it was Monday now, she figured—would anyone come to the church on a Monday morning? She should move on. But she was still exhausted. There was a small enclosure, a kind of porch, where someone had left a pile of used clothing. She tugged on a cotton sweater over the black tank top, wadded up a pair of overalls to make a pillow, and curled up on the painted boards. She was oh, so, so tired....

When a pair of thick legs in gray work pants loomed up in the dim light she opened her eyes wide: Where was she? A leg kicked her ankle, a hand clasped her arm, and she staggered up. The face was scarred, the nose a red bulb, the chin full of straggly black hairs. It was the ugliest face she'd ever seen. She tried to shake off the hand and run back down the steps.

But the hand held her fast.

# TWENTY-ONE

IT WAS AS IF a party was going on in Ruth's house Tuesday noon and she hadn't been invited. Someone had broken out her best glasses and the wine was going round, hand to hand. "Hey there!" Boadie cried, as if Ruth were a newcomer. "Have a glass."

Even the potbellied pig was sopping up dribbles of wine and cracker crumbs off the floor. Maggie's mongrel had Ruth's favorite barn cat cowering, whining, on top of the refrigerator. She declined the wine—it wasn't her own, after all, it was something homemade, rescued from the charred bowels of the trailer. Darren was in high spirits, a ninety-degree switch from the hysteria of two nights before. When she raised an eyebrow—she'd had to do all the barn work herself—he just grinned at her.

"New trailer," he said. "I mean, new old trailer. Gift of some church, yep. Your girl Sharon told 'em about the fire—somebody who knew somebody had this trailer he wasn't using no more, and he's bringing it round tonight. Bigger'n ours, with a new toilet and brand-new tires. We can hitch her up to the pickup and move back in."

"Well," Ruth said. It was good news and bad. Good news because she'd have her house back, and bad news because it meant the travellers would be staying on in the pasture. Not that she was swayed by all those letters to the editor, the small town prejudice and superstition, but, well, she'd just plain had enough. She wanted her old life back. She wanted her hired man, Tim, and her comfortable companionate cows, and her son, Vic, in his old room, and Emily in hers. She wanted Colm spending quiet nights in her bed. She might consider marrying him, as he asked once a week.

She gave a quick laugh. She wanted the moon—but who could reach that far? It wasn't made out of cheese, either.

The kitchen door flew open and Tormey Leary stomped in, followed by the dragging feet of young Keeley. Tormey had discovered a dent in the farm truck Ritchie had borrowed to take Nola to the hospital; he'd just gotten it back from the New York State Police. They had located it in a Utica garage, held it for evidence, and finding no blood or gore, had let the Vermont authorities have it. "And Christ, no gas," he complained, "just made it out here from town when it hit empty. I'll have to fill up with your gas. Do it for me, will ya, Darren? Oh, and you'll have to drive it back to Tonawanda for me. I can't drive two vehicles at once."

Darren nodded, rolled his eyes, poured himself another glass of wine, and went into the living room, where Maggie was holding a miniconcert of sentimental Irish songs. A moment later Ruth heard the buffo and blow of Darren's accordion. Boadie wandered after Darren with her leashed pig. Liz pulled a bottle of ginger ale out of the fridge and followed Boadie.

Ruth had planned to draw Maggie aside to discuss the gold cross, but allowed that this was not a good time. For one thing, she had other guests. Her past conditioning made her invite the uncle and Keeley to have a drink. Tormey nodded, of course; Keeley gave no reply. The boy was examining a spot on the floor where the dog had thrown up and no one had bothered to clean it.

"Careful there," Ruth said, and wiped it up with a wad of paper toweling. Keeley moved slowly into the living room, hands clasped behind his back. He glanced back furtively, as though he were being pursued.

The uncle was sitting at the kitchen table, reaching for a sugar doughnut. He was looking mad, very mad. "The sumbitches," he said. "Darren, too, and I done everything for that boy. He's in for the works now in the will, and would he go and put gas in my truck when I ask 'im? Answer me that. Would he? No, he's in there with his friggin' accordion."

In the living room the accordion made a loud off-key squawk.

"I'll see that you get enough gas to get you back to town," Ruth said. "There's a Mobil on Main Street." She wasn't going to get into a feud between uncle and nephew.

The song ended in the living room with a flurry of applause and Maggie burst back into the kitchen, followed by Liz. Seeing the uncle, she spit on the floor, grabbed a bottle of wine, and whirled back into the living room. Liz picked up a doughnut, her face expressionless, and left the room again. Ruth looked from one to the other: there was something similar about the curve of the eyebrows, the full upper lip that formed a kind of bow. Family resemblances, she supposed: travellers often married first cousins. And according to Sharon, Liz was Ritchie's daughter with Maggie's sister. She shouldn't make too much of these family relationships. And surely Keeley was no kin to the uncle. There seemed to be little affection for Tormey Leary on Keeley's part.

Still, there had to be a reason for Maggie's spitting. Ruth reached for another paper towel and swabbed the floor.

"Wouldn't put it past Maggie to of set the fire herself," Tormey grumbled. "Her and the old lady always complained about that trailer. Wanted me to give 'em a house. Thought I was made of money. Well, I told 'em they could wait till I kick off, then they'll have my house. I'd let Darren stay there now but for that crazy crew Maggie brought with her. Pigs! They belong in barns, not houses." He stood up, went to the living room door. "Darren? We need to talk, damn it. Put down that Christly accordion."

Maggie came back into the kitchen to "pour Keeley a drink. He won't do for hisself." She carefully avoided looking at the uncle. Ruth saw that she was wearing a miniature gold cross

similar to the one Franny had found. Maggie saw Ruth looking at it. "When'll the cops give back Nola's?" Maggie asked.
"I don't see why they have to keep it." The words brought on
a weeping spell. She pointed an accusing finger at Ruth. "You
haven't done anything to bring her back though you said you
wanted to."

Ruth put an arm around Maggie, patted her back. True, she
hadn't done anything to bring the woman back. But what could
she have done? There was a big confusing world out there,
where was Ruth to look? Except along the route between Branbury, Vermont, and Tonawanda, New York, and the police were
doing that. New York police were even on the Tonawanda farm,
keeping a lookout there in case Nola showed up. Colm had seen
to that. Ruth's arms fell to her sides. It was as if the government had taken away her muscles and her heart, with the quarantining of her cows.

Even her land was contaminated, according to the USDA.
And the Friesian calves they called sick—though not wholly
proven—had never left the calf pen! In what way was her land
contaminated? Unusable for six years, the feds threatened.
"Mad Cow is untreatable. Fatal. How can you sleep nights
knowing you might be spreading it?" the Leafmiller woman had
said when Ruth complained. Was she in cahoots with Bertha?

"Hel-lo, ladies, how are we all today?" Here was Colm, rush-
ing like a fresh breeze through the kitchen door. He was wearing a green plaid shirt, short khaki pants that revealed his bony
untanned legs, and high black socks—one higher than the other.
Ruth suppressed a giggle. But she disliked the word "ladies."
She'd reminded him of that before but he never remembered.

His greeting was met by a sob from Maggie. "Gimme back
Nola's cross, you nasty cop-cousin," she moaned. "I won't go
away with it—I just wanna wear it. As a good luck charm for
Nola. To keep her safe on the road." She held out her arms in
dumb appeal. "It's what we do, we travellers. It's our way."

Colm smiled and said she'd get it back—"when they let us.

It's still evidence—found at the scene. Forensic's got a back-log of work, too," he said, nodding at Ruth. They were still waiting for a report on the DNA found on the reins.

"What evidence? I don't understand," Maggie cried, and Colm appealed to Ruth. He grabbed a honey doughnut and stuffed it into his mouth.

"It was found at the scene of the murder—you know that," Ruth said, patting Maggie's shoulder. "It means Nola was there—if it was Nola's cross. It means—"

"Of course it's Nola's! You think I don't know Nola's cross? We got 'em after we graduated parochial school. Sister Maria hung 'em round our necks. I made Nola the leather strap. Afterward we went out and celebrated. We brought home Cokes and sucked out of each other's straws. It was a beautiful moment. Beautiful! We told each other secrets...."

"And I heard you one time down home." It was Keeley, coming in the room, smiling for the first time Ruth had seen him—a charming shy smile. "You were blabbing away and I couldn't sleep. I heard one of your secrets. Something you stole from—"

"You did not!" Maggie cried, turning on him, swatting his rear end. "We never talked in front of you."

"Heard through the wall. I had ears."

"But no brain," she said. "You don't know what you heard." Maggie pushed the boy into the living room where the TV was blaring away now, some actress crying, "It was you who betrayed me! You who—" And the living room door slammed.

"Good," said Colm. "I have news. Didn't want to talk in front of her." He dropped into a chair and stuffed a doughnut into his mouth. "No time for breakfas'—need my honey fix," he mumbled through the doughnut. Honey glistened at the corner of his lip. "Chief called seven o'clock, wanna—"

"It'd better be good news. Don't tell me if it isn't."

"Well, not bad news anyway. Not exactly good, either, but encouraging—"

"Say it then."

"I'm trying, Ruthie, gimme a chance to swallow."

She waited. He swallowed. Finally it came. The cops in a town called Minesville had located Nola. A woman had brought her to the police department. "But the stupid woman left her in the car. Nola got out, ran into a mall—and damn it, they lost her."

"How could they lose her? Probably two or three trained men and one woman in a green print dress. If she was still wearing that dress."

"She wasn't. Not then. Seems she got into a dress shop and stole some black pants and a shirt. And got away before the saleswoman could catch her."

"Good for her!"

"Ruthie, do you want to find Nola or not? I thought we decided we had to. To end all this—this—" He waved his arms vaguely in the direction of the burnt trailer.

Of course she did, what was her problem? Ruth hardly knew herself these days. Nola was key to everything. Ritchie's murder, the whole plaguish nightmare that was taking over her farm.

"Then what? Where did she go? Surely they could close her in. She must still be in that town. She didn't have a car. Unless she got a ride…"

"They don't know." He traced a tiny cross in the sugar the doughnuts had dropped on the table. "She just disappeared. They stopped all the cars going out, alerted the whole town. Nothing. It's like she flew into thin air. Houdini-like." He snapped his fingers and crumbs sprayed her cheek.

Ruth leaned her elbows on the table. "Where would she go if she were still in town?"

"Ruthie, love, no one's owned up. I mean who would take a chance on—well, not just a murderer but a woman who they think might be contagious with—you know."

"Colm. We've got to stop talking in euphemisms. She might have the human form of Mad Cow. Might. That *is* scary." The "mights" were killing her. Killing both Ruth and Nola. Ruth had a moment of true compassion for the woman. If she had strangled her lover it was understandable. He was a bastard, according to everyone—even the uncle. Even his half brother, Darren, who'd come east to escape him. "Poor Keeley," she said, hearing someone in the next room call the boy's name.

"You talked with the kid yet?" Colm asked. "Squeezed any information out of him?"

"Not much. Not really. He's almost pathologically shy. You want to try and talk to him? Keeley might have more to say about the uncle. We haven't written off Tormey yet in this murder. He despised Ritchie. Would have written him out of his will, I gather, but for something maybe that Ritchie had over him. And he wasn't about to leave the farm to Nola."

"Poor kid," Colm said. "Such a beautiful woman. I saw the photo of her down at the station. One the hospital took—and one Maggie gave them. Of Nola and Maggie, in fact, arms around each other—schoolgirl stuff."

"Maggie wants that back, too," Ruth said. "She should have it, if not the cross. Get it for her, will you, Colm? They've surely had copies made." He shrugged and she returned to her earlier thought. "We still haven't addressed my question. Where would she go to find sanctuary of some kind? Let's think."

"Lots of places. Counseling service, a shrink. Church, of course—that's the big one. Though no place is really safe. Remember that guy at the church down in Brattleboro? Ran in for help and the cops shot him something like eight times?"

"He'd pulled a knife. Still, it seemed like overkill. Church, yes. That cross—a Catholic church. Most towns over nine hundred will have a Catholic church. Priests are supposed to keep what you say confidential." She scraped back her chair, ran to the phone. "What was the name of that town?"

"Minesville. You planning to contact the Catholic church?"

She put down the phone. "No, go there, I think. Don't want to alert her in some way. Couldn't be over five or six hours by car, could it?"

"It's crazy, Ruthie. And who runs the farm?" He looked at his watch. "Almost milking time, isn't it?"

As if on cue, Darren appeared in the kitchen. "Reckon I'll head out to the barn. You coming?"

She had an important errand, she told him. "But Sharon's on call. She'll help. And so will Colm."

"Wait a minute now," Colm said. "I've got a five o'clock appointment. Lady wanting a condo—a sure sale if I can wangle it."

"Are you sure she's a 'lady'?"

"She was wearing a skirt, wasn't she?"

"Long or short?"

"Well, short," he admitted with a grin. "Very short. She'll keep. You sure you don't want me to come with you? A cop can be a useful companion."

She smiled. "Then pull yourself together, love. I'll call Sharon." She dialed East Branbury.

"Of course I'll come back and help," Sharon shouted over the cries of small children and a squawking goose. "And I *want* Colm to go with you. He wouldn't be much help in the barn anyway. I mean, you've seen him in action...." She giggled. "Darren and I can handle it."

"Thanks, sweetie. What would I do without you?" A wave of emotion came over Ruth for her daughter. She could count on Sharon. It was worth all the struggles of childhood and adolescence. It was more than worth it. She was sorry for all the people in the world who didn't have daughters. Or sons—thinking wistfully of Vic, who would be home next week and who, like Emily, knew nothing at all about this latest plague. They'd phone home, and she'd pretend "nothing to declare." Good thing they never read newspapers. Or listened to the news—although sooner or later they'd find out. Someone would say, "Too bad about your mother's cows...." She'd better prepare herself.

"And Mother. I forgot to tell you. I mean, I've been putting it off. Some agents came this morning when I was there—

when you were down in the pasture. I mean, they've been sneaking around for days now. Surveying the place. Seeing you don't spirit away the cows, I suppose. You can tell by the clean cars. Vermonters don't drive clean cars. But this morning, two guys came up and talked."

Ruth felt a stab in the belly. She couldn't get out the question, just waited for the answer.

"They mean to come and take the cows. Just for closer surveillance, they say.... Oh, wait—not yet. Next week sometime. They'll give you warning, they said. They were most apologetic. There was one woman with them, she seemed really sorry.... Mother? Are you still there, Mother?"

Ruth wasn't sure if she was still here or not. She thanked Sharon for filling in, hung up the phone, and poured herself a tall glass of Otter Creek Ale. She drank it in a gulp.

"Closer surveillance my foot," she told the barn cat, who'd jumped up on her lap. "They've made up their minds my cows are sick. They want to kill my beautiful organic cows."

Now she'd got the cat's fur soaking wet.

NOLA WAITED FOR the priest to come out of the confessional with a tall gaunt woman who'd looked at her oddly. But then, she was paranoid, ready to jump at every footstep. The janitor who'd brought her inside yesterday morning was a mute—the man had frightened her with his gruntings and harsh manner. Yet when she tripped on the threshold, he helped her up, looked close into her face. When the priest arrived in his office where the janitor had left her, he'd found a shaking, babbling woman who'd literally fallen at his feet. "Help me," she'd wept, clinging to his knees, "help me." And he had.

She'd confessed everything from recent events—the clothing she'd stolen: "Return them for me, will you, Father?" The apples and vegetables she'd taken, the mare she'd ridden off on. "But I left it in good hands, someone will return it." The tricks she'd played on the sisters at parochial school, the envy she'd had of her cousin Maggie. And harder to talk about, she spoke of the "remorse" she felt over Ritchie: "He had a bad upbringing, I can't tell you all of it, but he was damaged. And when he hit me I suppose he was hitting his—his abusers. But I hated him, hated him! Forgive me, Father, for that hate. Oh, forgive me, forgive me, Father—I've sinned badly."

And after all that outpouring he'd offered forgiveness, though she was altogether undeserving.

For she hadn't told everything. She'd mentioned the uncle, the hate she'd felt for him, even more than for Ritchie—but not why. She hadn't told about the fantasy she often had—of cutting off Tormey's penis. One summer night she'd found him asleep in a chair beside the small round swimming pool he'd set up behind the farmhouse. He was stark naked, legs wide apart—his penis huge and reddish-purple in its nest of coarse black fur. A butcher knife lay on the barbecue stand near his lounge chair. She'd picked it up. Then she heard Keeley calling for her, his voice coming closer, and she dropped the knife and ran back around the house. She heard Tormey call, "Huh? What? Who's there?—" but she kept on running till she found Keeley and hugged him till he cried, "Stop, Ma, quit it!"

But the fantasies kept on, and turned into cruel dreams.

"Are you sure you've told me everything?" he'd said again.

But no, she hadn't confessed everything.

The priest was coming back into his office now, a short, plump, twinkly-faced man with eyes the shade of the blue stole he wore, and best of all, an Irish name: Hannigan. She'd been lucky for once. He made her sit down, though her knees were rigid from the fright and the running and not knowing what would happen next, or where. She'd slept the past two nights on a cot in his mother's house. The mother had been nice enough, but she was the talkative kind who loved the sound of her own voice and didn't listen to you at all—though that was okay with Nola. Nola did hear her complain once about the "strays" he brought in. But the priest called it "a safe house" and she had to trust him. He'd introduced her simply as "one of the homeless—and we must help." He'd given her rosary beads to replace the missing ones. She'd grabbed them gratefully from him, like a starved puppy, and sat down at once to say the rosary. For a time she was happy—in the sanctuary with its lit candles and the fragrance of incense.

Her knees buckled under and she sat down. He had news she might be interested in, he said, something his mother had read in yesterday's paper—"but hidden back on page six, many won't have read it."

He handed her the paper and she read it, though her eyes would hardly focus. The one fact she could gather was that Uncle was now in Branbury, Vermont, on the Willmarth farm, and he had Keeley with him. She sat there a moment, breathing heavily, and then jumped up. The priest grabbed her hand as though he thought she might run out the door, do something rash. When she just had to stand, try to digest the news, what it meant. Where she'd have to go now. What she'd have to do.

She remembered the letter from her neighbor, Penny. She'd read it, horrified, then stashed it away in her box—the box she'd given Maggie for safekeeping. Something Penny suspected, and confronted Keeley with, and the boy burst into tears. Penny was like a surrogate mother to him.

"This is bad news, my girl?" Father didn't ask about the uncle: who and what he was to her. She'd merely told him she was on her way to find her son on the farm where they'd lived. The article had outlined Nola's escape from the Minesville police, and in the last paragraph the fact that the Willmarth cows, like Tormey Leary's, were to be removed "for the good of all."

She was sorry for the cows. But it was the fact that Uncle had Keeley with him that set her in motion: heart, nerves, feet, hands—all in a quiver.

"I got to make a phone call," she said. "I've no money—I'll have to send it to you."

He indicated the telephone on his desk. "To Vermont?" he said.

She shook her head and dialed the Tonawanda number. She had it by heart. Penny was her lifeline to Keeley. She needed to know—things. She looked up at the priest and he nodded and left the room. She was thankful for that.

Penny was there, thank God. Penny had read about Nola, had been expecting her, praying she'd make it safe to Tonawanda. "But now Keeley's gone to Vermont," Penny said, in her high sweet quavery voice that sounded an alarm inside Nola. "And you'd better get him away from Tormey."

She explained why—and Nola already knew, but felt her body turn inside out.

"I got to be on my way," Nola told Father Hannigan when he returned, and she headed for the door. He didn't try to stop her. He just said, "If you walk out now, they'll take you to prison. You'd better think through what you'll do."

She turned back to him. "What would you do, huh, Father, in my case? With the whole world thinking you're a thief and a murderer ready to spread disease through the whole wide world?" She heard her voice shrill at the end—hardly her own voice.

She promised the priest she would turn herself in for testing. But she had to rescue Keeley first. Had to! How long had he been alone already with Tormey Leary? And worse even, Tormey not knowing who Keeley was.

"Give yourself in. Now," the priest said. "I'll go with you, if you like. It will go better for you, my girl." He took her hand, looked penetratingly into her eyes. He wasn't impervious to her looks, she knew that—priest or no priest. It was a curse, this face and body. She'd gained five pounds at least from the mother's starchy cooking, she looked healthier.

"I will, Father, but not yet." She was suddenly suspicious of his motives. They were all alike, these men—the priests, the Ritchies, the Uncles of the world. This man wasn't going to help her. He was just toeing the party line. If he really cared about her welfare he'd have offered to drive her out of town, set her on her way. But he only wanted her to give herself up.

He didn't understand about Uncle and Keeley, and she couldn't bring herself to tell him.

She pulled back her hand and went to the door. "Think about it," he said, his voice sounding passionate. "Don't be hasty. Consider your soul."

She kept on going but he didn't pursue her. When she turned at the door to thank him, tell him she *would* turn herself in—in time, that is—he gave a sad smile and made the sign of the cross. Another soul lost, the sad smile said. He'd done all he could. It was time for the next victim. The woman who'd been in the confessional was tiptoeing toward him with an adoring look on her face. She'd obey him. *Her* soul would be saved.

Out on the back porch a hand grabbed Nola's. She knew the rough grip of it, she turned to face the janitor. He motioned her toward his motorbike that was leaning against the back fence. He took off his light jacket and handed it to her. It had a hood and she pulled it up over her hair. It was a risk and she had to take it, she was that desperate.

His hands were warm and strong on her back. He smelled of pipe tobacco and honest dirt and motor oil. They sped down Main Street and no one called out.

THE PRIEST WAS frustratingly true to his calling. He would divulge no confidences to Ruth and Colm. He would only repeat, "She was here, and she's gone. Two hours ago perhaps. I asked her to give herself in and she said she would—'in time,' she said." He spread his hands, what more could he say? He had a dimple in his left cheek. With his blondish hair he resembled a youthful Santa Claus. But there was a hard glint in the blue eyes. Don't mess with me, don't push me, the eyes said.

Yet as Ruth and Colm left his office, and he ushered them out the back way, he patted Ruth on the shoulder and said, "I can't tell you which way she'd have gone, but I did show her the news clipping. She seemed angry, upset. She made a, well, a gagging sound when she came to the end of the article."

"What did it say?" Ruth asked. She couldn't read all the papers. The local *Independent* was enough—maybe the *Free Press*—now and then the Sunday *Times*. But did she want to know what the world was saying about her and her cows?

He was creasing his brow, trying to remember. "She took my copy. But I believe it was something about her uncle's farm—and yours." He patted her shoulder again; she could smell the incense on him, that high church aroma that always struck her when she attended funerals in those ritualistic places. After a while, she supposed, it got into the bones. He spread his faith as he walked.

He snapped his fingers, a surprising gesture, almost childlike. "Keeley. It was the name Keeley that surprised her. She repeated the name with her lips. I read lips," he explained. "My janitor is deaf and dumb—a period of torture in Vietnam. But he can move his lips. He observes."

"Is he around?" Colm asked. "He might be able to help us."

The priest smiled indulgently. "Can you read lips?" he asked.

"Oh," said Colm. "But you can. If we ask him questions?"

"I'm afraid he's taken leave as well." The priest poked a thoughtful tongue into his cheek. "I heard his motorbike drive off." He caught Ruth's eye "It's unusual for him to take off in the morning. He hasn't cleaned the sanctuary yet."

"I see." Ruth thanked the priest and he held his hands palms up, as though he had a soul caught in them, but was giving it space to fly off. The eyes looked softer now, like summer lakes.

"By the way, Mrs. Willmarth"—they turned obediently at the door—"if you do catch up with Miss Donahue, you might want to be sure the, um, uncle she worked for is not around. I can't tell you why, of course—and she never said exactly—it was all in the reaction, the attitude. But, well, be warned." Wishing them luck, he turned to greet a tall woman who was waiting in the doorway with a lit candle.

"East, I presume," Colm asked as they walked around front to her truck.

"East, of course, Colm. Toward Vermont. To find Keeley. And the uncle—before she does."

# TWENTY-TWO

SHARON WAS BESIDE HERSELF. A part of her was swabbing the barn floor like one of the ancient furies; the other replaying the whirlwind visit of the feds—oh, the terror and outrage of it! Darren was bringing in the first of the cows for the late afternoon milking: Zelda as always in the lead, then Jane Eyre, Dolly, and Oprah, all with red circles painted on their foreheads. Death circles! That's what the red meant. They were destined for the slaughterhouse. And all because of two calves who tested—so they thought—positive. Yet positive, she'd read, was not positive at all because there was no science to this, just fear, possibility, what they called probability—a list of ifs and maybes.

She gave an angry shout and hurled her mop across the room. It struck Charlotte 2's heifer calf in the butt. The calf wailed and she rushed to apologize. At least this one had no red circle. The feds had passed it by when they came—just after her mother left with Colm, thank God—her mother would have gone mad again. Maybe Charlotte had hid it behind a bush. She'd take this one home if her mother would let her, breed a new herd of cows. A brave new herd for her mother out of Charlotte Bronte's belly.

Pigtailed Willa came running into the barn, grabbed Sharon around the smelly waist, and whimpered. "It's all right, baby, all right, sweetheart, Mommy's just mad, that's all. They painted red circles on Rooster's cows."

"Red circles?" The child's eyes widened.

"Not play circles. Real circles. They want to take the cows away."

"Take Rooster's cows away?" Willa stood a moment, head cocked in thought, a girl in red shorts and halter, small for her age—a throwback to a five-foot grandmother. Then she howled, a whirlpool of tears and rage. Sharon pulled her into her arms, hugged her, let the tears soak her flowered shirt.

"We won't let them do that, will we, Mama?" The green eyes implored, a pool of protest.

"No," said Sharon. "We won't. We'll get help." She didn't know why she hadn't called for help before this. Her mother had been so scattered; she helped everyone else but never asked for help herself. Some had offered, of course, but Ruth hadn't asked them. Well, Sharon would remedy that. She'd call the neighbors, everyone her mother had helped—and others besides. It was time they put their money where their mouths were, as the saying went. She would summon an army. They would lock the gates against the enemy, defend the castle to the last stone.

In the kitchen, armed with a hot chocolate—Sharon had a weakness for chocolate—she made a list of her mother's closest friends and neighbors. There were crotchety old Glenna down the road and her kooky relative Fay who rented a scrawny cow for her farm B&B. There were Moira Earthrowl and husband, Stan, who owned the orchard Ruth had liberated from a poisoner. There were beekeeper Gwen and her volatile husband who would bring along some of his Abenaki cronies—they knew what it was to have one's land and animals taken away! There were Henrietta and Franny, the latter still mourning her precious mare and ready for a good fight. There was Carol, whose sheep and mama llama as she called it, were still grazing on Ruth's land but quarantined, kept to a two-acre radius. There was old Lucien Larocque, whose assailants Ruth had brought to justice, though he'd been forced to sell his farm, and was living now with his bossy daughter. There was that man with the sheep—James Perlman—surely he'd want to help? He might soon need a neighbor's help himself if the feds kept pursuing everyone who'd ever breathed in the same stratosphere with Nola Donahue.

And there were the Irish travellers. Already, sympathetic clan members had been popping up on the pasture like Jacks and Jills from their boxy pickups, contributing pillows, curtains, rugs, and shawls, along with pans of apple crisp, mashed turnip, brownies, and what else Sharon didn't know—she'd only seen the cargo disappearing into the new used trailer.

Then there was Aunt Bertha, tripping up the steps this very minute in her shiny black pumps, knee-length pleated blue skirt, and scarlet lipstick that made her look all mouth. Which she was, of course.

"Sharon! Where's Ruth? I need to see her. I don't want her thinking for one single minute we set that fire. Because we didn't, Sharon, we wouldn't!"

"Who did, then?" Sharon asked, sweeping doughnut crumbs off the table into her palm and onto the floor. She'd vacuum before her mother returned.

"Why, God! It was God's will, Sharon, who else could you think was responsible?" Bertha plumped down on a chair, legs slightly apart in their coffee-colored stockings—Sharon could see clear up to her baggy cotton underwear, and it wasn't a pretty sight. Bertha thrust a doughnut into the red ring of her mouth.

Here, Sharon thought, is a true miscreant. She's the one should be sent to the knackers. "He just sent down a zigzag of lightning, did he, Bertha?"

"Yes, yes, that's what He did, absolutely! Retribution! 'I will punish the world for their evil and the wicked for their iniquity.' Isaiah 13:11," she quoted.

"But you helped, huh, Bertha? I mean, God needed a helping hand, right? From you and your lady friends, who left your charming signs down in front of the trailer?"

"Oh, no, not that, Sharon, I didn't. I told you it was—"

"But if God didn't want those people there, why did he send

them a new trailer? Through a church charity, as well. A group of Unitarians—"

"Oh, Unitarians have no connection with God," Bertha said, "oh no. They don't kneel to anyone. Why, pagans meet in that place! Just read the paper, Sharon, they make no bones about it. They teach free choice and take in colored people. And innocent children—a hundred of them, I heard. What are they teaching those poor children?!" Bertha poured herself a glass of milk and swilled it down.

Sharon decided right then to send her children to that church. "Now, Bertha, if you don't mind, I've phone calls to make. I'm helping here while Mother's away."

"But I need to talk to her, Sharon. Where is she anyway?"

"Gone off with Colm," Sharon said. "A sort of honeymoon, you know?"

Bertha's hands clutched her chest as though she'd been shot. "Honeymoon?" she gasped. "But Ruth has only been divorced a few months."

"Two years," Sharon said. "Four years since your brother left her. How is dear Violet, by the way?"

"Now, Sharon, I know you're upset about that woman, but it wasn't Peter's fault. Violet was possessed. Absolutely possessed! You know by who. And it wasn't our Lord, Sharon, it was—"

The phone rang. "I know who set that fire," a shrill voice said. "And you'd better look to other things he might've done."

"Who is this?" Sharon asked. But the anonymous voice went on—thinking, most likely, that Sharon was her mother. The voice didn't wait to make certain, just rushed on with her accusations. "He hates your travellers, you should know that. He hates the Irish. Despises us!"

"Who despises us?" Sharon said, wholly confused, but the voice shouted on.

"He's a small man, he's done that sort of thing before. Well, not a fire exactly, but back in Buffalo where—well, he did something terrible. Terrible! I won't tell you what, I'll just warn you. It was in the papers back there. Those travellers would of read it—that man who owned that farm where they all worked. And he was afraid! Afraid of people knowing around here. He'd do anything, I tell you, to keep them from finding out!"

"He? Who's he? And finding out what?" Sharon was getting a headache. Two kooks in one hour were two too many. But the phone went dead. Where was her mother anyway? Why did she have to go running off to upstate New York when all hell was breaking loose at home?

At last, Bertha was on her way out, the black pumps tapping a slow exit while the tongue wagged on about retribution, God's will, the triumph of evil. Sometimes Sharon wished she were adopted, bore no relationship to this bigoted woman.

She slammed the door on the black heels, then picked up the phone and dialed the Branbury Farm B&B. "Glenna?" she said. "Is that you?"

"Who else would it be? I'm busy as hell cleaning up a mess Fay's hound made on the floor," the octogenarian said. "Damn beast chewed up a bunch of garlic I had hanging—knocked it down with his skinny tail. Serve him right if he gets bad breath." She let out a great belly laugh.

Sharon explained the situation, and Glenna hollered, "You just tell me when they show up and I'll be there with a pitchfork. I won't have them screwing that good woman. I won't have it! But just in case they bring in the army and we can't hold the fort, I've got a pregnant goat here. Ruth can use my land, raise goats. You can milk 'em, you know."

Goats, Sharon thought. It was an idea all right. Sharon loved goats. She loved the way they frisked about the hillside, like elves, munching up the grass. She and her mother could hire them out—Goats 'R' Us they'd call themselves. Anyway, her mother had options now. Sharon liked the thought of options. Her mother had been obsessed with cows. She'd tried Christmas trees and maple syrup, but never any other kind of animal.

It was time to break loose, move in other directions. Sharon would tell her mother that. Sometimes good came out of the bad.

Though she knew her mother would never listen. What could you do with a woman who put her cows practically on a par with her own children?

"It's not fair to equate cows with people," Sharon told the bowl of doughnuts on the kitchen table. "'S not fair," as she stuffed one into her mouth.

"Hello?" she said when the phone rang again, and then "What?"

"A court order," the voice repeated. It was a friend of her mother's who worked at the local phone company. "I thought your mom should know. So she can be, like, careful from now on, you know, when she talks on the phone?"

"Oh God," Sharon said when she hung up. "Oh dear God. Now they're having the phone bugged."

Who was bugging it—the USDA or the FBI? Or did it matter? Any way you looked at it, it was the feds.

COLM WANTED to send out a warning to the police about a deaf-mute and a woman on a motorbike, but Ruth argued against it. "If the police pick Nola up, we'll have no way to question her ourselves. And there's Keeley. The boy needs her right now more than the police. Think of that, Colm."

"Mmmm." Colm was wolfing down a ham and cheese sandwich they'd bought in a 7-Eleven in Gloversville, and he could only mumble through the fatty thick of it. Ruth had a tuna salad roll but didn't want to eat it while it was her turn to drive.

"Anyway," Ruth said, "she wouldn't be on the thruway—not if she's on that motorbike. They don't allow motorbikes on thruways, do they?"

"Sure," Colm mumbled through the cheese, "y' see motorcycles alla time. Jeez, I hate gettin' behind 'em, they're in an' outa traffic like flies. Oughta be banned."

Ruth turned onto Route 29. For three hours now she'd kept

her eyes peeled for a motorbike but seen only cars and trucks. How many routes and back roads the couple could take! And the roads were so thick with summer traffic that a motorbike could easily get lost to view. Already they'd passed more than three dozen motorcycles and bicycles along the route. And who knew how far Nola would ride with that deaf-mute? Or if they'd even ride at all while it was light. Only now, with nightfall, might they dare move out on the main roads.

They were passing a motel, and Colm was pointing with his sandwich. It was tempting, but Ruth shook her head. "The important thing now, I think, is to get home before she does."

"Warn the uncle?"

"Well, I don't know. He might take flight if we do. It's entirely possible he killed Ritchie. And that somehow she knows it."

"Why? What's the motive?"

"I don't know that. We'll have to find out, won't we? I've got to talk to Keeley. Nola's dislike of the uncle must have something to do with the boy." She didn't want to think the worst, but it was possible. Sometimes it was hard not to pre-judge, bring the ugly scenarios alive in the mind. "Tormey doesn't have an alibi for the night Ritchie died, does he? Your police were going to check."

"In process. They're checking with the hired hand back in Tonawanda, all the neighbors. To find out when he left the farm. He was here the next day—Friday. He was at the farm when Darren called about Ritchie?"

"Darren called a cell phone. Tormey told Darren he was in some New York burg or other looking for his pickup."

"Likely story," said Colm. "Anyhow, we should have a full report on his whereabouts, the alibi—all that—when we get home. I'll call the department."

They let the subject go for the next hour; were quiet except for small talk: William Hanna's prostate problems, the aggravating Bertha, the usual pleas from Colm to move in permanently.

"Will I even have a home," she asked, "after the feds get

through with me? If they quarantine the land, will they keep me out of my house?"

Colm laughed through the Mars bar he was chewing. He'd bought two of them, ostensibly one for her, knowing she didn't eat them and he'd have to make the sacrifice. "How could they do that? You didn't bring the cows in your kitchen, did you?" Though he wouldn't put it past her, he said. "It wouldn't surprise me to see a heifer sitting at the table, munching a doughnut."

She didn't respond to that silliness. She loved her cows, but preferred them in the barn or out-of-doors. "Well, I'm not quitting," she said stubbornly. "I know you want me to buy a place in town, work in an ice cream shop or something. But you're mistaken, my friend. I'll wait it out. Till I get my land back."

"Six years? And do what?" He put a hand on her knee and stroked it. "Aw, Ruthie, love."

She didn't know, she couldn't think past today. Couldn't think past getting home, finding out what had happened since they'd left early this morning. The agents might have come already, loaded the cows into a truck—how many trucks would it take for thirty cows? She was sick at the thought. She was angry all over again at Nola. Bertha, she had to admit, had gotten to her. Nola, who might or might not have variant CJD, had to be the cause. Yes, the fear and hate and superstition had all started with Nola's coming. She said this out loud to Colm and he snorted.

"It was Tormey Leary at the root of it. He was the one sold you the Friesian calves."

"And whose relative was he?" She was whining now, she hated the sound of her voice. But she couldn't help it. It was Colm at the root of it, she started to say, but bit back the words. It wasn't Colm's fault. The travellers had come on to him, claimed blood ties. Colm, in his easygoing, hospitable, want-to-be-liked-by-everyone manner, had simply acquiesced. Wouldn't she have done the same?

"I'm sorry. Hit me when I get this way," she said, gripping

his thigh. "It's nobody's fault. Certainly not Nola's! It's fate. That's what plague is, isn't it? Fate? The Furies, grabbing and clutching and cutting off the life threads? I mean, the world's so small we can fly in hours from Beijing, China, to Burlington, Vermont, and spread a deadly disease to all the passengers. We're all potential carriers. And victims, too."

"Easy, lady," he said, loosening her fingers, which were crawling near his groin, pressing hard. "You're getting close to the roots here. The family jewels. Careful now."

She had to laugh at the way he looked at her. That largish nose, the unruly gray-black hair, the fullish lips, the watery blue eyes—Irish eyes, she thought, shaking her head. She tried to move her hand, but he had it, wouldn't let go.

"If we run into a tree it's your fault," she told him.

"I'll take my chances."

"Okay. You're in the passenger seat." She took a deep, shuddering breath. There was some weird sense of foreboding. It was already nine o'clock, and at least an hour and a half to the Champlain bridge. She pressed down on the accelerator. She *had* to get to Branbury before Nola.

AFTER MILKING the next morning, Ruth ran down into the pasture and discovered the red circles. And it wasn't Bertha's group this time. It was as if her cows were in a Walt Disney film, were slowly turning into bovine devils. A red horn would grow out of each circle. Here was Zelda, casting a mad eye on her. Was she still Zelda? Or had she already metamorphosed into a she-devil?

But here was sweet Jane Eyre, bounding over to greet her. No red circle could alter maternal Jane. Jane's calf was loping along beside her, the circle smaller on her forehead. It was like her ancestor's concept of original sin—the innocent offspring tainted at birth. She clenched her fists. What fiend had declared this sweet calf a monster? A calf fed on fresh grass and clover and mother's milk. Ruth dropped to her knees to embrace the creature.

And found herself sobbing into its white flank. The heifer bawled with her. Jane came along to butt Ruth on the rear end, knocking her down, and the trio were locked in a warm, mewling embrace. "I can't let you go, I won't," Ruth sobbed.

She got up to see Keeley over by the fence, watching her. She smiled, and beckoned to him. There was still no sign of Nola, but she should warn the boy that his mother was on her way.

"Darren sent me," he said. "He left his clippers here. He's back there. Gonna let me take a turn on the tractor." Through the haze of sun Ruth could see the Allis tractor pulling its tank spreader of thick oozy manure, painting the meadow a dark liquid brown. Beyond him in the John Deere, Sharon was sitting, ready to reload the tank. Spreading and loading, the process would go on all morning—a normal summer day on the farm. And her cows, the reason for all this hot hard labor, were wearing red circles on their brows, like openings into a house of death.

Keeley saw what she was looking at and watched with her. "They did that to Uncle's cows, too," he said.

Neither spoke for a few minutes. The sun was growing hotter although it was only seven in the morning. Bertha would tell Ruth she was already entering the gates of hell, and Ruth would begin to believe it.

Keeley turned to leave, and Ruth came back to life. "Wait," she said. She would seize the moment. "Can we talk a minute? I want to tell you about your mother."

The boy reeled back, as though she'd lassoed him. His face looked white as milk in the morning haze. "You saw her?"

"No, but I just missed her. I'm pretty sure she's on her way back here." She told the boy about the priest and the deaf-mute who, it seemed, had taken her up on his motorbike—"if not all the way here, at least partway. She should be back before long."

The boy's eyes opened wide as if already he were seeing his mother. His lips twitched into a half smile.

"I think," said Ruth, "that Nola is unhappy with your uncle. He's—"

"Not *my* uncle," the boy interrupted. "We just call him that. He makes us."

"No, no, I realize that. With Tormey, then, um, Mr. Leary."

The boy looked wary. He backed off a little, shuffled his feet on the grass. The feet appeared too large for the rest of him. He'd surely grow up to them one day.

"Do you know any reason why she might be, well, upset with him?"

Keeley leaned down to pull a piece of longish grass and sucked on it. He wouldn't look at her.

"Keeley? I know I shouldn't pressure you, but it might be important for me to know. I mean, for when your mother returns. Which could be—very soon, like I said."

"I think," the boy began, "I think—she thinks he wants to hurt us. Her and me."

"Hurt you? In what way?"

The boy's face was pinkening with the heat and his confusion. He was shaking his head rapidly, as though he'd shake away bad thoughts. His mouth was opening and shutting, the hands pulling at his shirt buttons. "Did he ever—hurt you?" Ruth suggested. "Touch you maybe—and Nola saw?"

"No, she didn't see! Uncle made sure she wasn't around when he—" His mouth opened into a wide O, his whole face seemed to shrink into that circle of anguish. He was backing away now, still staring at her, unable to articulate his thoughts.

"It's all right," she said, "you don't have to tell. I think I understand. But you'll have your mother back soon, and she'll watch over you. You won't have to go back to Uncle's. Soon there may not be any cows to milk there, anyway."

She had a choking feeling in her chest to say that—a moment's awareness that if there were no cows at the uncle's, there might soon be none here. And how was Nola to watch over Keeley when she would be taken into custody, returned to the hospital for testing, then indicted for Ritchie's murder?

Keeley was still standing there, a little off balance, like a newborn calf. He was staring beyond Ruth at Jane Eyre and her calf—as though any minute Jane would turn into Nola and roll Keeley gently against her. Esmeralda had moved down to stand behind Jane, then Charlotte Bronte behind Esmeralda, and then pregnant Elizabeth. The cows made a semicircle around Ruth and the boy; they were like circling wagons, a congregation of mothers. Ruth's beloved bovines with their liquidy brown eyes, watching, waiting—with red dye on their foreheads.

Only Zelda kept her distance, like a watchful sentry. Would she bellow out a warning when the feds came for her? When Nola arrived? If Nola knew that Tormey Leary had been abusing Keeley—for that's what he'd been doing, it seemed clear to Ruth—what would she do? Perhaps this was what the priest had been warning. Ruth must stop any violence before it happened.

When she turned back to speak to Keeley, the boy was already gone, loping across the fields, scurrying toward the Allis tractor and the tank spreader that Sharon was loading up with thick brown manure. The corn would grow tall and green on the fertilized land. But would the cows be here to feed on the corn?

It might be a last supper before the hanging.

COLM WAS STANDING by the wall phone in the kitchen, his back to the door, the receiver clapped to his ear. Ruth knew at once whom he was talking to. He was in his cop mode. Playing his conscience, as he called it. He turned and winked when he saw her, held out an arm to encircle her waist, and she let him. He knew the phone was bugged, she'd warned him, but he just shrugged. "Cops and robbers," the optimistic fellow said, as if the feds were just playing a game. She could hear Chief Fallon's voice on the other end: he had a husky, booming voice. He didn't need a loudspeaker, Colm would joke, to converse anywhere in town.

"Leary's got the alibi," Colm mouthed, though she could hear Roy Fallon anyway, booming on about a hired hand and a man in a local Tonawanda bar who had occupied the adjacent stool on Thursday night. Tormey Leary could not have killed his nephew Ritchie.

"Who then?" she asked for the umpteenth time when Colm got off the line.

"A vandal, a random kind of killing," Colm said. "Some guy wanting the horse. Maybe Ritchie tried to trade it or something and the deal went bad. Could be drugs involved—he seemed the type, even if he is my relative. Though very distant," he reminded her.

"Yes, dear. We all have strange relations," she said, thinking of Bertha. "Mine are worse than yours, I think. Of course, Bertha's my ex-husband's sister, not mine."

"Uh-huh." He gave a slight smile.

"It could still be Nola," she said, "though it doesn't seem plausible. Nola did end up with the horse, after all—so that would shoot your horse-trading theory."

"So Fallon says he'll put out a warning to New York cops. Woman headed east, not west. And on a motorbike."

She reeled out of his arms. "Damn it, we agreed you wouldn't say that! We agreed you'd let her come here first. To see Keeley." She grabbed his hands. "The boy needs her, Colm. He needs to see her before any police ship her off under police protection to the hospital. Then lock her behind bars." She heard her voice pleading. But what good did her pleading do? It was too late. He'd given the orders.

"Remember what the priest said, Ruthie. About her reaction to the news clipping, his warning about Tormey Leary— Nola's attitude toward him."

"Oh. Well, sit down and I'll tell you about it. I just talked with Keeley." She related the conversation in the meadow. "I mean, it's all pretty clear now. Nola probably suspects something. And then when she read the account in the newspaper— about Tormey and Keeley coming here..."

"She doesn't have a gun, does she?"

"I would doubt it. But a knife can do a lot of damage. Look what those terrorists did with a box cutter."

"You're calling Nola a terrorist?"

"Of course not, Colm! Look, we have to be sure Tormey's not here when she arrives."

"If."

"All right, if. Though I'd say 'when.' She's managed to elude the police so far. It's"—she looked at the kitchen clock—"eight-thirty. Tormey's probably breakfasting in the Branbury Inn. We need to keep him there. She'll come here first, and we can reason with her, let her talk to Keeley. Keep a lid on things until—"

He was looking at her, his eyes probing. "Until what?" his lips said.

She couldn't answer that. She went to the phone, asked the inn for Tormey Leary. She waited. Listened. Then hung up, sighed heavily.

"He's not there," Colm said, and she nodded.

# TWENTY-THREE

NOLA WANTED TO PAY the janitor for his time and trouble but could only turn out her empty pockets. He shrugged and got back on his motorbike. It had broken down en route, delaying the already long, back road journey for another several hours, and he would have to get to a garage. They were in Crown Point, in a parking lot beside the old revolutionary fort. He would have driven her over the bridge, but it was getting dark and she didn't want him to go any farther. Besides, they were not far from Branbury, and the police might be on the lookout for a man and woman on a motorbike. She didn't know whether the priest had seen them leave, but even if not, he would have figured it out from the way the man had gazed at Nola. Once during the breakdown period, when they'd decided to catch a few hours' sleep in an abandoned barn, she'd had to discourage his attentions. But admonished, he'd kept to himself, and all she could do in the end was thank him.

She put her hands in the pockets of the thin jacket he'd lent her. It was hot on her sweaty back, but with daylight, she was grateful for the hood that hid half her face and hair. When she pulled out her hands she drew out a five-dollar bill. It hadn't been there before, she knew, and she waved her arms at the motorbike that was already around the bend, stirring up dust and fumes. There was no response, and in minutes he was out of sight.

She trudged over the Champlain bridge behind an elderly man and his grandson, keeping close so they'd look a family. Once the boy turned around but she smiled, and the boy turned quickly back and walked on, swaggering a little. On the Vermont side of the lake she skirted the Chimney Point Museum and kept to the edge of Route 125 that would lead her across Route 22A, she recalled, and then over to Branbury and Cow Hill Road. It was fifteen miles, according to a sign—that could take her five or six hours if she kept up a steady pace. Though she couldn't, could she, when she had to duck into the bushes every time a car came by? Already there had been a dozen cars.

Even when she got to Branbury, she didn't know what she was going to do. Go at once to the trailer, she supposed—she couldn't risk The Willmarth with her policeman friend. She wasn't sure about Darren, either. He and Ritchie never got along, she knew, but blood was blood and she couldn't take a chance.

She'd have to see Maggie. Maggie would know what to do, how to get Keeley away from Tormey Leary.

For she didn't want to see Tormey. She didn't know what she'd do—face-to-face with him. The hate was too thick. The hate would blind her.

But what did it matter now? She was already a criminal, a fugitive. All that really mattered was Keeley. And the only hope for Keeley was Maggie. Maggie would have to care for the boy, get him away from his father, keep him safe till he reached majority. This was Nola's plan now, she couldn't see beyond it. Maggie must be persuaded to take Keeley. Maybe Darren would agree. For Keeley and Darren had blood ties, too.

The thought of seeing Keeley and Maggie kept her going even though her body was flagging, her breath coming harder in the hot sunlight, her head throbbing at the thought of returning to the farm where she might see the hated uncle. And if he was there, if he did have Keeley in thrall—she might have to kill him.

Kill him. Would that be so hard to do?

No, not if he didn't kill her first.

KEELEY WAS STAYING in the new trailer. Maggie insisted on it, and the boy seemed relieved to be invited. This trailer was bigger than the old one, and The Willmarth had offered a futon for his bed. Maggie was laying a sheet on it now—it was still too hot for a blanket; all the boy needed was a sheet over him, and a pillow. For that she used a sofa pillow that Boadie had embroidered a pink pig on—Keeley smiled at that. The Willmarth said he could use her son's room, but the kid was coming home soon and Keeley's visit might be permanent.

Maggie didn't know why she used that word, "permanent"—it was just a hunch of hers. The boy was Tormey Leary's son, according to the old letter from the midwife in Nola's box—and that was a shock! It was like in the old days at birth when you had to tell who the father was, and Nola told. The auntie wanted to know if Nola had told the uncle yet, and thought that maybe she should. It'd be for Nola's sake, her letter said, so the boy would be in Tormey's will. The auntie knew Tormey, she said—he'd use any excuse to keep the boy from getting what was rightly his.

Nola had told Maggie only that the rapist had come in the night, that she didn't know who he was. And Maggie believed her then, because they were blood sisters. But she couldn't hold the lie against her friend. There were things even blood sisters couldn't share.

"She's on her way, she'll come here first. Maybe this evening," she told Keeley. He was lying on the Salvation Army sofa, feet up on the split arm, guzzling a Pepsi, leafing through a copy of *Model Railroader*. Keeley had a passion for trains—Maggie didn't know where it came from. But when Nola couldn't find him or he'd skipped school again, she'd usually head down to the roundhouse near their farm where they repaired old engines and there he'd be, sitting in a corner, listening to the train talk.

"It'll be good to see her, right?" Maggie said.

Keeley didn't respond, but she saw the quiver in the jaw, the way the page rustled in his fingers.

If the worst happened and she couldn't care for Keeley, who

then? Boadie? No, too old. There was Boadie now, sound asleep in her chair, mouth open wide enough to swallow a baseball. The foolish pig was at her feet, along with the twelve-gauge shotgun, for Boadie was ready at a minute's notice, she said, to defend the cows. Not to mention the bloody pig. Maggie took the gun and laid it on a shelf by the trailer door. It was loaded; she didn't want Liz or Keeley picking it up.

She repeated the question to herself. Who would care for Keeley if the worst happened and she wasn't around?

It would have to be Darren. Darren would have to know who Keeley was. When he came in from the barn she'd tell him. It was already seven-thirty, he should be in soon. She'd give him dinner—his favorite ham and grits. She had a sudden wild yearning for Darren. She loved the fellow, he was a good man—crazy sometimes, silly, a kind of swaggerer, but a good fellow. He'd never cheated on her, she was sure of that. If he looked funny at Nola sometimes, he never did anything about it. If Darren walked into the trailer this minute she'd take him in her arms, squeeze so tight he'd holler.

Maggie wanted nothing more in life than to live it out with tall, gawky, sweet-faced Darren. And he was coming home to her, she heard his voice outside in the meadow.

But not alone—there was someone with him. She knew the voice, that hoarse rasp like angry bees when you blundered into their nest. Oh sweet Jesus save me—it's Tormey Leary. He isn't welcome in this place. No.

She threw a silk shawl over her bare shoulders and met the men in the doorway. Darren looked apologetic, he knew how she felt about Tormey. But Tormey was his uncle. Darren was soft that way. If Tormey invited himself over for a drink, Darren would let him in. The uncle would remind Darren he was in the will, and Darren felt he had to be grateful. Though he'd risked being cut out by not going back to the farm—she had to give him that.

But there was no working farm, was there? Would Tormey

want to stay here in town? If so, they'd move on, Darren said. At the same time he'd wavered. Maggie couldn't always trust Darren's staying power. Maggie was the tough one in this family. She had to be.

"Darren invited me in for a beer," Tormey said. "Besides, I got Keeley's train magazine, he left it in my room at the inn."

Maggie saw Keeley freeze over on the sofa, pull his legs up, like he'd make himself invisible. She stepped back to shield the boy. "Kid's resting. He worked with Darren all day in the fields. Go lie on the futon," she told the boy.

Tormey just laughed, and threw down the magazine and a five-dollar bill on the sofa. "There's a fiver for you, kid," he said. "You can go downtown and have yourself some fun."

Keeley picked up the magazine, but he left the money on the sofa. He went behind the charred screen without looking at the uncle.

The uncle—his father, Maggie thought, and scrunched up her skirt with her fists.

"You got Rolling Rock?" Tormey bellowed, and Darren went to get it. Tormey followed and stumbled over the pig. The pig screeched and Boadie's hand shot out for the gun. But it wasn't there, and now Maggie was sorry she'd put it on the shelf. "Go to bed, he'll be gone soon," Maggie told her grandmother—there was no reason for her to pussyfoot in front of this SOB.

"I'm not tired. I need air, I need a walk," Boadie said. "Where's Liz?"

"At the movies. Some friend she met in town." Maggie was tempted to follow Boadie out, but she didn't want to leave Keeley alone. Not that Uncle would do anything with Darren nearby, but, well, she wanted to be here, that's all.

She lit a cigarette and sat in Boadie's rocker and rocked hard. Rocked and smoked and rocked while the men brought their beers back to the sofa and sat together like old cronies. She knew who'd invited who for a drink, but she didn't give a damn.

She didn't look at Darren, though he kept taking side glances at her. Darren had made a goof and he was going to pay for it.

"Thought maybe I'd sell the farm—they could put a hundred houses on it," Tormey was saying. "You can make a bundle offa that land. One day it'll be yours, Darren."

Darren was looking interested; Maggie didn't like that. Darren was a good man, sure, but he was easily managed. It was Maggie who'd had to psyche him up to leave the Tonawanda farm. She said, "Darren's talking about staying here in Vermont. Buying a small farm of his own, right, Darren?"

"Darren can't afford it, I don't think. Not while I'm alive," Tormey said before Darren could speak. He smiled his twisty smile at Maggie. He knew she disliked him. He knew she knew something about him. He was ignoring her signals, he was cottoning up to her. It wouldn't be the first time he'd tried to brainwash. To blackmail.

"The Willmarth's going to help us," Maggie lied. "And Colm's dad. He's Darren's relation, too, you know. He's an undertaker. Undertakers have money."

Tormey laughed out loud—a laugh that made Maggie want to hit him. "Sure, undertakers always have work. But Christ, that don't mean they'll lend you their precious money. I know that for a fact! Well, you want the truth, I'm thinking of settling here myself. Starting over again. Maybe a little land over by the lake. It's flat there, good soil. You could help, Darren. We'd give Keeley a home—don't look like Nola's coming back to take him. Not when she killed Ritchie. Seems pretty damn clear to me—"

"You won't have Keeley!" Maggie shouted. She was furious now; she jumped to her feet—caught her skirt hem in her polished toenails. Let it rip, what the hell. "You can live alone on that farm. You won't have Darren. You won't have Keeley. We know what you been doing to the child. Taking advantage. Penny next door saw."

"She's lying," Tormey said, his face the color of a turnip.

"Nobody saw. A little wrestling, that's all, trying to make a man of him—sniveling baby, he is."

"We know. Darren knows. Why you think he won't come back? One of the reasons, anyhow." She looked at Darren, but he was hanging his head, like he was in shock. Maybe Darren didn't know.... Or knew and felt guilty that he didn't tell.

"Darren never saw such a thing!" Tormey bawled. "He never! I been good to the boy. Brung him into my house. Give him treats."

"What treats? What sort of nasty treats?" Maggie cried, rich with fury. "Doing it to your own son!"

"What? Not my son!" Tormey cried, his skin going ashen. "No, I'd never—"

"Your son, yes." It was Nola, barging into the trailer, her hair fall of burrs, prickers, and leaves like she'd been rolling or sleeping in them—and probably had. She pointed a shaky finger at Tormey. He was sitting upright now, the beer in his left hand, the right palm held up like some flag of truce. He was shaking his head, trying to smile. He got up out of his chair and moved toward her—face like a clown mask. "Oh come on, woman," he said. "*Your* son. Some fellow got to you when you was seventeen. You said that, sure you did. It was that fellow's son."

"Wasn't any other fellow. Was you. Down home, when I was seventeen. You got me outside that diner, in the bushes. I fought you off but you took me."

"You wanted it. I'd bought you a fine meal."

"I never wanted it. Oh you villain—you—" Nola was choking on the words. "I—I hated you. I hate you now. Worse for what you done to my child." She took a deep, gasping breath and went on. "You'll never have him. Never!"

Nola rushed at him, flailing her arms. She moved so fast Maggie could see only the motion of her plunging body and the muzzle of the loaded shotgun she'd grabbed from its perch on the shelf. When Tormey took another step toward her with his clenched fists, she leveled the gun at his chest. He lunged and tried to wrestle the gun from her. It went off and he dropped to the floor.

It was like one of those fake killings you see in the comic shows, Maggie thought. The actor writhes and collapses and gets up again and finally somebody kicks him and he's down.

In a minute, she thought, her own leg poised to kick, he'll get up again.

But he didn't get up.

Darren was feeling for a pulse, listening for a heartbeat. Blood was seeping into the trailer floor, staining the linoleum a bright red. Nola was collapsed against the door, like she'd run a race and couldn't go another step, win or lose. Keeley came out from behind the screen and ran to his mother. They embraced—like they were locked together and somebody'd thrown away the key. Keeley never looked at the man lying there on the floor. Maggie thought of her cat killed on the road once, and the cat's sibling moved past it, wouldn't look at it, like it'd never lived.

Boadie panted back into the trailer. She pushed Darren aside, pronounced Tormey "Dead. He's garbage now. Serve him right. I seen him once, pawing the boy."

"Why didn't you say something?" Maggie yelled, finding her voice at last.

"What could I do, anyway? What could anybody do except kill him? I almost did. Now you best get rid of him 'fore somebody calls the cops." She glanced about, like she might try to stuff the body into the kitchen trash can or under a bed where it would slowly rot.

Too late for that. Here was The Willmarth, breathing hard, and behind her, Colm Hanna. The farmwoman looked at the body and then at Nola, who was standing there, a scarecrow in the wind, her arms tight around Keeley, like she'd dare anyone to try and take him from her. The shotgun was at her feet. Sure, Maggie thought, and her fingerprints still on it.

"I killed him," Nola said, her eyes blinking and blinking. "I killed him—I had to. But that's not why I came. I came to find

Keeley. To see you, Mag. Look, I want you to take him. Bring him up, you know?"

"Aw, sweetie," said Maggie, throwing her arms around Nola and the boy—she could hear the boy whimpering. "You just tell the cops what he done, they'll let you off. You'll have Keeley back."

"Not that easy," Nola said, twisting her head to look at Colm, "right?"

Colm nodded. "But I know a good lawyer here in town."

"Not that youngster Franny was complaining about," said Ruth. "He still hasn't located her mare."

"Different guy. Hotshot fellow by the name of Bingham. He'll help. You'll live to be with Keeley again." Colm moved over by the sink, unclipped his cell phone. The cops, Maggie thought. The coroner. No one wanted to touch the body; it was like somebody'd thrown up on the floor, everyone stepping around it, not wanting to look, step in it.

Maggie watched Nola gaze at the boy like she wanted to memorize him—what he still looked like as a youth. If she got out, she might be an old lady, Keeley a grown man.

Nola was fingering the cross on Maggie's neck, though her eyes were on Keeley. "You're still wearing it," she said.

It wasn't Nola's cross, the one Maggie had been wearing all these years—the police had that one. Maggie had recently bought a new, cheaper one with performance money she'd saved, and had it engraved. "Sure," she said. "I thought I lost it. But it was in the grass, you know. Here in the pasture."

"In the swamp, by Ritchie's body," The Willmarth said, the first time she'd spoken. Maggie saw a dozen expressions cross the farmer's face—from horror at the thing on the floor to something that looked like she'd just waked up, was putting things together. Maggie stepped back, ice cubes down her spine. Already a cop had said he was coming to look at Maggie's shoes—she could hide the one without a heel, but would it help? She supposed he'd want her prints.

How long could she hide her part in it? She couldn't let Nola take all the blame. She'd blocked it out all these long days. And now the reality of Ritchie's death was surfacing, like something you flush down the toilet but it keeps coming up.

"It was my cross," Nola said—almost shouted, like she'd cover up her mistake of mentioning the cross. "I'm the one would've lost it."

"We exchanged crosses when we mixed our blood. I know what you're thinking," Maggie said, addressing The Willmarth—feeling breathless, like her lungs weren't pumping enough air. "But I was wearing Nola's cross. She's still got mine." She pulled the cross out from under her friend's black shirt, turned it over. "See? It's got my initials on it." She was sweating, she stubbed out her cigarette and pulled out another. Darren came over, put an arm around her. She barely felt it she was sweating so hard.

"And we know where you lost yours, Maggie," The Willmarth said. "The police have the prints from it. The DNA on the reins. They'll want samples from you. I'm sorry."

Maggie lit the cigarette with shaky fingers, curled her sandaled toes.

"Why don't we go up to my house and talk about it?" The Willmarth said. "Darren can stay with the body."

"But I need Darren!" Maggie cried, reaching for him.

"I'm here, baby," he said, and squeezed her hand.

"You all go up there. I'll stay," Boadie said. "I want to see the garbage dragged off."

"If you really want to know," Maggie said, feeling desperate, squinting at The Willmarth, "it was Uncle killed Ritchie. He as much as admitted it to me, yeah, he did. Ritchie knew about a guy Uncle stole money from, and threatened to tell, right, Darren? Threatened to tell what Uncle did to him as a kid...."

Darren slowly nodded; his face was the color of Maggie's hair. "And Uncle knew he had a sick cow on his farm. He sent the calves here with me on purpose. He was mad as hell 'cause

I wouldn't go back to the farm." When Ruth looked at him, horrified: "I mean, hell, *I* didn't know till Ritchie come back and told me—*after* the feds took the calves. I swear, I'd never of brought the calves otherwise. No way! I swear it! Never!" He went over to The Willmarth, shook her arm hard, like he'd make her believe him.

"So now Uncle's got his, and we're even," Maggie said, taking a long trembly suck on her cigarette—she needed it to keep her balance. "What do we have to go up to your house for? There's nothing more to talk about."

"Sorry to burst your bubble, cousins," Colm said, clipping the cell phone back on his belt. "But Tormey O'Neill was in the Horizons Bar in Buffalo the night Ritchie was killed. With a dozen witnesses identifying him. New one just came through." He nodded at The Willmarth and she gave a half smile. They both knew all the time!

Maggie dropped her cigarette stub and Boadie ran to crush it with a slippered foot. "You want to start another fire?" the old lady shouted. She pulled her pig up into her arms. The stupid thing burbled like Boadie was its mother.

A siren shrilled up on Cow Hill Road. Cop cars slowed down, jamming on their brakes, making the turn into the farm. They were coming for Uncle. They were coming for Nola. They were coming maybe for Maggie.

"Wait," said Nola when The Willmarth started out the door after Colm. She grabbed the farmwoman by the blue sleeve. "Look, I already killed one man. What's one more?" Her face was like burnt ashes. She was holding on to The Willmarth, as though the farmwoman was the Last Judgment. The farmwoman waited, looked down at the defiant Nola. Her eyes were soft and watery, like she was on Nola's side.

But she wasn't, Maggie knew. She was on the side of what happened. You killed somebody and you paid for it. She wouldn't stop till she knew all the truth, Maggie realized that. It was the way of that woman. Maggie had heard the stories.

"You were both there in the swamp that night," The Willmarth said, like she was trying to prime the pump, get Nola to talk even as the sirens quit up in the drive, the cops already on their way down to the trailer. "It was only one set of prints on that cross, Maggie. I don't think they were Nola's. I mean, we'll find out." She glanced at Colm and he nodded. "You were there as well, weren't you?"

"I was and I—" Maggie began, but Nola interrupted.

"Maggie came to find me," Nola said, talking fast like somebody'd wound her up. "Mag followed Ritchie back after he went to talk with Darren. Ritchie and I were, like, camping out for a night, lying low, like Ritchie said. He wanted to unload the mare he stole. I was waiting for my chance to escape, but he'd take my clothes with him each time he left. He said he'd kill me if I tried to leave."

"Yeah, I came," Maggie broke in, "and Nola was sleeping. She looked so pathetic, curled up like a kid on that miserable mat. You could see the bruises on her arms and neck where he'd hit her."

You could see something worse, near the scar on her breast, Maggie thought, but couldn't even think the words.

Everyone was looking at her now, and she went on. "I watched Ritchie awhile, hoping he'd leave a minute so I could grab Nola and run. I saw him polish off a quart, then start on another. He just sat there, drinking. I was furious at Ritchie for doing all that to Nola. I—I lost my temper. I grabbed a stick and ran to hit him with it."

"I woke," Nola said, grabbing The Willmarth's arm, making her turn her eyes from Maggie, "and they were fighting. Ritchie'd got Maggie and dragged her down. He was trying to—"

"Rape me," Maggie said. "Kill me maybe, I don't know."

"He was drunk, sure," Nola said. "Mag was screaming, trying to fight him off. I went to help—Maggie's my blood sister. I got the reins off the mare, dropped them round his neck. He was drunk enough not to notice."

"And we pulled on the reins. Hard," Maggie said.

"No!" Nola cried. "Not you. *I* pulled. You were on th
ground. You just pushed up on him. I choked him with thos
reins. Not you. It was me."

Maggie was holding Nola, letting Nola sob into her shoul
der. "You know damn well I helped pull those reins," Maggi
whispered into her ear, but Nola only shushed her, pushed he
off, pulled her back, and stared hard into her eyes. "*I* kille
him," she said in a fierce hoarse voice that stilled Maggie. "
strangled Ritchie. *You* got to take Keeley. Promise to take car
of Keeley."

Maggie felt her lungs filling with breath, her veins with nev
blood. "I will. You know I will."

"It was self-defense," Maggie shouted as the cops arrive
and took Nola away in handcuffs—what need was there fo
handcuffs? "I saw it. Tormey was trying to kill Nola!"

"You can save your breath for the trial, lady," one of the cop
said, and lifted a grizzled eyebrow at The Willmarth.

If looks could kill, Maggie thought, The Willmarth's woul
"You be careful of her," the farmwoman told the cop, "she's ha
a hard time. She's been through more than most of us in a life
time." She turned to Nola. "We'll be in to see you. We'll pu
up a fight for you. But get that test, in the hospital. That's par
amount. Get the test. I'll see that she does," she told the grou
after the door slammed behind Nola and the cops. "We'll a
pray she comes out clean. Now how about coffee, up in m
kitchen?"

Maggie heard Keeley, who'd gone behind the screen. He wa
sobbing, funny little sobs, like an engine trying to start up bu
not catching on. She'd bring the boy with her, he was hers now
Well, for the time being anyhow. He was the child she couldn'
seem to conceive, even though she'd thrown away the pills.

"Come on, love," she said. "The Willmarth's got hot choc
olate. And Darren, bring your beer. We'll have a gig to cele
brate Nola's return. Tomorrow, Keel, we'll go see your mom.

She led the boy out the back door of the trailer. She didn't want him to see the coroner, who was bending over the uncle's body, pronouncing him dead of a gunshot wound to anyone who would listen. Which, in the end, was only Boadie and the pig.

"Garbage," Boadie said, "take the garbage away."

# TWENTY-FOUR

THE FEDS WERE COMING for Ruth's cows in twenty-four hours: the call came the next morning from the state veterinarian. Ruth wasn't surprised; she'd expected it. She held the dead phone numbly in her hand, its buzzing as senseless as what was happening to her cows. Darren, Liz, and Boadie were back in the barn after breakfast; they'd spent the night upstairs—the trailer was wrapped in yellow crime scene tape. The cops had taken the shotgun, and Boadie complained loudly. What was she going to use against the feds?

What, indeed, Ruth thought. Most likely the agents would bring in armed men. It seemed a lost cause. "Tell the neighbors not to come," she warned Sharon when her daughter appeared, "dying" for coffee. "Someone will get hurt if they try to keep the agents out."

"Uh-huh," said Sharon, which meant "I'm listening but not listening."

"I mean it," Ruth said, and sat in the kitchen rocker, resigned to her fate. She was drinking a cup of Irish coffee Colm had brewed: coffee, whipped cream, honey, and Colm's "moonshine whiskey." She and Darren had finished the milking, got Boadie and Liz out of the house with a promise to stay away from the trailer—a promise they probably wouldn't keep. Now she just wanted to sit here and gestate, sink slowly into some kind of oblivion, a self-administered tranquillizer.

"Uh-huh," Sharon said again, and ran out to the barn with a full cup of coffee. Black coffee, she emphasized, "none of that lethal stuff you're drinking, Mother."

A moment later Sharon's head popped back in. "I meant to tell you, Mother. That Leafmiller woman called. There are three conditions you'll have to meet when they come tomorrow. You ready for them?"

Ruth grunted. She was never ready, but guessed she'd have to listen.

"Number one," Sharon said. "Make a five-foot-wide path to lead the cows through to the truck."

"Mmm."

"Number two: no llamas."

"Ha! They're afraid they'll get spit on."

"Right. Their nice starched shirts. Number three: no third parties. Which translated, means no demonstrators—no opposition."

"Just what I told you, Sharon, remember?"

"Sure. And number four—"

"You said three conditions."

"Well I forgot. There are four. Number four: no media. No reporters. No embarrassment for the feds. They want this swept under the rug as quick as possible."

"Sounds familiar," Ruth said. "Okay. You run along now. Your coffee's getting cold."

There were still unanswered questions, Ruth thought as she sat alone and sipped the moonshine coffee. She had to think about the murder—it would take her mind off all those conditions. Although cows and murder were somehow linked, weren't they? The travellers coming, the suspect calves from Tormey Leary, the sick woman, Nola, and her possible CJD. And then Ruth's own farm pronounced unclean. The plague. The fear and superstition and hate at the heart of it....

Had Ritchie really been in the swamp when he accosted Maggie? Why would he be? How had his body ended up there? How much of a part had Maggie actually played? Would the judge believe Nola if she claimed she'd done the killing alone?

In any event, Maggie had to be considered an accomplice. What would happen to Keeley?

Footsteps ran lightly down the back stairs and there was Maggie, in the red and yellow skirt and halter top she'd worn the night before. "Sit down," Ruth said, and blurted out her questions.

Maggie held up a palm, as if she were taking the fifth.

"They'll ask you in court," Ruth said. "You'll have to take an oath. You could call this a rehearsal." She poured the young woman a cup of black coffee, put away the moonshine. It wouldn't do to have two of them in their cups.

Maggie took a deep breath and let it out with a whoosh. "He was in a clearing, not far from that healing place I knew Nola was in—I'd gone looking for her. Near the swamp—not in it. I hit him and he yelled and knocked me down. He was laughing, drunk. He'd always been after me. You might call him a stalker—next thing to it anyhow. I hated him. I hated that Nola stayed with him. I could of drawn and quartered him, I was that full of rage!"

"So you both struggled with him? Tightened the reins around his neck?"

Maggie was nodding and talking right through Ruth's questions. Her passion told Ruth that what she was saying was truth. "I saw he was dead. I guess we were shocked at that. It happened so fast! But we didn't want to leave him there for the world to see. I mean, Nola needed to get away, she needed time. She thought she'd take the mare as far as she could without somebody seeing. She thought the swamp was the safest place to hide."

"You didn't take the mare into the swamp?"

"Sure we did. Partway anyhow—we hoisted the body up over the horse. You ever pick up a dead body? Weighs like ten tons! The mare had a hard time in that swamp, so we dragged the body the rest of the way. Look, Willmarth, I hated the bastard but I wouldn't of, like, wanted to kill him. Not in my right mind, anyway. But then he waved that letter at me—after I hit him, before he came down on me, that was. Bragging, you know, like only Ritchie could do—"

"Letter?"

"Yeah, the one Ritchie wanted me to give Darren." Maggie sipped her coffee, then poured in milk to cool it down. "He was going to send it to you. Tell you Darren knew about the calves being sick. He was trying to blackmail Darren, get him to leave here. So Uncle would keep Ritchie in his will—'stead of leaving it all to Darren. I mean, Uncle never knew he had a son— Nola kept that from him. From all of us! And then Uncle knowing Ritchie killed that guy in the bar—all that bad stuff, you know. Everybody blackmailing everybody else. But nobody, I mean nobody was going to blackmail my Darren!"

"You have that letter?"

"Tore it up afterward. Little shreds. Wind's got it."

"Mmm." Ruth gulped her coffee. "But why did Nola want to kill him?" She was beginning to feel the moonshine. Maggie's voice was sounding far away.

"I told you! He was after *me*. It was part of Nola's and my blood bond. If anyone tried to hurt one of us, the other would come running. That's when Nola wrapped the reins around his neck. Nola and I—we're bound together, like I said. I pulled too—I did! I couldn't help it. That filthy man! I should go to prison with her. I should!"

Keeley tramped down the stairs and Maggie stopped talking. The boy looked up shyly at the two women. Maggie put an arm around him, fussed over his breakfast. Keeley looked like a bull calf Ruth had treated once with an injured leg. She'd cured him, only to see him shipped off to the slaughterhouse. She couldn't keep bull calves, no matter how much her son pleaded. Not for long, anyway.

"He was trying to hurt you," Ruth said to Maggie. "He was trying to hurt Nola. He'd already endangered her life taking her out of that hospital. He was a woman beater, I gather?"

Maggie nodded. "Not as bad as some, but yeah. The verbal abuse! You know, a control freak."

"He tried to force you. It was self-defense for both of you. We'll make a case out of that. Get a good lawyer—that Bingham fellow Colm knows."

Maggie was hugging Keeley, weeping over him. They were both weeping.

Finally Ruth said, "Nola was the one who put the reins around his neck. You only helped drag the body into the swamp. They'll get you on that, but you won't be away long. We'll keep Keeley here with us for that short time."

Even without the cows, she thought, she could keep the boy. He might be a companion for Vic—he was only a year or two younger.

"What about Darren?" Maggie asked. "If I'm in the lockup and you've lost your cows? What'll Darren do?"

Ruth couldn't answer that question.

RUTH WALKED OUT of the barn after milking and into a sea of faces. It was five-thirty the next morning, the sun a lemony glaze on the Green Mountains. She stopped, and stared. Forty people here at least, holding a candlelight vigil. And more arriving on motorbikes, in pickups, and old cars. Franny and Henrietta riding together on a large chestnut Morgan, like a bicycle built for two. Glenna Flint and her kooky cousin Fay squatting on the porch with Fay's rescued greyhound—the beast with a red flag tied to its scrawny tail. Carol and her son Wilder leading the llama up from the pasture. So much for conditions number one and two, Ruth thought.

Leroy Boulanger careening in on his bicycle, a hive of bees in his hand—oh dear, that could mean trouble. Gwen Woodleaf and her husband, Russell—the latter in full Abenaki regalia, wielding a spear. Their son, Brown Bear, drawing a red circle on his forehead, calling others to his palette. Old Lucien Larocque hobbling on his cane, shaking a fist: "We'll get 'em!

There's fight in the old man yet!" Moira Earthrowl with a pail full of apples; her husband, Stan, shaking his crutch.

These were people Ruth had helped in the past, come to help her in turn. She felt the tears push against her eyeballs. To hell, she thought, with her resolution not to fight. To hell with the feds' four conditions.

A pickup crammed with colorful travellers veered into the driveway—cousins, double cousins, would-be cousins, no doubt, to Maggie and Darren—all hugging and weeping and shouting. Boadie danced among them, brandishing a pitchfork, like she was godmother to the world's cows, calves, and pigs. Here was the media: *Free Press, Branbury Independent,* a WCAX television truck: men and women leaping out with cameras, notebooks, cell phones—already working the crowd.

And then—unbelievably—her son, Vic, came running up to hug her, long knock-kneed legs outgrowing his pants, hair a pile of hay in the wind; furious he'd had no word until Sharon called him. "Jezum crow, you were gonna leave me out of all this? Unfair, Mom! Am I your son or not? You're not gonna let 'em take our cows, are you?"

"Our cows," Ruth thought. Her son, who said he wanted nothing to do with cows, called them "our" cows! Ruth was weeping buckets, she couldn't help it. Vic was here! And all these friends and neighbors and sympathizers. It was like old home week. Only daughter Emily was missing. Why, Emily would love this. Ruth was always doing the wrong thing. Keeping things from her children. What kind of mother was she? She wept for her failings. She wept for the joy of reunion. She would call Emily tonight.

"You're impossible but I love you," Ruth told Sharon, who was emerging from the kitchen door with coffee, lemonade, and cookies to distribute to the crowd—as though they were all here for a tea party or a breakfast brunch—not a battle with the feds.

Sharon grinned at her mother and went on passing the treats. "Everyone should have a red circle!" she shouted, and Vic and

Leroy lent painterly hands to Brown Bear. Soon everyone's forehead was painted with red dye—except for Glenna, who said she was "goddamned if I'll look like an aborigine." Until Glenna's niece Hartley rode in on a bicycle and planted a red lipsticky kiss on the stubborn lady's forehead. And Glenna left the lipstick mark there.

"Hey!" It was Colm at the upstairs window, pulling on a T-shirt. Seeing the crowd, he hollered, "Jeez, I'll be right down. Feds here yet?"

"No, and they said 'dawn,' and it's already after six o'clock so they might not come after all," Ruth shouted back. "You're a cop. You going to let the crowd get away with this?"

"Fifty against one, you crazy?" Colm hollered back, and disappeared from view. Moments later he was outside in sunglasses, straw hat, a pair of denim cutoffs that were too short for his bony legs.

"Listen, listen everyone. Listen!" Ruth yelled, and waved her arms. Then blinked, for fifty-odd persons with red dots on their foreheads were staring at her. It was as if they'd all floated down out of outer space and she was the only rational being left on earth. She planted her legs farther apart for balance. "They'll bring marshals—armed marshalls. That's what they did up in East Warren at that sheep farm. Your pitchforks and bees and apples won't do anything against bullets. I appreciate your concern, your coming here to help me—"

She was close to tears again and she tried a new tack: "I mean, thank you from the bottom of my heart. Thank you. But don't try to attack the authorities. You'll just get hurt. Dragged off to jail—do you want that?"

A loud "Goddammit, why not?" from octogenarian Glenna. "Always said I wanted to experience everything in my lifetime. Never been to jail."

"Free the cows or jail! Free the cows or jail!" the crowd chanted. They were getting out of control, there was nothing Ruth could do. Even Colm was chanting with them. Franny was on her high horse—King Harry in the field: "They took my mare," she screeched, "are we going to let them get away with that? Are we going to sit here and let them take these healthy cows? Cows fed on grass and grain? Put an end to a farm that's been here eight generations?"

"Four generations," Ruth murmured, but no one heard her.

"Well, are we? Yes or no?" Franny shouted and the crowd shouted back "No! No!" A voice hollered, "Free the slaves!" And Russell Leblanc waved his spear; his silver earrings gleamed in the early sun. "They come here with their plagues and kill my people. We're not gonna let 'em do it again!"

People cheered. Cameras flashed. Sharon was dancing in and out of the throng, urging them on. Colm flung an arm around Ruth. "You might's well get with it, Ruthie. You can't win against this crowd." His arm was squeezing her waist, pumping it.

"You're the cop," she said. "Remember that."

"Not today. Got on my real estate hat. My undertaker's cap."

"Don't say that! We don't want any mortalities here. I mean, someone can get hurt. Crowds have a weird mentality. Individuals get lost in the shuffle."

"Not as long as you're here, Ruthie. But better get ready for a fight 'cause here they come!"

Two cattle trucks: rumbling into the driveway. A dozen SUVs behind them—agents jumping out—Colm was counting out loud. Thirteen USDA agents in black Carharts and coveralls; the Leafmiller woman in a blood-red suit. And then the local police. Whose side were they on?

Ruth's heart was a sump pump, it wouldn't quit. The protesters were on their feet, moving toward the feds, signs and placards waving, voices at high pitch. The red dye on the foreheads: they were Abenaki on the attack. Boadie rammed into a Carhart with her pitchfork, the llama kicked loose and spit buckets. Apples flew through the air like bees. Or were they bees?

Ruth was an Amazon now, waving her arms at the crowd to

"Get back. Let me handle this!" She faced the feds: the anger up in her toes, knees, elbows, neck, throat. "If you want my cows you'll have to go down in the pasture and get them. You'll have to go *through* them. Run the gauntlet."

She flailed her arms at the crowd. The protesters thought she was waving them on, and they rushed the truck. Boadie's pitchfork stabbed at the huge tires. Russell's spear forced a pair of agents back in their car. Franny's stallion charged the steel monster: "We won't let them take any more innocents!" When the pair tried to get out the back door, Fay sicked her rented greyhound on them. "Go git 'em, baby, git 'em, I said!"

"Killer bees!" Leroy screamed. They were only honey bees, but they were angry; they flew at the crowd, stung unprotected necks and faces. Glenna shrieked and took to the house. "Damn fool! Now see what you've gone and done!"

Darren came running up from the barn. "I hid that unmarked calf, ma'am. They won't get him. Like you said, cows are still in the pasture. Feds'll have to go down there if they want 'em."

"Good," she said. "But I don't think the feds are going anywhere this minute. The crowd has them—well—"

"Cowed," Colm said with a grin, and Ruth laughed at the pun. She felt exhilarated from the cheering and protesting and hollering. She was part of the crowd now. She knew that excitement, that cry for blood, for revolution. When Vic drew a red circle on her own forehead, she let it stay.

It wasn't right. It wasn't fair. "Hey hey, USDA," she yelled with the crowd, "how many farms did you wreck today? Hey, hey, USDA…" There might be a hundred people here now, folk dropping in from the sky, it seemed, cars and pickups all over her lawn. The trucks would never get out. She could hardly speak, swallow even, with the thrill of it. She wanted to fall on her knees and hug each one.

"Love you," she shouted, flinging her arms in the air, "love you all!" Colm grabbed her, held her tight against him. "And I love you," he said. "But don't look. Don't look, because here come the big guns. The armed feds. Twenty-six," he counted, "no, twenty-seven of 'em. Black leather jackets. Guns. Jeez. You were right. We got to calm this crowd."

"What did I tell you?" Ruth cried, her moods shifting like shadows on a windy day. "Stop!" she screamed at the crowd. "Sharon—help me! It's the Big Guns. Someone will get hurt. Leroy, Russell, Franny, Boadie, all of you—stop, I said! You've done all you can. You can't win over guns. We'll have to fight it some other way—some peaceful way." She felt like she'd fallen two hundred feet out of a giant pine. Only hurt and humiliation when she hit bottom. That awful awareness of how small you are, how helpless in the face of guns and billy clubs and black-jacketed authority.

Sharon and Colm were circulating among the crowd, shouting for order. Gwen wrestled the spear out of Russell's hands—but not before he gave one of the feds a jab with it. Folk were dodging out of the range of Boadie's pitchfork. Agents forced back the crowd with their weapons. A fed sprayed tear gas, and everyone screamed. Out of their cars now, the agents rushed down to the pasture, herded the bewildered cows up the hill, into the trucks. Uniformed men hustled away the pierced tires; feds trampled signs and feet that got in the way. Everyone was hollering. Ruth could hardly tell human beings from the bawling, bellowing, kicking cows. Cows and protesters, all with red dye on their foreheads. All of us, Ruth thought: victims.

Charlotte, Jane Eyre, Esmeralda, Dolly, Oprah, Elizabeth, Amelia—Ruth thrust through the crowd, to hug each one. When they brought up Zelda, bucking and bawling, it was the final blow. Ruth flung her arms about the irrepressible beast, wept another full bucket. "Don't let them take you, Zel," she cried. "Don't let them!"

Zelda reared on her hind legs and shot a hefty kick at her captor. The man yelped, and clutched his groin. The cow ran at a second agent who'd come to help the first. "Go, girl!" the crowd cheered. "Go go go!"

A shot rang out and Zelda fell, in midkick. Ruth dropped to her knees, her mouth a silent O. The wild eye pierced her own. And then went cold.

Ruth was keening. She wept for Zelda, she wept for all her beloved cows whom she might not ever see again. She wept for innocent victims everywhere: humans and animals, trampled underfoot; tortured, slaughtered.

She wept for herself. What was she going to do now? Where was she going to go? How was she going to make a living?

Colm was holding her, people were trying to embrace her, make promises, give options, offer barns and land. "Damn it all, girl, pull yourself together." It was old Glenna, rasping in her ear. "Come over tomorrow and see me. I got thirty acres and only Fay's rented cow keeping down the dandelions. We'll have a scotch. We can talk. We can work out a deal."

Slowly the old lady's face came into focus. That face like a waterfall, that crisscross of deep lines, the white hair like a cyclone had hit it. That foolish red lipstick on the withered forehead. She was beautiful.

But Ruth couldn't think about scotch and small talk. She couldn't give any answers.

"Zelda" was all she could think to say, leaning back against a pliant birch. "Oh, my poor darling Zelda."

# TWENTY-FIVE

MAGGIE RAN INTO the farmhouse kitchen with Keeley in tow, and held up a pair of charred shoes. "They were in his room. At that inn!" she shouted. "I went with Keeley to get his train model and there were the shoes. The chambermaid was shoving 'em into a plastic bag with his other stuff. I didn't want Tormey's old pants and shirts—told her to take 'em if she got somebody can wear 'em. But the shoes. Look!"

Ruth looked. But she couldn't seem to focus. It had been just two days since the seizure of her cows and she was still in deep mourning. The emptiness down in the pasture… What did she want with a pair of shoes that looked like they'd been through a holocaust?

Maggie was waving a black shoe in her ringed hand. "It was Uncle set that fire, burned our trailer. Oh you bet! To get back at Darren for leaving the farm. Keeley knows, right, Keel? Keeley 'members him coming in late at night, drunk, stinking like a furnace, right?"

"Oh," said Ruth, realizing. "Why didn't you tell us, Keeley?"

"Uncle was still alive," Maggie said softly, and the women's eyes connected. Stupid woman, Ruth told herself. Of course. The boy was afraid.

There was the glimmer of a smile on Keeley's lips. His demeanor had altered since the uncle's death. It was as though a hundred pounds had been lifted from his shoulders. Though the scars would remain, Ruth knew. And there was his mother, awaiting trial. Awaiting the verdict, as well, from the hospital where they'd taken her for testing.

The jury was still out on Maggie. Sooner or later she, too, would be brought to trial.

It was some small compensation at least to know there would be no more damage from the uncle. But it didn't undo what had already been done.

And so with my cows, Ruth thought. She recalled an Irish play she'd read in college about a mother who'd lost her last fisher son to the sea; and the woman was almost relieved because there would be no more sons to worry about. For Ruth, Zelda was gone, her remaining cows taken away for testing. And in the morning paper, a Canadian cow tested positive for Mad Cow: "Although BSE has not been shown to be transmitted among cows in a herd, as a precaution the entire herd is being destroyed."

Still, she had to hope, Colm kept telling her. Soon Darren would leave—he had found a job with a farmer over in Bridport. He and Maggie would take Keeley with them. Ruth had invited the boy to stay, but he shook his head. He needed his blood family, and Ruth understood. She'd contacted Emily, who would arrive on Saturday—upset that she hadn't known about the summer's happenings, but longing to be "home with family."

Outside the window Boadie was leading a spindly-legged black-and-white calf across the grass—Charlotte 2's calf that Darren had saved from the red dye. Keeley ran out to join them, and Maggie followed. Ruth would begin again—somewhere—with that adorable creature. Looking at Boadie, she wished she could paint. She would entitle the picture *Old Woman and Calf*. She would paint all the beauty of the pair onto canvas.

But Ruth wasn't an artist, she could hardly draw a line. Ruth was a farmer. When Glenna phoned again that night just as Ruth was climbing into bed, Ruth listened. It was a second invitation for her to use Glenna's hundred acres. "What do I want with a hundred acres?" the octogenarian said. "I'm happy just sitting on the porch with a bottle of scotch. Contemplating my navel, you know?" She burst into her rich belly laugh. "But I'm a Vermonter, too. Can't see land going to waste. Look, girl, you can put anything you damn please on it. Cows, goats, sheep—horses—llamas if you want!"

"I love llamas," Ruth said, smiling to think of Carol's llama, soaking the front of a Carhart jacket. "But they do spit. And I don't know anything about horses. I'll leave horses to Franny." Franny had got her Ophelia back after Nola went for testing—her child lawyer had seen to that-but the mare was being "carefully monitored," according to the feds. Franny had to be content with that.

"But no birds," Glenna warned. "I draw the line at birds. You know that emu farm down on Route 125? Well, one of 'em got loose—those friggin' big wings—those long skinny legs! Sprayed my clothes basket when I was hanging clothes. I had to wash 'em all over again."

Ruth thought of the agents leaving the farm, frantically spraying their government vehicles with disinfectant, as though everything on the Willmarth farm—people, grass, vehicles—was contaminated. And then James Perlman, driving slowly past, windows closed though it was ninety degrees outside, safe in his sterile car. She hadn't seen his face among the demonstrators.

"No birds, she's right," Colm said. As a four-year-old, Colm had been attacked by a cranky turkey; he was still phobic. Even a sparrow in his path, he said, gave him hives.

"All I have now is a heifer calf," Ruth told Glenna. "I suppose I could begin with her. But there's an outside chance I may get my cows back. The use of my land. Who knows? I mean, look, Glenna, I don't know anything about raising goats."

"They mow the lawn," Glenna said, "they give milk."

"Yes, there is that," Ruth said thoughtfully. "You can milk them."

"Good girl," Glenna said. "You bring that little critter over tomorrow, okay? We'll introduce her to Daffodil. Though Fay's thinking of buying that foolish beast. All that rent going out every month—just so she can call the place a farm B&B?" The belly laugh came again, rich and mellow out of the old lady's gut. "It's settled then. See you tomorrow. I'll break out the scotch."

"She thinks I've agreed," Ruth said, hanging up the phone.

"Jeez, Ruthie. A golden apple falls off a tree and you'd let it rot?" Colm reached for her. He was wearing his blue pajama top with no bottoms. His hair was a gray-brown scarecrow on his head. He was taking those little sips again from her lips, like a calf nursing its mother. She had to laugh. She was laughing when the phone rang and it was Chief Fallon from the local police station. Colm grabbed it and she couldn't help but hear; Fallon, it seemed, had a built-in loudspeaker in his throat.

"Hey!" Colm said, then "Wow! Fantastic! Here, tell Ruthie." He handed over the phone, but she'd already heard. The hospital had called. Nola had passed the test. She wasn't sick with Creutzfeldt-Jakob disease. She wasn't a carrier—"Doesn't seem to be. But she killed a guy, right? Two guys?" Roy Fallon shouted. "Oughta have those DNA tests soon."

"Self-defense?" Ruth suggested, and Fallon shouted, "What do I know? You say both guys threatened that traveller woman—that's why she did 'em in? Christ, you'll need a helluva good lawyer to prove it happened same way twice." He gave a chugging heh heh heh laugh, like a train picking up speed.

Colm grabbed the receiver from Ruth. "We got one," he said. "A good lawyer. We'll give 'em a fight."

"You're a cop. You gotta be objective, remember?" Fallon said, and Colm said, "Yeah, oh sure. Well, g'night then," and hung up.

He grabbed Ruth and lifted her up off the bed, shouting, "Hallelujah, your woman's clean!" and danced her on top of the bed.

"Stop it, stop, you animal!" Ruth cried. "Good news for Nola, though she's still facing a stone wall. And they haven't cleared my Friesian calves. They haven't brought back my cows."

"Think positive," said Colm, the optimist.

This was true. Nola was clean, she was healthy—there had never been any contamination—not in that quarter anyway. So Ruth should be glad of that. Colm released her and she stood on the mattress and flung her arms high. "Praise be for something, anyhow," she cried—"if not for the cows, at least for Nola's health. Praise be for my unmarked calf. I'll call her Eve!"

Colm put his arms around her; she hung on for life while they did a pirouette. They fell back laughing on the bed—and the slats gave way. Omigod, the whole bedful of slats! "Too bloody short for the bed," Colm hollered as they went down together in a bang and crash. Like an army being routed, Ruth thought; like a fort felled, a town liberated from an enemy.

They were still on the mattress after making love, though it had sunk below the sides of the bed. But it was all right, they'd stay the night this way, Ruth told him. She was too exhausted to get up.

"And a damn good thing," Colm said. "I haven't got strength to pick up a single slat. Not tonight. Not after I moved three boxes full of clothes and books over here this afternoon."

"You what?"

"You're not going to stay here alone, are you? Cows gone, Emily in college, Vic off with friends half the time. You need somebody to keep you company, right? Somebody to come home to after a long day of goat tending over at Glenna's? I mean, baby, I'm your man."

Before she could answer he was leaning over her: those hot slurpy kisses, sucking up her resistance. "You *can* milk goats," he reminded her when they came up for air. "Goats eat anything—you won't have to recycle your tin cans. You don't have to worry about planting corn. They're easier than cows."

"But they're not cows," she said. "They don't have those big brown liquid eyes. They're not like Zelda. Or Jane Eyre. Or Dolly. Or Elizabeth. Oh, my poor Elizabeth," she murmured.

"Elizabeth's pregnant. Who's going to help her freshen next month? She has that narrow passage. She'll need help."

"She'll be back by then. You'll get her back. You watch."

"You think so?"

"I do."

She gave in to him then. There was always the fairy tale after the plague. "London bridge is falling down…ashes, ashes…" she sang softly. A play song for children. A way to forget until the next time. Like sleep. She nestled into the curve of her lover's shoulder, she fit there nicely. His flesh was warm. Warm as summer sun on the bare back. Warm as a cow's fleshy flank.

"They slept with their cows back in the old days," she said. "Winters anyway. Your forebears and mine—wherever they were living—Ireland, Scotland, Vermont. It was the way to keep warm. Man, woman, and beast, curled up together."

"Moo-oo," Colm murmured, and dropped off to sleep.

Outdoors the first rain of the season splattered against the window glass, nourishing the corn that Ruth would store in one of the old stave silos. "Just in case," she told the rain.

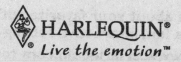

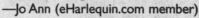

# e◆HARLEQUIN.com

The Ultimate Destination for Women's Fiction

The ultimate destination for women's fiction.
Visit eHarlequin.com today!

## GREAT BOOKS:
- We've got something for everyone—and at great low prices!
- Choose from new releases, backlist favorites, Themed Collections and preview upcoming books, too.
- Favorite authors: Debbie Macomber, Diana Palmer, Susan Wiggs and more!

## EASY SHOPPING:
- Choose our convenient "bill me" option. No credit card required!
- Easy, secure, 24-hour shopping from the comfort of your own home.
- Sign-up for free membership and get $4 off your first purchase.
- Exclusive online offers: FREE books, bargain outlet savings, hot deals.

## EXCLUSIVE FEATURES:
- Try Book Matcher—finding your favorite read has never been easier!
- Save & redeem Bonus Bucks.
- Another reason to love Fridays— Free Book Fridays!

## Shop online
## at www.eHarlequin.com today!